Gothic documents

Gothic documents

A sourcebook 1700–1820

edited by

E.J. Clery

and

Robert Miles

Manchester University Press

Manchester and New York

distributed exclusively in the USA by St. Martin's Press

Published by Manchester University Press
Oxford Road, Manchester M13 9NR, UK
and Room 400, 175 Fifth Avenue, New York, NY 10010, USA
http://www.man.ac.uk/mup

Distributed exclusively in the USA by
St. Martin's Press, Inc., 175 Fifth Avenue, New York,
NY 10010, USA

Distributed exclusively in Canada by
UBC Press, University of British Columbia, 6344 Memorial Road,
Vancouver, BC, Canada V6T 1Z2

British Library Cataloguing-in-Publication Data
A catalogue record for this book is available from the British Library

Library of Congress Cataloging-in-Publication Data applied for
ISBN 0 7190 4026 4
0 7190 4027 2

First published 2000

06 05 04 03 02 01 00 10 9 8 7 6 5 4 3 2 1

Typeset by Florence Production Ltd, Stoodleigh, Devon.
Printed in Great Britain
by Biddles Ltd, Guildford and King's Lynn

Contents

Acknowledgements

We would like to thank the following publishers for permission to use extracts from modern editions: Associated University Presses; Clarendon Press; Cornell University Press; Folio Press; Longman; Oxford University Press; Penguin; Routledge & Kegan Paul; University of California Press; University of Delaware Press; Yale University Press.

The idea for a Gothic anthology was the brainchild of Anita Roy of Manchester University Press. For this, and for her inspirational enthusiasm, we thank her. But, like another well-known creator, she didn't stick around to face the consequences. That was left to her successor at MUP, Matthew Frost, who has been a marvel of patient supportiveness and unflagging belief. Chris Baldick and Gary Kelly lent valuable assistance at a critical juncture. Fred Botting gave advice on selection, and commented encouragingly on an early draft. Matthew Steggle aided us with translations from Latin and Greek and identification of sources. Karen Morton ably supplemented our trawls in the library.

The research and preparation of texts for the book have been generously supported by a grant from the British Academy.

Note on the text

In our selection of texts we have tried to balance the needs of the student with the interests of the scholar. Where we have included excerpts from texts which are now frequently taught, we have used modern editions, to facilitate further reading (subject to publishers' permission). In other cases, we have chosen either first editions, or ones in common use in the period, or editions of special significance. We have retained original spelling, such as the manifold forms of 'Shakespeare'. We have also kept archaic conventions, notably the use of initial capitals, except in those cases where a modernised edition has been used as source. However archaic grammar (e.g. the possessive 'it's'), and obvious typographic errors have been silently corrected, apart from three instances where the errors have some significance and are noted (in 4.4, 4.5a, and 4.9). Notes by the original authors are shown as footnotes.

Introduction

The aim of the present collection is to make available a body of texts connected with the cultural phenomenon known as Gothic writing. Some of the texts document the ideological and aesthetic environment which gave rise to the new form of writing – its conditions of possibility. Others indicate its political inflections. We include many of the critical writings and reviews which helped to constitute Gothic as a distinct genre, by revisions of the standards of taste, by critique and by outright attack. Together, this material represents a substantial part of the discursive hinterland of Gothic.

The selections are not intended to illustrate an overarching thesis about the origins or development of Gothic writing. On the contrary, our hope is that ready access to contextual material will serve to open up critical debate. We hope, in particular, that it will encourage students to follow new routes, make new connections, and enable them to read set works on the syllabus in more adventurous and historically informed ways.

Some of the choices of text will be predictable. The chapters on supernaturalism, on the aesthetics of Gothic, and on opposition to Gothic contain a number of the standard references in any history of the genre, which it would be perverse to exclude. But here they will be juxtaposed with other more novel items of journalism, religious propaganda, folk tradition, non-fictional narrative, poetry, and so on – writings not usually viewed in connection with a mode regarded, for the most part, as consisting of prose fiction alone.

There are perhaps two points to make here. In the first place, we want to emphasise the permeable nature of Gothic, and indeed of any literary category. In the period surveyed, Gothic is in the process of becoming a discrete discursive form, but it shares in the intertextual nature of all writing. Second, and relatedly, the sense of relevance within each chapter is determined not by looking backwards from a point at which the 'Gothic novel' becomes visible as an achieved product, but rather in terms of a set of generative historical problems. On what terms could the supernatural or the marvellous be represented in the literature of an enlightened age? What authority might license an aesthetic of reckless originality? What social or moral justification – a requisite for eighteenth-century cultural theory – could be found for the experience of artificial terror? These implicit interrogations have encouraged us to broaden the policy of selection.

The chapters on the politics of Gothic, before and after the French Revolution, will prove more surprising, perhaps even controversial. Anyone interested in the significance of the word 'Gothic' before Walpole employed it to describe his tale *The Castle of Otranto* will want to know more about the word's existing political, ideological and cultural meanings. The view that the English owe the peculiar perfection of their institutions, manners and customs to the Gothic tribes who settled in Britain is at the heart of the matter. We have therefore included extracts from Tacitus and Montesquieu, the authorities eighteenth-century commentators most often referred to. However, this material was, by its nature, extremely pliable, and highly controversial. It was often bent into contrasting, even opposing, positions. Before the French Revolution it was used by establishment Whigs and radical Dissenters alike. Moreover, the story of Britain's Gothic origins, although implicitly progressivist, was to be re-fashioned in the cultural and sociological theories critical of modern society: that vital eighteenth-century trend known as primitivism. Here, too, we have included examples. This overtly political material coexists and overlaps with the more familiar literary and aesthetic material within the semantic constellation of the 'Gothic'. The precise nature of the interrelation of aesthetics and politics we leave to the reader to explore. But the correspondences are many and overt. John Aikin's translation of Tacitus's *Germania* and his authorship of the Gothic fragment 'Sir Bertrand' is just one example. The controversy surrounding 'Ossian', the careers as Whig Members of Parliament of three pioneers of the Gothic novel – Walpole, Beckford and Lewis – and the Dissenting background of Ann Radcliffe all suggest in various ways the importance of this neglected dimension of Gothic writing.

Matters are more clear-cut after the French Revolution, when radicals like Mary Wollstonecraft and Thomas Paine attacked the feudal social practices celebrated with increasing stridency by Tories and apostate Whigs, most notably Edmund Burke. For the English Jacobins, such 'Gothic' survivals as primogeniture or the code of chivalry were the tools of aristocratic privilege and abuse. An awareness of the terms of this political debate, conducted by means of works like *The Rights of Man* on an unprecedented scale, is, we would argue, necessary to any reading of the products of the Gothic craze of the 1790s. The romance-writers' obsessive return to the scene of aristocratic crime on the one hand, and urgent repetitions of the restitution of social hierarchy on the other, could not be free of revolutionary resonances. This is not to say that the popular terror fictions of the time are coherent polemics. But they undeniably form part of a general socio-cultural problematic regarding Gothic manners and institutions, with pressing contemporary relevance.

The last chapter broadly covers the period from the height of the Gothic vogue (in the mid-1790s) to the mid nineteenth century, and reprises the main themes of the previous sections: the supernatural and the ethic of probability, the claim to artistic licence, the artificial cultivation of terror, historical constructions of Gothic times, political stratagems around narratives of Gothic vice or virtue. The intention is to show how these issues and discursive practices persist and undergo transformation. Experimental tales of the marvellous modulate into the established literary type of the ghost story; the supernatural takes on a phantasmal aspect; Walter Scott undertakes the re-invention of chivalry for a post-revolutionary Britain; the boundary between romance and novel is reinvoked but constantly redrawn. The texts in this section suggest that, even while the Gothic genre gains definition and a degree of acceptance as a literary category, it continues to be the locus of a broad set of tensions and negotiations.

Although the aim throughout has been to open out and diversify the picture of literary Gothic in relation to its conditions of production, we are aware that some areas have been emphasised at the expense of others. The exclusions might, indeed, warrant a second volume of Gothic documents: the ubiquitous discourse of sensibility; sensitivity to the sublime in landscape; changing conceptions of the passions, particularly the question of representing the psychology of villainy; the ideological meanings of Gothic architecture. All of these are touched on here, but could be illustrated far more extensively. However, part of our justification would be that sensibility, the natural sublime and the 'Gothic revival' in architecture are already the subject of many substantial monographs. We have chosen to linger on those areas which we felt were either indispensable or seriously neglected.

After this brief summary of the principles of selection, a few words about the presentation of the texts. As regards the overall shape of the work, it documents a period of roughly one hundred years, extending from the early eighteenth century to the early nineteenth century. The chapters are divided thematically and arranged for the most part chronologically. Thematic divisions are of course artificial: the issues we illustrate do not naturally arise in isolation, and individual texts similarly defy compartmentalisation. We have tried to encourage a more fluid approach to the material by cross-referencing. But there are gains to tracing ideas roughly relating to different aspects of the Gothic phenomenon over a span of fifty or so years at a time, and the chapters have an internal chronological arrangement for this reason.

In the headnotes to each item we give some contextual information and draw attention to a few salient features, providing a slightly fuller account when the text is especially significant, or apparently tangential to the Gothic. However, since the purpose is always to make possible new and more creative readings of Gothic, rather than impose a ready-made theory, we have resisted offering interpretations. Notes by the authors are given as footnotes; our annotations – which are occasional, added where most needed, rather than exhaustive – are placed as endnotes after every chapter. In a few cases we have taken the texts from modern editions, and included or adapted some notes (see the Acknowledgements page).

1 Supernaturalism: religion, folklore, Shakespeare

1.1 Daniel Defoe (1600?–1731), *A True Relation of the Apparition of One Mrs. Veal* (1706)

This is the most famous example of the 'apparition narrative', a genre that developed from the late seventeenth century in response to a crisis in religious belief. The intention was to counteract the influence of the Hobbes and materialist philosophy, and persuade sceptics about the reality of the after-life and divine providence, by detailed and carefully authenticated accounts of spectral visitations. Titles such as *Saducismus Triumphatus: or, Full and Plain Evidence Concerning Witches and Apparitions* (1681; by Joseph Glanvill), *The Certainty of the World of Spirits* (1691; by Richard Baxter) and *The Secrets of the Invisible World Disclos'd: or, An Universal History of Apparitions, &c.* (1727; by Defoe himself), make clear a serious 'theologico-propagandic' purpose which is absent from the line of super-natural fiction beginning with *The Castle of Otranto* in 1764. And yet, as Coleman O. Parsons (1956) has shown, apparition narratives provided a stepping-stone from a largely oral and popular culture of ghost stories to a new literary tradition led by enthusiastic consumer demand. Defoe's *A True Relation* bears the hallmark of philosophical debate in its emphasis on authen-ticity, but there are also not-so-discreet references to the marketability of its subject. From its first appearance as a pamphlet it was reissued at an average rate of a new edition each week, and when it was appended to *The Christian's Defence Against the Fears of Death* by Charles Drelincourt in 1707, the latter was, as Defoe put it, 'bought up strangely'. A comparison of *A True Relation* with other accounts of the celebrated ghost of Mrs Veal demonstrates Defoe's superior skill in the art of story-telling (Schonhorn, 1965). Like a number of other strange tales published for didactic purposes, it later found its way into literary anthologies.

Source: [Daniel Defoe] (1706), *A True Relation of the Apparition of One Mrs. Veal*, London: B. Bragg.

★

The Preface

This relation is Matter of Fact, and attended with such Circumstances as may induce any Reasonable Man to believe it. It was sent by a Gentleman, a Justice of Peace at Maidstone in Kent, *and a very Intelligent Person, to his Friend in* London, *as it is here Worded; which Discourse is attested by a very sober and understanding Gentlewoman, a Kinswoman of the said Gentlemans, who lives in* Canterbury, *within a few Doors of the House in which the within named Mrs.* Bargrave *lives; who believes his Kinswoman to be of so discerning a Spirit, as not to be put upon by any Fallacy, and who possitively assured him, that the whole Matter, as it is here Related and laid down, is what is really True; and what She her self had in the same Words (as near as may be) from Mrs.* Bargraves *own Mouth, who she knows had no Reason to Invent and publish such a Story, nor any design to forge and tell a Lye, being a Woman of much Honesty and Virtue, and her whole Life a Course as it were of Piety. The use which we ought to make of it is, to consider, That there is a Life to come after this, and a Just God, who will retribute to every one according to the Deeds done in the Body; and therefore, to reflect upon our Past course of Life we have led in the World; That our Time is Short and Uncertain, and that if we would escape the Punishment of the Ungodly, and receive the Reward of the Righteous, which is the laying hold of Eternal Life, we ought for the time to come, to turn to God by a speedy Repentance, ceasing to do Evil and Learning to do Well: To seek after God Early, if happily he may be found of us, and lead such Lives for the future, as may be well pleasing in his sight.*

A True Relation of the Apparition of One Mrs. Veal

This thing is so rare in all its Circumstances, and on so good Authority, that my Reading and Conversation has not given me any thing like it; it is fit to gratifie the most Ingenious and Serious Enquirer. Mrs. *Bargrave* is the Person to whom Mrs. *Veal* Appeared after her Death; she is my Intimate Friend, and I can avouch for her Reputation, for these last fifteen or sixteen Years, on my own Knowledge; and I can confirm the Good Character she had from her Youth, to the time of my Acquaintance. Tho' since this Relation, she is Calumniated by some People, that are Friends to the Brother of Mrs. *Veal* who Appeared; who think the Relation of this Appearance to be a Reflection, and endeavour what they can to Blast Mrs. *Bargrave*'s Reputation; and to Laugh the Story out of Countenance. But the Circumstances thereof, and the Chearful Disposition of Mrs. *Bargrave*, notwithstanding the unheard of ill Usage of a very Wicked Husband, there is not the least sign of Dejection in her Face; nor did I ever hear her let fall a Desponding or Murmuring Expression; nay, not when actually under her Husbands Barbarity; which I have been Witness to, and several other Persons of undoubted Reputation.

Now you must know, that Mrs. *Veal* was a Maiden Gentlewoman of about 30 Years of Age, and for some Years last past, had been troubled with Fits; which were perceived coming on her, by her going from her Discourse very abruptly, to some impertinence: She was maintain'd by an only Brother, and kept his House in *Dover*. She was a very Pious Woman, and her Brother a very Sober Man to all appearance: But now he does all he can to Null or Quash the Story. Mrs. *Veal* was intimately acquainted with Mrs. *Bargrave* from her Childhood. Mrs. *Veals* Circumstances were then Mean; her Father did not take care of his Children as he ought, so that they were exposed to Hardships: And Mrs. *Bargrave* in those days, had as Unkind a Father, tho' She wanted for neither Food nor Cloathing, whilst Mrs. *Veal* wanted for both: So that it was in the Power of Mrs. *Bargrave* to be very much her Friend in several Instances, which mightily endear'd Mrs. *Veal*; insomuch that she would often say, Mrs. *Bargrave you are not only the Best, but the only Friend I have in the World; and no Circumstances of Life, shall ever dissolve my Friendship*. They would often Condole each others adverse Fortune, and read together, *Drelincourt upon Death*, and other good Books: And so like two Christian Friends, they comforted each other under their Sorrow.

Sometime after, Mr. *Veals* Friends got him a Place in the Custom-House at *Dover*, which occasioned Mrs. *Veal* by little and little, to fall off from her Intimacy with Mrs. *Bargrave*, tho' there was never any such thing as a Quarrel; but an Indifferency came on by degrees, till at last Mrs. *Bargrave* had not seen her in two Years and a half; tho' above a Twelve Month of the time, Mrs. *Bargrave* had been absent from *Dover*, and this last half Year, has been in *Canterbury* about two Months of the time, dwelling in a House of her own.

In this House, on the Eighth of *September* last, *viz*. 1705, She was sitting alone in the Forenoon, thinking over her Unfortunate Life, and arguing her self into a due Resignation to Providence, tho' her condition seem'd hard. And said she, *I have been provided for hitherto, and doubt not but I shall be still; and am well satisfied, that my Afflictions shall end, when it is most fit for me*: And then took up her Sewing-Work, which she had no sooner done, but she hears a Knocking at the Door; she went to see who it was there, and this prov'd to be Mrs. *Veal*, her Old Friend, who was in a Riding Habit: At that Moment of Time, the Clock struck Twelve at Noon.

Madam says Mrs. *Bargrave*, I am surprized to see you, you have been so long a stranger, but told her, she was glad to see her and offer'd to Salute her, which Mrs. *Veal* complyed with, till their Lips almost touched, and then Mrs. *Veal* drew her hand cross her own Eyes, and said, *I am not very well*, and so waved it. She told Mrs. *Bargrave*, she was going a Journey, and had a great mind to see her first: But says Mrs. *Bargrave*, *how came you to take a Journey alone? I am amaz'd at it, because I know you have so fond a Brother.* O! says Mrs. *Veal, I gave my Brother the Slip, and came away, because I had so great a Mind to see you before I took my Journy.* So Mrs. *Bargrave* went in with her, into another Room within the first, and Mrs. *Veal* sat her self down in an Elbow-chair, in which Mrs. *Bargrave* was sitting when she heard Mrs. *Veal* Knock. Then says Mrs. *Veal, My Dear Friend, I am come to renew our Old Friendship again, and to beg your Pardon for my breach of it, and if you can forgive me you are one of the best of Women. O!* says Mrs. *Bargrave, don't mention such a thing, I have not had an uneasie thought about it, I can easily forgive it.* What did you think of me says Mrs. *Veal*? Says Mrs. *Bargrave, I thought you were like the rest of the World, and that Prosperity had made you forget your self and me.* Then Mrs. *Veal* reminded Mrs. *Bargrave* of the many Friendly Offices she did her in former Days, and much of the Conversation they had with each other in the time of their Adversity; what Books they Read, and what Comfort in particular they received from *Drelincourt's Book of Death*, which was the best she said on that Subject, was ever Wrote. She also mentioned Dr. *Sherlock*, and two *Dutch* Books which were Translated, Wrote upon Death, and several others: But *Drelincourt* she said, had the clearest Notions of Death, and of the Future State, of any who have handled that Subject. Then she asked Mrs. *Bargrave*, whether she had *Drelincourt*; she said yes. Says Mrs. *Veal* fetch it, and so Mrs. *Bargrave* goes up Stairs, and brings it down. Says Mrs. *Veal*, Dear Mrs. *Bargrave, If the Eyes of our Faith were as open as the Eyes of our Body, we should see numbers of Angels about us for our Guard: The Notions we have of Heaven now, are nothing like what it is, as* Drelincourt *says. Therefore be comforted under your Afflictions, and believe that the Almighty has a particular regard to you; and that your Afflictions are Marks of Gods Favour: And when they have done the business they were sent for, they shall be removed from you.* And believe me my Dear Friend, believe what I say to you, *One Minute of future Happiness will infinitely reward you for all your Sufferings. For I can never believe,* (and claps her Hand upon her Knee, with a great deal of Earnestness, which indeed ran through all her Discourse) *that ever God will suffer you to spend all your Days in this Afflicted State: But be assured, that your Afflictions shall leave you, or you them in a short time.* She spake in that Pathetical and Heavenly manner, that Mrs. *Bargrave* wept several times; she was so deeply affected with it. Then Mrs. *Veal* mentioned Dr. *Hornecks Ascetick*, at the end of which, he gives an account of the Lives of the Primitive Christians. *Their Pattern she recommended to our Imitation;* and said, *their Conversation was not like this of our Age. For now* (says she) *there is nothing but frothy vain Discourse, which is far different from theirs. Theirs was to Edification, and to Build one another up in the Faith: So that they were not as we are, nor are we as they are; but* said she, *We might do as they did. There was a hearty*

Friendship among them, but where is it now to be found? Says Mrs. *Bargrave, 'tis hard indeed to find a true Friend in these days.* Says Mrs. *Veal*, Mr. *Norris* has a Fine Coppy of Verses, call'd *Friendship in Perfection*, which I wonderfully admire, have you seen the Book says Mrs. *Veal*? No, says Mrs. *Bargrave, but I have the Verses of my own writing out. Have you*, says Mrs. *Veal, then fetch them*; which she did from above Stairs, and offer'd them to Mrs. *Veal* to read, who refused, and wav'd the thing, saying, *holding down her Head would make it ake*, and then desired Mrs. *Bargrave* to read them to her, which she did. As they were admiring Friendship, Mrs. *Veal* said, Dear Mrs. *Bargrave*, I shall love you for ever: In the Verses, there is twice used the Word *Elysium*. Ah! says Mrs. *Veal*, *These Poets have such Names for Heaven.* She would often draw her Hand cross her own Eyes; and say, Mrs. *Bargrave Don't you think I am mightily impaired by my Fits?* No, says Mrs. Bargave, I think you look as well as ever I knew you.

After all this discourse, which the Apparition put in Words much finer than Mrs. *Bargrave* said she could pretend to, and was much more than she can remember (for it cannot be thought, that an hour and three quarters Conversation could all be retained, tho' the main of it, she thinks she does.) She said to Mrs. *Bargrave, she would have her write a Letter to her Brother, and tell him she would have him give Rings to such and such; and that there was a Purse of Gold in her Cabinet, and that she would have Two Broad Pieces given to her Cousin Watson.* Talking at this Rate, Mrs. *Bargrave* thought that a Fit was coming upon her, and so placed her self in a Chair, just before her Knees, to keep her from falling to the Ground, if her Fits should occasion it; for the Elbow Chair she thought would keep her from falling on either side. And to divert Mrs. *Veal* as she thought, she took hold of her Gown Sleeve several times, and commended it. Mrs. *Veal* told her, it was a Scower'd Silk, and newly made up. But for all this Mrs. *Veal* persisted in her Request, and told Mrs. *Bargrave* she must not deny her: and she would have her tell her Brother all their Conversation, when she had an opportunity. Dear Mrs. *Veal*, says Mrs. *Bargrave*, *this seems so impertinent, that I cannot tell how to comply with it; and what a mortifying Story will our Conversation be to a Young Gentleman?* Well, says Mrs. *Veal, I must not be deny'd.* Why, says Mrs. *Bargrave, 'tis much better methinks to do it your self*, No, says Mrs. *Veal; tho' it seems impertinent to you now, you will see more reason for it hereafter.* Mrs. *Bargrave* then to satisfie her importunity, was going to fetch a Pen and Ink; but Mrs. *Veal* said, *let it alone now, and do it when I am gone; but you must be sure to do it*: which was one of the last things she enjoin'd her at parting; and so she promised her.

Then Mrs. *Veal* asked for Mrs. *Bargraves* Daughter; she said she was not at home; but if you have a mind to see her says Mrs. *Bargrave*, I'le send for her. Do, says Mrs. *Veal*. On which she left her, and went to a

Neighbours, to send for her; and by the Time Mrs. *Bargrave* was returning, Mrs *Veal* was got without the Door in the Street, in the face of the *Beast-Market* on a Saturday (which is Market Day) and stood ready to part, as soon as Mrs. *Bargrave* came to her. She askt her, *Why she was in such hast?* she said, *she must be going; tho' perhaps she might not go her journey till Monday.* And told *Mrs.* Bargrave *she hoped she should see her again, at her Cousin* Watsons *before she went whither she was a going.* Then she said, *she would not take her Leave of her*, and walk'd from Mrs. *Bargrave* in her view, till a turning interrupted the sight of her, which was three quarters after One in the Afternoon.

Mrs. *Veal* Dyed the 7th of *September* at 12 a Clock at Noon, of her Fits, and had not above four hours Senses before her Death, in which time she received the Sacrament. The next day after Mrs. *Veals* appearing being Sunday, Mrs. *Bargrave* was mightily indisposed with a Cold, and a Sore Throat, that she could not go out that day: but on Monday morning she sends a person to Captain Watsons to know if Mrs. *Veal* were there. They wondered at Mrs. *Bargraves* enquiry, and sent her Word, that she was not there, nor was expected. At this Answer Mrs. *Bargrave* told the Maid she had certainly mistook the Name, or made some blunder. And tho' she was ill, she put on her Hood, and went her self to Captain *Watsons*, tho' she knew none of the Family, to see if Mrs. *Veal* was there or not. They said, they wondered at her asking, for that she had not been in Town; they were sure, if she had, she would have been there. Says Mrs. *Bargrave, I am sure she was with me on Saturday almost two hours.* They said it was impossible, for they must have seen her if she had. In comes Captain *Watson*, while they were in Dispute, and said that Mrs. *Veal* was certainly Dead, and her Escocheons[1] were making. This strangely surprised Mrs. *Bargrave*, who went to the Person immediately who had the care of them, and found it true. Then she related the whole Story to Captain *Watsons* Family, and what Gown she had on, and how striped. And that Mrs. *Veal* told her it was Scowred. Then Mrs. *Watson* cry'd out, *you have seen her indeed, for none knew but Mrs.* Veal *and my self, that the Gown was Scowr'd*; and Mrs. *Watson* own'd that she described the Gown exactly; for, said she, *I helpt her to make it up.* This, Mrs *Watson* blaz'd all about the Town, and avouch'd the Demonstration of the Truth of Mrs. *Bargraves* seeing Mrs. *Veal*'s Apparition. And Captain *Watson* carried two Gentlemen immediately to Mrs. *Bargraves* House, to hear the Relation from her own Mouth. And then it spread so fast, that Gentlemen and Persons of Quality, the Judicious and Sceptical part of the World, flock't in upon her, which at last became such a Task, that she was forc'd to go out of the way. For they were in general, extreamly satisfyed of the truth of the thing; and plainly saw, that Mrs. *Bargrave* was no Hypochondriack, for she always appears with such a chearful Air, and pleasing Mien, that she has gain'd the favor and esteem of all the Gentry. And its thought a great favor if they can but get the Relation from her own Mouth. I should have told you before, that Mrs. *Veal* told Mrs. *Bargrave*, that her Sister and Brother in Law, were just come down from *London* to see her. Says Mrs. *Bargrave, how came you to order matters so strangely? it could not be helpt* said Mrs. *Veal*; and her Sister and Brother did come to see her, and entred the Town of *Dover*, just as Mrs. Veal was *expiring*. Mrs. *Bargrave* asked her, whether she would not drink some Tea. Says Mrs. *Veal*, *I do not care if I do: But I'le Warrant this Mad Fellow* (meaning Mrs. *Bargraves* Husband,) *has broke all your Trinckets*. But, says Mrs. *Bargrave*, *I'le get something to Drink for all that;* but Mrs. *Veal* wav'd it, and said, *it is no matter, let it alone*, and so it passed.

All the time I sat with Mrs. *Bargrave*, which was some Hours, she recollected fresh sayings of Mrs. *Veal*. And one material thing more she told Mrs. *Bargrave*, that Old Mr. *Breton* allowed Mrs. *Veal* Ten pounds a Year, which was a secret, and unknown to Mrs. *Bargrave*, till Mrs. *Veal* told it her. Mrs. *Bargrave* never varies in her Story, which puzzles those who doubt of the Truth, or are unwilling to believe it. A Servant in a Neighbours Yard adjoining to Mrs. *Bargraves* House, heard her talking to some body, an hour of the Time Mrs. *Veal* was with her. Mrs. *Bargrave* went out to her next Neighbours the very Moment she parted with Mrs. *Veal*, and told what Ravishing Conversation she had with an Old Friend, and told the whole of it. *Drelincourt's Book of Death* is, since this happened, Bought up strangely. And it is to be observed, that notwithstanding all this Trouble and Fatigue Mrs. *Bargrave* has undergone upon this Account, she never took the value of a Farthing, nor suffer'd her Daughter to take any thing of any Body, and therefore can have no Interest in telling the Story.

But Mr. *Veal* does what he can to stifle the matter, and said he would see Mrs. *Bargrave*; but yet it is certain matter fact, that he has been at Captain *Watsons* since the Death of his Sister, and yet never went near Mrs. *Bargrave*; and some of his Friends report her to be a great Lyar, and that she knew of Mr. *Breton*'s Ten Pounds a Year. But the Person who pretends to say so, has the Reputation of a Notorious Lyar, among persons which I know to be of undoubted Repute. Now Mr. *Veal* is more a Gentleman, than to say she Lyes; but says, a bad Husband has Craz'd her. But she needs only to present her self, and it will effectually confute that Pretence. Mr. *Veal* says he ask'd his Sister on her Death Bed, whether she had a mind to dispose of any thing, and she said, No. Now what the things which Mrs. *Veals* Apparition would have disposed of, were so Trifling, and nothing of Justice aimed at in their disposal, that the design of it appears to me to be only in order to make Mrs. *Bargrave*, so to demonstrate the Truth of her Appearance, as to satisfie the World of the Reality thereof, as to what she had seen and heard: and to secure her Reputation among the Reasonable and understanding part of Mankind. And then again, Mr. *Veal* owns that there was a Purse of Gold; but it was not found in her Cabinet, but in a Comb-Box. This looks improbable, for that Mrs. *Watson* own'd that Mrs. *Veal* was so very careful of the Key of her Cabinet, that she would trust no Body with it. And if so, no doubt she would not trust her Gold out of it. And Mrs. *Veals* often drawing her hand over her Eyes, and asking Mrs. *Bargrave*, whether her Fits had not impair'd her; looks to me, as if she did it on purpose to remind Mrs. *Bargrave* of her Fits, to prepare her not to think it strange that she should put her upon Writing to her Brother to dispose of Rings and Gold, which looks so much like a dying Persons Bequest; and it took accordingly with Mrs. *Bargrave*, as the effect of her Fits coming upon her; and was one of the many Instances of her Wonderful Love to her, and Care of her, that she should not be affrighted: which indeed appears in her whole management; particularly in her coming to her in the day time, waving the Salutation, and when she was alone; and then the manner of her parting, to prevent a second attempt to Salute her.

Now, why Mr. *Veal* should think this Relation a Reflection, (as 'tis plain he does by his endeavouring to stifle it) I can't imagine, because the Generality believe her to be a good Spirit, her Discourse was so Heavenly. Her two great Errands were to comfort Mrs. *Bargrave* in her Affliction, and to ask her Forgiveness for her Breach of Friendship, and with a Pious Discourse to encourage her. So that after all, to suppose that Mrs. *Bargrave* could Hatch such an Invention as this from *Friday-Noon*, till *Saturday-Noon*, (supposing that she knew of Mrs. *Veals* Death the very first Moment) without jumbling Circumstances, and without any Interest too; she must be more Witty, Fortunate, and Wicked too, than any indifferent Person I dare say, will allow. I asked Mrs. *Bargrave* several times, *If she was sure she felt the Gown.* She answered Modestly, *if my Senses be to be relied on, I am sure of it.* I asked her, *If she heard a Sound, when she claps her Hand upon her Knee*: She said, *she did not remember she did*: And she said, *she Appeared to be as much a Substance as I did, who talked with her. And I may* said she, *be as soon persuaded that your Apparition is talking to me now, as that I did not really see her; for I was under no manner of Fear, I received her as a Friend, and parted with her as such. I would not*, says she, *give one Farthing to make any one believe it, I have no Interest, in it; nothing but trouble is entail'd upon me for a long time for ought that I know: and had it not come to Light by Accident, it would never have been made Publick.* But now she says, *she will make her own Private Use of it, and keep her self out of the way as much as she can.* And so she has done since. She says, *she had a Gentleman who came thirty Miles to her to hear the Relation; and that she had told it to a Room full of People at a time.* Several particular Gentlemen have had the Story from Mrs. *Bargraves* own Mouth.

This thing has very much affected me, and I am as well satisfied, as I am of the best grounded Matter of Fact. And why should we dispute Matter of Fact, because we cannot solve things, of which we can have no certain or demonstrative Notions, seems strange to me: Mrs. *Bargrave*'s Authority and Sincerity alone, would have been undoubted in any other Case.

Advertisement

Drelincourts's Book of the Consolations against the Fears of Death, *has been four times Printed already in English, of which many Thousands have been Sold, and not without great Applause: And its bearing so great a Character in this Relation, the Impression is near Sold off.*

1.2 Joseph Addison (1672–1719), *The Spectator*, Nos. 12 and 110 (1711)

Addison wrote a number of essays on superstition for the highly influential journal *The Spectator* (cf. particularly no. 117 on witchcraft). Later he would write a play, *The Drummer: or, The Haunted House* (1715), based on the case of the ghostly Drummer of Tedworth, which takes a sceptical stance on the supernatural through the device of a mock-ghost. But in the following essays his approach to the question of ghost-belief is more tentative. He follows Locke in opposing the transmission of popular superstitions, on the grounds that they disorder the faculty of reason in young minds. However, this view is tempered by the desire to articulate a more rational mode of spiritualism, in response to the danger of materialism. In both essays he assumes the character of 'Mr Spectator', the quintessential city-dweller and observer of social mores. In no. 110, another representative figure comes into play: Sir Roger de Coverley, member of the landed gentry.

Source: *The Spectator*, nos. 12 and 110 (14 March and 6 July 1711), from Donald F. Bond, ed. (1965) *The Spectator*, 5 vols, Oxford: Oxford University Press, vol. I, pp. 52–5, 453–6.

★

No. 12 (Wednesday 14 March 1711)

. . . *Veteres avias tibi de pulmone revello.*

Per.[2]

At my coming to London, it was some time before I could settle my self in a House to my likeing. I was forced to quit my first Lodgings, by reason of an officious Land-lady, that would be asking me every Morning how I had slept. I then fell into an honest Family, and lived very happily for above a Week; when my Land-lord, who was a jolly good-natur'd Man, took it into his Head that I wanted Company, and therefore would frequently come into my Chamber to keep me from being alone. This I bore for Two or Three Days; but telling me one Day that he was afraid I was melancholy, I thought it was high time for me to be gone, and accordingly took new Lodgings that very Night. About a Week after, I found my jolly Land-lord, who, as I said before was an honest hearty Man, had put me into an Advertisement of the *Daily Courant*, in the following Words. *Whereas a melancholy Man left his Lodgings on* Thursday *last in the afternoon, and was afterwards seen going toward* Islington; *If any one can give notice of him to* R. B. *Fishmonger in the* Strand, *he shall be very well rewarded for his Pains.* As I am the best Man in the World to keep my own Counsel, and my Land-lord the Fishmonger not knowing my Name, this Accident of my Life was never discovered to this very Day.

I am now settled with a Widow-woman, who has a great many Children, and complies with my Humour in every thing. I do not remember that we have exchang'd a Word together these Five Years; my Coffee comes into my Chamber every Morning without asking for it; if I want Fire I point to my Chimney, if Water to my Bason: Upon which my Land-lady nodds, as much as to say she takes my Meaning, and immediately obeys my Signals. She has likewise model'd her Family so well, that when her little Boy offers to pull me by the Coat or prattle in my Face, his eldest Sister immediately calls him off and bids him not disturb the Gentleman. At my first entering into the Family, I was troubled with the Civility of their rising up to me every time I came into the Room; but my Land-lady observing that upon these Occasions I always cried pish and went out again, has forbidden any such Ceremony to be used in the House; so that at present I walk into the Kitchin or Parlour without being taken notice of, or giving any Interruption to the Business or Discourse of the Family. The Maid will ask her Mistress (tho' I am by) whether the Gentleman is ready to go to Dinner, as the Mistress (who is indeed an excellent Housewife) scolds at the Servants as heartily before my Face as behind my Back. In short, I move up and down the House and enter into all Companies, with the same Liberty as a Cat or any other domestick Animal, and am as little suspected of telling any thing that I hear or see.

I remember last Winter there were several young Girls of the Neighbourhood sitting about the Fire with my Land-lady's Daughters, and telling Stories of Spirits and Apparitions. Upon my opening the Door the young Women broke off their Discourse, but my Land-lady's Daughters telling them that it was no Body but the Gentleman (for that is the Name which I go by in the Neighbourhood as well as in the Family) they went on without minding me. I seated my self by the Candle that stood on a Table at one End of the Room; and pretending to read a Book that I took out of my Pocket, heard several dreadful Stories of Ghosts as pale as Ashes that had stood at the Feet of a Bed, or walked over a Church-yard by Moon-light: And of others that had been conjured into the *Red-Sea*, for disturbing People's Rest, and drawing their Curtains at Midnight; with many other old Womens Fables of the like Nature. As one Spirit raised another, I observed that at the End of every Story, the whole Company closed their Ranks and crouded about the Fire: I took Notice in particular of a little Boy, who was so attentive to every Story, that I am mistaken if he ventures to go to bed by himself this Twelvemonth. Indeed they talked so long, that the Imaginations of the whole Assembly were manifestly crazed, and I am sure will be the worse for it as long as they live. I heard one of the Girls, that had looked upon me over her Shoulder, asking the Company how long I had been in the Room, and whether I did not look paler than I used to do. This put me under some Apprehensions that I should be forced to explain my self if I did not retire; for which Reason I took the Candle in my Hand, and went up into my Chamber, not without wondering at this unaccountable Weakness in reasonable Creatures, that they should love to astonish and terrify one another. Were I a Father, I should take a particular Care to preserve my Children from these little Horrours of Imagination, which they are apt to contract when they are young, and are not able to shake off when they are in Years. I have known a Soldier that has enter'd a Breach, affrighted at his own Shadow; and look pale upon a little scratching at his Door, who the Day before had march'd up against a Battery of Cannon. There are Instances of Persons, who have been terrify'd, even to Distraction, at the Figure of a Tree or the shaking of a Bull-rush. The Truth of it is, I look upon a sound Imagination as the greatest Blessing of Life, next to a clear Judgment and a good Conscience. In the mean Time, since there are very few whose Minds are not more or less subject to these dreadful Thoughts and Apprehensions, we ought to arm our selves against them by the Dictates of Reason and Religion, *to pull the old Woman out of our Hearts* (as *Persius* expresses it in the Motto of my Paper,) and extinguish those impertinent Notions which we imbibed at a Time that we were not able to judge of their Absurdity. Or if we believe, as many wise and good Men have done, that there are such Phantoms and Apparitions as those I have been speaking of, let us endeavour to establish to our selves an Interest in him who holds the Reins of the whole Creation in his Hand, and moderates them after such a Manner, that it is impossible for one Being to break loose upon another without his Knowledge and Permission.

For my own Part, I am apt to join in Opinion with those who believe that all the Regions of Nature swarm with Spirits; and that we have Multitudes of Spectators on all our Actions, when we think our selves most alone: But instead of terrifying my self with such a Notion, I am wonderfully pleased to think that I am always engaged with such an innumerable Society in searching out the Wonders of the Creation, and joining in the same Consort of Praise and Adoration.

Milton has finely described this mixed Communion of Men and Spirits in Paradise; and had doubtless his Eye upon a Verse in old *Hesiod*, which is almost Word for Word the same with his third Line in the following Passage

> . . . Nor think, though Men were none,
> That Heav'n would want Spectators, God want Praise:
> Millions of spiritual Creatures walk the Earth
> Unseen, both when we wake and when we sleep;
> All these with ceaseless Praise his Works behold
> Day and Night. How often from the Steep
> Of echoing Hill or Thicket, have we heard
> Celestial Voices to the midnight Air,
> Sole, or responsive each to others Note,
> Singing their great Creator: Oft in Bands,
> While they keep Watch, or nightly Rounding walk,
> With heav'nly Touch of instrumental Sounds,
> In full harmonick Number join'd, their Songs
> Divide the Night, and lift our Thoughts to Heaven.[3]

No. 110 (Friday 6 July 1711)

Horror ubique animos, simul ipsa silentia terrent.
Virg.[4]

At a little Distance from Sir ROGER's House, among the Ruins of an old Abby, there is a long Walk of aged Elms; which are shot up so very high, that when one passes under them, the Rooks and Crows that rest upon the Tops of them seem to be Cawing in another Region. I am very much delighted with this Sort of Noise, which I consider as a kind of natural Prayer to that Being who supplies the Wants of his whole Creation, and who in the beautiful Language of the *Psalms*, feedeth the young Ravens that call upon him. I like this Retirement the better, because of an ill Report it lies under of being *haunted*; for which Reason (as I have been told in the Family) no living Creature ever walks in it besides the Chaplain. My good Friend the Butler desired me with a very grave Face not to venture myself in it after Sun-set, for that one of the Footmen had been almost frighted out of his Wits by a Spirit that appeared to him in the Shape of a black Horse without an Head; to which he added, that about a Month ago one of the Maids coming home late that Way with a Pail of Milk upon her Head, heard such a Rustling among the Bushes that she let it fall.

I was taking a Walk in this Place last Night between the Hours of Nine and Ten, and could not but fancy it one of the most proper Scenes in the World for a Ghost to appear in. The Ruins of the Abby are scattered up and down on every Side, and half covered with Ivy and Eldar-Bushes, the Harbours of several solitary Birds which seldom make their Appearance till the Dusk of the Evening. The Place was formerly a Church-yard, and has still several Marks in it of Graves and Burying-Places. There is such an Eccho among the old Ruins and Vaults, that if you stamp but a little louder than ordinary you hear the Sound repeated. At the same Time the Walk of Elms, with the Croaking of the Ravens which from time to time are heard from the Tops of them, looks exceeding solemn and venerable. These Objects naturally raise Seriousness and Attention; and when Night heightens the Awfulness of the Place, and pours out her supernumerary Horrours upon every thing in it, I do not at all wonder that weak Minds fill it with Spectres and Apparitions.

Mr. *Lock*, in his Chapter of the Association of Ideas, has very curious Remarks to shew how by the Prejudice of Education one Idea often introduces into the Mind a whole Set that bear no Resemblance to one another in the Nature of things. Among several Examples of this Kind he produces the following Instance. *The Ideas of Goblins and Sprights have really no more to do with Darkness than Light; yet let but a foolish Maid inculcate these often on the Mind of a Child, and raise them there together, possibly he shall never be able to separate them again so long as he lives, but Darkness shall ever afterwards bring with it those frightful Ideas, and they shall be so joyned, that he can no more bear the one than the other.*[5]

As I was walking in this Solitude, where the Dusk of the Evening conspired with so many other Occasions of Terrour, I observed a Cow grazing not far from me, which an Imagination that is apt to *startle* might easily have construed into a black Horse without an Head; and I dare say the poor Footman lost his Wits upon some such trivial Occasion.

My Friend Sir ROGER has often told me with a great deal of Mirth, that at first coming to his Estate he found three Parts of his House altogether useless; that the best Room in it had the Reputation of being haunted, and by that Means was locked up; that Noises had been heard in his long Gallery, so that he could not get a Servant to enter it after eight a Clock at Night; that the Door of one of his Chambers was nailed up, because there went a Story in the Family that a Butler had formerly hanged himself in it; and that his Mother, who lived to a great Age, had shut up half the Rooms in the House, in which either her Husband, a Son, or Daughter had died. The Knight seeing his Habitation reduced to so small a Compass, and himself in a Manner shut out of his own House, upon the Death of his Mother ordered all the Apartments to be flung open, and *exorcised* by his Chaplain, who lay in every Room one after another, and by that Means dissipated the Fears which had so long reigned in the Family.

I should not have been thus particular upon these ridiculous Horrours, did not I find them so very much prevail in all Parts of the Country. At the same Time I think a Person who is thus terrify'd with the Imagination of Ghosts and Spectres much more reasonable, than one who contrary to the Reports of all Historians sacred and prophane, ancient and modern, and to the Traditions of all Nations, thinks the Appearance of Spirits fabulous and groundless: Could not I give my self up to this general Testimony of Mankind, I should to the Relations of particular Persons who are now living, and whom I cannot distrust in other Matters of Fact. I might here add, that not only the Historians, to whom we may joyn the Poets, but likewise the Philosophers of Antiquity have favoured this Opinion. *Lucretius* himself, though by the Course of his Philosophy he was obliged to maintain that the Soul did not exist separate from the Body, makes no Doubt of the Reality of Apparitions, and that Men have often appeared after their Death. This I think very remarkable; he was so pressed with the Matter of Fact which he could not have the Confidence to deny, that he was forced to account for it by one of the most absurd unphilosophical Notions that was ever started. He tells, us, That the Surfaces of all Bodies are perpetually flying off from their respective Bodies, one after another; and that these Surfaces or thin Cases that included each other whilst they were joined in the Body like the Coats of an Onion, are sometimes seen entire when they are separated from it; by which Means we often behold the Shapes and Shadows of Persons who are either dead or absent.

I shall dismiss this Paper with a Story out of *Josephus*, not so much for the Sake of the Story it self, as for the moral Reflections with which the Author concludes it, and I shall here set down in his own Words.[6] '*Glaphyra* the Daughter of King *Archilaus*, after the Death of her first Husbands (being married to a third, who was Brother to her first Husband, and so passionately in Love with her that he turn'd off his former Wife to make Room for this Marriage) had a very odd kind of Dream. She fancied that she saw her first Husband coming towards her, and that she embraced him with great Tenderness; when in the Midst of the Pleasure which she expressed at the Sight of him, he reproached her after the following Manner: *Glaphyra*, says he, thou hast made good the old Saying, That Women are not to be trusted. Was not I the Husband of thy Virginity? have I not Children by thee: How couldst thou forget our Loves so far as to enter into a second Marriage, and after that into a third, nay to take for thy Husband a Man who has so shamelessly crept into the Bed of his Brother? However, for the Sake of our passed Loves, I shall free thee from thy present Reproach, and make thee mine for ever. *Glaphyra* told this Dream to several Women of her Acquaintance, and died soon after. I though this Story might not be impertinent in this Place, wherein I speak of those Kings: Besides that, the Example deserves to be taken Notice of, as it contains a most certain Proof of the Immortality of the

Soul, and of Divine Providence. If any Man thinks these Facts incredible, let him enjoy his Opinion to himself, but let him not endeavour to disturb the Belief of others, who by Instances of this Nature are excited to the Study of Virtue.'

1.3 Thomas Parnell (1679–1718), 'A Night Piece on Death' (1721)

The so-called 'Graveyard School' of poetry follows Addison in attempting to elevate or abstract superstitious fears for moral and religious purposes. The period 1740 to 1752 was the heyday of melancholy verse (Sickels, 1969, p. 4). Edward Young's *The Complaint, or Night Thoughts on Life, Death, and Immortality* (1742–3), Robert Blair's *The Grave* (1743) and James Hervey's prose *Meditations Among the Tombs* (1746–7) all dwell luxuriously on the horror and mystery of death before ending with a call to faith and fortitude. They were immensely popular, and '*Youngisme*' became a European phenomenon (McManners, 1985, p. 337). Parnell's poem, published after his death, anticipated the trend, and displays its characteristic features, but, being uncharacteristically brief, can be included here in its entirety.

Source: *The Collected Poems of Thomas Parnell*, eds Claude Rawson and F. P. Lock (1989), Delaware: University of Delaware Press; London and Toronto: Associated University Presses.

By the blue Tapers trembling Light,
No more I waste the wakeful Night,
Intent with endless view to pore
The Schoolmen and the Sages o'er:
Their Books from Wisdom widely stray,
Or point at best the longest Way.
I'll seek a readier Path, and go
Where Wisdom's surely taught *below*.

How deep yon Azure dies the Sky!
Where Orbs of Gold unnumber'd lye,
While thro' their Ranks in silver pride
The nether Crescent seems to glide.
The slumb'ring Breeze forgets to breathe,
The Lake is smooth and clear beneath,
Where once again the spangled Show
Descends to meet our Eyes below.
The Grounds which on the right aspire,

In dimness from the View retire:
The Left presents a Place of Graves,
Whose Wall the silent Water laves.
The Steeple guides thy doubtful sight
Among the livid gleams of Night.
There pass with melancholy State,
By all the solemn Heaps of Fate,
And think, as softly-sad you tread
Above the venerable Dead,
Time was, like thee they life possest,
And Time shall be, that thou shalt Rest.

Those Graves, with bending Osier bound,
That nameless heave the crumbled Ground,
Quick to the glancing Thought disclose
Where *Toil* and *Poverty* repose.

The flat smooth Stones that bear a Name,
The Chissels slender help to Fame,
(Which e'er our Sett of Friends decay
Their frequent Steps may wear away.)
A middle Race of Mortals own,
Men, half ambitious, all unknown.

The Marble Tombs that rise on high,
Whose Dead in vaulted Arches lye,
Whose Pillars swell with sculptur'd Stones,
Arms, Angels, Epitaphs and Bones,
These (all the poor Remains of State)
Adorn the *Rich*, or praise the *Great*;
Who while on Earth in Fame they live,
Are sensless of the Fame they give.

Ha! while I gaze, pale *Cynthia* fades,
The bursting Earth unveils the Shades!
All slow, and wan, and wrap'd with Shrouds,
They rise in visionary Crouds,
And all with sober Accent cry,
Think, Mortal, what it is to dye.

Now from yon black and fun'ral Yew,
That bathes the Charnel House with Dew,
Methinks I hear a *Voice* begin;
(Ye Ravens, cease your croaking Din,
Ye tolling Clocks, no Time resound

O'er the long Lake and midnight Ground)
It sends a Peal of hollow Groans,
Thus speaking from among the Bones.

When Men my Scythe and Darts supply,
How great a *King of Fears* am I!
They view me like the last of Things:
They make, and then they dread, my Stings.
Fools! if you less provok'd your Fears,
No more my Spectre-Form appears.
Death's but a Path that must be trod,
If Man wou'd ever pass to God:
A Port of Calms, a State of Ease
From the rough Rage of swelling Seas.

Why then thy flowing sable Stoles,
Deep pendent Cypress, mourning Poles,
Loose Scarfs to fall athwart thy Weeds,
Long Palls, drawn Herses, cover'd Steeds,
And Plumes of black, that as they tread,
Nod o'er the 'Scutcheons of the Dead?[7]

Nor can the parted Body know,
Nor wants the Soul, these Forms of Woe:
As men who long in Prison dwell,
With Lamps that glimmer round the Cell,
When e'er their suffering Years are run,
Spring forth to greet the glitt'ring Sun:
Such Joy, tho' far transcending Sense,
Have pious Souls at parting hence.
On Earth, and in the Body plac't,
A few, and evil Years, they wast:
But when their Chains are cast aside,
See the glad Scene unfolding wide,
Clap the glad Wing and tow'r away,
And mingle with the Blaze of Day.

1.4 William Mallet (1705?–65), 'William and Margaret' (1724)

Mallet's poem played an influential part in the revival of interest in ballads, which was linked in turn to the contemporary intellectual trends of anti-quarianism and primitivism. Like *The Castle of Otranto*, the poem was originally published as an anonymous work of some antiquity (see Percy, 1966, vol. 3, p. 309). But in a later edition of his works, Mallet explained how its composition was inspired by the coincidence of reading an old ballad reproduced in *The Knight of the Burning Pestle* ('Fair Margaret and Sweet William', which also appears in Percy's *Reliques*), and his first-hand knowledge of a similar tragedy: 'It was then midnight. All around me was still and quiet. The concurring circumstances worked my soul to a powerful melancholy. I could not sleep. And at that time I finished my little poem, such as you see it here' (cited in Percy, 1893, p. 569). The combination of sentiment and supernaturalism in the story of broken love vows proved popular. From the 1720s Allan Ramsay was engaged in similar renovations of Scottish ballads, many of them concerned with popular superstitions, which would have an influence on William Collins (see section 1.9) and Robert Burns. Thomas Percy's *Reliques of Ancient English Poetry* (1765) contained three versions of this ballad: one traditional, another Mallet's and the third taken from Ramsay's *Tea-table Miscellany*. In the 1790s, two immensely successful poems offered sensational variations on a similar theme: M. G. Lewis's 'Alonso the Brave and the Fair Imogene' (from *The Monk*) and Gottfried August Bürger's 'Lenore' (3.13).

Source: First published in *The Plain Dealer*, no. 36 (July 1724). Quoted from Roger Lonsdale, ed. (1984) *The New Oxford Book of Eighteenth-century Verse*, Oxford and New York: Oxford University Press, pp. 159–61.

★

'Twas at the silent, solemn hour,
  When night and morning meet;
In glided Margaret's grimly ghost,
  And stood at William's feet.

Her face was like an April morn,
  Clad in a wintry cloud:
And clay-cold was her lily hand,
  That held her sable shroud.

So shall the fairest face appear,
  When youth and years are flown:
Such is the robe that kings must wear,
  When death has reft their crown.

Her bloom was like the springing flower,
  That sips the silver dew;
The rose was budded in her cheek,
  Just opening to the view.

But love had, like the canker-worm,
  Consumed her early prime:
The rose grew pale, and left her cheek;
  She died before her time.

'Awake!' she cried, 'thy true love calls,
  Come from her midnight grave;
Now let thy pity hear the maid
  Thy love refused to save.

'This is the dumb and dreary hour,
  When injured ghosts complain;
When yawning graves give up their dead
  To haunt the faithless swain.

'Bethink thee, William, of thy fault,
  Thy pledge, and broken oath:
And give me back my maiden vow,
  And give me back my troth.

'Why did you promise love to me,
  And not that promise keep?
Why did you swear my eyes were bright,
  And leave those eyes to weep?

'How could you say my face was fair,
  And yet that face forsake?
How could you win my virgin heart,
  Yet leave that heart to break?

'Why did you say my lip was sweet,
  And made the scarlet pale?
And why did I, young, witless maid,
  Believe the flattering tale?

'That face, alas! no more is fair;
  Those lips no longer red;
Dark are my eyes, now closed in death,
  And every charm is fled.

'The hungry worm my sister is;
  This winding-sheet I wear:
And cold and weary lasts our night,
  Till that last morn appear.

'But hark! – the cock has warned me hence;
A long and late adieu!
Come, see, false man, how low she lies,
Who died for love of you.'

The lark sung loud; the morning smiled,
And raised her glistering head;
Pale William quaked in every limb,
And raving left his bed.

He hied him to the fatal place
Where Margaret's body lay:
And stretched him on the grass-green turf,
That wrapped her breathless clay.

And thrice he called on Margaret's name,
And thrice he wept full sore:
Then laid his cheek to her cold grave,
And word spake never more.

1.5 Anon., 'Political Vampyres' (1732)

The vampire superstitions of Eastern Europe first became known in Britain in 1732, as a result of an official enquiry by the Austrian government into strange events surrounding the death of Arnold Paole, a Serbian soldier. The resulting report gave rise to numerous embellished versions, in the form of pamphlets and periodical articles, and these in turn aroused considerable debate (Frayling, 1991, pp. 19–36). According to Horace Walpole, King George II became convinced of the existence of vampires. This item is from *The Craftsman*, a journal fiercely opposed to the Prime Minister Robert Walpole (father of the author of *The Castle of Otranto*). It rehearses the standard charges made against the Whig government, centring on financial corruption. In doing so, it incidentally displaces the opposition of credulity and scepticism with a materialist interpretation of the case reminiscent of Franco Moretti's well-known Marxist reading of *Dracula* (Moretti, 1983, pp. 83–108). The piece could be regarded simply as an elaborate joke, but the reading of superstitious fictions as allegories of political oppression remained an option for early readers of Gothic (cf. Hurd, 2.6; and see Clery, 1995, pp. 68–9).

Source: First published: *The Craftsman*, no. 307 (20 May 1732). Quoted from *Gentleman's Magazine*, May 1732, pp. 750–2.

★

In the *London Journal*, Mar. 11. p. 631 was an Account of a Prodigy discover'd at *Madreyga* in *Hungary*, namely of *dead Bodies* sucking, as it were, the Blood of *Living*; the *latter* visibly drying up, while the *former* are fill'd with Blood. They are call'd *Vampyres*; see the Story of *Paul Arnold*, p. 681.

Mr. D'anvers was in company where a Dispute happen'd upon this extraordinary Narrative, between a grave *Doctor of Physick* and a beautiful young *Lady*, an Admirer of strange Occurrences. The Doctor ridicul'd such romantick Stories, as common Artifices of News-writers to fill up their Papers; The Lady insisted on the Truth of this Relation, which stood attested by unexceptionable Witnesses, 4 of them Surgeons, and 2 Officers of the Army. The Doctor replied that all the Surgeons and Soldiers in the Universe should never make him believe, that a dead inanimate Body, could torment the Living by *sucking their Blood*; it being contrary to the Principles, Philosophy, and the Laws of Nature. The Lady, a little nettled, returned, – 'Sure, Doctor, you cannot have forgot the Story of the famous Rabbit-Woman of Godalmin, which you persuaded us to believe'.[8] This produc'd a Laugh on the Lady's Side, who turning to *Mr. D'anvers* with an Air of Triumph, said, 'I am sure, Mr. *D'anvers*, You are of my Opinion, and believe there may be Vampyres'. – Mr. *D'anvers* answer'd,

I must agree with the learned Doctor, that an inanimate Corpse cannot perform any vital Functions; yet, agree with the Lady that there are Vampyres. This Account, you'll observe, comes from the Eastern Part of the World, always remarkable for the *Allegorical Style*. The States of *Hungary* are in *Subjection* to the *Turks* and *Germans*, and govern'd by a pretty hard Hand; which obliges them to couch all their Complaints under *Figures*. This Relation seems to be of the same kind.

These *Vampyres* are said to torment and kill the Living by sucking out all their Blood; and a *ravenous Minister*, in this part of the World, is compared to a *Leech* or a *Blood-sucker*, and carries his Oppressions beyond the Grave, by anticipating the *publick Revenues*, and entailing a Perpetuity of *Taxes*, which must gradually drain the Body Politick of its Blood and Spirits.

In like manner, Persons who groan under the Burthens of such a *Minister*, by selling or mortgaging their Estates, torment their unhappy Posterity, and become *Vampyres* when dead.

Paul Arnold, who is call'd a *Heyduke*,[9] was only a *ministerial Tool*, because it is said he had kill'd but 4 Persons; whereas, if he had been a *Vampyre* of any Rank, we shou'd probably have heard of his *Ten Thousands*. It may be objected that his Body, after it had been buried 40 Days, was free from Corruption. It is the *Mind*, not the *Body* is the Author of all Wickedness; and a Man can no more carry his bad Qualities, than his Riches with him to the Grave. His Corruption and the Fruits of it remains to stinck in the Nostrils of his Posterity.

As to the driving a Stake thro' the Heart of *Arnold*, at which he gave an horrid Groan and lost a great deal of Blood. This seems an Argument that the whole Story is a *Fable*, us'd to convey a satirical Invective against some *living Oppressor*; for it is impossible that a dead Corpse should be sensible of any Pain, or express it by any Sounds. The Blood which *Arnold* lost in driving the Stake thro' his Heart, might figurate the making him refund the *corrupt Wages*, which he had suck'd out of the Veins of his Countrymen. History, especially our own, supplies us with so many Instances of *Vampyres* in this Sense, that it wou'd fill Volumes to enumerate them. The *Gavestons, Spencers, De la Poles, Empson* and *Dudley, Wolsey*, and *Buckingham*,[10] were *Vampyres* of the first Magnitude; nor do we want later Instances.

Private Persons may be Vampyres, or Blood-suckers, i.e. Sharpers, Usurers, and Stockjobbers, fraudulent Guardians, unjust Stewards, and the dry Nurses of great Estates; a noble Colonel lately deceas'd, some *S. Sea Directors*,[11] and the Managers of the *Charitable Corporation*; but nothing less that the Power of a Tr[easu]ry can raise up a compleat *Vampyre*.

'Tis somewhere observed, that *Cecil*, E. of *Salisbury* was the last good Treasurer, and the first bad one, since Q. *Elizabeth*'s Reign; perhaps this is too severe; for we are told the Bp *Juxton* accompted with the utmost Exactness, and the Earls of *Godolphin* and *Oxford* went out of their Office with *clean Hands*, and died *poor*. *Mezeray* tells us of one *Girard de Possi*, who being seized with a Remorse of Conscience for having robb'd his Master, refunded it into the Exchequer of his own Accord: But the Historian adds, *he believes this Example will always remain singular*.

1.6 Horace Walpole (1717–97), on the Cock Lane ghost (1762)

For a few weeks in January and February 1762, the newspapers carried reports of a haunting at a lodging house in the East End of London. Walpole was one of numerous visitors who went to witness a spirit that knocked in response to questions from the curious. Samuel Johnson was among those who hoped the phenomenon would provide proof of the afterlife, while Oliver Goldsmith wrote a pamphlet, *The Mystery Revealed* (1762), exposing it as a fraud. The most intriguing and significant aspect of the case, however, was the recasting of the ghost into a form of fashionable spectacle; a development to which Walpole testifies. He ignores the religious and philosophical debate on the supernatural, and focuses instead on the entertainment value of the marvellous (not, unfortunately, to be manifested on this particular evening).

Source: from a letter to George Montagu. 29 January 1762 in *The Yale Edition of Horace Walpole's Correspondence*, ed. W. S. Lewis, 48 vols (1937–83), New Haven: Yale University Press, vol. 10, pp. 5–7.

★

I could send you volumes on the ghost; I went to hear it – for it is not an *apparition*, but an *audition*. – We set out from the Opera, changed our clothes at Northumberland House, the Duke of York, Lady Northumberland, Lady Mary Coke, Lord Hertford, and I, all in one hackney coach, and drove to the spot; it rained torrents; yet the lane was full of mob, and the house so full we could not get in – at last they discovered it was the Duke of York, and the company squeezed themselves into one another's pockets to make room for us. The house, which is borrowed, is wretchedly small and miserable; when we opened the chamber, in which were fifty people, with no light but one tallow candle at the end, we tumbled over the bed of the child to whom the ghost comes, and whom they are murdering there by inches in such insufferable heat and stench. At the top of the room are ropes to dry clothes – I asked, if we were to have rope dancing[12] between the acts? – we had nothing; they told us, as they would at a puppet-show, that it would not come that night till seven in the morning – that is, when there are only prentices and old women. We stayed, however, till half an hour after one.

1.7 John Wesley (1703–91), 'Narrative drawn up by Mr John Wesley, and published by him in the *Arminian Magazine*' (1784)

Eighteenth-century debate on superstition was punctuated by a series of *causes célèbres,* which tended to highlight the division between popular and elite culture. The cases of Mary Tofts (who allegedly gave birth to a litter of rabbits), of Elizabeth Canning (succoured by angels), and of the poltergeist in Cock Lane (1.6) stratified opinion. The Methodists shared the interest of Glanvill (see headnote to 1.1) and Defoe in authenticating miracles as a spur to religious faith. Methodists were active in publicising the Cock Lane ghost in 1762; many years earlier, in 1716, the family of John Wesley, founder of Methodism, had experienced a haunting in their own home. A detailed record of events was kept by Wesley's father Samuel, the Rector of Epworth, and eventually Wesley, who had been absent at the time, used it as the basis for a journal article. In the latter part of the narrative, not included here, the poltergeist is named as 'Old Jeffries', 'the name of one that died in the house'; after two months, the disturbances suddenly ceased.

Source: A. Clarke (1823), *Memoirs of the Wesley Family*, London: J. Kershaw, pp. 166–72; extract pp. 166–9.

★

When I was very young, I heard several letters read, wrote to my elder brother by my father, giving an account of strange Disturbances, which were in his house at Epworth, in Lincolnshire.

When I went down thither, in the year 1720, I carefully enquired into the particulars. I spoke to each of the persons who were then in the house, and took down what each could testify of his or her own knowledge. The sum of which was this.

On Dec. 2, 1716, while Robert Brown, my father's servant, was sitting with one of the maids a little before ten at night, in the dining room which opened into the garden, they both heard one knocking at the door. Robert rose and opened it, but could see nobody. Quickly it knocked again, and groaned. 'It is Mr. Turpine,' said Robert: 'he has the stone, and uses to groan so.' He opened the door again twice or thrice, the knocking being twice or thrice repeated. But still seeing nothing, and being a little startled, they rose and went up to bed. When Robert came to the top of the garret stairs, he saw a handmill, which was at a little distance, whirled about very swiftly. When he related this he said, 'Nought vexed me, but that it was empty. I thought, if it had but been full of malt he might have ground his heart out for me.' When he was in bed, he heard as it were the gobbling of a turkey-cock, close to the bed-side: and soon after, the sound of one stumbling over his shoes and boots, but there were none there; he had left them below. The next day, he and the maid related these things to the other maid, who laughed heartily, and said, 'What a couple of fools are you! I defy any thing to fright me.' After churning in the evening, she put the butter in the tray, and had no sooner carried it into the dairy, than she heard a knocking on the shelf where several puncheons of milk stood, first above the shelf, then below. She took a candle, and searched both above and below; and being able to find nothing, threw down butter, tray and all, and run away for life. The next evening between five and six o'clock my sister Molly, then about twenty years of age, sitting in the dining room, reading, heard as if it were the door that led into the hall open, and a person walking in, that seemed to have on a silk night-gown, rustling and trailing along. It seemed to walk round her, then to the door, then round again: but she could see nothing. She thought, 'it signifies nothing to run away: for whatever it is, it can run faster than me.' So she rose, put her book under her arm, and walked slowly away. After supper, she was sitting with my sister Sukey, (about a year older than her,) in one of the chambers, and telling her what had happened, she quite made light of it; telling her, 'I wonder you are so easily frighted; I would fain see what would fright me.' Presently a knocking began under the table. She took the candle and looked, but could find nothing. Then the iron casement began to clatter, and the lid of a warming pan. Next the latch of the door moved up and down without ceasing. She started up, leaped into the bed without undressing, pulled the bed clothes over her head, and never ventured to look up till next morning. A night or two after, my sister Hetty, a year younger than my sister Molly, was waiting as usual between nine and ten, to take away my father's candle, when she heard one coming down the garret stairs, walking slowly by her, then going down the best stairs, then up the back stairs, and up the garret stairs. And at every step it seemed the house shook from top to bottom. Just then my father knocked. She went in, took his candle, and got to bed as fast as possible. In the morning she told this to my eldest sister, who told her, 'You know, I believe none of these things. Pray let me take away the candle to-night, and I will find out the trick.' She accordingly took my sister Hetty's place; and had no sooner taken away the candle, than she heard a noise below. She hastened down stairs to the hall, where the noise was. But it was then in the kitchen. She ran into the kitchen, where it was drumming on the inside of the screen. When she went round it was drumming on the outside, and so always on the side opposite to her. Then she heard a knocking at the back kitchen door. She ran to it; unlocked it softly; and when the knocking was repeated, suddenly opened it: but nothing was to be seen. As soon as she had shut it, the knocking began again. She opened it again, but could see nothing: when she went to shut the door, it was violently thrust against her; she let it fly open, but nothing appeared. She went again to shut it, and it was again thrust against her: but she set her knee and her shoulder to the door, forced it too, and turned the key. Then the knocking began again: but she let it go on, and went up to bed. However, from that time she was throughly convinced that there was no imposture in the affair.

The next morning my sister telling my mother what had happened, she said, 'If I hear any thing myself, I shall know how to judge.' Soon after, she begged her to come into the nursery. She did, and heard in the corner of the room, as it were the violent rocking of a cradle: but no cradle had been there for some years. She was convinced it was preternatural, and earnestly prayed it might not disturb her in her own chamber at the hours of retirement; and it never did. She now thought it was proper to tell my father. But he was extremely angry, and said, 'Sukey, I am ashamed of you: these boys and girls fright one another: but you are a woman of sense, and should know better. Let me hear of it no more.'

At six in the evening, he had family prayers as usual. When he began the prayer for the king, a knocking began all round the room; and a thundering knock attended the Amen. The same was heard from this time every morning and evening, while the prayer for the King was repeated. As both my father and mother are now at rest, and incapable of being pained thereby, I think it my duty to furnish the serious Reader with a key to this circumstance.

The year before King William died, my father observed my mother did not say Amen to the prayer for the King. She said she could not; for she did not believe the Prince of Orange was King. He vowed he never would cohabit with her till she did. He then took his horse, and rode away; nor did she hear any thing of him for a twelvemonth. He then came back, and lived with her as before. But I fear his vow was not forgotten before God.

1.8 The example of Shakespeare

In the course of the eighteenth century, Shakespeare became established in critical opinion as the pre-eminent national poet. However, there was continuing controversy about aspects of his plays which failed to meet the rules of neo-classical decorum; among them, his use of the supernatural, especially in *Hamlet* and *Macbeth* (see Babcock, 1964, pp. 70–7).

1.8a Arthur Murphy, *The Entertainer* (1754)

Murphy follows Addison in seeing the tendency to superstition as a peculiarly English characteristic (see 3.3). But he takes a firmly rationalist stance against it, only slightly linking representation of the supernatural to imaginative creativity towards the end of this account. Shakespeare is held to share the enlightened view; the spectres in *Hamlet* and *Macbeth* are psychological projections.

Source: *The Entertainer*, no. 11 (12 November 1754). Quoted from Brian Vickers, ed. (1976), *Shakespeare: The Critical Heritage*, vol. 4, London, Boston and Henley: Routledge & Kegan Paul, pp. 156–8.

★

This nation has in all ages been much more addicted to folly and superstition than any other whatever. The belief of GHOSTS and APPARITIONS is at present as strongly implanted in the minds of the major part of the inhabitants of this kingdom as it was in the days when ignorance and want of knowledge and experience blinded the eyes of men. I have always looked upon this foible as the creation of guilt or weakness. FEAR is the centre of both, and this continually fills our thoughts with unreal objects, full of darkness and horror. I have had frequent opportunities to realize this remark: several times have I gone through a CHURCH-YARD by night in company with persons whom I know to be much given to melancholy and horrid thoughts. I have oft seen them start at the least noise, and when the glimpses of the MOON formed their own shadow upon the ground I could behold them suddenly stop and gaze at it with looks full of wildness and amazement.

SHAKESPEARE seems to have selected his *Hamlet* chiefly to shew the horrors and gloomy sights that continually croud upon the mind of a weak or malancholy person. FEAR and SADNESS are the characters of HAMLET, and the black suggestions of his imagination appear in several scenes of that PLAY, especially when he goes to see his MOTHER by night and breaks out in this reflection:

'Tis now the very witching time of night,
When church-yards yawn, and hell itself breathes out
Contagion to the world:

[III.ii.378ff.]

This short passage alone is sufficient to demonstrate whence proceed all the frightful objects that appear before us when our hearts are stung with SORROW and overwhelmed with GRIEF.

In the tragedy of *Macbeth* the bard has finely pictured the condition of a guilty mind, and the scene when MACBETH goes to murder DUNCAN is one of the strongest proofs that a GHOST or APPARITION proceeds either from GUILT or FEAR or is a mixture of both. The thoughts of MACBETH are solely engaged by the deed he is going to act. That unhappy prince, we are told, was a virtuous man until, corrupted by his wife and misled by AMBITION, he is prompted to murder the KING, his benefactor. His foresaken virtue fills him with fear, and makes him sensible of his guilt; it presents to his view a DAGGER in the AIR leading him to DUNCAN, at which he starts and addresses it thus:

Is this a dagger which I see before me,
The handle tow'rd my hand? come, let me clutch thee.
I have thee not, and yet I see thee still.
Art thou not, fatal vision, sensible
To feeling, as to sight? or art thou but
A dagger of the mind, a false creation
Proceeding from the heat-oppressed brain?
I see thee yet in form as palpable
As this which now I draw –
Thou marshal'st me the way that I was going;
And such an instrument I was to use.
Mine eyes are made the fools o'th'other senses,
Or else worth all the rest – I see thee still;
And on thy blade and dudgeon, gouts of blood,
Which was not so before.

[II.i.33ff.]

Then he summons his reason to his aid, and prevails upon himself to believe it is the bloody purpose only that works upon his imagination; after which a secret horror takes possession of his SOUL, and he says

Now o'er half the world
Nature seems dead, and wicked dreams abuse
The curtain'd sleep; now witchcraft celebrates
Pale Hecate's offerings: and wither'd murder,
(Alarm'd by his sentinel, the wolf,
Whose howl's his watch) thus with his stealthy pace,
With Tarquin's *ravishing strides; tow'rds his design*
Moves like a ghost –

[II.i.49ff.]

Then he goes to murder DUNCAN; and LADY MACBETH enters, full of the same guilty thoughts as her husband, her imagination filled with BLOOD and DEATH, and as she comes forth every noise appalls her and engages her attention. Then she cries out

Hark! – peace? –
It was the owl that shriek'd, the fatal bell-man,
Which gives the stern'st good-night. –

[II.ii.2ff.]

All this is finely imagined, and worthy of SHAKESPEARE. The whole is natural, and when I see Mr GARRICK in the character of MACBETH I cannot help starting with him at the visionary DAGGER and partake of his amazement.

1.8b Elizabeth Montagu (1720–1800), 'On the Praeternatural Beings' (1769)

In the charged atmosphere produced by the Seven Years War between Britain and France, Voltaire launched a number of attacks against the plays of Shakespeare, contrasting them unfavourably to the work of Corneille and Racine. British responses were self-consciously patriotic. One of the earliest was Horace Walpole's Preface to the second edition of *The Castle of Otranto* (3.7b). Elizabeth Montagu's treatise was more fully argued and illustrated. In her chapter on 'Praeternatural Beings', she does not attempt to explain away Shakespeare's supernaturalism, but instead vindicates it as an expression of the British nation's popular tradition, arguing in addition that the ghost scenes from *Hamlet* have superior dramatic logic to the ghost scenes of classical tragedy. Her statement, 'Shakespear saw how useful the popular superstitions had been to the ancient poets: he felt what they were necessary to poetry itself', gave tacit support to modern-day writers experimenting with supernaturalism, such as William Collins (1.9), Thomas Gray and Horace Walpole (1.6). Also notable is Montagu's objection to the use of supernatural fantasy as allegory in order to figure philosophical ideas, on the grounds that it dissipates the emotional impact of the marvellous. Although her examples are taken from classical and Renaissance literature, 'supernatural machinery' remained a popular mode, and her argument has a direct bearing on contemporary poetic practice (see Swedenberg, 1938, and Spacks, 1962).

Source: [Elizabeth Montagu] (1769), *An Essay on the Writings and Genius of Shakespear, Compared with the Greek and French Dramatic Poets, with Some Remarks upon the Misrepresentations of Mons. de Voltaire*, London: Cadell et al., pp. 133–41, 142–51, 152–4, 158–60, 163–4.

★

As the genius of Shakespear, through the whole extent of the poet's province, is the object of our enquiry, we should do him great injustice, if we did not attend to his peculiar felicity, in those fictions and inventions, from which poetry derives its highest distinction, and from whence it first assumed its pretensions to divine inspiration, and appeared the associate of religion.

The ancient poet was admitted into the synod of the Gods: he discoursed of their natures, he repeated their counsels, and, without the charge of impiety or presumption, disclosed their dissensions, and published their vices. He peopled the woods with nymphs, the rivers with deities; and, that he might still have some being within call to his assistance, he placed responsive echo in the vacant regions of air.

In the infant ages of the world, the credulity of ignorance greedily received every marvellous tale: but, as mankind increased in knowledge, and a long series of traditions had established a certain mythology and history, the poet was no longer permitted to range, uncontrolled, through the boundless dominions of fancy, but became restrained, in some measure, to things believed or known. – Though the duty of poetry to please and to surprise still subsisted, the means varied with the state of the world, and it soon grew necessary to make the new inventions lean on the old traditions. – The human mind delights in novelty, and is captivated by the marvellous, but even in fable itself requires the credible. – The poet, who can give to splendid inventions, and to fictions new and bold, the air and authority of reality and truth, is master of the genuine sources of the Castalian spring,[13] and may justly be said to draw his inspiration from *the well-head of pure poesy.*

Shakespear saw how useful the popular superstitions had been to the ancient poets: he felt that they were necessary to poetry itself. One needs only to read some modern French heroic poems to be convinced how poorly epic poetry subsists on the pure elements of history and philosophy: Tasso, though he had a subject so popular, at the time he wrote, as the deliverance of Jerusalem, was obliged to employ the operations of magic, and the interposition of angels and daemons, to give the marvellous, the sublime, and, I may add, that religious air to his work, which ennobles the enthusiasm, and sanctifies the fiction of the poet. Ariosto's excursive muse wanders through the regions of romance, attended by all the superb train of chivalry, giants, dwarfs, and enchanters; and however these poets, by the severe and frigid critics may have been condemned for giving ornaments not purely classical, to their works; I believe every reader of taste admires, not only the fertility of their imagination, but the judgment with which they availed themselves of the superstition of the times, and of the customs and modes of the country, in which they laid their scenes of action.

To recur, as the learned sometimes do, to the mythology and fables of other ages, and other countries, has ever a poor effect: Jupiter, Minerva, and Apollo, only embellish a modern story, as a print from their statues adorns the frontispiece. – We admire indeed the art of the sculptors who give their images with grace and majesty; but no devotion is excited, no enthusiasm kindled, by the representations of characters whose divinity we do not acknowledge.

When the Pagan temples ceased to be revered, and the Parnassian mount existed no longer, it would have been difficult for the poet of later times to have preserved the divinity of his muse inviolate, if the western world too had not had its sacred fables. While there is any national superstition which credulity has consecrated, any hallowed tradition long revered by vulgar faith; to that sanctuary, that asylum, may the poet resort. – Let him tread the holy ground with reverence; respect the established doctrine; exactly observe the accustomed rites, and the attributes of the object of veneration; then shall he not vainly invoke an inexorable or absent deity. Ghosts, fairies, goblins, elves, were as propitious, were as assistant to Shakespear, and gave as much of the sublime, and of the marvellous, to his fictions, as nymphs, satyrs, fawns, and even the triple Geryon,[14] to the works of ancient bards. Our poet never carries his praeternatural beings beyond the limits of the popular tradition. It is true, that he boldly exerts his poetic genius and fascinating powers in that magic circle, *in which none e'er durst walk but he*: but as judicious as bold, he contains himself within it. He calls up all the stately phantoms in the regions of superstition, which our faith will receive with reverence. He throws into their manners and language a mysterious solemnity, favorable to superstition in general, with something highly characteristic of each particular being which he exhibits. His witches, his ghosts, and his fairies, seem spirits of health or goblins damn'd; *bring with them airs from heaven, or blasts from hell*. His ghosts are sullen, melancholy, and terrible. Every sentence, utter'd by the witches, is a prophecy or a charm; their manners are malignant, their phrases ambiguous, their promises delusive. – The witches cauldron is a horrid collection of what is most horrid in their supposed incantations. Ariel is a spirit, mild, gentle, and sweet, possess'd of supernatural powers, but subject to the command of a great magician.

The fairies are sportive and gay; the innocent artificers of harmless frauds, and mirthful delusions. Puck's enumeration of the feats of a fairy is the most agreeable recital of their supposed gambols.

To all these beings our poet has assigned tasks, and appropriated manners adapted to their imputed dispositions and characters; which are continually developing through the whole piece, in a series of operations conducive to the catastrophe. They are not brought in as subordinate or casual agents, but lead the action, and govern the fable; in which respect our countryman has entered more into theatrical propriety than the Greek tragedians.

Every species of poetry has its distinct duties and obligations. The drama does not, like the epic, admit of episode, superfluous persons, or things incredible; for, as it is observed by a critic of great ingenuity and taste,* 'that which passes in representation, and challenges, as it were, the scrutiny of the eye, must be truth itself, or something very nearly approaching it.' It should indeed be what our imagination will adopt, though our reason would reject it. Great caution and dexterity are required in the dramatic poet to give an air of reality to fictitious existence.

In the bold attempt to give to airy nothing a local habitation and a person, regard must be paid to fix it in such scenes, and to display it in such actions, as are agreeable to the popular opinion. – Witches holding their sabbath, and saluting passengers on the blasted heath; ghosts, at the midnight hour, visiting the glimpses of the moon, and whispering a bloody secret, from propriety of place and action, derive a credibility very propitious to the scheme of the poet. Reddere personae – convenientia cuique,[15] cannot be less his duty in regard to these superior and divine, than to human characters. Indeed, from the invariableness of their natures, a greater consistency and uniformity is necessary; but most of all, as the belief of their intervention depends entirely on their manners and sentiments suiting with the preconceived opinion of them.

The magician Prospero raising a storm; witches performing infernal rites; or any other exertion of the supposed powers and qualities of the agent, were easily credited by the vulgar.

The genius of Shakespear informed him that poetic fable must rise above the simple tale of the nurse; therefore he adorns the beldame tradition with flowers gathered on classic ground, but still wisely suffering those simples of her native soil, to which the established superstition of her country has attributed a magic spell, to be predominant . . .

[Montagu cites a passage from *The Tempest* to illustrate Shakespeare's adaptation of the lore concerning magicians.]

* [Richard] Hurd, on Dramatic Imitation.

The incantations of the witches in Macbeth are more solemn and terrible than those of the Erichtho of Lucan, or of the Canidia of Horace. It may be said, indeed, that Shakespear had an advantage derived from the more direful character of his national superstitions.

A celebrated writer in his ingenious letters on chivalry,[16] has observed, that the Gothic manners, and Gothic superstitions, are more adapted to the uses of poetry, than the Grecian. The devotion of those times was gloomy and fearful, not being purged of the terrors of the Celtic fables. The priest often availed himself of the dire inventions of his predecessor, the Druid. The church of Rome adopted many of the Celtic superstitions; others, which were not established by it as points of faith, still maintained a traditional authority among the vulgar. Climate, temper, modes of life, and institutions of government, seem all to have conspired to make the superstitions of the Celtic nations melancholy and terrible. Philosophy had not mitigated the austerity of ignorant devotion, or tamed the fierce spirit of enthusiasm. As the bards, who were our philosophers and poets, pretended to be possessed of the dark secrets of magic and divination, they certainly encouraged the ignorant credulity, and anxious fears, to which such impostures owed their success and credit. The retired and gloomy scenes appointed for the most solemn rites of devotion; the austerity and rigour of druidical discipline and jurisdiction; the fasts, the penances, the sad excommunications from the comforts and privileges of civil life; the dreadful anathema, whose vengeance pursued the wretched beyond the grave, which bounds all human power and mortal jurisdiction, must deeply imprint on the mind all those forms of superstition such an hierarchy presented. The bard, who was subservient to the druid, had mixed them in his heroic song; in his historical annals; in his medical practice: genii assisted his heroes; daemons decided the fate of the battle; and charms cured the sick, or the wounded. After the consecrated groves were cut down, and the temples demolished, the tales that sprung from thence were still preserved with religious reverence in the minds of the people.

The poet found himself happily situated amidst enchantments, ghosts, goblins; every element supposed the residence of a kind of deity; the genius of the mountain, the spirit of the floods, the oak endued with sacred prophecy, made men walk abroad with a fearful apprehension 'Of powers unseen, and mightier far than they'. On the mountains, and in the woods, stalked the angry spectre; and in the gayest and most pleasing scenes, even within the cheerful haunts of men, amongst villages and farms, 'Tripp'd the light fairies and the dapper elves'.

The reader will easily perceive what resources remained for the poet in this visionary land of ideal forms. The general scenery of nature, considered as inanimate, only adorns the descriptive part of poetry; but being, according to the Celtic traditions, animated by a kind of intelligences, the bard could better make use of them for his moral purposes. That awe of the immediate presence of the deity, which, among the rest of the vulgar, is confined to temples and altars, was here diffused over every object. They passed trembling through the woods, and over the mountain, and by the lakes, inhabited by these invisible powers; such apprehensions must indeed

> Deepen the murmur of the falling floods,
> And shed a browner horror on the woods;

give fearful accents to every whisper of the animate or inanimate creation, and arm every shadow with terrors.

With great reason, therefore, it was asserted, that the western bards had advantage over Homer in the superstitions of their country. The religious ceremonies of Greece were more pompous than solemn; and seemed as much a part of their civil institutions, as belonging to spiritual matters: nor did they impress so deep a sense of invisible beings, and prepare the mind to catch the enthusiasm of the poet, and to receive with veneration the phantoms he presented.

Our countryman has another superiority over the Greek poets, even the earliest of them, who, having imbibed the learning of mysterious Egypt, addicted themselves to allegory; but our Gothic bard employs the potent agency of sacred fable, instead of the mere amusive allegory. When the world becomes learned and philosophical, fable refines into allegory. But the age of fable is the golden age of poetry; when the beams of unclouded reason, and the steady lamp of inquisitive philosophy, throw their penetrating rays upon the phantoms of imagination, they discover them to have been mere shadows, formed by ignorance. The thunderbolts of Jove, forged in Cimmerian caves;[17] the cestus[18] of Venus, woven by hands of the attracting Graces, cease to terrify and allure. Echo, from an amorous nymph, fades into voice, and nothing more; the very threads of Iris's scarf are untwisted; all the poet's spells are broken, his charms dissolved: deserted on his own enchanted ground, he takes refuge in the groves of philosophy; but there his divinities evaporate in allegory, in which mystic and insubstantial state they do but weakly assist his operations. By associating his muse with philosophy, he hopes she may establish with the learned the worship she won from the ignorant; so makes her quit the old traditional fable, from whence she derived her first authority and power, to follow airy hypothesis, and chimerical systems. Allegory, the daughter of fable, is admired by the fastidious wit, and abstruse scholar, when her mother begins to be treated as superannuated, foolish, and doting; but however well she may please and amuse, not being worshipped as divine, she does not awe and terrify like sacred mythology, nor ever can establish the same fearful devotion, nor assume such arbitrary power over the mind. Her person is not adapted to the stage, nor her qualities to the business and end of dramatic representation. L'Abbe du Bos has judiciously distinguished the reasons why allegory is not fit for the drama. What the critic investigated by art and study, the wisdom of nature unfolded to our unlettered poet, or he would not have resisted the prevalent fashion of his allegorizing age; especially as Spencer's Fairy Queen was the admired work of the times.

Allegorical beings, performing acts of chivalry, fell in with the taste of an age that affected abstruse learning, romantic valour, and high-flown gallantry. Prince Arthur, the British Hercules, was brought from ancient ballads and romances, to be allegorized into the knight of magnanimity, at the court of Gloriana. His knights followed him thither, in the same moralized garb, and even the questynge beast received no less honour and improvement from the allegorizing art of Spencer, as has been shewn by a critic of great learning, ingenuity, and taste, in his observations on the Fairy Queen.[19]

Our first theatrical entertainments, after we emerged from gross barbarism, were of the allegorical kind. The Christmas carol, and carnival shews, the pious pastimes of our holy-days, were turned into pageantries and masques, all symbolical and allegorical. – Our stage rose from hymns to the virgin, and encomiums on the patriarchs and saints: as the Grecian tragedies from the hymns to Bacchus. Our early poets added narration and action to this kind of psalmody, as Aeschylus had done to the song of the goat. Much more rapid indeed was the progress of the Grecian stage towards perfection. – Philosophy, poetry, eloquence, all the fine arts, were in their meridian glory, when the drama first began to dawn at Athens, and gloriously it shone forth, illumined by every kind of intellectual light.

Shakespear, in the dark shades of Gothic barbarism, had no resources but in the very phantoms that walked the night of ignorance and superstition: or in touching the latent passions of civil rage and discord; sure to please best his fierce and barbarous audience, when he raised the bloody ghost, or reared the warlike standard. His choice of these subjects was judicious, if we consider the times in which he lived; his management of them so masterly, that he will be admired in all times . . .

Indeed if we compare our countryman, in this respect, with the most admired writers of antiquity, we shall perhaps, not find him inferior to them. – Aeschylus, with greater impetuosity of genius than even our countryman, makes bold incursions into the blind chaos of mingled allegory and fable, but he is not so happy in diffusing the solemn shade; in casting the dim, religious light that should reign there. When he introduces his furies, and other supernatural beings, he exposes them by too glaring a light; causes affright in the spectator, but never rises to imparting that unlimited terror which we feel when Macbeth to his bold address,

How now! ye secret, foul, and midnight hags,
What is't ye do?

is answered,

A deed without a name.

The witches of the forest are as important in the tragedy of Macbeth, as the Eumenides in the drama of Aeschylus; but our poet is infinitely more dexterous and judicious in the conduct of their part. The secret, foul, and midnight hags are not introduced into the castle of Macbeth; they never appear but in their allotted region of solitude and night, nor act beyond their sphere of ambiguous prophecy, and malignant sorcery. The Eumenides, snoring in the temple of Apollo, and then appearing as evidences against Orestes in the Areopagus, seem both acting out of their sphere, and below their character. It was the appointed office of the venerable goddesses, to avenge the crimes unwhipt of justice, not to demand the public trial of guilty men. They must lose much of the fear and reverence in which they were held for their secret influence on the mind, and the terrors they could inflict on criminal conscience, when they were represented as obliged to have recourse to the ordinary method of revenge, by being witnesses and pleaders in a court of justice, to obtain the corporal punishment of the offender. Indeed, it is possible, that the whole story of this play might be allegorical, as thus, that Orestes, haunted by the terrors which pursue the guilty mind, confessed his crime to the Areopagus, with all the aggravating circumstances remorse suggested to him, from a pious desire to expiate his offence, by submitting to whatever sentence this respectable assembly should pronounce for that purpose. The oracle, which commanded him to put Clytemnestra to death, would plead for him with his judges: their voices being equal for absolving or punishing, wisdom gives her vote for absolving him . . .

[Montagu argues that the play was understood by its original audience as an allegorical representation of the history of Athens.]

It has been just now observed, that Shakespear has an advantage over the Greek poets, in the more solemn, gloomy, and mysterious air of his national superstitions; but this avails him only with critics of deep penetration and true taste, and with whom sentiment has more sway than authority. The learned have received the popular tales of Greece from their poets; ours are derived to them from the illiterate vulgar. The phantom of Darius, in the tragedy of the Persians, evoked by ancient rites, is beheld with reverence by the scholar, and endured by the bel esprit. To these the ghost of Hamlet is an object of contempt or ridicule. Let us candidly examine these royal shades, as exhibited to us by those great masters in the art of exciting pity and terror, Aeschylus and Shakespear; and impartially decide which poet throws most of the sublime into the praeternatural character; and, also, which has the art to render it most efficient in the drama. This enquiry may be more interesting, as the French wits have often mentioned Hamlet's ghost as an instance of the barbarism of our theatre. The Persians, of Aeschylus, is certainly one of the most august spectacles that ever was represented on a theatre; nobly imagined, happily sustained, regularly conducted, deeply interesting to the Athenian people, and favorable to their great scheme of resisting the power of the Persian monarch. It would be absurd to depreciate this excellent piece, or to bring into a general comparison with it, a drama of so different a kind as the tragedy of Hamlet. But it is surely allowable to compare the Persian phantom with the Danish ghost; and to examine, whether any thing but prejudice, in favour of the ancients, protects the superstitious circumstances relative to the one, from the ridicule with which those accompanying the other are treated. Atossa, the widow of Darius, relates to the sages of the Persian council, a dream and an omen; they advise her to consult the shade of her dead lord, upon what is to be done in the unfortunate situation of Xerxes just defeated by the Greeks. In the third act she enters offering to the Manes a libation composed of milk, honey, wine, oil, &c. upon this Darius issues from his tomb. Let the wits, who are so smart on our ghost's disappearing at the cock's crowing, explain why, in reason, a ghost in Persia, or in Greece, should be more fond of milk and honey, than averse, in Denmark, to the crowing of a cock. Each poet adopted, in his work, the superstition relative to his subject; and the poet who does so, understands his business much better than the critic, who, in judging of that work, refuses it his attention . . .

[A description of the role of the apparition of Darius, with criticism of the lack of sublime effect.]

The first propriety in the conduct of this kind of machinery, seems to be, that the praeternatural person be intimately connected with the fable; and the increase the interest, add to the solemnity of it, and that his efficiency, in bringing on the catastrophe, be in some measure adequate to the violence done to the ordinary course of things in his visible interposition. These are points peculiarly important in dramatic poetry, as has been before observed. To these ends it is necessary this being should be acknowledged and revered by the national superstition, and every operation that developes the attributes, which the vulgar opinion, or nurse's legend, taught us to ascribe to him, will augment our pleasure; whether we give the reins to imagination, and, as spectators, willingly yield ourselves up to pleasing delusion, or, as critics, examine the merit of the composition. I hope it is not difficult to shew, that in all these capital points our author has excelled . . .

[The discussion ends with an enthusiastic summary, including long quotations, of the scenes in which the ghost appears in Act I of *Hamlet*.]

1.9 William Collins, 'An Ode on the Popular Superstitions of the Highlands of Scotland, considered as the Subject of Poetry' (1749–50)

The poem is addressed to the Scottish dramatist John Home, who was on a visit to London in 1749 when Collins met him. Collins was by this time established as a poet of passion and sentiment, and as a specialist in the ode, a form connected with imaginative flight because of its metrical irregularity. When in later life he became insane, contemporaries felt that Collins's fervent interest in the supernatural and the terrible must have been a contributing factor (see also 3.5). A number of the superstitions described in the poem are drawn from *Description of the Western Islands of Scotland* (1706) by Martin Martin, a work which Samuel Johnson also consulted on his visit to the Western Isles in 1773 (Lonsdale, 1969, p. 500). Although Collins ostensibly eschews the use of such 'false themes' for himself, his emotive treatment of the supernatural material he recommends to Home makes him a precursor of the Gothic novelists, and in the 1790s Ann Radcliffe frequently cited his poetry in her fiction and journals. The poem could be compared interestingly with Robert Burns's 'Hallowe'en' (1785) and 'Tam O'Shanter' (1790), employing Scottish superstitions to comic effect. It was not published in Collins's lifetime. An incomplete copy in manuscript was discovered in the early 1780s and published in the *Transactions of the Royal Society of Edinburgh*, March 1788; this remains the only authoritative version. Gaps in the manuscript are shown as blanks in the following text.

Source: Roger Lonsdale, ed. (1969), *The Poems of Thomas Gray, William Collins, Oliver Goldsmith*, London and Harlow: Longman, pp. 501–19.

★

1

H[ome], thou return'st from Thames, whose Naiads long
  Have seen thee lingering, with a fond delay,
  Mid those soft friends whose hearts some future day,
Shall melt, perhaps, to hear thy tragic song.
Go, not unmindful of that cordial youth,[20]
  Whom, long endeared, thou leav'st by Lavant's side;
Together let us wish him lasting truth,

And joy untainted with his destined bride.
Go! nor regardless, while these numbers boast
My short-lived bliss, forget my social name;
But think far off how, on the southern coast,
I met thy friendship with an equal flame!
Fresh to that soil thou turn'st, whose every vale
Shall prompt the poet and his song demand:
To thee thy copious subjects ne'er shall fail;
Thou need'st but take the pencil to thy hand,
And paint what all believe who own thy genial land.

2

There must thou wake perforce thy Doric[21] quill,
'Tis Fancy's land to which thou sett'st thy feet;
Where still, 'tis said, the fairy people meet
Beneath each birken shade on mead or hill.
There each trim lass that skims the milky store
To the swart tribes their creamy bowl allots;
By night they sip it round the cottage-door,
While airy minstrels warble jocund notes.
There every herd, by sad experience, knows
How, winged with fate, their elf-shot arrows fly,
When the sick ewe her summer food foregoes,
Or, stretched on earth, the heart-smit heifers lie.
Such airy beings awe the untutored swain:
Nor thou, though learned, his homelier thoughts neglect;
Let thy sweet muse the rural faith sustain:
These are the themes of simple, sure effect,
That add new conquests to her boundless reign,
And fill with double force her heart-commanding strain.

3

Even yet preserved, how often may'st thou hear,
Where to the pole the Boreal mountains run,
Taught by the father to his listening son
Strange lays, whose power had charmed a Spenser's ear.
At every pause, before thy mind possessed,
Old Runic[22] bards shall seem to rise around
With uncouth lyres, in many-coloured vest,
Their matted hair with boughs fantastic crowned:
Whether thou bidd'st the well-taught hind repeat
The choral dirge that mourns some chieftain brave,
When every shrieking maid her bosom beat,
And strewed with choicest herbs his scented grave;
Or whether, sitting in the shepherd's shiel,[23]

Thou hear'st some sounding tale of war's alarms;
When at the bugle's call, with fire and steel,
The sturdy clans poured forth their bonny swarms,
And hostile brothers met to prove each other's arms.

4

'Tis thine to sing how, framing hideous spells,
In Skye's lone isle the gifted wizard seer,
Lodged in the wintry cave with
Or in the depth of Uist's dark forests dwells;
How they, whose sight such dreary dreams engross,
With their own visions oft astonished droop,
When o'er the watery strath[24] or quaggy moss
They see the gliding ghosts unbodied troop.
Or if in sports, or on the festive green,
Their glance some fated youth descry,
Who, now perhaps in lusty vigour seen
And rosy health, shall soon lamented die.
For them the viewless forms of air obey,
Their bidding heed and at their beck repair.
They know what spirit brews the stormful day,
And heartless, oft like moody madness stare
To see the phantom train their secret work prepare.

[Stanza 5 missing]

6

[8 lines missing.]

What though far off, from some dark dell espied,
His glimmering mazes cheer the excursive sight,
Yet turn, ye wanderers, turn your steps aside,
Nor choose the guidance of that faithless light![25]
For watchful, lurking mid the unrustling reed,
At those mirk hours the wily monster lies,
And listens oft to hear the passing steed,
And frequent round him rolls his sullen eyes,
If chance his savage wrath may some weak wretch surprise.

7

Ah, luckless swain, o'er all unblest indeed!
Whom late bewildered in the dank, dark fen
Far from his flocks and smoking hamlet then!
To that sad spot his
On him enraged the fiend, in angry mood,

Shall never look with pity's kind concern,
But instant, furious, rouse the whelming flood
O'er its drowned banks, forbidding all return.
Or, if he meditate his wished escape
To some dim hill that seems uprising near,
To his faint eye the grim and grisly shape
In all its terrors clad shall wild appear.
Meantime the watery surge shall round him rise,
Poured sudden forth from every swelling source.
What now remains but tears and hopeless sighs?
His fear-shook limbs have lost their youthly force,
And down the waves he floats, a pale and breathless corse.

8

For him, in vain, his anxious wife shall wait,
Or wander forth to meet him on his way;
For him, in vain, at to-fall[26] of the day,
His bairns shall linger at the unclosing gate
Ah, ne'er shall he return! Alone,[27] if night
Her travelled[28] limbs in broken slumbers steep,
With dropping willows dressed, his mournful sprite
Shall visit sad, perhaps, her silent sleep:
Then he, perhaps, with moist and watery hand,
Shall fondly seem to press her shuddering cheek,
And with his blue swoll'n face before her stand,
And, shivering cold, these piteous accents speak:
'Pursue, dear wife, thy daily toils pursue
At dawn or dusk, industrious as before;
Nor e'er of me one hapless thought renew,
While I lie weltering on the osiered shore,
Drowned by the Kaelpie's[29] wrath, nor e'er shall aid thee more.'

9

Unbounded is thy range; with varied style
Thy Muse may, like those feathery tribes which spring
From their rude rocks, extend her skirting wing
Round the moist marge of each cold Hebrid isle,
To that hoar pile which still its ruin shows:
In whose small vaults a pigmy-folk is found,
Whose bones the delver with his spade upthrows,
And culls them, wondering, from the hallowed ground!
Or thither, where beneath the showery west
The mighty kings of three fair realms are laid;
Once foes, perhaps, together now they rest.

  No slaves revere them and no wars invade:
Yet frequent now, at midnight's solemn hour,
  The rifted mounds their yawning cells unfold,
And forth the monarchs stalk with sovereign power
  In pageant robes, and wreathed with sheeny gold,
And on their twilight tombs aerial council hold.

10

But O, o'er all, forget not Kilda's race,[30]
  On whose bleak rocks, which brave the wasting tides,
  Fair Nature's daughter, Virtue, yet abides!
Go, just as they, their blameless manners trace!
Then to my ear transmit some gentle song
  Of those whose lives are yet sincere and plain,
Their bounded walks the ragged cliffs along,
  And all their prospect but the wintry main.
With sparing temperance, at the needful time,
  They drain the sainted spring or, hunger-pressed,
Along the Atlantic rock undreading climb,
  And of its eggs despoil the solan's[31] nest.
Thus blest in primal innocence they live,
  Sufficed and happy with that frugal fare
Which tasteful toil and hourly danger give.
  Hard is their shallow soil,   and bare;
Nor ever vernal bee was heard to murmur there!

11

Nor needs't thou blush that such false themes engage
  Thy gentle mind, of fairer stores possessed;
  For not alone they touch the village breast,
But filled in elder time the historic page.
  There Shakespeare's self, with every garland crowned,
In musing hour his Wayward Sisters found,
  And with their terrors dressed the magic scene.
From them he sung, when mid his bold design,
  Before the Scot afflicted and aghast,
The shadowy kings of Banquo's fated line,
  Through the dark cave in gleamy pageant passed
Proceed, nor quit the tales which, simply told,
  Could once so well my answering bosom pierce;
Proceed, in forceful sounds and colours bold
  The native legends of thy land rehearse;
To such adapt thy lyre and suit thy powerful verse.

12

In scenes like these, which, daring to depart
From sober Truth, are still to Nature true,
And call forth fresh delights to Fancy's view,
The heroic Muse employed her Tasso's art![32]
How have I trembled when, at Tancred's stroke,
Its gushing blood the gaping cypress poured;
When each live plant with mortal accents spoke,
And the wild blast upheaved the vanished sword!
How have I sat, where piped the pensive wind,
To hear his harp by British Fairfax strung.
Prevailing poet, whose undoubting mind
Believed the magic wonders which he sung!
Hence at each sound imagination glows;
Hence his warm lay with softest sweetness flows;
Melting it flows, pure, numerous, strong and clear,
And fills the impassioned heart and lulls the harmonious ear.

13

All hail, ye scenes that o'er my soul prevail,
Ye firths and lakes which, far away,
Are by smooth Annan filled, or pastoral Tay,
Or Don's romantic springs, at distance, hail!
The time shall come when I perhaps may tread
Your lowly glens, o'erhung with spreading broom,
Or o'er your stretching heaths by Fancy led:
Then will I dress once more the faded bower,
Where Jonson sat in Drummond's shade;[33]
Or crop from Tiviot's dale[34] each
And mourn on Yarrow banks
Meantime, ye powers, that on the plains which bore
The cordial youth,[35] on Lothian's plains attend,
Where'er he dwell, on hill or lowly muir,[36]
To him I lose your kind protection lend,
And, touched with love like mine, preserve my absent friend.

Notes

1 A funeral shield attached to the door of the house of the deceased.
2 Persius, *Satires*, 5.92: 'I pluck the old wives' notions from your breast.'
3 Milton, *Paradise Lost*, 675–88.
4 Virgil, *Aeneid*, 2.755: 'All things were full of Horrour and Affright, / And dreadful ev'n the silence of the Night' (in Dryden's translation).

5 John Locke, *Essay Concerning Human Understanding*, 2.33.
6 Flavius Josephus (37–c.98), Roman military commander and historian; author of *History of the Jewish War* and of *Antiquities of the Jews*, from which the tale of Glaphyra is taken (13.4).
7 See note 1 above.
8 In 1726 Mary Tofts was examined by a Court doctor who confirmed her claim that she had given birth to a litter of rabbits.
9 A mercenary soldier, with an overlapping meaning of robber or brigand (see Frayling, 1991, p. 20).
10 Examples of infamous Court favourites from British history.
11 A reference to the crash of South Sea Company stocks in 1720 known as the 'South Sea bubble'; a byword for financial corruption.
12 Tightrope-walking.
13 On Mount Parnassus, sacred to Apollo and the Muses.
14 The tenth labour of Hercules was to slay the monster Geryon, with three bodies and one pair of legs, and capture the herd of oxen he guarded.
15 Post-classical Latin. The meaning is unclear.
16 Richard Hurd, *Letters on Chivalry and Romance* (1762); see 2.6.
17 The fabled tribe of Cimmerii lived in perpetual darkness.
18 Girdle.
19 Thomas Warton, *Observations on the Fairie Queene of Spenser* (1754).
20 A reference to a mutual friend, Thomas Barrow, like Collins resident in Chichester, 'by Lavant's side'.
21 Rustic; but also used with reference to Scottish dialect.
22 Usually referring to ancient Scandinavian language or mythology; the latter a favourite subject of the contemporary poet Thomas Gray.
23 Hut.
24 Scottish term for a valley through which a river runs.
25 Will-o'-the-wisp, a delusory effect of light created in swampland.
26 The close.
27 Except.
28 Wearied.
29 In Scottish folklore, the 'kaelpie' or kelpie is a malignant water-spirit that usually takes the form of a horse.
30 The people of St Kilda, the most barren and remote of the Western Isles.
31 Solan-goose, or gannet.
32 Torquato Tasso (1544–95), Italian poet, author of the romantic epic *Rinaldo*, and himself a legendary figure who for a period was imprisoned for insanity.
33 Ben Jonson visited the poet William Drummond in 1619, at Hawthornden near Edinburgh.
34 The valley of the river Teviot in the Scottish Lowlands, the setting for many of the Border Ballads.
35 Here referring to Home.
36 Moor (Scottish).

2 Gothic origins

2.1 Cornelius Tacitus (55 to after 115 AD), *Germania* (trans. 1777), translated by John Aikin

The Gothic aesthetic in architecture, poetry and fiction did not emerge in a vacuum. In the words of one authority, 'the history of the "Gothic" begins not in the eighteenth but in the seventeenth century, not in aesthetic but in political discussion' (Kliger, 1945, p. 1). From the seventeenth century onwards, British historians, legal commentators and political philosophers showed a deep interest in the historical role of the Germanic tribes, collectively known as the Goths, which had invaded Britain in the fifth century AD. The impact of Gothic customs and institutions on the evolution of British political and legal structures remained a topic for impassioned debate; a debate which reached a climax in the 1790s, at the very moment when the Gothic novel achieved its greatest popularity (see Chapter 5).

What was at stake in these discussions was the elaboration of persuasive myths of the nation's past as a means of influencing its present and future course. In general terms, the myth of Gothic origins was fundamental to an emergent sense of British national distinctiveness; favourite historical sources tended to represent the Goths as valorous and virtuous, innately inclined to venerate women, and with a strong attachment to liberty and justice, displayed in their representative system of government and their invention of the jury system. Most of these features are described in the work by the Roman historian Tacitus, from which the following extracts are taken.

But there were other, more precise and contentious political meanings attached to the Gothic. The Glorious Revolution of 1688, which saw King James II deposed by a cabal of Whig grandees, was in part legitimated by reference to an 'ancient constitution' deriving from the 'Witenagemot' or Parliament of the Saxons. According to this precedent, the chief did not rule by right of inheritance, but by the consent of the representatives of his people. Conversely, the Tories, in opposition to the Whigs, maintained the principle that the monarch ruled by right of the Norman conquest, an event which nullified the Saxon constitution. Meanwhile, outside of official politics, a tradition within popular radicalism developed, which held that the Gothic constitution supported the case for universal manhood suffrage, for instance, and that the present political structure was a mere continuation of the 'Norman Yoke' (see Hill, 1954, pp. 42–54). Such opinions were often associated with the disenfranchised Nonconformist community. Some radicals went well beyond the Whig principle of a balance between parliament and crown, and argued that the king was an elected official at any time removable by the will of the people, should the monarch threaten their ancient rights.

There were two important classical sources for the political debate on the Goths. One was Julius Caesar's *De Bello Gallico* (*Commentaries on The Gallic War*); the other, longer and more influential source was the *Germania* of Tacitus.[1] John Aikin, the translator of the edition used here,[2] was, perhaps not incidentally, both a Dissenter and one of the pioneers of literary Gothic writing. With his sister Anna Laetitia Aikin (later Barbauld), he published *Miscellaneous Pieces* (1773), which contained a fragment of an experimental tale of terror and a number of relevant critical essays (3.8). In his preface to Tacitus, Aikin notes (p. vii) that the

> *Treatise on the Manners of the Germans* has ever been esteemed as one of the most precious relics of the political or historical writings of antiquity; and by the course of events has been rendered more important to modern times than its author probably expected, who could scarcely forsee that the government, policy, and manners of the most civilized parts of the globe, were to originate from the woods and deserts of Germany.

The text is from the first edition. The title page reads: '*Warrington*, printed by W. Eyres, for J. Johnson, St. Paul's Churchyard, London, 1777'. Warrington was the most significant of the eighteenth-century Dissenting academies. W. Eyres was the 'house' publisher for the Warrington Academy, while Joseph Johnson was the leading London radical publisher. Aikin substantially revises his later editions, mainly for stylistic reasons. In the first edition Aikin ignores Tacitus's divisions by chapter, but later inserts them. For ease of reference we have included the chapter references in square brackets.

Source: Cornelius Tacitus ([98 AD] 1777), *A Treatise on the Situation, Manners, and Inhabitants of Germany, & the Life of Agricola*, trans. John Aikin, London: J. Johnson, pp. 1–3, 3–6, 10–11, 21–4, 35–7, 37–41, 44–53, 53–5, 55–5, 55–9, 75–7.

[*I*] Germany is separated from Gaul, Rætia,* and Pannonia,† by the rivers Rhine and Danube; from Sarmatia and Dacia, by mountains‡ and mutual dread. The rest is surrounded by an ocean forming extensive bays, and

* Rætia comprehended the country of the Grisons, with parts of *Suabia* and *Bavaria*.

† *Lower Hungary* and parts of *Austria*.

‡ The *Crapack Mountains* in *Upper Hungary*.

including vast insular tracts,* in which our military expeditions have lately discovered various nations and kingdoms. The Rhine, issuing from the inaccessible and precipitous summit of the Raetic Alps,† after a moderate flexure to the West, flows into the Northern Ocean. The Danube, poured from the easy and gentle elevation of the mountain Abnoba,‡ visits several nations in its course, till at length it disembogues by six channels into the Pontic Sea:§ a seventh is lost in marshes.

[*II*] I should imagine that the people of Germany are indigenous, without having received any mixture from the emigrations or visits of foreigners. For the emigrants of former ages performed their expeditions not by land, but by water; and that immense, and, if I may so call it, hostile ocean, is rarely navigated by ships from our world. Then, besides the dangers of a boisterous and unknown sea, who would relinquish Asia, Africa, or Italy, to settle in Germany; a land rude in its surface, rigorous in its climate, cheerless to every beholder and cultivator, unless it were his native country? In their ancient songs, which are their only records or annals, they celebrate the god Tuisto, sprung from the earth, and his son Mannus, as the fathers and founders of their race. . . .

[*IV*] I concur in opinion with those who suppose the Germans never to have intermarried with other nations; but to be a people, peculiar, unmixed, and resembling one another alone. Hence the same constitution of body pervades the whole, though their numbers are so great: – fierce blue eyes; ruddy hair; large bodies, powerful in sudden exertions, but less firm under toil and labour, least of all capable of sustaining thirst and heat. Cold and hunger they are accustomed by their climate and soil to endure.

[*VII*] In the election of kings they have regard to birth; in that of military commanders, to valour. Their kings have not an absolute or unlimited power;¶ and their generals command less through the force of authority, than of example. If they are daring, adventurous, and conspicuous in action, they procure obedience from the admiration their inspire. None, however, but the priests are to chastise delinquents, to inflict bonds or stripes; that it may appear not as a punishment, or in consequence of the general's order, but as the instigation of the god whom they suppose present with warriors. They also carry with them to battle, images and

* *Scandinavia* and *Finland*, of which the Romans had a very slight knowledge, were supposed to be islands.

† The mountains of the *Grisons*. That in which the Rhone rises is at present called *Vogelberg*.

‡ Now called *Schwartz-wald* or the *Black Forest*.

§ Now the *Black Sea*.

¶ Hence Amborix, King of the Eburones, declared that 'the nature of his authority was such, that the people had no less power over him, than he over the people.' Caesar, *Bell. Gall. V*. The Authority of the North American chiefs is almost exactly similar.

standards taken from the sacred groves. It is a principal incentive to their courage, that their squadrons and battalions are not formed by men fortuitously collected, but by the assemblage of families and clans. Near them are ranged the dearest pledges of their affection; so that they have within hearing the yells of their women, and the cries of their children. These, too, are the most respected witnesses, the most liberal applauders, of the conduct of each. To their mothers and wives they bring their wounds; and these are not shocked at counting, and even requiring them. They also carry food and encouragement to those who are engaged.

[*VIII*] Tradition relates, that armies beginning to give way have been brought again to the charge by the women, through the earnestness of their entreaties, the opposition of their bodies, and the pictures they have drawn of imminent slavery, a calamity which these people bear with more impatience on their women's account than their own; so that those states who have been obliged to give among their hostages the daughters of noble families, are the most effectually engaged to fidelity. They even suppose somewhat of sanctity and prescience to be inherent in the female sex; and therefore neither despise their counsels, nor disregard their responses. . . .

[*XI*] On affairs of smaller moment, the chiefs consult; on those of greater importance, the whole community; yet with this circumstance, that what is referred to the decision of the people, is maturely discussed by the chiefs.* They assemble, unless upon some sudden emergency, upon stated days, either at the full or change of the moon, which they account the most auspicious season for beginning any enterprise . . . An inconvenience produced by their liberty is, that they do not all assemble punctually to the same time, as if it were in obedience to a command; but two or three days are lost in the delays of convening. When the number appears sufficient, they sit down armed. Silence is proclaimed by the priests, who have on this occasion a coercive power. Then king or chief, with such as are conspicuous for age, birth, military renown, or eloquence, are heard; and gain attention rather from their ability to persuade, than their authority to command. If a proposal displease, the assembly reject it by an inarticulate murmur; if it prove agreeable, they clash their javelins; for the most honourable expression of assent among them is the sound of arms.

[*XII*] Before this council, it is likewise allowed to exhibit accusations, and to prosecute capital offences. Punishments are varied according to the

* This remarkable passage, so curious in political history, is commented on by Montesquieu in his *Spirit of Laws*, xi, 6. That celebrated author expresses his surprize at the existence of such a balance between liberty and authority in the forests of Germany; and traces the origin of the English Constitution from this source. Tacitus again mentions the German form of government in his *Annals*, iv, 33.

nature of the crime. Traitors and deserters are hung upon trees: cowards, effeminate persons, and those guilty of unnatural practices, are suffocated in mud under a hurdle. This difference of punishment has in view the principle, that villainy should be exposed while it is punished, but turpitude concealed. The penalties annexed to slighter offences are also proportioned to the delinquency. The culprits are fined in horses and cattle: part of the mulct goes to the king or state; part to the injured person, or his relations. In the same assemblies chiefs are also elected, to administer justice through the cantons and districts. A hundred *companions*, chosen from the people, attend each of them, to assist them as well with their advice as their authority.

[*XIV*] In the field of battle, it is disgraceful for the chief to be surpassed in valour; it is disgraceful for the companions not to equal their chief; but it is reproach and infamy during a whole succeeding life to retreat from the field surviving him. To aid, to protect him; to place their own gallant actions to the account of his glory, is their first and most sacred engagement. The chiefs fight for victory; the companions for their chief. If their native country be long sunk in peace and inaction, many of the young nobles repair to some other state, then engaged in war. For, besides that repose is ungrateful to their dispositions, and toils and perils afford them a better opportunity of distinguishing themselves; they are unable, without war and violence, to maintain a large train of followers. The companion requires from the liberality of his chief, the warlike steed, the bloody and conquering spear: and in place of pay, he expects to be supplied with a table, homely indeed, but plentiful.* The funds for this munificence must be in war and rapine: nor are they so easily persuaded to cultivate the earth, and await the produce of the seasons, as to challenge the foe, and hazard wounds; for they think it base and spiritless to earn by sweat, what they might purchase with blood.

[*XVIII*] The matrimonial bond is, nevertheless, strict and severe among them; nor are their manners in any other respect more deserving of praise.† Almost singly among the barbarians, they content themselves with one wife; a very few of them excepted, who, not through incontinence, but because their alliance is solicited on account of their rank, practice polygamy. The wife does not bring a dowry to her husband, but receives one from him. The parents and relations interpose, and pass their appro-

* From hence Montesquieu (*Spirit of Laws*, xxx, 3) justly derives the origin of *vassalage*. At first, the prince gives to his nobles arms and provision: as avarice advanced, money, and then lands were required, which from benefices became at length hereditary possessions, and were called *fiefs*. Hence the establishment of the *feudal system*.

† The chastity of the Germans, and their strict regard to the laws of marriage, are witnessed by all their antient codes of law. The purity of their manners in this respect afforded a striking contrast to the licentiousness of the Romans in the decline of the empire; and is exhibited in this light by Salvian, in his treatise *De Gubernatione*, DCI, L. VII.

bation on the presents – presents not adapted to please a female taste, or decorate the bride; but a yoke of oxen, a caparisoned steed, a shield, spear and sword. By virtue of these, the wife is espoused; who on her part also makes a present of armour to her husband. This they consider as the firmest bond of union; these, the sacred mysteries, the conjugal deities. That the woman may not think herself excused from exertions of fortitude, or exempt from the casualties of war, she is admonished by the very ceremonial of her marriage, that she comes to her husband as a partner in toils and dangers; an equal both to suffer and to dare, in peace and in war: this is indicated by the yoked oxen, the harnessed steed, the offered arms. Thus she is to live; thus to die. She receives what she is to return inviolate and honoured to her children; what her daughters-in-law are to receive, and again transmit to her grandchildren.

[*XIX*] They live, therefore, in a state of well-guarded chastity; corrupted by no seducing spectacles,* no convivial incitements. Men and women are alike ignorant of the secret methods of corresponding by letters. Adultery is extremely rare among so numerous a people. Its punishment is instant, and at the pleasure of the husband. He cuts off the hair of the offender, strips her, and in presence of her relations expels her from his house, and pursues her with stripes through the whole village. Nor is any indulgence shown to a prostitute. Neither beauty, youth, nor riches can procure her a husband: for none there looks on vice with a smile; nor calls mutual seduction the way of the world. Still more exemplary is the practice of those states in which none but virgins marry, and the expectations and wishes of a wife are at once brought to a period. Thus they take one husband as one body and one life; that no thought, no desire, may reach beyond him; and he may be loved not only as their husband, but as their marriage. To limit the increase of children, or put to death any of the husband's blood, is accounted infamous: and virtuous manners have there more efficacy than good laws elsewhere.

[*XXVII*] Lending money upon interest, and increasing it by usury, is unknown amongst them; and this ignorance more effectually prevents the practice than a prohibition would do. The lands are occupied by townships, in allotments proportional to the number of cultivators; and are afterwards parcelled out among the individuals of the district, in shares according to the rank and condition of each person. The wide extent of plain facilitates this partition. The arable lands are annually changed, and a part left fallow; nor do they attempt to make the most of the fertility and plenty of the country, by their own industry in planting orchards,

* Seneca speaks with great force and warmth on this subject. 'Nothing is so destructive to morals as loitering at public entertainments; for vice most easily insinuates itself into the heart when suffused in pleasure. What shall I say? I return from them more covetous, ambitious, and luxurious.' *Epist.* Vii.

enclosing meadows, and watering gardens. Corn is the only product required from the earth: hence their year is not divided into so many seasons as ours; for while they know and distinguish by name Winter, Spring, and Summer, they are unacquainted equally with the appellation and bounty of Autumn.

2.2 James Thomson (1700–48), *Liberty* (1734–6)

In Thomson's poem, Liberty narrates her progress down the ages, from Greece, through Rome, and finally to Britain, where she is patriotically represented as achieving perfection in the form of the matchless British Constitution. Thomson's version of liberty's progress is Whiggish in the most general sense: it depicts a process of gradual improvement; it achieves fruition in the shape of a constitutional monarchy; and the final result is a blend of the best that has gone before.

Source: James Thomson, *Poetical Works,* ed., with notes, J. Logie Robertson, London: Oxford University Press [1908], 1951: Part 4, ii. 624–820.

'Now turn you view, and mark from Celtic night*
To present grandeur how my Britain rose.
'Bold were those Britons, who, the careless sons
Of nature, roamed the forest-bounds, at once
Their verdant city, high-embowering fane,
And the gay circle of their woodland wars:
For by the Druid taught, that death but shifts†
The vital scene, they that prime fear despised;
And, prone to rush on steel, disdained to spare
An ill-saved life that must again return.
Erect from nature's hand, by tyrant force
And still more tyrant custom unsubdued,
Man knows no master save creating heaven,
Or such as choice and common good ordain.
This general sense, with which the nations I
Promiscuous fire, in Britons burned intense,
Of future times prophetic. Witness, Rome,
Who saw'st thy Caesar from the naked land,
Whose only fort was British hearts, repelled,

* Great Britain was peopled by the Celtae or Gauls.

† The Druids among the ancient Gauls and Britons had the care and direction of all religious matters.

To seek Pharsalian wreaths. Witness the toil,
The blood of ages, bootless to secure
Beneath an empire's yoke* a stubborn isle,
Disputed hard and never quite subdued.
The north remained untouched, where those who scorned
To stoop retired; and, to their keen effort
Yielding at last, recoiled the Roman power.
In vain, unable to sustain the shock,
From sea to sea desponding legions raised
The wall immense† – and yet, on summer's eve,
While sport his lambkins round, the shepherd's gaze.
Continual o'er it burst the northern storm;‡
As often, checked, receded – threatening hoarse
A swift return. But the devouring flood
No more endured control, when, to support
The last remains of empire, was recalled§
The weary Roman, and the Briton lay
Unnerved, exhausted, spiritless, and sunk.
Great proof! how men enfeeble into slaves.
The sword behind him flashed; before him roared,
Deaf to his woes, the deep.¶ Forlorn, around
He rolled his eye – not sparkling ardent flame
As when Caractacus** to battle led
Silurian swains, and Boadicea†† taught
Her raging troops the miseries of slaves.
'Then (sad relief!) from the bleak coast that hears
The German Ocean roar, deep-blooming, strong,
And yellow-haired, the blue-eyed Saxon came.
He came implored, but came with other aim
Than to protect. For conquest and defence
Suffices the same arm. With the fierce race

* The Roman Empire.

† The wall of Severus, built upon Adrian's rampart, which ran for eighty miles quite across the country, from the mouth of the Tyne to Solway Frith.

‡ Irruptions of the Scots and Picts.

§ The Roman empire being miserably torn by the northern nations, Britain was for ever abandoned by the Romans in the year 426 or 427.

¶ The Britons applying to Aetius, the Roman general, for assistance, thus expressed their miserable condition: – 'We know not which way to turn us. The Barbarians drive us to sea, and the sea forces us back to the Barbarians; between which we have only the choice of two deaths, either to be swallowed up by the waves, or butchered by the sword.'

** King of the Silures, famous for his great exploits, and accounted the best general Great Britain had ever produced. The Sulures were esteemed the bravest and most powerful of all the Britons: they inhabited Herefordshire, Radnorshire, Brecknockshire, Monmouthshire, and Glamorganshire.

†† Queen of the Iceni: her story is well known.

Poured in a fresh invigorating stream,
Blood, where unquelled a mighty spirit glowed.
Rash war and perilous battle their delight;
And immature, and red with glorious wounds,
Unpeaceful death their choice* – deriving thence
A right to feast and drain immortal bowls
In Odin's hall, whose blazing roof resounds
The genial uproar of those shades who fall
In desperate fight or by some brave attempt;
And, though more polished times the martial creed
Disown, yet still the fearless habit lives.
Nor were the surly gifts of war their all.
Wisdom was likewise theirs, indulgent laws,
And calm gradations of art-nursing peace,
And matchless orders, the deep basis still
On which ascends my British reign. Untamed
To the refining subtleties of slaves,
They brought a happy government along;
Formed by that freedom which, with secret voice,
Impartial nature teaches all her sons,
And which of old through the whole Scythian mass
I strong inspired. Monarchical their state,
But prudently confined, and mingled wise
Of each harmonious power: only, too much,
Imperious war into their rule infused,
Prevailed their general-king and chieftain-thanes.
'In many a field, by civil fury stained,
Bled the discordant Heptarchy;† and long
(Educing good from ill) the battle groaned
Ere, blood-cemented, Anglo-Saxons saw
Egbert‡ and peace on one united throne.

* It is certain, that an opinion was fixed and general among them (the Goths) that death was but the entrance into another life; that all men who lived lazy and unactive lives, and died natural deaths, by sickness or by age, went into vast caves under ground, all dark and miry, full of noisome creatures usual to such places, and there for ever grovelled in endless stench and misery. On the contrary, all who gave themselves to warlike actions and enterprises, to the conquest of their neighbours and the slaughter of their enemies, and died in battle, or of violent deaths upon bold adventures or resolutions, went immediately to the vast hall or palace of Odin, their god of war, who eternally kept open house for all such guests, where they were entertained at infinite tables, in perpetual feasts and mirth, carousing in bowls made of the skulls of their enemies they had slain; according to the number of whom, every one in these mansions of pleasure was the most honoured and best entertained. – *Sir William Temple's Essay on Heroic Virtue*.

† The seven kingdoms of the Anglo-Saxons, considered as being united into one common government, under a general in chief or monarch, and by the means of an assembly general, or wittenagemot.

‡ Egbert, King of Wessex, who, after having reduced all the other kingdoms of the Heptarchy under his dominion, was the first king of England.

'No sooner dawned the fair disclosing calm
Of brighter days, when lo! the north anew,
With stormy nations black, on England poured
Woes the severest e'er a people felt.
The Danish raven* lured by annual prey,
Hung o'er the land incessant. Fleet on fleet
Of barbarous pirates, unremitting tore
The miserable coast. Before them stalked,
Far seen, the demon of devouring flame;
Rapine, and murder, all with blood besmeared,
Without or ear or eye or feeling heart:
While close behind them marched the sallow power
Of desolating famine, who delights
In grass-grown cities and in desert fields;
And purple-spotted pestilence, by whom
Even friendship scared, in sickening horror sinks
Each social sense and tenderness of life.
Fixing at last, the sanguinary race
Spread, from the Humber's loud resounding shore
To where the Thames devolves his gentle maze,
And with superior arm the Saxon awed.
But superstition first, and monkish dreams
And monk-directed cloister-seeking kings
Had eat away his vigour, eat away
His edge of courage, and depressed the soul
Of conquering freedom which he once respired.
Thus cruel ages passed; and rare appeared
White-mantled Peace, exulting o'er the vale;
As when, with Alfred,† from the wilds she came
To policed cities and protected plains.
Thus by degrees the Saxon empire sunk,
Then set entire in Hastings' bloody field.‡
'Compendious war! (on Britain's glory bent,
So fate ordained) in that decisive day,
The haughty Norman seized at once an isle
For which through many a century in vain
The Roman, Saxon, Dane had toiled and bled.
Of Gothic nations this the final burst;

* A famous Danish standard was called Reafan, or Raven. The Danes imagined that, before a battle, the Raven wrought upon this standard clapped its wings or hung down its head, in token of victory or defeat.

† Alfred the Great, renowned in war, and no less famous in peace for his many excellent institutions, particularly that of juries.

‡ The battle of Hastings, in which Harold II, the last of the Saxon kings, was slain, and William the Conqueror made himself master of England.

And, mixed the genius of these people all,
Their virtues mixed in one exalted stream,
Here the rich tide of English blood grew full.
'Awhile my spirit slept; the land awhile,
Affrighted, drooped beneath despotic rage.
Instead of Edward's equal gentle laws,
The furious victor's partial will prevailed.
All prostrate lay; and, in the secret shade,
Deep-stung but fearful, Indignation gnashed
His teeth. Of freedom, property, despoiled,
And of their bulwark, arms; with castles crushed,
With ruffians quartered o'er the bridled land –
The shivering wretches, at the curfew sound,*
Dejected shrunk into their sordid beds,
And, through the mournful gloom, of ancient times
Mused sad, or dreamt of better. Even to feed
A tyrant's idle sport the peasant starved:
To the wild herd the pasture of the tame,
The cheerful hamlet, spiry town was given,
And the brown forest roughened wide around.†
'But this so dead, so vile submission long
Endured not. Gathering force, my gradual flame
Shook off the mountain of tyrannic sway.
Unused to bend, impatient of control,
Tyrants themselves the common tyrant checked.
The church, by kings intractable and fierce,
Denied her portion of the plundered state,
Or, tempted by the timorous and weak,
To gain new ground first taught their rapine law.
The Barons next a nobler league began,
Both those of English and of Norman race,
In one fraternal nation blended now,
The nation of the free! Pressed by a band
Of Patriots, ardent as the summer's noon
That looks delighted on, the tyrant see!
Mark! how with feigned alacrity he bears
His strong reluctance down, his dark revenge,
And gives the charter by which life indeed
Becomes of price, a glory to be man.‡

* The Curfew-Bell (from the French Couvrefeu) which was rung every night at eight of the clock, to warn the English to put out their fires and candles, under the penalty of a severe fine.

† The New Forest in Hampshire; to make which, the country for above thirty miles in compass was laid waste.

‡ On June 5, 1215, King John, met by the Barons on Runnemede, signed the Great Charter of Liberties or Magna Charta.

Through this, and through succeeding reigns affirmed
These long-contested rights, the wholesome winds
Of opposition hence began to blow;
And often since have lent the country life.
Before their breath corruption's insect-blights,
The darkening clouds of evil counsel, fly;
Or, should they sounding swell, a putrid court,
A pestilential ministry, they purge,
And ventilated states renew their bloom.
'Though with the tempered monarchy here mixed
Aristocratic sway, the people still,
Flattered by this or that, as interest leaned,
No full protection knew. For me reserved,
And for my commons,* was that glorious turn.
They crowned my first attempt – in senates rose,
The fort of freedom! Slow till then, alone
Had worked that general liberty, that soul
Which generous nature breathes, and which, when left
By me to bondage was corrupted Rome,
I through the northern nations wide diffused.
Hence many a people, fierce with freedom, rushed
From the rude iron regions of the north,
To Libyan deserts swarm protruding swarm,
And poured new spirit through a slavish world.
Yet, o'er these Gothic states, the king and chiefs
Retained the high prerogative of war,
And with enormous property engrossed
The mingled power. But on Britannia's shore
Now present, I to raise my reign began
By raising the democracy, the third
And broadest bulwark of the guarded state.
Then was the full the perfect plan disclosed
Of Britain's matchless constitution, mixed
Of mutual checking and supporting powers,
Kings, lords, and commons; not the name of free
Deserving, while the vassal-many dropped:
For, since the moment of the whole they form,
So, as depressed or raised, the balance they
Of public welfare and of glory cast.
Mark from this period the continual proof.'

* The commons are generally thought to have been first represented in parliament towards the end of Henry III's reign. To a parliament called in the year 1264, each county was ordered to send four knights, as representatives of their respective shires: and to a parliament called in the year following, each county was ordered to send, as their representatives, two knights, and each city and borough as many citizens and burgesses. Till then, history makes no mention of them; whence a very strong argument may be drawn, to fix the original of the House of Commons to that era.

2.3 Anon., *Common Sense* (1739)

Among the many interesting aspects of the following extract, three in particular stand out. It is an early example of the revolution in architectural taste, where the aesthetic value of the Gothic rises at the expense of classical and Italianate models; it echoes William Blackstone's famous metaphor of the English law as a renovated 'Gothic Castle' (Clery, 1995, p. 124); and it exemplifies the interpenetration of aesthetic, legal and political discourses.

Source: First published in *Common Sense*, no. 150 (15 December 1739). Quoted from *Gentleman's Magazine*, vol. 9 (1739), pp. 640, 641.

★

Building and Gardening, though in one Light not so injurious to the Publick (the whole Expence being made within ourselves, and the Property only changing Hands) yet in another Light the State may probably not be less affected by it, since, by impairing or ruining the Fortunes of those to whom the Care of Government is committed, it facilitates the Progress of Corruption. . . .

Every Man now, be his Fortune what it will, is to be *doing something at his Place*, as the fashionable Phrase is; and you hardly meet with any Body, who, after the first Compliments, does not inform you, that he is *in Mortar* and *moving of Earth*; the modest Terms for Building and Gardening. *One large Room*, *a Serpentine River*, and *a Wood*, are become the most absolute necessaries of Life, without which a Gentleman of the smallest Fortune thinks he makes no Figure in his Country. . . .

But, independently of the Expence and other ill Consequences of this modern Taste, I own I am always griev'd to see the venerable Paternal Castle of a Gentleman of an antient Family, and a competent Fortune, *tasted* and dwindled down into and imperfect Imitation of an *Italian Villa*, and the good old profitable Orchard laid out into a Waste of Green, bounded by fruitless Trees. Methinks there was something respectable in those old hospitable *Gothick* Halls, hung round with the Helmets, Breast-Plates, and Swords of our Ancestors; I entered them with a Constitutional Sort of Reverence, and look'd upon those Arms with Gratitude, as the Terror of former Ministers, and the Check of Kings. Nay, I even imagin'd that I here saw some of those good swords, that had procured the confirmation of *Magna Charta*, and humbled *Spencers* and *Gavestons*. And when I see these thrown by, to make way for some tawdry Gilding and Carving, I can't help considering such an Alteration as ominous even to our Constitution. Our old *Gothick* constitution had a noble Strength and

Simplicity in it, which was well enough represented by the bold Arches, and the solid Pillars of the Edifices of those Days. And I have not observed that the modern Refinements in either have in the least added to their Strength and Solidity.

2.4 Charles-Louis de Secondat Montesquieu (1689–1755), *Spirit of the Laws* (trans. 1750)

Montesquieu was one of the most influential historians of the eighteenth century. His impact on the Scottish Enlightenment was especially noticeable. Four features particularly distinguished Montesquieu's practice: he saw history as cycles of progress and corruption; he stressed the role of environment; his method was implicitly sociological, in that he considered, not just events, but the social complex in which they occurred (this third point is really an extension of the second); and he was systematic.

Although the contested belief that the English constitution had its ancient origins in the customs of Anglo-Saxons was a common one,[1] Montesquieu's prestige renewed the currency of the belief when he asserted (in a passage frequently echoed) that we learn from Tacitus that the English derived their 'idea of political government' from the Germans, from their 'beautiful system . . . invented first in the woods'. Like many other Continental thinkers at the time, Montesquieu held a high opinion of England, viewing it as the one nation 'in the world that has for the direct end of its constitution political liberty' (vol. I, p. 162). Montesquieu defined political liberty as 'a tranquillity of mind arising from the opinion each person has of his safety. In order to have this liberty, it is requisite the government be so constituted as one man need not be afraid of another' (p. 163). Political liberty was 'to be found only in moderate governments' (p. 161). The key to such moderation was a constitution in which the principal powers of government (the executive, the legislative, and the judiciary) were separate and balanced, characteristics Montesquieu found perfectly exhibited in Britain's constitutional monarchy. Montesquieu clearly influenced the architects of the American constitution who built in 'checks and balances' as an integral feature of their design. But Montesquieu was averse to democracy, as he was, indeed, to aristocracy: 'Democratic and aristocratic states are not in their own nature free' (p. 161). Montesquieu's carefully balanced position meant that his political legacy was a tricky one for admiring Britons. Radical Whigs could take comfort from Montesquieu's assertion that the spirit governing England's laws was the principle of political liberty, one arising out of the manners of the Gothic tribes, while conservative Whigs, such as Edmund Burke, could

[1] See R. J. Smith, *The Gothic Bequest: Medieval Institutions in British Thought, 1688–1863*, Cambridge: Cambridge University Press, 1987, pp. 6, 12, 61–5.

point to Montesquieu's endorsement of the view that political liberty could only arise within the evolving framework of existing constitutional structures, such as the historic division between an hereditary nobility and commoners.

The Spirit of the Laws devotes two chapters to the subject of the English constitution, 'XI: 6', which concentrates on theory, and 'XIX: 27', which focuses on the English system as it worked in practice. The following excerpts are from 'XI: 6' and 'XI: 8', which contain Montesquieu's two most extended references to Tacitus. The beginning of 'XI: 6' expands on the theory of separated powers. The following extract, representing Montesquieu's conclusion, ends with a disquisition on the vexed question of a standing army, a much debated issue in eighteenth-century political theory. The logic of Montesquieu's argument is not as random as it may at first seem, as it was one of Tacitus's contentions that the German tribes were, effectively, a nation of warrior-citizens, one of the possibilities canvassed by Montesquieu.

The translation, by Thomas Nugent, was the standard one throughout the eighteenth century.

Source: Charles-Louis de Secondat Montesquieu ([1748, trans. 1750] 1878), *The Spirit of the Laws*, translated by Thomas Nugent, two vols. London: George Bell & Sons, vol I, pp. 162–3; 171–5.

★

6. – *Of the Constitution of England.**

In every government there are three sorts of power: the legislative; the executive in respective to things dependent on the law of nations; and the executive in regard to matters that depend on the civil law.

By virtue of the first, the prince or magistrate enacts temporary or perpetual laws, and amends or abrogates those that have been already enacted. By the second, he makes peace or war, sends or receives embassies, establishes the public security, and provides against invasions. By the third, he punishes criminals, or determines the disputes that arise between individuals. The latter we shall call the judiciary power, and the other simply the executive power of the state. . . .

Here then is the fundamental constitution of the government we are treating of. The legislative body being composed of two parts, they check one another by the mutual privilege of rejecting. They are both restrained by the executive power, as the executive is by the legislative.

These three powers should naturally form a state of repose or inaction. But as there is a necessity for movement in the course of human affairs, they are forced to move, but still in concert.

* The greater part of the principles produced in this chapter by Montesquieu is derived from Locke's Treatise upon Civil Government, xii. – Ed.

As the executive power has no other part in the legislative than the privilege of rejecting, it can have no share in the public debates. It is not even necessary that it should propose, because as it may always disapprove of the resolutions that shall be taken, it may likewise reject the decisions on those proposals which were made against its will.

In some ancient commonwealths, where public debates were carried on by the people in a body, it was natural for the executive power to propose and debate in conjunction with the people, otherwise their resolutions must have been attended with a strange confusion.

Were the executive power to determine the raising of public money, otherwise than by giving its consent, liberty would be at an end; because it would become legislative in the most important point of legislation.

If the legislative power was to settle the subsidies, not from year to year, but for ever, it would run the risk of losing its liberty, because the executive power would be no longer dependent; and when once it was possessed of such a perpetual right, it would be a matter of indifference whether it held it of itself or of another. The same may be said if it should come to a resolution of intrusting, not an annual, but a perpetual command of the fleets and armies to the executive power.

To prevent the executive power from being able to oppress, it is requisite that the armies with which it is intrusted should consist of the people, and have the same spirit as the people, as was the case at Rome till the time of Marius. To obtain this end, there are only two ways, either that the persons employed in the army should have sufficient property to answer for their conduct to their fellow-subjects, and be enlisted only for a year, as was customary at Rome: or if there should be a standing army, composed chiefly of the most despicable part of the nation, the legislative power should have a right to disband them as soon as it pleased; the soldiers should live in common with the rest of the people; and no separate camp, barracks, or fortress should be suffered.

When once an army is established, it ought not to depend immediately on the legislative, but on the executive, power; and this from the very nature of the thing, its business consisting more in action than in deliberation. . . .

In perusing the admirable treatise of Tacitus 'On the Manners of the Germans,'* we find it is from that nation the English have borrowed the idea of their political government. This beautiful system was invented first in the woods.

* *De minoribus rebus principes consultant, de majoribus omnes; ita tamen ut ea quoque quorum penes plebem arbitrium est, apud principes pertractentur.* [This translates as 'On affairs of smaller moment, the chiefs consult; on those of greater importance, the whole community; yet with this circumstance, that what is referred to the decision of the people, is first maturely discussed by the chiefs.' Translated by John Aikin (see section 2.1, above, p. 51).]

As all human things have an end, the state we are speaking of will lose its liberty, will perish. Have not Rome, Sparta and Carthage perished? It will perish when the legislative power shall be more corrupt than the executive.

It is not my business to examine whether the English actually enjoy this liberty or not. Sufficient it is for my purpose to observe that it is established by their laws; and I inquire no further.

8. – Why the Ancients had not a clear Idea of Monarchy.

The ancients had no notion of a government founded on a body of nobles, and much less on a legislative body composed of the representatives of the people. The republics of Greece and Italy were cities that had each their own form of government, and convened their subjects within their walls. Before Rome had swallowed up all the other republics, there was scarcely anywhere a king to be found, no, not in Italy, Gaul, Spain, or Germany; they were all petty states or republics. Even Africa itself was subject to a great commonwealth: and Asia Minor was occupied by Greek colonies. There was, therefore, no instance of deputies of towns or assemblies of the states; one must have gone as far as Persia to find a monarchy.

I am not ignorant that there were confederate republics; in which several towns sent deputies to an assembly. But I affirm that there was no monarchy on that model.

The first plan, therefore, of the monarchies we are acquainted with was thus formed. The German nations that conquered the Roman empire were certainly a free people. Of this we may be convinced only by reading Tacitus 'On the Manners of the Germans.' The conquerors spread themselves over all the country; living mostly in the fields, and very little in towns. When they were in Germany, the whole nation was able to assemble. This they could no longer do, when dispersed through the conquered provinces. And yet as it was necessary that the nation should deliberate on public affairs, pursuant to their usual method before the conquest, they had recourse to representatives. Such is the origin of the Gothic government amongst us. At first it was mixed with aristocracy and monarchy – a mixture attended with this inconvenience, that the common people were bondmen. The custom afterwards succeeded of granting letters of enfranchisement, and was soon followed by so perfect a harmony between the civil liberty of the people, the privileges of the nobility and clergy, and the prince's prerogative, that I really think there never was in the world a government so well tempered as that of each part of Europe, so long as it lasted. Surprising that the corruption of the government of a conquering nation should have given birth to the best species of constitution that could possibly be imagined by man!

2.5 Henry Brooke (1700–83), *The Fool of Quality, or, The History of Henry, Earl of Morland* (1765)

The Fool of Quality, by the Irish writer Henry Brooke, is a rambling novel of sensibility. The eponymous fool is Harry Clinton, a young nobleman. In the following extract, he is given a lesson in British history by Mr Fenton, his merchant uncle, who has undertaken Harry's education on principles drawn from Rousseau. In his discourse on the origins of British liberty and of 'the incomparable beauties of the Britannic constitution', the character Fenton goes beyond Tacitus to cite Julius Ceasar's commentaries on pre-Roman Britain; in other words, the origins of the constitution go back so far that it amounts to a state of nature. The Goths appear here as latecomers (constitutionally speaking), and (contrary to Tacitus's emphasis on racial purity) as an assortment of different nations. They have contributed to Britain a spirit of independence and, more specifically, the model of the modern Parliament. However, it is clear that Fenton does not wish to be taken for a radical. He argues that, in spite of appearances to the contrary, feudalism was not absolutist, and praises it in terms analogous to the Whig ideal of constitutional monarchy.

Source: Henry Brooke (1765), *The Fool of Quality, or, The History of Henry, Earl of Morland*, 4 vols, Dublin: Dillon Chamberlaine, vol. 4, pp. 121–8.

★

How deplorable, then, my *Harry*, is the *suppression* of these rights, now nearly *universal* throughout the earth! But when people, from their infancy, and from generation to generation, have been habituated to bondage, oppression, and submission, without any tradition or memorial delivered down to them, of a happier or more equitable manner of life; they are accustomed to look on themselves, their possessions, and their progeny, as the rightful property of their rulers, to be disposed of at pleasure; and they no more regret the want of Liberty that they never knew, than the blind-born regret the want of the light of the sun.

Before I give up this paper that I have in my hand, this epitome or picture in miniature of the incomparable beauties of the Britannic constitution, it may be requisite to premise a few matters.

Travellers, when they survey a grand *Egyptian* pyramid, are apt to inquire by whom the stupendous pile was erected, and how long it has stood the assaults of time? But, when nothing of this can be developed, imagination runs back through antiquity without bounds; and thence contemplates an object with peculiar veneration, that it appears as it were to have had no beginning.

Such a structure is the constitution of *Great Britain*! No records discover when it had a commencement; neither can any annals specify the time at which it was not.

William the *Norman*, about seven hundred years ago, on his entering into the original contract with the people, engaged to govern them according to the *bonae et approbate antiquae Regni Leges*, the good well-approved and ancient laws of the kingdom, this constitution was therefore ancient, even in ancient times.

More than eighteen hundred years are now elapsed since Julius Caesar, in the sixth book of his Commentaries, bore testimony as well to the antiquity as excellency of the system of laws of Britain. He tells us that the venerable order of the Druids, who then administered justice throughout Gaul, derived their system of government from Britain; and that it was customary for those, who were desirous of being versed in the said ancient institutions, to go over to Britain for that purpose.

Caesar seems to recommend, while he specifies, one of the laws that was then peculiar to the constitution of Britain. He tells you that, if a woman was suspected of the death of her husband, she was questioned thereupon with severity by *her neighbours*; and that, if she was found guilty, she was tied alive to a stake, and burned to death. The very trial used in Britain, *by a jury of neighbours*, to this day.

It is, hence, very obvious that our *Gothic* ancestors either adopted what they judged excellent in the British constitution, or rather superadded what was deemed to be excellent in their own.

The people who went under the general name of *Goths* were of many different nations, who, from the *Northern*, poured down on the more *Southern* parts of Europe.

Their kings were, originally, chiefs or generals, appointed to lead voluntary armies, or colonies, for the forming of new settlements in foreign lands; and they were followed by a free and independent multitude, who had previously stipulated that they should share and enjoy the possessions which their valour should conquer.

Next to the general, in order, the officers or principal men of the army were attended, on such expeditions, by their kinsfolk, friends, and dependants, who chose to attach themselves to their persons and fortunes, respectively; and such attachments gave these officers great power and consideration . . .

Independent of the military services above reserved, the prince or chief, further, reserved the civil service or personal attendance of his feudatory officers, at certain times, and for certain terms, at his general or national court. This court was composed of *three estates*, the *prince*, the *nobles*, and such of the *priesthood*, whether Pagan or Christian, as held in *fief* from the prince; and from this *national council* our *parliament* took its origin . . .

If we look back upon one of those *Fief* or *Feudal* kings, seated high on his throne, and encircled with all the ensigns of royalty; when we find him entitled the sole proprietor of all the lands within his dominions; when we hear his subjects acknowledge that he, alone, is the fountain from whence are derived all possessions, rights, titles, distinctions, and dignities; when we see his most potent prefects and nobles, with lifted hands and bended knees, swearing fealty at his feet; who would not take him for an arbitrary and most absolute prince?

Such a judgement, however, would have been very premature. No prince could be more limited. He had not the licence of doing hurt to the person or property of the meanest vassal throughout his dominions. But, was he the less powerful, think you, for being less absolute? quite the contrary. While he acted within the sphere of his compact with the people, he acted in all the persons and powers of the people. Tho' prescribed with respect to evil; the extent of his beneficence was wholly unconfined. He was not dreaded indeed, but, on that account, he was the more revered and beloved by his subjects. He was a part of themselves; the principal member of their body. In him they beheld, with delight, their own dignity and strength so gloriously represented; and, by being the proprietor of all their hearts, he became the master of all their hands . . .

. . . How hath the invention of nature been stretched! how have the veins of the valiant been exhausted, to form, support, reform, and bring to maturity this unexampled constitution, this coalescence and grand effort of every human virtue, *British Liberty*.

2.6 Richard Hurd (1720–1808), *Letters on Chivalry and Romance* (1762)

Bishop Hurd's *Letters* are an exercise in cultural revaluation. He was one of a number of critics and antiquarians who in the 1750s and 1760s began to show a new appreciation of the literature of the past, partly as a means of challenging the supremacy of Pope and neo-classical principles within contemporary literary culture (see also extracts 2.7, 2.8, 2.9 and 3.7a). The most striking feature of the *Letters* is Hurd's insistence that Gothic art has its own distinct logic, derived from the social structure of feudalism, and its cultural expression, chivalry. This was already a bold departure from the commonplace denigration of all aspects of the Gothic era as senseless barbarism. But Hurd goes further and claims that Gothic art and literature follow aesthetic principles which are wholly different from those of classicism, but no less valid. Using Spenser's *The Faerie Queene* as his chief example, he claims that Gothic romance is to be preferred to the classical epic for its flights of fancy and sublimity. The 'good sense' of the modern age is a poor compensation.

Hurd uses the term 'Gothic' in the loose sense, to mean medieval, or outside the classical current (which was revived by the Renaissance). By making feudalism its defining feature, he appears to dissociate his argument from the Whig political discourse on the ancient constitution, which concerns the pre-Norman, pre-feudal Germanic nation of 'Goths'. Hurd draws much of his information about the Middle Ages from an alternative source: the French antiquarian Sainte-Palaye. However the emphasis on gallantry and veneration of women maintains one component of the political myth of the Goth, while the attention given to the religious spirit of Gothic as opposed to classical art looks forward to the fully fledged Gothic Revival of the early nineteenth century.

Source: Richard Hurd (1911), *Letters on Chivalry and Romance*, ed. Edith J. Morley, London: H. Frowde, pp. 79–81, 82–5, 85–93, 107–8, 114–17, 118–19, 121–2, 138–9, 154–5.

★

Letter I

The ages, we call barbarous, present us with many a subject of curious speculation. What, for instance, is more remarkable than the Gothic CHIVALRY? or than the spirit of ROMANCE, which took its rise from that singular institution?

Nothing in human nature, my dear friend, is without its reasons. The modes and fashions of different times may appear, at first sight, fantastic and unaccountable. But they, who look nearly into them, discover some latent cause of their production, 'Nature once known, no prodigies remain,' as sings our philosophical bard; but to come at this knowledge, is the difficulty. Sometimes a close attention to the workings of the human mind is sufficient to lead us to it: sometimes more than that, the diligent observation of what passes without us, is necessary.

This last I take to be the case here. The prodigies, we are now contemplating, had their origin in the barbarous ages. Why then, says the fastidious modern, look any farther for the reason? Why not resolve them at once into the usual caprice and absurdity of barbarians?

This, you see, is a short and commodious philosophy. Yet barbarians have their *own*, such as it is, if they are not enlightened by our reason. Shall we then condemn them unheard, or will it not be fair to let them have the telling of their own story?

Would we know, from what causes the institution of *Chivalry* was derived? The time of its birth, the situation of the barbarians, amongst whom it arose, must be considered: their wants, designs and policies must be explored: we must inquire when, and where, and how it came to pass that the western world became familiarised to this *Prodigy*, which we now start at.

Another thing is full as remarkable, and concerns us more nearly. The spirit of Chivalry, was a fire which soon spent itself: but that of *Romance*, which was kindled at it, burnt long, and continued its light and heat even to the politer ages.

The greatest geniuses of our own and foreign countries, such as Ariosto and Tasso in Italy, and Spenser and Milton in England, were seduced by these barbarities of their forefathers; were even charmed by the Gothic Romances. Was this caprice and absurdity in them? Or, may there not be something in the Gothic Romance peculiarly suited to the views of a genius and to the ends of poetry? And may not the philosophic moderns have gone too far, in their perpetual ridicule and contempt of it?

To form a judgment in the case, the rise, progress, and genius of Gothic Chivalry must be explained.

The circumstances in the Gothic fictions and manners, which are proper to the ends of poetry (if any such there be) must be pointed out.

Reasons, for the decline and rejection of the Gothic taste in later times must be given.

You have in these particulars both the SUBJECT, and the PLAN of the following Letters.

Letter II

I look upon Chivalry, as on some mighty River, which the fablings of the poets have made immortal. It may have sprung up amidst rude rocks, and blind deserts. But the noise and rapidity of its course, the extent of country it adorns, and the towns and palaces it ennobles, may lead a traveller out of his way and invite him to take a view of those dark caverns,

undè supernè
Plurimus Eridani per sylvam volvitur amnis.[4]

I enter without more words, on the subject I began to open to you in my last Letter.

The old inhabitants of these North-West parts of Europe were extremely given to the love and exercise of arms. The feats of Charlemagne and our Arthur, in particular, were so famous as in later times, when books of Chivalry were composed, to afford a principal subject to the writers of them.*

But CHIVALRY, properly so called; and under the idea 'of a distinct military order, conferred in the way of investiture, and accompanied with the solemnity of an oath and other ceremonies, as described in the old historians and romancers' was of later date, and seems to have sprung immediately out of the FEUDAL CONSTITUTION.

* See a discourse at the end of *Love's Labour Lost* in Warb. Ed. of Shakespear; in which the *origin*, *subject*, and *character* of these books of Chivalry (or *Romances*, properly so called) are explained with an exactness of learning, and penetration, peculiar to the writer.

The first and most sensible effect of this constitution, which brought about so mighty a change in the policies of Europe, was the erection of a prodigious number of petty tyrannies. For, though the great barons were closely tied to the services of their Prince by the conditions of their tenure, yet the power which was given them by it over their own numerous vassals was so great, that, in effect, they all set up for themselves; affected an independency; and were, in truth, a sort of absolute Sovereigns, at least with regard to one another. Hence, their mutual aims and interests often interfering, the feudal state was, in a good degree, a state of war: the feudal chiefs were in frequent enmity with each other: the several combinations of feudal tenants were so many separate armies under their head or chief: and their castles were so many fortresses, as well as palaces, of these puny princes.

In this state of things one sees, that all imaginable encouragement was to be given to the use of arms, under every different form of attack and defence, according as the safety of these different communities, or the ambition of their leaders, might require. And this condition of the times, I suppose, gave rise to that military institution, which we know by the name of CHIVALRY.

FURTHER, there being little or no security to be had amidst so many restless spirits and the clashing views of a neighbouring numerous and independent nobility, the military discipline of their followers, even in the intervals of peace, was not to be relaxed, and their ardour suffered to grow cool by a total disuse of martial exercises. And hence the proper origin of JUSTS and TURNAMENTS; those images of war, which were kept up in the castles of the barons and, by an useful policy, converted into the amusement of the knights, when their arms were employed on no serious occasion.

I call this the *proper origin* of Justs and Turnaments; for the date of them is carried no higher, as far as I can find even in France (where unquestionably they made their first appearance) than the year 1066; which was not till after the introduction of the feudal government into that country. Soon after, indeed, we find them in England and in Germany; but not till the feudal policy had spread itself in those parts and had prepared the way for them.

You see, then, my notion is, that Chivalry was no absurd and freakish institution, but the natural and even sober effect of the feudal policy; whose turbulent genius breathed nothing but war, and was fierce and military even in its amusements.

I leave you to revolve this idea in your own mind. You find, I believe, a reasonable foundation for it in the history of the feudal times, and in the spirit of the feudal government.

Letter III

If the conjecture, I advanced, of the rise of Chivalry, from the circumstances of the feudal government, be thought reasonable, it will now be easy to account for the several CHARACTERISTICS of this singular profession.

I. 'The passion for arms; the spirit of enterprize; the honour of knighthood; the rewards of valour; the splendour of equipages'; in short, every thing that raises our ideas of the prowess, gallantry, and magnificence of these sons of Mars is naturally and easily explained on this supposition.

Ambition, interest, glory all concurred, under such circumstances, to produce these effects. The feudal principles could terminate in nothing else. And when, by the necessary operation of that policy, this turn was given to the thoughts and passions of men, use and fashion would do the rest; and carry them to all the excesses of military fanaticism, which are painted so strongly, but scarcely exaggerated in the old Romances ...

II. 'Their romantic ideas of justice; their passion for adventures; their eagerness to run to the succour of the distressed; and the pride they took in redressing wrongs, and removing grievances'; all these distinguishing characters of genuine Chivalry are explained on the same principle. For, the feudal state being a state of war, or rather of almost perpetual violence, rapine, and plunder, it was unavoidable that, in their constant skirmishes, stratagems, and surprizes, numbers of the tenants or followers of one Baron should be seized upon and carried away by the followers of another: and the interest, each had to protect his own, would of course introduce the point of honour in attempting by all means not only to retaliate on the enemy, but to rescue the captive sufferers out of the hands of their oppressors.

It would be meritorious, in the highest degree, to fly to their assistance, when they knew where they were to be come at; or to seek them out with diligence, when they did not. This last service they called, *Going in quest of adventures*; which at first, no doubt, was confined to those of their own party, but afterwards, by the habit of acting on this principle, would be extended much farther. So that, in process of time, we find the Knights errant, as they were now properly styled, wandering the world over in search of occasions on which to exercise their generous and disinterested valour ...

III. 'The courtesy, affability, and gallantry, for which these adventurers were so famous, are but the natural effects and consequences of their situation.'

For the castles of the Barons were, as I said, the courts of these little sovereigns, as well as their fortresses; and the resort of their vassals thither, in honour of their chiefs, and for their own proper security, would make that civility and politeness, which is seen in courts and insensibly prevails there, a predominant part in the character of these assemblies ...

Further, the free commerce of the ladies, in those knots and circles of the great, would operate so far on the sturdiest knights as to give birth to the attentions of gallantry. But this gallantry would take a refined turn, not only from the necessity there was of maintaining the strict forms of decorum, amidst a promiscuous conversation under the eye of the Prince and in his own family; but also from the inflamed sense they must needs have of the frequent outrages committed, by their neighbouring clans of adversaries, on the honour of the Sex, when by chance of war they had fallen into their hands. Violations of chastity being the most atrocious crimes they had to charge on their enemies, they would pride themselves in the glory of being its protectors: and as this virtue was, of all others, the fairest and strongest claim of the sex itself to such protection, it is no wonder that the notions of it were, in time, carried to so platonic an elevation . . .

Not but the foundation of this refined gallantry was laid in the antient manners of the German nations. Caesar tells us how far they carried their practice of chastity, which he seems willing to account for on political principles. However that be, their consideration of the sex was prodigious, as we see in the history of their irruptions into the Empire; where, among all their ravages and devastations of other sorts, we find they religiously abstained from offering any violence to the honour of the women.

IV. It only remains to account for that 'character of Religion', which was so deeply imprinted on the minds of all knights and was essential to their institution. We are even told, that *the love of God and of the Ladies* went hand in hand, in the duties and ritual of Chivalry.

Two reasons may be assigned for this singularity,

First, the superstition of the Times, in which Chivalry arose; which was so great that no institution of a public nature could have found credit in the world, that was not consecrated by the Churchmen, and closely interwoven with religion.

Secondly, the condition of the Christian world; which had been harassed by long wars, and had but just recovered a breathing-time from the brutal ravages of the Saracen armies. The remembrance of what they had lately suffered from these grand enemies of the faith, made it natural and even necessary to engage a new military order on the side of religion . . .

Such was the state of things in the western World, when the crusades to the holy land were set on foot. Whence we see how well prepared the minds of men were for engaging in that enterprize. Every object, that had entered into the views of the institutors of chivalry, and had been followed by its professors, was now at hand to inflame the military and religious ardor of the knights, to the utmost. And here, in fact, we find the strongest and boldest features of their genuine character: *daring* to madness, in enterprises of hazard: burning with zeal for the delivery of the *oppressed*; and, which was deemed the height of *religious* merit, for the rescue of the holy city out of the hands of infidels: and, lastly exalting their honour of *chastity* so high as to profess celibacy; as they constantly did, in the several orders of knighthood created on that extravagant occasion.

Letter VI

Let it be no surprize to you that, in the close of my last Letter, I presumed to bring the *Gerusalemme liberata*[5] into competition with the *Iliad.*

So far as the heroic and Gothic manners are the same, the pictures of each, if well taken, must be equally entertaining. But I go further, and maintain that the circumstances, in which they differ, are clearly to the advantage of the Gothic designers.

You see, my purpose is to lead you from this forgotten chivalry to a more amusing subject, I mean the Poetry we still read, and which was founded upon it.

Much has been said, and with great truth, of the felicity of Homer's age, for poetical manners. But as Homer was a citizen of the world, when he had seen in Greece, on the one hand, the manners he has described, could he, on the other hand, have seen in the west the manners of the feudal ages, I make no doubt but he would certainly have preferred the latter. And the grounds of this preference would, I suppose, have been '*The improved gallantry of the feudal times*; and the *superior solemnity of their superstitions.*'

If any great poet, like Homer, had lived amongst, and sung of, the Gothic knights . . . this preference, I persuade myself, had been very sensible. But their fortune was not so happy.

> *omnes illacrymabiles*
> *Urgentur, ignotique longâ*
> *Nocte, carent quia vate sacro.*[6]

As it is, we may take a guess of what the subject was capable of affording to real genius from the rude sketches we have of it, in the old Romancers. And it is but looking into any of them to be convinced that the *gallantry*, which inspirited the feudal times, was of a nature to furnish the poet with finer scenes and subjects of description in every view, than the simple and uncontrolled barbarity of the Grecian. . . .

Letter VII

But nothing shews the difference of the two systems under consideration more plainly, than the effect they really had on the two greatest of our

Poets; at least the Two which an English reader is most fond to compare with Homer, I mean SPENSER and MILTON.

It is not to be doubted but that each of these bards had kindled his poetic fire from classic fables. So that, of course, their prejudices would lie that way. Yet they both appear, when most inflamed, to have been more particularly rapt with the Gothic fables of chivalry.

Spenser, tho' he had been long nourished with the spirit and substance of Homer and Virgil, chose the times of chivalry for his theme, and fairy land for the scene of his fictions. He could have planned, no doubt, an heroic design on the exact classic model: or, he might have trimmed between the Gothic and Classic, as his contemporary Tasso did. But the charms of *fairy* prevailed . . .

Under this idea then of a Gothic, not classical poem, the *Faery Queen* is to be read and criticized. And on these principles, it would not be difficult to unfold its merit in another way than has been hitherto attempted.

Milton, it is true, preferred the classic model to the Gothic. But it was after long hesitation; and his favourite subject was *Arthur and his Knights of the round table*. On this he had fixed for the greater part of his life. What led him to change his mind was, partly, as I suppose, his growing fanaticism; partly, his ambition to take a different rout from Spenser; but chiefly perhaps, the discredit into which the stories of chivalry had now fallen by the immortal satire of Cervantes. Yet we see thro' all his poetry, where his enthusiasm flames out most, a certain predilection for the legends of chivalry before the fables of Greece.

This circumstance, you know, has given offence to the austerer and more mechanical critics. They are ready to censure his judgment, as juvenile, and unformed, when they see him so delighted, on all occasions, with the Gothic romances. But do these censors imagine that Milton did not perceive the defects of these works, as well as they? No: it was not the *composition* of books of chivalry, but the *manners* described in them, that took his fancy . . .

The conduct then of these two poets may incline us to think with more respect, than is commonly done of the *Gothic manners*, I meant as adapted to the uses of the greater poetry.

I say nothing of Shakespear, because the sublimity (the divinity, let it be, if nothing else will serve) of his genius kept no certain rout, but rambled at all hazard into all the regions of human life and manners. So that we can hardly say what he preferred, or what he rejected, on full deliberation. Yet one thing is clear, that even he is greater when he uses Gothic manners and machinery, than when he employs classical: which brings us again to the same point, that the former have, by their nature and genius, the advantage of the latter in producing the *sublime*.

Letter VIII

I spoke 'of criticizing Spenser's poem, under the idea, not of a classical but Gothic composition'.

It is certain much light might be thrown on that singular work, were an able critic to consider it in this view. For instance, he might go some way towards explaining, perhaps justifying, the general plan and *conduct* of the Faery Queen, which, to classical readers has appeared indefensible.

I have taken the fancy, with your leave, to try my hand on this curious subject.

When an architect examines a Gothic structure by Grecian rules, he finds nothing but deformity. But the Gothic architecture has its own rules, by which when it comes to be examined, it is seen to have its merit, as well as the Grecian. The question is not, which of the two is conducted in the simplest or truest taste: but, whether there be not sense and design in both, when scrutinized by the laws on which each is projected.

The same observation holds of the two sorts of poetry. Judge of the Faery Queen by the classic models, and you are shocked with its disorder: consider it with an eye to its Gothic original, and you find it regular. The unity and simplicity of the former are more complete: but the latter has that sort of unity and simplicity, which results from its nature.

The Faery Queen then, as a Gothic poem, derives its METHOD, as well as the other characters of its composition, from the established modes and ideas of chivalry. . . .

If you ask then, what is this *Unity* of Spenser's Poem? I say, it consists in the relation of its several adventures to one common *original*, the appointment of the Faery Queen; and to one common *end*, the completion of the Faery Queen's injunctions. The knights issued forth on their adventures on the breaking up of this annual feast; and the next annual feast, we are to suppose, is to bring them together again from the achievement of their several charges.

This, it is true, is not the classic Unity, which consists in the representation of one entire action: but it is an Unity of another sort, an unity resulting from the respect which a number of related actions have to one common purpose. In other words, it is an unity of *design*, and not of action.

This Gothic method of design in poetry may be, in some sort, illustrated by what is called the Gothic method of design in Gardening. A wood or grove cut out into many separate avenues or glades was amongst the most favourite of the works of art, which our fathers attempted in this species of cultivation. These walks were distinct from each other, had, each, their several destination, and terminated on their own proper objects. Yet the whole was brought together and considered under one view by the relation which these various openings had, not to each other, but to their common and concurrent center. You and I are, perhaps, agreed that this sort of gardening is not of so true a taste as that which *Kent and Nature* have brought us acquainted with;[7] where the supreme art of the Designer consists in disposing his ground and objects into an *entire landskip*; and grouping them, if I may use the term, in so easy a manner, that the careless observer, tho' he be taken with the symmetry of the whole, discovers no art in the combination . . .

Letter IX

. . . [French neo-classical critics] aspired to a sort of supremacy in Letters; and finding the Italian language and its best writers standing in their way, they have spared no pains to lower the estimation of both.[8]

Whatever their inducements were, they succeeded but too well in their attempt. Our obsequious and over modest critics were run down by their authority. Their taste of Letters, with some worse things, was brought amongst us at the Restoration. Their language, their manners, nay their very prejudices were adopted by our Frenchified king and his Royalists. And the more fashionable wits, of course, set their fancies, as my Lord Molesworth[9] tells us the people of Copenhagen in his time did their clocks, by the court-standard. . . .

Letter X

. . . But the source of bad criticism, as universally of bad philosophy, is the abuse of terms. A poet, they say, must follow *Nature*; and by Nature we are to suppose can only be meant the known and experienced course of affairs in this world. Whereas the poet has a world of his own, where experience has less to do, than consistent imagination.

He has, besides, a supernatural world to range in. He has Gods, and Faeries, and Witches at his command: and,

—O! who can tell
The hidden *pow'r* of herbes, and might of magic spell?
Spenser. B.i.C.2.

Thus in the poet's world, all is marvellous and extraordinary; yet not *unnatural* in one sense, as it agrees to the conceptions that are readily entertained of these magical and wonder-working Natures.

This trite maxim of *following* Nature is further mistaken in applying it indiscriminately to all sorts of poetry.

In those species which have men and manners professedly for their theme, a strict conformity with human nature is reasonably demanded.

> *Non hic Centauros, non Gorgonas, Harpyiasque*
> *Invenies: hominem pagina nostra sapit:*[10]

is a proper motto to a book of Epigrams, but would make a poor figure at the head of an epic poem.

Still further, in those species that address themselves to the heart and would obtain their end, not thro' the Imagination, but thro' the *Passions*, there the liberty of transgressing nature, I mean the real powers and properties of human nature, is infinitely restrained; and *poetical* truth is, under these circumstances, almost as severe a thing as *historical*.

The reason is, we must first *believe*, before we can be *affected*.

But the case is different with the more sublime and creative poetry. This species, addressing itself solely or principally to the Imagination; a young and credulous faculty, which loves to admire and to be deceived; has no need to observe those cautious rules of credibility so necessary to be followed by him, who would touch the affections and interest the heart. . . .

Letter XII

. . . Under this form [of allegory] the tales of faery kept their ground, and even made their fortune at court; where they became, for two or three reigns, the ordinary entertainment of our princes. But reason, in the end, (assisted however by party, and religious prejudices) drove them off the scene, and would endure these *lying wonders*, neither in their own proper shape, nor as masked in figures.

Henceforth, the taste of wit and poetry took a new turn: and *fancy*, that had wantoned it so long in the world of fiction, was now constrained, against her will, to ally herself with strict truth, if she would gain admittance into reasonable company.

What we have gotten by this revolution, you will say, is a great deal of good sense. What we have lost, is a world of fine fabling; the illusion of which is so grateful to the *charmed Spirit*; that, in spite of philosophy and fashion, *Faery* Spenser still ranks highest among the Poets; I mean with all those are either come of that house, or have any kindness for it.

Earth-born critics, my friend, may blaspheme,

> But all the Gods ravish'd with delight
> Of this celestial Song, and music's wondrous might.

2.7 Thomas Warton (1728–90), '*The History of English Poetry* (1778)

Thomas Warton's *History* included the fullest critical consideration of 'Gothic' (i.e. medieval) literature that had yet been attempted. Although its judgements continue to be inflected by neo-classical views, the following extract shows the same admiration for Gothic art as was found in Hurd (Warton refers to the 'gorgeous veil of Gothic invention' (I, p. cclxix)), albeit qualified by a sense of historical progress. In this passage scholarly assessment gradually mutates into a rallying-cry for a new, non-classical aesthetic. In terms of debate about Gothic origins, Warton's other main contribution was his controversial claim that romance (the defining narrative form of the Gothic period) was ultimately of Saracen origin. Many authorities accepted that the taste for marvellous adventures was imported into the West by the Crusaders returning from the Orient. In 'Of the Origin of Romantic Fiction in Europe', one of the dissertations prefixed to his history, Warton argued for an even earlier point of Oriental influence: the Moorish conquest of Spain. Hugh Blair, Clara Reeve and Thomas Percy responded, eager to defend the native tradition of Northern romance.

Source: Thomas Warton (1778), *The History of English Poetry from the Close of the Eleventh to the Commencement of the Eighteenth Century. To Which are prefixed, Three Dissertations, etc.*, vol. II, London: J. Dodsley, pp. 462–3.

★

. . . The customs, institutions, traditions, and religion, of the middle ages, were favorable to poetry. Their pageaunts, processions, spectacles, and ceremonies, were friendly to imagery, to personification and allegory. Ignorance and superstition, so opposite to the real interests of human society, are the parents of imagination. The very devotion of the Gothic times was romantic. The catholic worship, besides that its numerous exteriour appendages were of a picturesque and even of a poetical nature, disposed the mind to a state of deception, and encouraged, or rather authorized, every species of credulity: its visions, miracles, and legends, propagated a general propensity to the Marvellous, and strengthened the belief of spectres, demons, witches, and incantations. These illusions were heightened by churches of a wonderful mechanism, and conformed on such principles of inexplicable architecture as had a tendency to impress the soul with every false sensation of religious fear. The savage pomp and the capricious heroism of the baronial manners, were replete with incident, adventure, and enterprise: and the intractable genius of the feudal policy, held forth those irregularities of conduct, discordancies of interest, and dissimilarities of situation, that framed rich materials for the minstrel muse. The tacit compact of fashion, which promotes civility by diffusing habits of uniformity, and therefore destroys peculiarities of character and situation, had not yet operated upon life: nor had domestic convenience abolished unwieldy magnificence. Literature, and a better sense of things, not only banished these barbarities, but superseded the mode of composition which was formed upon them. Romantic poetry gave way to the force of reason and inquiry; as its own inchanted palaces and gardens instantaneously vanished, when the Christian champion displayed the shield of truth, and baffled the charm of the necromancer. The study of the classics, together with a colder magic and a tamer mythology, introduced method into composition: and the universal ambition of rivalling those new patterns of excellence, the faultless models of Greece and Rome, produced that bane of invention, IMITATION. Erudition was made to act upon genius. Fancy was weakened by reflection and philosophy. The fashion of treating every thing scientifically, applied speculation and theory to the arts of writing. Judgment was advanced above imagination, and rules of criticism were established. The brave eccentricities of original genius, and the daring hardiness of native thought, were intimidated by metaphysical sentiments of perfection and refinement. Setting aside the consideration of the more solid advantages, which are obvious, and are not the distinct object of out contemplation at present, the lover of true poetry will ask what have we gained by this revolution? It may be answered, much good sense, good taste, and good criticism. But, in the mean time, we have lost a set of manners, and system of machinery, more suitable to the purposes of poetry than those which have been adopted in their place. We have parted with extravagancies that are above propriety, with incredibilities that are more acceptable than truth, and with fictions that are more valuable than reality. . . .

2.8 Hugh Blair (1718–1800), *A Critical Dissertation on the Poems of Ossian, The Son of Fingal* (1763)

In 1762 James Macpherson published what he claimed was an ancient Scottish epic in translation: *Fingal*, by the bard Ossian. In fact the prose poem was the product of creative editing. There was dispute about its origins from the start, but at the same time *Fingal* and its sequel *Temora* achieved immense international popularity. Hugh Blair, a friend of Macpherson, was one of the earliest and most vehement champions of the authenticity of Ossian.

Blair was a Scottish divine and professor of rhetoric in Edinburgh. His *Critical Dissertation* 'subjoined' to the third edition of Macpherson's work elaborates on the revisionist history of poetry already sketched by Hurd and Warton. Nowhere in eighteenth-century criticism is it more fully stated that primitive societies are most conducive to the powers of imagination, and with civilisation comes an inevitable decline. Blair grants that the Goths had their poets, but he is nevertheless at pains to depict the society of the Celts as primitivism of a different order; an ideal blend of aboriginal vigour and refined civility. This odd equivocation in his argument may be a concession to Enlightenment progressivism, or the result of a Scottish nationalist bias.

The works of 'Ossian' appeared at the same time as the first Gothic fictions, and together they represented a new area of taste within literary culture. In the novel *Maria* (1785) by Elizabeth Blower, one character, a Miss Hampden, looking forward to a house party in a renovated castle, 'is impatient to enjoy the delightful horrors of Gothic galleries, winding avenues, gaping chimnies, and dreary vaults; and by way of enlivening the scene, she intends to take with her the tragedies of Eschylus, the poems of Ossian, Castle of Otranto, &c. &c. . . . – Are you,' she asks the heroine of the story, 'a lover of this kind of sublimity?'

Source: Hugh Blair (1765), *A Critical Dissertation on the Poems of Ossian, The Son of Fingal* from James Macpherson, *The Works of Ossian, the Son of Fingal*, 2 vols, trans. (from the Gaelic), 3rd edn, London, II, pp. 313–18, 332–5; 340.

★

Among the monuments remaining of the ancient state of nations, few are more valuable than their poems or songs. History, when it treats of remote and dark ages, is seldom very instructive. The beginnings of society, in every country, are involved in fabulous confusion; and though they were not, they would furnish few events worth recording. But, in every period of society, human manners are a curious spectacle; and the most natural pictures of ancient manners are exhibited in the ancient poems of nations. These present to us, what is much more valuable than the history of such transactions as a rude age can afford, the history of human imagination and passion. They make us acquainted with the notions and feelings of our fellow-creatures in the most artless ages; discovering what objects they admired, and what pleasures they pursued, before those refinements of society had taken place, which enlarge indeed, and diversify the transactions, but diversify the manners of mankind.

Besides this merit, which ancient poems have with philosophical observers of human nature, they have another with persons of taste. They promise some of the highest beauties of poetical writing. Irregular and unpolished we may expect the productions of uncultivated ages to be; but abounding, at the same time, with that enthusiasm, that vehemence and fire, which are the soul of poetry. For many circumstances of those times which we call barbarous, are favourable to the poetical spirit. That state, in which human nature shoots wild and free, though unfit for other improvements, certainly encourages the high exertions of fancy and passion.

In the infancy of societies, men live scattered and dispersed, in the midst of solitary rural scenes, where the beauties of nature are their chief entertainment. They meet with many objects, to them new and strange; their wonder and surprise are frequently excited; and by the sudden changes of fortune occurring in their unsettled state of life, their passions are raised to the utmost. Their passions have nothing to restrain them: their imagination has nothing to check it. They display themselves to one another without disguise: and converse and act in the uncovered simplicity of nature. As their feelings are strong, so their language, of itself, assumes a poetical turn. Prone to exaggerate, they describe every thing in the strongest colours; which of course renders their speech picturesque and figurative. Figurative language owes its rise chiefly to two causes; to the want of proper names for objects, and to the influence of imagination and passion over the form of expression. Both these causes concur in the infancy of society. Figures are commonly considered as artificial modes of speech, devised by orators and poets, after the world had advanced to a refined state. The contrary of this is the truth. Men never have used so many figures of style, as in those rude ages, when, besides the power of a warm imagination to suggest lively images, the want of proper and precise terms for the ideas they would express, obliged them to have recourse to circumlocution, metaphor, comparison, and all those substituted forms of expression, which give a poetical air to language. An American chief, at this day, harangues at the head of his tribe, in a more bold metaphorical style than a modern European would adventure to use in an Epic poem.

In the progress of society, the genius and manners of men undergo a change more favourable to accuracy than to sprightliness and sublimity. As the world advances, the understanding gains ground upon the imagination; the understanding is more exercised; the imagination, less. Fewer objects occur that are new or surprising. Men apply themselves to trace the causes of things; they correct and refine one another; they subdue or disguise their passions; they form their manners upon one uniform standard of politeness and civility. Human nature is pruned according to method and rule. Language advances from sterility to copiousness, and at the same time, from fervour and enthusiasm, to correctness and precision. Style becomes more chaste; but less animated. The progress of the world in this respect resembles the progress of age in man. The powers of imagination are more vigorous and predominant in youth; those of the understanding ripen more slowly, and often attain not their maturity, till the imagination begin to flag. Hence, poetry, which is the child of imagination, is frequently most glowing and animated in the first ages of society. As the ideas of our youth are remembered with a peculiar pleasure on account of their liveliness and vivacity; so the more ancient poems have often proved the greatest favourites of nations.

Poetry has been said to be more ancient than prose: and however paradoxical such an assertion may seem, yet, in a qualified sense, it is true.

Men certainly never conversed with one another in regular numbers; but even their ordinary language would, in ancient times, for the reasons before assigned, approach to a poetical style; and the first compositions transmitted to posterity, beyond doubt, were, in a literal sense, poems; that is, compositions in which imagination had the chief hand, formed into some kind of numbers, and pronounced with a musical modulation or tone. Musick or song has been found coeval with society among the most barbarous nations. The only subjects which could prompt men, in their first rude state, to utter their thoughts in compositions of any length, were such as naturally assumed the tone of poetry; praises of their gods, or of their ancestors; commemorations of their own warlike exploits; or lamentations over their misfortunes. And before writing was invented, no other compositions, except songs or poems, could take such hold of the imagination and memory, as to be preserved by oral tradition, and handed down from one race to another.

Hence we may expect to find poems among the antiquities of all nations. It is probable too, that an extensive search would discover a certain degree of resemblance among, all the most ancient poetical productions, from whatever country they have proceeded. In a similar state of manners, similar objects and passions operating upon the imaginations of men, will stamp their productions with the same general character. Some diversity will, no doubt, be occasioned by climate and genius. But mankind never bear such resembling features, as they do in the beginnings of society. Its subsequent revolutions give rise to the principal distinctions among nations; and divert, into channels widely separated, that current of human genius and manners, which descends originally from one spring. What we have been long accustomed to call the oriental vein of poetry, because some of the earliest poetical productions have come to us from the East, is probably no more oriental than occidental; it is characteristical of an age rather than a country; and belongs, in some measure to all nations at a certain period. Of this the works of Ossian seem to furnish a remarkable proof.

Our present subject leads us to investigate the ancient poetical remains, not so much of the east, or of the Greeks and Romans, as of the northern nations; in order to discover whether the Gothic poetry has any resemblance to the Celtic or Galic, which we are about to consider. Though the Goths, under which name we usually comprehend all the Scandinavian tribes, were a people altogether fierce and martial, and noted, to a proverb, for their ignorance of the liberal arts, yet they too from the earliest times, had their poets and their songs. Their poets were distinguished by the title of *Scalders* and their songs were termed *Vyses* . . .

. . . This is such poetry as we might expect from a barbarous nation. It breathes a more ferocious spirit. It is wild, warm and irregular; but at the same time animated and strong; the style, in the original, full of inventions, and, as we learn from some of Olaus's notes, highly metaphorical and figured.

But when we open the works of Ossian, a very different scene presents itself. There we find the fire and the enthusiasm of the most early times, combined with an amazing degree of regularity and art. We find tenderness, and even delicacy of sentiment, greatly predominant over fierceness and barbarity. Our hearts are melted with the softest and at the same time elevated with the highest ideas of magnanimity, generosity, and true heroism. When we turn from the poetry of Lodbrog to that of Ossian, it is like passing from a savage desart, into a fertile and cultivated country. How is this to be accounted for? Or by what means to be reconciled with the remote antiquity attributed to these poems? This is a curious point; and requires to be illustrated.

That the ancient Scots were of Celtic original, is past all doubt. Their conformity with the Celtic nations in language, manners and religion, proves it to a full demonstration. The Celtae, a great and mighty people, altogether distinct from the Goths and Teutones, once extended their dominion over all the west of Europe; but seem to have had their more full and compleat establishment in Gaul. Wherever the Celtae or Gauls are mentioned by ancient writers, we seldom fail to hear of their Druids and their Bards; the institution of which two orders, was the capital distinction of their manners and policy. The Druids were their philosophers and priests; the Bards, their poets and recorders of heroic actions: And both there orders of men, seem to have subsided among them, as chief members of the date, from time immemorial. We must not therefore imagine the Celtae to have been altogether a gross and rude nation. They possessed from very remote ages a formed system of discipline and manners, which appears to have had a deep and lasting influence. Ammianus Marcellinus gives them this express testimony, that there flourished among them the study of the most laudable arts; introduced by the bards, whose office it was to sing in heroic verse, the gallant actions of illustrious men; and by the Druids, who lived together in colleges or societies, after the Pythagorean manner, and philosophising upon the highest subjects, asserted the immortality of the human soul. Though Julius Caesar in his account of Gaul, does not expressly mention the Bards, yet it is plain that under the title of Druids, he comprehends that whole college or order; of which the Bards, who, it is probable, were the disciples of the Druids, undoubtedly made a part. It deserves remark, that according to his account, the Druidical institution first took rise in Britain, and passed from thence into Gaul; so that they who aspired to be thorough makers of that learning were wont to resort to Britain. He adds too, that such as were to be initiated among the Druids, were obliged to commit to their memory a great number of verses, in so much that some employed twenty years in this course of education; and that they did not think it lawful to record these poems in writing, but sacredly handed them down by tradition from race to race.

So strong was the attachment of the Celtic nations to their poetry and their Bards, that amidst all the changes of their government and manners, even long after the order of the Druids was extinct, and the national religion altered, the Bards continued to flourish; not as a set of strolling songsters, like the Greek Αοιδοι [Bards] or Rhapsodists in Homer's time, but as an order of men highly respected in the state, and supported by a public establishment. We find them, according to the testimonies of Strabo and Diodorus,[11] before the age of Augustus Caesar; we find them remaining under the same name, and exercising the same functions as of old, in Ireland, and in the north of Scotland, almost down to our own times. It is well known that in both these countries, every *Regulus* or chief had his own Bard, who was considered as an officer of rank in his court; and had lands assigned him, which descended to his family. . . .

The manners of Ossian's age, so far as we can gather them from his writings, were abundantly favourable to a poetical genius. The two dispiriting vices, to which Longinus imputes the decline of poetry, covetousness and effeminacy, were as yet unknown. The cares of men were few. They lived a roving indolent life; hunting and war their principal employments; and their chief amusements, the musick of bards and the 'feast of shells'. . . .

2.9 James Beattie (1735–1803), *The Minstrel; or, The Progress of Genius* (1770–4)

James Beattie was professor of moral philsophy at Marischal College, Aberdeen. His poem takes up where 'Ossian' leaves off, and was almost as celebrated as *Fingal* during the last decades of the eighteenth century. It reinforced the reputation of Scotland as the homeland of the sublime, anciently peopled by a race remarkable for virtue, simplicity and sensibility. However, Beattie characterises the era depicted in the poem as 'Gothic', and gives his hero the Anglo-Saxon name Edwin: perhaps a rebuke to Blair's divisive insistence on the singularity of the Celts?

The Minstrel concerns the unfolding of poetic genius; along with Thomas Gray's *The Bard* and, much later, Walter Scott's *The Lay of the Last Minstrel*, it helped to define, in a generically Gothic form, the persona of the modern poet: an alienated, 'romantic' individual, at odds with social conventions and the march of civilisation. It was one of Wordsworth's favourite works, and sustained him in his sense of poetic vocation. Especially notable in Beattie is his emphasis on landscape-viewing as a formative influence on the developing mind, and as a means of emotional release or consolation. Ann Radcliffe was another writer profoundly impressed by this vision, and acknowledges her debt in numerous quotations from *The Minstrel*, especially in *The Romance of the Forest* and *The Mysteries of Udolpho*. Her first novel, *The Castles of Athlin and Dunbayne*, set in the Scottish Highlands, was clearly written under the influence of 'Ossian' and Beattie.

In addition, the poem pioneered the revival of the Spenserian stanza, a Gothic form Beattie felt obliged to defend in his Preface:

> To those who may be disposed to ask what could induce me to write in so difficult a measure, I can only answer, that it pleases my ear, and seems, from its Gothic structure and original, to bear some relation to the subject and spirit of the poem. It admits both simplicity and magnificence of sound and of language, beyond any other stanza I am acquainted with.

The Spenserian stanza was to be a favourite of the second generation of Romantic poets.

Source: George Gilfillan, ed. (1854) *The Poetical Works of Beattie, Blair, and Falconer*, Edinburgh, London and Dublin: James Nichol, James Nisbet and W. Robertson, Part 1, stanzas 11–22, 32, 33.

There lived in Gothic days, as legends tell,
A shepherd-swain, a man of low degree;
Whose sires, perchance, in Fairyland might dwell,
Sicilian groves, or vales of Arcady;
But he, I ween, was of the north countrie;*
A nation famed for song and beauty's charms;
Zealous, yet modest; innocent, though free;
Patient of toil; serene amidst alarms;
Inflexible in faith; invincible in arms.

The shepherd swain of whom I mention made,
On Scotia's mountains fed his little flock;
The sickle, scythe, or plough he never sway'd:
An honest heart was almost all his stock;
His drink the living water from the rock:
The milky dams supplied his board, and lent
Their kindly fleece to baffle winter's shock;
And he, though oft with dust and sweat besprent,
Did guide and guard their wanderings, whereso'er they went.

From labour, health, from health, contentment, springs;
Contentment opes the source of every joy.
He envied not, he never thought of kings;

* There is hardly an ancient ballad, or romance, wherein a minstrel or a harper appears, but he is characterized, by way of eminence, to have been 'of the north countrie.' It is probable, that under this appellation were formerly comprehended all the provinces to the north of the Trent. – See *Percy's Essay on the English Minstrels*.

Nor from those appetites sustain'd annoy,
That chance may frustrate, or indulgence cloy;
Nor Fate his calm and humble hopes beguiled;
He mourn'd no recreant friend, nor mistress coy,
For on his vows the blameless Phoebe smiled,
And her alone he loved, and loved her from a child.

No jealousy their dawn of love o'ercast,
Nor blasted were their wedded days with strife;
Each season look'd delightful, as it pass'd,
To the fond husband, and the faithful wife.
Beyond the lowly vale of shepherd life
They never roam'd: secure beneath the storm
Which in Ambition's lofty hand is rife,
Where peace and love are canker'd by the worm
Of pride, each bud of joy industrious to deform.

The wight whose tale these artless lines unfold,
Was all the offspring of this humble pair:
His birth no oracle of seer foretold;
No prodigy appear'd in earth or air,
Nor aught that might a strange event declare.
You guess each circumstance of Edwin's birth;
The parent's transport, and the parent's care;
The gossip's prayer for wealth, and wit, and worth;
And one long summer day of indolence and mirth.

And yet poor Edwin was no vulgar boy;
Deep thought oft seem'd to fix his infant eye.
Dainties he heeded not, nor gaude, nor toy,
Save one short pipe of rudest minstrelsy:
Silent when glad; affectionate, though shy;
And now his look was most demurely sad;
And now he laugh'd aloud, yet none knew why.
The neighbours stared and sigh'd, yet bless'd the lad:
Some deem'd him wondrous wise, and some believed
him mad.

But why should I his childish feats display?
Concourse, and noise, and toil he ever fled;
Nor cared to mingle in the clamorous fray
Of squabbling imps; but to the forest sped,
Or roam'd at large the lonely mountain's head,
Or, where the maze of some bewilder'd stream
To deep untrodden groves his footsteps led,

There would he wander wild, till Phoebus' beam,
Shot from the western cliff, released the weary team.

The exploit of strength, dexterity, or speed,
To him nor vanity nor joy could bring.
His heart, from cruel sport estranged, would bleed
To work the woe of any living thing,
By trap, or net; by arrow, of by sling:
These he detested; those he scorn'd to wield;
He wish'd to be the guardian, not the king,
Tyrant far less, or traitor of the field.
And sure the sylvan reign unbloody joy might yield.

Lo! where the stripling, wrapt in wonder, roves
Beneath the precipice o'erhung with pine;
And sees, on high, amidst the encircling groves,
From cliff to cliff the foaming torrents shine:
While waters, woods, and winds in concert join,
And Echo swells the chorus to the skies.
Would Edwin this majestic scene resign
For aught the huntsman's puny craft supplies?
Ah! no; he better knows great Nature's charms to prize.

And oft he traced the uplands, to survey,
When o'er the sky advanced the kindling dawn,
The crimson cloud, blue main, the mountain gray,
And lake, dim-gleaming on the smoky lawn:
Far to the west the long long vale withdrawn,
Where twilight loves to linger for a while;
And now he faintly kens the bounding fawn,
And villager abroad at early toil.
But lo! the Sun appears, and heaven, earth, ocean smile!

And oft the craggy cliff he loved to climb,
When all in mist the world below was lost.
What dreadful pleasure! there to stand sublime,
Like shipwreck'd mariner on desert coast,
And view the enormous waste of vapour, toss'd
In billows, lengthening to the horizon round,
Now scoop'd in gulfs, with mountains now emboss'd!
And hear the voice of mirth and song rebound,
Flocks, herds, and waterfalls, along the hoar profound!

In truth he was a strange and wayward wight,
Fond of each gentle, and each dreadful scene.

In darkness, and in storm, he found delight:
Nor less than when on ocean-wave serene
The southern Sun diffused his dazzling sheen,*
Even sad vicissitude amused his soul:
And if a sigh would sometimes intervene,
And down his cheek a tear of pity roll,
A sigh, a tear, so sweet, he wish'd not to control.

[. . .]

When the long sounding curfew from afar
Loaded with loud lament the lonely gale
Young Edwin, lighted by the evening star,
Lingering and listening, wander'd down the vale.
There would be he dream of graves, and corses pale,
And ghosts that to the charnel-dungeon throng,
And drag a length of clanking chain, and wail,
Till silenced by the owl's terrific song,
Or blast that shrieks by fits the shuddering aisles along.

Or, when the setting Moon, in crimson dyed
Hung o'er the dark and melancholy deep,
To haunted stream, remote from man, he hied,
Where fays of yore their revels wont to keep;
And there let Fancy rove at large, till sleep
A vision brought to his entrancèd sight.
And first, a wildly murmuring wind 'gan creep
Shrill to his ringing ear; then tapers bright,
With instantaneous gleam, illumed the vault of night.

2.10 James Beattie (1735–1803), *On Fable and Romance* (1783)

Beattie's essay usefully reviews opinions which had by the late eighteenth century become standard, including one of the most repeated clichés: that the taste for Gothic romances had been extinguished by the satire of Cervantes' *Don Quixote* (its two parts first published in 1605 and 1615). This assertion provided a convenient date for marking the end of the Gothic era, and the dawning of the modern (reinforced for British critics by the near-coincidence with the year of Shakespeare's death in 1616).

Source: James Beattie (1783), *Dissertations Moral and Critical*, vol. 2 of *The Philosophical and Critical Works of James Beattie*, London: W. Strahan and T. Cadell; Edinburgh: W. Creech, pp. 525–7, 540–4, 549, 550–1, 562–3.

* 'Dazzling sheen': Brightness, splendour. The word is used by some late writers, as well as by Milton.

★

. . . A third peculiarity in the character of these people [Gothick warriors] is, their attention to their women. With us, the two sexes associate together, and mutually improve and polish one another: but in Rome and Greece they lived separate; and the condition of the female was little better than slavery; as it still is, and has been from very early times, in many parts of Asia, and in European and African Turkey. But the Gothick warriors were in all their expeditions attended by their wives; whom they regarded as friends and faithful counsellors, and frequently as sacred persons, by whom the gods were pleased to communicate their will to mankind. This in part accounts for the reverence wherewith the female sex were always treated by those conquerors: and, as Europe still retains many of their customs, and much of their policy, this may be given as one reason of that polite gallantry, which distinguishes our manners, and has extended itself through every part of the world that is subject to European government.

Another thing remarkable in the Gothick nations, was an invincible spirit of liberty. Warm and fruitful countries, by promoting indolence and luxury, are favourable to the views of tyrannical princes; and commonly were in antient, as many of them are in modern times, the abode of despotism. But the natives of the north, more active and valiant, are for the most part more jealous of their privileges. Exceptions may be found to all general theories concerning the influence of climate in forming the human character: but this will be allowed to have been true of the antient Germans, and those other nations, whereof I now speak. All the Gothick institutions were, in their purest form, favourable to liberty. The kings, or generals, were at first chosen by those who were to obey them: and though they acknowledged, and indeed introduced, the distinctions of superiour and vassal, they were careful to secure the independence, and respective rights of both, as far as the common safety would permit. To them there is reason to believe that we are indebted for those two great establishments, which form the basis of British freedom, a parliament for making laws, and juries for trying criminals, and deciding differences. . . .

[Beattie dwells on the characteristics of the Goths: the first two being religious piety and valour.]

3. Their passion for strange adventures is another trait in the character of the knights of chivalry. The world was then little known, and men (as I observed before) were ignorant and credulous. Strange sights were expected in strange countries; dragons to be destroyed, giants to be humbled, and enchanted castles to be overthrown. The caverns of the mountain were believed to be inhabited by magicians; and the depth of the forest gave shelter to the holy hermit, who, as the reward of his piety,

was supposed to have the gift of working miracles. The demon yelled in the storm, the spectre walked in darkness, and even the rushing of water in the night was mistaken for the voice of a goblin. The castles of the greater barons, reared in a rude but grand style of architecture; full of dark and winding passages, of secret apartments, of long uninhabited galleries, and of chambers supposed to be haunted with spirits; and undermined by subterraneous labyrinths as places of retreat in extreme danger; the howling of winds through the crevices of the walls, and other dreary vacuities; the grating of heavy doors on rusty hinges of iron; the shrieking of bats, and the screaming of owls, and other creatures, that resort to desolate or half-inhabited buildings: – these, and the like circumstances, in the domestick life of the people I speak of, would multiply their superstitions, and increase their credulity; and, among warriors, who set all danger at defiance, would encourage a passion for wild adventure, and difficult enterprise.

Consider, too, the political circumstances of the feudal barons. They lived apart, in their respective territories, where their power was like that of petty kings; and in their own fortified castles, where they kept a train of valiant friends and followers: and, in the economy and splendor of their household, they imitated royal magnificence. An offender, who had made his escape, either from the publick justice of his county, or from the vengeance of some angry chief, was sure of a place of refuge, if he could find admittance into the castle of any other lord. Hence publick justice was eluded, and the authority of the law despised: and a wicked and powerful baron, secure within his own castle, would even defy the power of the sovereign himself, or perhaps with hostile intention meet him in the field, at the head of an army of determined followers . . .

Hence a conjecture may be formed of the distracted state of those feudal governments, in which the nobility had acquired great power, and high privileges. The most daring enormities were daily committed, to gratify the resentment, or the rapacity, of those Chieftains: castles were invaded, and plundered, and burned: depredations by the vassals of one lord were made upon the grounds and castle of another; and horrid murders and other cruelties perpetrated. Rich heiresses, and women of distinguished beauty, were often seized upon, and compelled to marry the ravisher. Royalty itself was not secure from these outrages . . . Nay, in those days, there were outlaws and robbers, who, possessing themselves of mountains and forests, got together a little army of followers, and lived by rapine; while the power of the kingdom was employed in vain to dislodge, and bring them to justice. Such, in England, were the famous Adam Bell, and Robin Hood, and others who are still celebrated in ballads . . . In a word, the western world was in those feudal times full of extraordinary events, and strange vicissitudes of fortune. And therefore we need not wonder, that a passion for adventures and warlike enterprize should have been universal among the knights of chivalry.

4. They were also distinguished by a zeal for justice: and, as the laws were so ineffectual, professed to take up arms in vindication of the rights of mankind; to punish the oppressor; to set at liberty the captive; to succour the distressed damsell; and to rid the world of those false knights, who wandered about in armour, to accomplish wicked purposes. These were noble designs; and, while society was so insecure, and the laws so openly violated must have been attended with good effects. – If you ask, how this heroick part of their character is to be accounted for; I answer that they seem to have derived it, partly front their northern ancestors who were lovers of liberty, and generous in their behaviour to the weaker sex; and partly front their attachment to the Christian religion whereof they were the declared champions, and which, disfigured as it then was by superstition, would still be a restraint upon the passions of those who were willing to attend to its dictates . . .
5. The fifth and last characteristick of chivalry, is the courtesy of the knights who professed it. I remarked, that the founders of the feudal system were distinguished, among all the nations then known in Europe or Asia, by the peculiarity of their behaviour to their women; whom they regarded and loved, as their friends, and faithful counsellors, and as invested with something of a sacred character. Accordingly we are told by some authors, that in all their conquests they were never guilty of violence, where the female sex was concerned. This delicacy they transmitted to their descendants; among the greater part of whom, whatever outrages might now and then be committed by individuals, it seems to have been a point of honour, to be generous and respectful in their attentions to women. This was at least an indispensable part of the duty of a knight errant. By the statutes of Chivalry, the love of God was the first virtue, and devotion to the ladies the second. But that devotion has nothing licentious in it; being delicate to a degree that bordered on extravagance, if not on impiety. For the true knight did not expect condescension on the part of his mistress, till he had proved himself worthy of her, by deeds of arms, and performed many acts of heroism as her champion and admirer . . .

I have endeavoured to trace out the distinguishing features of that extraordinary character, a knight errant; and to account for each of them, from the nature of the institution, and the manners of the times. The true Knight was religious, valiant, passionately fond of strange adventures, a lover of justice, a protector of the weak, a punisher of the injurious; temperate, courteous, and chaste; and zealous, and respectful, in his attentions to the fair sex. And this is the character assigned him in all those old romances and poems, that describe the adventures of chivalry.

Knight-errantry, however respectable in its first institution, soon became dangerous. The Gothick armour was a complete covering to the whole person: and under that disguise many warriours went through the world as knights errant, who were really nothing better than robbers; and who, instead of being patrons of mankind, were pests of society. The true knight, therefore, thought himself bound in honour to inquire into the character of those who might appear in the same garb; so that two knights, who were strangers to each other, could hardly meet without fighting. And we may warrantably suppose, that even the better sort of these wanderers would sometimes attack an innocent man, without necessity, in order to signalise their valour, and do honour to the lady of their affections . . .

But the old spirit of chivalry was not extinguished: and what remained of it was inflamed by the books called Romances, which were now common in Europe, and, being written in the vulgar toungues, and filled with marvellous adventures, could not fail to be eagerly sought after and read, at a time when books were rare and men credulous . . .

But the final extirpation of chivalry and all its chimeras was now approaching. What laws and force could not accomplish, was brought about by the humour and satire of one writer. This was the illustrious Miguel de Cervantes Saavedra. He was born at Madrid in the year one thousand five hundred and forty-nine.[12] He seems to have had every advantage of education, and to have been a master in polite learning. But in other respects fortune was not very indulgent. He served many years in the armies of Spain, in no higher station, than that of a private soldier. In that capacity he fought at the battle of Lepanto, under Don John of Austria, and had the misfortune, or, as he rather thought, the honour, to lose his left hand. Being now disqualified for military Service, he commenced author; and wrote many Dramatick pieces, which were acted with applause on the Spanish theatre, and acquired him both money and reputation. But want of economy and unbounded generosity dissipated the former: and he was actually confined in prison for debt, when he composed the first part of *The History of Don Quixote*; a work, which every body admires for its humour; but which ought also to be considered as a most useful performance, that brought about a great revolution in the manners and literature of Europe, by banishing the wild dreams of chivalry, and reviving a taste for the simplicity of nature. In this view, the publication of Don Quixote forms an important era in the history of mankind . . .

This work no sooner appeared, than chivalry vanished, as snow melts before the sun. Mankind awoke as from a dream. . . .

2.11 John Pinkerton (dates unknown), *A Dissertation on the Origin and Progress of the Scythians or Goths* (1787)

In the *Dissertation,* Pinkerton takes issue with earlier writers on a variety of points, including the place of origin of the Goths, which he locates in Scythia, in the Middle East. In the following passage, he takes the customary belief in the Norman Conquest as a watershed of the Gothic era, and gives it an openly radical edge by distinguishing between a pure stage of feudalism based on a democratic political structure, and a corrupt stage of feudalism characterised by aristocratic tyranny. In this schema the romances of chivalry figure as a literature of protest, and Cervantes the satirist of romance is represented, somewhat bizarrely, as a dangerous misanthrope.

Source: John Pinkerton (1787), *A Dissertation on the Origin and Progress of the Scythians or Goths, Being an Introduction to the Ancient and Modern History of Europe,* London: John Nichols, pp. 137–8.

... The Feudal System has been treated of by many writers, but so uncommon a quality is penetration, that all of them to this day have confounded two grand divisions in its history, which are totally dissimilar. These divisions are, 1. The Feudal System. 2. The Corrupted Feudal System. The former extends from the earliest account of time, thro the early history of Greece and Rome, till the progress of society changed the manners of these nations: and thro the early history of the Goths and Germans who overturned the Roman empire, down to the eleventh century. At this period commenced the Corrupted Feudal System, and lasts till the fifteenth century, when the Feudal System began after its corruption to dissolve quite away. The Corruption of the Feudal System took place soon after the petty kingdoms of the former ages were united into great monarchies, as the heptarchies in England became subject to our monarch; and so in other countries. This corruption is no more the Feudal System than any other corruption is the substance preceding corruption, that is quite the reverse: and yet, such is modern superficiality, that it has been termed The Feudal System, κατ εξοχην; and all writers estimate the Feudal System by its corruption only, just as if we should judge of a republic by its condition when changed into an aristocracy! About the eleventh century, by the change of small kingdoms into one great monarchy, and by a concatenation of other causes, which it would require a volume to detail, the Feudal System corrupted, (and *curruptio optimi pessima*)[13] into a state of aristocratic tyranny, and oppression. Before that period no such matter can be found. The greatest cause was, that nobility and estates annexed were not hereditary till that time, so that the great were kept in perpetual awe; and that check was removed, before the cities had attained such privileges and powers, as to balance the nobility. In Ancient Greece, and Italy, confined spots, cities were from the first the grand receptacles of society. To the want of cities the subjection of the people is owing. To cities the ruin of the Corrupted Feudal System (generally called the Feudal System), is solely to be ascribed. Of the Corrupted Feudal System nothing shall be added here; as it commenced at a late period, and is foreign to my work; save one or two remarks on Chivalry, an institution quite misunderstood. It was so heterogeneous to the Feudal System, that, had the latter lasted pure, chivalry would never have appeared. But as it is often so decreed that, out of the corruption of a constitution, a remedy for that corruption springs, such was the case with chivalry, an institution which does honour to human nature. The knighthood was not hereditary, but an honour of personal worth. Its possessors were bound to help the oppressed, and curb the tyrannic spirit of the hereditary great, those giants of power, and of romance. Had the ridicule of Cervantes appeared three centuries sooner, we must have branded him as the greatest enemy of society that ever wrote. As it is, a sensible French writer well observes, that it now begins to be questioned whether his book is not worthy of execration. All professions have their foibles; but ridicule ought never to be exerted against the benefits of society. Cervantes envied the success of the romances; but ought not to have derided an institution so beneficial, because even fables concerning it had the fortune to delight his contemporaries.

2.12 Samuel Taylor Coleridge (1732–1834), 'General Character of the Gothic Mind in the Middle Ages', and 'General Character of the Gothic Literature and Art' (1818)

In 1818 Coleridge delivered a series of public lectures at Bristol. The following excerpts come from lecture notes taken by members of the audience.[14] The lectures constitute a recapitulation of eighteenth-century accounts of the Gothic era, with some new elements imported from the German Romantics F. W. Schlegel and Friedrich Schiller. The consistent valorising of Gothic manners and aesthetics over those of ancient Greece or Rome has obvious nationalist implications.

Source: S. T. Coleridge (1936), *Miscellaneous Criticism*, ed. T. M. Raysor, London: Constable, pp. 6–8, 11–13.

★

Lecture I: General Character of the Gothic Mind in the Middle Ages

... [Coleridge] proceeded to describe the generic character of the Northern nations, and defined it as an independence of the whole in the freedom of the individual, noticing their respect for women, and their consequent chivalrous spirit in war; and how evidently the participation in the general council laid the foundation of the representative form of government, the only rational mode of preserving individual liberty in opposition to the licentious democracy of the ancient republics.

He called our attention to the peculiarity of their art, and showed how it entirely depended on a symbolical expression of the infinite, – which is not vastness, nor immensity, nor perfection, but whatever cannot be circumscribed within the limits of actual sensuous being. In the ancient art, on the contrary, every thing was finite and material. Accordingly, sculpture was not attempted by the Gothic races till the ancient specimens were discovered, whilst painting and architecture were of native growth amongst them. In the earliest specimens of the paintings of modern ages, as in those of Giotto and his associates in the cemetery at Pisa, this complexity, variety, and symbolical character are evident, and are more fully developed in the mightier works of Michel Angelo and Raffael. The contemplation of the works of antique art excites a feeling of elevated beauty, and exalted notions of the human self; but the Gothic architecture impresses the beholder with a sense of self-annihilation; he becomes, as it were, a part of the work contemplated. An endless complexity and variety are united into one whole, the plan of which is not distinct from the execution. A Gothic cathedral is the petrifaction of our religion. The only work of truly modern sculpture is the Moses of Michel Angelo.[15]

The northern nations were prepared by their own previous religion for Christianity; they, for the most part, received it gladly, and it took root as in a native soil. The deference to woman, characteristic of the Gothic races, combined itself with devotion in the idea of the Virgin Mother, and gave rise in many beautiful associations ...

He also enlarged on the influence of female character on our education, the first impressions of our childhood being derived from women. Amongst oriental nations, he said, the only distinction was between lord and slave. With the antique Greeks, the will of every one conflicting with the will of all, produced licentiousness; with the modern descendants from the northern stocks, both these extremes were shut out, to reappear mixed and condensed into this principle or temper; – submission, but with free choice, – illustrated in chivalrous devotion to women as such, in attachment to the sovereign, &c. ...

Lecture II: General Character of the Gothic Literature and Art

. . . After a time, when the Goths, – to use the name of the noblest and most historical of the Teutonic tribes, – had acquired some knowledge of these arts from mixing with their conquerors, they invaded the Roman territories. The hardy habits, the steady perseverance, the better faith of the enduring Goth, rendered him too formidable an enemy for the corrupt Roman, who was more inclined to purchase the subjection of his enemy, than to go through the suffering necessary to secure it. The conquest of the Romans gave to the Goths the Christian religion as it was then existing in Italy; and the light and graceful building of Grecian, or Roman-Greek order, became singularly combined with the messy architecture of the Goths, as wild and varied as the forest vegetation which it resembled. The Greek art is beautiful. When I enter a Greek church, my eye is charmed, and my mind elated; I feel exalted, and proud that I am a man. But the Gothic art is sublime. On entering a cathedral, I am filled with devotion and with awe; I am lost to the actualities that surround me, and my whole being expands into the infinite; earth and air, nature and art, all swell up into eternity, and the only sensible impression left is, 'that I am nothing'![16] This religion, while it tended to soften the manners of the Northern tribes, was at the same time highly congenial to their nature. The Goths are free from the stain of hero worship. Gazing on their rugged mountains, surrounded by impassable forests, accustomed to gloomy seasons, they lived in the bosom of nature, and worshipped an invisible and unknown deity. Firm in his faith, domestic in his habits, the life of the Goth was simple and dignified, yet tender and affectionate.

The Greeks were remarkable for complacency and completion; they delighted in whatever pleased the eye; to them it was not enough to have merely the idea of a divinity, they must have it placed before them, shaped in the most perfect symmetry, and presented with the nicest judgement; and if we look upon any Greek production of art, the beauty of its parts, and the harmony of their union, the complete and complacent effect of the whole, are the striking characteristics.[17] It is the same in their poetry. In Homer you have a poem perfect in its form, whether originally so, or from the labour of after critics, I know not; his descriptions are pictures brought vividly before you, and as far as the eye and understanding are concerned, I am indeed gratified. But if I wish my feelings to be affected, if I wish my heart to be touched, if I wish to melt into sentiment and tenderness, I must turn to the heroic songs of the Goths, to the poetry of the middle ages. The worship of statues in Greece had, in a civil sense, its advantage, and disadvantage; advantage in promoting statuary and the arts; disadvantage, in bringing their gods too much on a level with human beings, and thence depriving them of their dignity, and gradually giving rise to scepticism and ridicule. But no statue, no artificial emblem, could satisfy the Northman's mind; the dark wild imagery of nature, which surrounded him, and the freedom of his life, gave his mind a tendency to the infinite, so that he found rest in that which presented no end, and derived satisfaction from that which was indistinct. . . .

Notes

1 The British Library lists only one previous English translation: *The Annals and History of Cornelius Tacitus: His Account of the Antient Germans; and the life of Agricola.* Made English by Diverse Hands [viz. John Dryden, W. Higden, Sir H. Savile, and others]. London: M. Gillyflower, 1698. There were several nineteenth-century translations, following on from Aikin's, which had gone through four editions by 1823.

2 The text translated by Aikin was M. Brotier's edition (Paris, 1771). The majority of the notes were also Brotier's. Aikin designated the few exceptions through the use of his initials, none of which are included here among the author's notes.

3 Tacitus. See 2.1.

4 'From where the great stream of the Eridanus rolls through forest towards the upper world [i.e. Hell]'. Virgil, *Aeniad,* book 6, line 659.

5 *Gerusalemme Liberata* or *Jerusalem Delivered*: an epic romance by Torquato Tasso first published in 1580.

6 'All are overwhelmed in unending night, unwept, unknown, because they lack a sacred bard'. Horace, *Odes,* 4.9.26.

7 William Kent (1685–1748) was a celebrated landscape designer and architect.

8 By 'both' Hurd means Ariosto and Tasso. Hurd's argument is that in order to assert their critical supremacy French neo-classical critics attacked the Italians' Gothic qualities, partly out of the same sort of French chauvinism that Charles II brought with him upon the Restoration.

9 Robert Molesworth (first Viscount) (1656–1725) was a political writer and diplomat from Dublin, a 'Commonwealth Man' or 'Old Whig'. Molesworth's *An Account of Denmark as it was in the Year 1692* (1694) was an inflammatory work which advocated the merits of the Glorious Revolution of 1688 by comparing free England with a despotic, monarchical Denmark. By aligning French neo-classicism with the Danish 'court-standard' Hurd is implicitly identifying Gothic aesthetic principles with the Whig ascendancy while underlining its native and therefore patriotic credentials.

10 'You will not find here Centaurs, Gorgons, and Harpies: my pages are to do with Man.'

11 Strabo was a Roman historian (b. c. 63 BC); Diodorus Siculus a Greek historian of the latter half of the first century BC.

12 Cervantes was in fact born in Alcalá in 1547.

13 'The worst corruption is the corruption of the best men.'

14 According to H. N. Coleridge, who first published them in *Literary Remains* (Raysor, p. 6). The report of Lecture I is reputedly by Joseph Henry Green; of Lecture II by William Hammond.

15 According to Raysor, 'This whole paragraph is loosely based on Schlegel's distinction of the classic and the romantic. Cf. *Werke,* v. 11–17; vi. 32–33, 161–62.

A reference to this part of Schlegel implies, of course, a further reference to Schiller's essay, "On Naive and Sentimental Poetry"' (p. 7, n. 1).

16 According to Raysor, Coleridge is again paraphrasing Schlegel (Raysor, p. 12).

17 According to Raysor, Coleridge is again paraphrasing Schlegel, and Schiller's 'On Naive and Sentimental Poetry' (Raysor, p. 12).

3 The Gothic aesthetic: imagination, originality, terror

3.1 John Dryden (1631–1700), 'Of Heroique Playes' (1670)

It is a commonplace that Gothic writing developed in reaction against the rules of neo-classical criticism. But although it is certainly true that writers like William Collins and Horace Walpole presented their fantastic fictions as transgressive of critical norms, the doctrine of neo-classicism had been challenged from its first introduction in the latter half of the seventeenth century, as Dryden's remarks show. At the heart of doctrine was the authority of Aristotle's *Poetics*, and the principle of mimesis derived from it: art should follow nature. The question of how poetry could be said to imitate nature, and how nature itself should be defined, left considerable room for debate. However, there was a general consensus that the fictions of the poet should be probable, true to life, and a number of technical prescriptions followed from this: the action, characters and dialogue of narrative fictions should all be credible and coherent; further, to aid this consistency, it was desirable to observe unities of action, time and place, limiting the scope of drama, specifically, to an orderly simplicity. In Britain, these tenets were adopted as a means of curbing the twin evils of English drama, crowd-pleasing sensationalism and scurrilous wit, and replacing it with a more morally responsible form of theatre.

In this passage prefixed to *The Conquest of Granada*, Part I, Dryden defends his own use of the marvellous in the play with a forceful declaration of independence for the imagination. He presents a lineage of 'Enthusiastick' poets, invoking the example of the past in order to justify rule-breaking by modern writers like himself. 'Enthusiasm', which literally means 'the state of being possessed by a god', would later in the century become roughly synonymous with the term 'original genius'. Alexander Gerard in his *Essay on Genius* defines it as 'elevation and warmth of imagination' (Gerard, 1774, p. 67). Yet it contained a troubling ambivalence, through its negative sense of religious fanaticism and superstition.

Source: John Dryden (1978), *The Works of John Dryden*, ed. H. T. Swedenberg, Berkeley, Los Angeles and London: University of California Press, vol. XI, pp. 12–13.

★

. . . For my part, I am of opinion, that neither *Homer*, *Virgil*, *Statius*, *Ariosto*, *Tasso*, nor our *English Spencer* could have form'd their Poems half so beautiful without those Gods and Spirits, and those Enthusiastick parts of Poetry, which compose the most noble parts of all their writings. And I will ask any man who loves Heroick Poetry, (for I will not dispute their tastes who do not) if the Ghost of *Polydorus* in *Virgil*, the Enchanted wood in *Tasso*, and the Bower of bliss, in *Spencer* (which he borrowed from the admirable *Italian*) could have been omitted without taking from their works some of the greatest beauties in them. And if any man object the improbabilities of a spirit appearing, or of a Palace rais'd by Magick,[1] I boldly answer him, that an Heroick Poet is not ty'd to a bare representation of what is true, or exceeding probable: but that he may let himself loose to visionary objects, and to the representation of such things, as depending not on sence, and therefore not to be comprehended by knowledge, may give him a freer scope for imagination. 'Tis enough that in all ages and Religions, the greatest part of mankind have believ'd the power of Magick, and that there are Spirits, or Spectres, which have appear'd. This I say is foundation enough for Poetry: and I dare farther affirm that the whole Doctrine of separated beings, whether those Spirits are incorporeal substances, (which Mr. *Hobbs*, with some reason thinks to imply a contradiction,[2]) or that they are a thinner and more Aerial sort of bodies (as some of the Fathers have conjectur'd) may better be explicated by Poets, than by Philosophers or Divines. For their speculations on this subject are wholy Poetical; they have onely their fancy for their guide, and that, being sharper in an excellent Poet, than it is likely it should in a phlegmatick, heavy gown-man,[3] will see farther, in its own Empire, and produce more satisfactory notions on those dark and doubtful Problems.

Some men think they have rais'd a great argument against the use of Spectres and Magique in Heroique Poetry, by saying, They are unnatural: but, whether they or I believe there are such things, is not material, 'tis enough that, for ought we know, they may be in Nature: and what ever is or may be, is not, properly, unnatural. . . .

3.2 John Dennis (1657–1734), *The Grounds of Criticism in Poetry* (1704)

The aim of Dennis's treatise as a whole was to show the necessary interdependence of religion and poetry, and the importance of strong emotions in both. The following passages put forward a theory of the sublime, a concept taken from a work of classical literary criticism, *On the Sublime*, attributed to Longinus and translated into French by Boileau (in 1674; the first English translation to have an influence was by Leonard Welsted, in 1712; see Monk, 1960, pp. 19–23). So extravagant was Dennis's championing of Longinus, that he was satirised as 'Sir Tremendous Longinus' by Pope and Gay in the play *Three Hours after Marriage*. Dennis was innovative not only in his religious emphasis but, more to the present purpose, in arguing the connection between the sublime and the emotion of *terror*; an anticipation of Burke (3.6). Terror is here categorised as one of the 'Enthusiastic Passions': passions belonging to the realm of contemplation and aesthetic taste, rather than to 'common life'.

Source: Scott Elledge, ed. (1961), *Eighteenth-century Critical Essays*, 2 vols, Ithaca, New York: Cornell University Press, vol. I, pp. 121–2 and 127–30.

★

. . . Let us now pass to the next enthusiastic passion, which is terror; than which, if it is rightly managed, none is more capable of giving a great spirit to poetry. This passion scarce ever goes by itself, but is always more or less complicated with admiration. For everything that is terrible is great at least to him to whom it is terrible. It is now our business to show two things: first, what this enthusiastic terror is; and secondly, from what ideas it is chiefly to be derived.

First let us show what this sort of enthusiasm is; and in order to do that, let us show as briefly as we can what the common passion is which we call terror. Fear then, or terror, is a disturbance of mind proceeding from an apprehension of an approaching evil, threatening destruction or very great trouble either to us or ours. And when the disturbance comes suddenly with surprise, let us call it terror; when gradually, fear. Things then that are powerful, and likely to hurt, are the causes of common terror; and the more they are powerful and likely to hurt, the more they become the causes of terror; which terror, the greater it is, the more it is joined with wonder, and the nearer it comes to astonishment. Thus we have shown what objects of the mind are the causes of common terror; and the ideas of those objects are the causes of enthusiastic terror.

Let us now show from what ideas this enthusiastic terror is chiefly to be derived. The greatest enthusiastic terror then must needs be derived from religious ideas, for since the more their objects are powerful and likely to hurt, the greater terror their ideas produce; what can produce a greater terror than the idea of an angry god? Which puts me in mind of that admirable passage of Homer, about the fight of the gods, in the Twentieth of the *Iliad*, cited by Longinus in his chapter of the loftiness of the conception.[4] . . .

[Dennis demonstrates with close textual reference to *On the Sublime* that religious ideas are central to Longinus's definition of the sublime.]

But to return to terror, we may plainly see by the foregoing precepts and examples of Longinus that this enthusiastic terror contributes extremely to the sublime, and secondly, that it is most produced by religious ideas.

First, ideas producing terror contribute extremely to the sublime. All the examples that Longinus brings of the loftiness of the thought consist of terrible ideas. And they are principally such ideas that work the effects which he takes notice of in the beginning of his treatise, viz., that ravish and transport the reader and produce a certain admiration mingled with astonishment and surprise. For the ideas which produce terror are necessarily accompanied with admiration (because everything that is terrible is great to him to whom it is terrible), and with surprise (without which terror cannot subsist), and with astonishment (because everything which is very terrible is wonderful and astonishing); and as terror is perhaps the violentest of all the passions, it consequently makes an impression which we cannot resist, and which is hardly to be defaced; and no passion is attended with greater joy than enthusiastic terror, which proceeds from our reflecting that we are out of danger at the very time that we see it before us.[5] And as terror is one of the violentest of all passions, if it is very great, and the hardest to be resisted, nothing gives more force nor more vehemence to a discourse.

But, secondly, it is plain from the same Longinus that this enthusiastic terror is chiefly to be derived from religious ideas. For all the examples which he has brought of the sublime in his chapter of the sublimity of the thoughts consists of most terrible and most religious ideas; and at the same time every man's reason will inform him that every thing that is terrible in religion is the most terrible thing in the world.

But that we may set this in a clearer light, let us lay before the reader the several ideas which are capable of producing this enthusiastic terror, which seem to me to be those which follow: viz., gods, demons, hell, spirits and souls of men, miracles, prodigies, enchantments, witchcrafts, thunder, tempests, raging seas, inundations, torrents, earthquakes, volcanoes, monsters, serpents, lions, tigers, fire, war, pestilence, famine, etc.

Now of all these ideas none are so terrible as those which show the wrath and vengeance of an angry God, for nothing is so wonderful in its effects; and consequently the images or ideas of those effects must carry a great deal of terror with them, which we may see was Longinus' opinion by the examples which he brings in his chapter of the sublimity of the thoughts. Now of the things which are terrible, those are the most terrible which are the most wonderful, because that seeing them both threatening and powerful, and not being able to fathom the greatness and extent of their power, we know not how far and how soon they may hurt us.

But further, nothing is so terrible as the wrath of Infinite Power, because nothing is so unavoidable as the vengeance designed by it. There is no flying nor lying hid from the great universal Monarch. He may deliver us from all other terrors, but nothing can save and defend us from Him. And therefore reason, which serves to dissipate our terrors in some other dangers, serves but to augment them when we are threatened by Infinite Power; and that fortitude, which may be heroic at other times, is downright madness then.

For the other ideas which we mentioned above, they will be found to be more terrible as they have more of religion in them. But we shall have so many necessary occasions of giving examples of them in the sequel of this treatise, that it will be altogether needless to do it now. But here it will be convenient to answer an objection: For how come some of the forementioned ideas which seem to have but little to do with religion to be terrible to great and to wise men – as it is plain that such, when they read the descriptions of them in Homer and Virgil, are terrified?

To which we answer that the care, which nature has inrooted in all, of their own preservation is the cause that men are unavoidably terrified with anything that threatens approaching evil. It is now our business to show how the ideas of serpents, lions, tigers, etc. were made by the art of those great poets to be terrible to their readers, at the same time that we are secure from their objects.

It is very plain that it is the apprehension of danger which causes that emotion in us which we call terror, and it signifies nothing at all to the purpose whether the danger is real or imaginary; and it is as plain, too, that the soul never takes the alarm from anything so soon as it does from the senses, especially those two noble ones of the eye and the ear, by reason of the strict affinity which they have with the imagination; and the evil always seems to be very near when those two senses give notice of it; and the nearer the evil is, the greater still is the terror. But now let us see how those two poets did, by virtue of their ideas, bring even absent terrible objects within the reach of those two noble senses. First then, to bring an absent terrible object before our sight, they drew an image or picture of it; but to draw an image or picture of a terrible object so as to surprise and astonish the soul by the eye, they never failed to draw it in violent action or motion; and in order to that, they made choice of words and numbers which might best express the violence of that action or motion. For an absent object can never be set before the eye in a true light unless it be shown in violent action or motion, because unless it is shown so, the soul has leisure to reflect upon the deceit. But violent motion can never be conceived without a violent agitation of spirit, and that sudden agitation surprises the soul and gives it less time to reflect, and at the same time causes the impressions that the objects make to be so deep, and their traces to be so profound, that it makes them in a manner as present to us, as if they were really before us. For the spirits being set in a violent emotion, and the imagination being fired by that agitation, and the brain being deeply penetrated by those impressions, the very objects themselves are set as it were before us, and consequently we are sensible of the same passion that we should feel from the things themselves. For the warmer the imagination is, the less able we are to reflect, and consequently the things are the more present to us of which we draw the images; and therefore when the imagination is so inflamed as to render the soul utterly incapable of reflecting, there is no difference between the images and the things themselves, as we may see, for example, by men in raging fevers. But those two great poets were not satisfied with setting absent objects before our eyes by showing them in violent motion, but if their motion occasioned any extraordinary sounds that were terrifying, they so contrived their numbers and expressions as that they might be sure to ring those sounds in the very ears of their readers. . . .

3.3 Joseph Addison (1672–1719), *The Spectator*, No. 419 (1712)

This essay appeared in the journal as one of a series of eleven papers under the general title 'The Pleasures of the Imagination' (nos. 409, 411–21), all of which are of interest as a context for Gothic writing. Here, Addison finds no need to apologise for purely imaginary works; instead he seems to suggest that the marvellous is the ultimate test of creative ability, and even proposes immersion in tales of superstition as an essential preparation for a poet. There are a number of links with other selections: the echo of Dryden in the sharp dismissal of 'men of cold fancies' who would argue that spirits are improbable and therefore unsuitable for representation (3.1; cf. 1.2a); the assertion that 'the *English* are naturally fanciful' and the use of Shakespeare as exemplar, looking forward to Montagu (1.8b); and the formulation 'a pleasing kind of horrour' directly prefiguring Burke's oxymoron of 'a sort of delightful horror, a sort of tranquillity tinged with terror' (3.6). The final remarks relate to the allegorical employment of 'supernatural machinery', the mode of supernaturalism that the Augustans found easiest to assimilate to their notions of literary decorum (again, cf. 1.8b). Other essays from *The Spectator* on questions of taste relevant to Gothic are no. 44, on effects of pity and terror in the theatre; nos. 70 and 74 on the ballad 'Chevy-Chase'; and no. 350 on the true and false sublime (by Richard Steele).

Source: *The Spectator*, no. 419 (1 July, 1712), from Donald F. Bond, ed. (1965), *The Spectator*, 5 vols, Oxford: Oxford University Press; vol. 3, pp. 570–3.

★

... mentis gratissimus Error.
Hor.[6]

There is a kind of Writing, wherein the Poet quite loses sight of Nature, and entertains his Reader's Imagination with the Characters and Actions of such Persons as have many of them no Existence, but what he bestows on them. Such are Fairies, Witches, Magicians, Demons, and departed Spirits. This Mr. *Dryden* calls *the Fairie way of Writing*,[7] which is, indeed, more difficult that any other that depends on the Poet's Fancy, because he has no Pattern to follow in it, and must work altogether out of his own Invention.

There is a very odd turn of Thought required for this sort of Writing, and it is impossible for a Poet to succeed in it, who has not a particular Cast of Fancy, and an Imagination naturally fruitful and superstitious. Besides this, he ought to be very well versed in Legends and Fables, antiquated Romances, and the Traditions of Nurses and old Women, that he may fall in with our natural Prejudices, and humour those Notions which we have imbibed in our Infancy. For, otherwise, he will be apt to make his Fairies talk like People of his own Species, and not like other Setts of Beings, who converse with different Objects, and think in a different manner from that of Mankind;

Sylvis deducti caveant, me Judice, Fauni
Ne veulut imati triviis ac paene forenses
Aut nimium teneris juventur versibus. ...
Hor.[8]

I do not say with Mr. *Bays* in the *Rehearsal*, that Spirits must not be confined to speak Sense,[9] but it is certain their Sense ought to be a little discoloured, that it may seem particular, and proper to the Person and the Condition of the Speaker.

These Descriptions raise a pleasing kind of Horrour in the Mind of the Reader, and amuse his Imagination with the Strangeness and Novelty of the Persons who are represented in them. They bring up into our Memory the Stories we have heard in our Child-hood, and favour those secret Terrours and Apprehensions to which the Mind of Man is naturally subject. We are pleased with surveying the different Habits and Behaviours of Foreign Countries, how much more must we be delighted and surprised when we are led, as it were, into a new Creation, and see the Persons and Manners of another Species? Men of cold Fancies, and Philosophical Dispositions, object to this kind of Poetry, that it has not Probability enough to affect the Imagination. But to this it may be answered, that we are sure, in general, there are many Intellectual Beings in the World besides our selves, and several Species of Spirits, who are subject to different Laws and Oeconomies from those of Mankind; when we see, therefore, any of these represented naturally, we cannot look upon the Representation as altogether impossible; nay, many are prepossest with such false Opinions, as dispose them to believe these particular Delusions; at least, we have all heard so many pleasing Relations in favour of them that we do no care for seeing through the Falshood, and willingly give our selves up to so agreeable an Imposture.

The Ancients have not much of this Poetry among them, for, indeed, almost the whole Substance of it owes its Original to the Darkness and Superstition of later Ages, when pious Frauds were made use of to amuse Mankind, and frighten them into a Sense of their Duty. Our Forefathers looked upon Nature with more Reverence and Horrour, before the World was enlightened by Learning and Philosophy, and loved to astonish themselves with the Apprehensions of Witchcraft, Prodigies, Charms and Enchantments. There was not a Village in *England* that had not a Ghost in it, the Churchyards were all haunted, every large Common had a Circle of Fairies belonging to it, and there was scarce a Shepherd to be met with who had not seen a Spirit.

Among all the Poets of this Kind our *English* are much the best, by what I have yet seen, whether it be that we abound with more Stories of this Nature, or that the Genius of our Country is fitter for this sort of Poetry. For the *English* are naturally Fanciful, and very often disposed by that Gloominess and Melancholly of Temper, which is so frequent in our Nation, to many wild Notions and Visions, to which others are not so liable.

Among the *English*, *Shakespear* has incomparably excelled all others. That noble Extravagance of Fancy, which he had in so great Perfection, throughly qualified him to touch this weak superstitious Part of his Reader's Imagination; and made him capable of succeeding, where he had nothing to support him besides the Strength of his own Genius. There is something so wild and yet so solemn in the Speeches of his Ghosts, Fairies, Witches, and the like Imaginary Persons, that we cannot forbear thinking them natural, tho' we have no Rule by which to judge of them, and must confess, if there are such Beings in the World, it looks highly probably they should talk and act as he has represented them.

There is another sort of Imaginary Beings, that we sometimes meet with among the Poets, when the Author represents any Passion, Appetite, Virtue or Vice, under a visible Shape, and makes it a Person or an Actor in his Poem. Of this Nature are the Descriptions of Hunger and Envy in *Ovid*, of Fame in *Virgil*, and of Sin and Death in *Milton*. We find a whole Creation of the like shadowy Persons in *Spencer*, who had an admirable Talent in Representations of this kind. I have discoursed of these Emblematical Persons in former Papers, and shall therefore only mention them in this Place. Thus we see how many ways Poetry addresses it self to the Imagination, as it has not only the whole Circle of Nature for its Province, but makes new Worlds of its own, shews us Persons who are not to be found in Being, and represents even the Faculties of the Soul, with her several Virtues and Vices, in a sensible Shape and Character.

I shall, in my two following Papers, consider in general, how other kinds of Writing are qualified to please the Imagination, with which I intend to conclude this Essay.

3.4 Georg Christoph Lichtenberg, Garrick's performance of the ghost scenes in *Hamlet* (1776)

Lichtenberg recorded his impressions of England for a periodical in Germany, and included the account of David Garrick's performance as Hamlet in his first instalment. As the two extracts in 1.8 have shown, the ghost scenes from *Hamlet* were considered a controversial aspect of Shakespeare's work. Garrick first played the part of the Prince in 1742, and from the beginning audiences were captivated by the naturalness of his portrayal of Hamlet's fear on encountering an apparition. Henry Fielding immortalised the scenes in *Tom Jones* (1749), Book 16, Chapter 5, but in a debunking rather than a sublime mode. Tom's companion Partridge responds excessively to Garrick's performance because he is naturally superstitious, and mistakes art for reality. In fact, as Lichtenberg shows, the power of Garrick's body language spread a universal contagion of terror among the audience, a general abandonment to the pleasure of strong sensation, not dependent on the issue of personal belief. It is a cultural moment which predicts the popular demand for fictions of supernatural terror from the 1790s onwards.

Source: Georg Christoph Lichtenberg (1938), *Lichtenberg's Visits to England as Described in His Letters and Diaries,* trans. and ed. Margaret L. Mare and W. H. Quarrell, Oxford: Clarendon Press, pp. 9–11.

★

. . . Hamlet appears in a black dress, the only one in the whole court, alas! still worn for his poor father, who has been dead scarce a couple of months. Horatio and Marcellus, in uniforms, are with him, and they are awaiting the ghost; Hamlet has folded his arms under his cloak and pulled his hat down over his eyes; it is a cold night and just twelve o'clock; the theatre is darkened, and the whole audience of some thousands are as quiet, and their faces as motionless, as though they were painted on the walls of the theatre; even from the farthest end of the playhouse one could hear a pin drop. Suddenly, as Hamlet moves towards the back of the stage slightly to the left and turns his back on the audience, Horatio starts, and saying: 'Look, my Lord, it comes,' points to the right, where the ghost has already appeared and stands motionless, before anyone is aware of him. At these words, Garrick turns sharply and at the same moment staggers back two or three paces with his knees giving way under him; his hat falls to the ground and both his arms, especially the left, are stretched out nearly to their full length, with the hands as high as his head, the right arm more bent and the hand lower, and the fingers apart; his mouth is open: thus he stands rooted to the spot, with legs apart, but no loss of dignity, supported by his friends, who are better acquainted with the apparition and fear lest he should collapse. His whole demeanour is so expressive of terror that it made my flesh creep even before he began to speak. The almost terror-struck silence of the audience, which preceded this appearance and filled one with a sense of insecurity, probably did much to enhance this effect. At last he speaks, not at the beginning, but at the end of a breath, with a trembling voice: 'Angels and ministers of grace defend us!' words which supply anything this scene may lack and make it one of the greatest and most terrible which will ever be played on any stage. The ghost beckons to him. With eyes fixed on the ghost, though he is speaking to his companions, freeing himself from their restraining hands, as they warn him not to follow and hold him back. But at length, when they have tried his patience too far, he turns his face towards them, tears himself with great violence from their grasp, and draws his sword on them with a swiftness that makes one shudder, saying: 'By Heaven! I'll make a ghost of he that lets me!' that is enough for them. Then he stands with his sword upon the guard against the spectre, saying: 'Go on, I'll follow thee,' and the ghost goes off the stage. Hamlet still remains motionless, his sword held out so as to make him keep his distance, and at length, when the spectator can no longer see the ghost, he begins to follow him, now standing still and then going on, with sword still upon guard, eyes fixed on the ghost, hair disordered, and out of breath, until he too is lost to sight. You can well imagine what applause accompanies this exit. It begins as soon as the ghost goes off the stage and lasts until Hamlet also disappears. What an amazing triumph it is. One might think that such applause in one of the first playhouses in the world, and from an audience of the greatest sensibility, would fan into flame every spark of dramatic genius in a spectator. But then one perceives that to act like Garrick and to write like Shakespeare are the effects of very deep-seated causes. They are certainly imitated; not they, but rather their phantom self, created by the imitator according to the measure of his own powers. He often attains to and even surpasses this phantom, and nevertheless falls far short of the true original. The house-painter thinks his work as perfect as, or even more so than that of the artist. Not every player who can always command the applause of a couple of hundred people or so is on that account a Garrick; and not every writer who has learnt the trick of blabbing a few of the so-called secrets of human nature in archaic prose, outraging language and propriety in his bombast, is on that account Shakespeare.

The ghost was played by Mr. Bransby. He looked, in truth, very fine, clad from head to foot in armour, for which a suit of steel-blue satin did duty; even his face is hidden, except for his pallid nose, and a little to either side of it. . . .

3.5 William Collins, 'Ode to Fear' (1746)

The originality of Collins's Ode lies in the fact that personified Fear is positively wooed rather than avoided by the aspiring poet. It can be measured against another, far more conventional, 'Ode to Fear' by Andrew Erskine (*Scots Magazine*, 25, (April 1763), pp. 218–19). Erskine uses a regular sonnet form for his stanzas, orders Fear 'Away with all thy rueful train', presents examples from Shakespeare who 'alone thy ghastly charms enjoy'd', and closes with the banishment of Fear and a restoration of serenity:

> Ye angels sent as guardians of the good,
>   Swift chase th'enthusiastic pow'r away,
> Clear the low cloud, each grief-charg'd thought exclude,
>   Drive hence the fiend that shuns the eye of day;
> Ah! calm and gentle sink us down to rest
>   Let Chearfulness the lonely void adorn,
> Let her mild radiance gild the fear-struck breast,
>   While we with air-form'd terrors cease to mourn;
> And in such raptur'd dreams the fancy steep,
> As render more endear'd the deity of Sleep.

Collins, in contrast, adopts the irregular form of the Pindaric Ode, and, as Roger Lonsdale notes, heightens this irregularity by using 'the calmer epode as a temporary relief of tension rather than as a final resolution', and employing a rugged, 'Gothic' vocabulary taken from Spenser (Lonsdale, 1969, p. 418). Here, as in the 'Ode on . . . Popular Superstitions' (1.9), folklore is cited as a source of inspiration. In addition Sophocles and Shakespeare are invoked, not simply as geniuses of the past, uniquely equipped to represent scenes of fear, but as objects of emulation for a writer of the present.

Source: Roger Lonsdale, ed. (1969), *The Poems of Thomas Gray, William Collins, Oliver Goldsmith*, London and Harlow: Longman, pp. 418–23.

★

> Thou, to whom the world unknown
> With all its shadowy shapes is shown;
> Who see'st appalled the unreal scene,
> While Fancy lifts the veil between:

Ah Fear! Ah frantic Fear!
I see, I see thee near.
I know thy hurried step, thy haggard eye!
Like thee I start, like thee disordered fly.
For lo, what monsters in thy train appear!
Danger, whose limbs of giant mould
What mortal eye can fixed behold?
Who stalks his round, an hideous form,
Howling amidst the midnight storm,
Or throws him on the ridgy steep
Of some loose hanging rock to sleep;
And with him thousand phantoms joined,
Who prompt to deeds accursed the mind;
And those, the fiends who near allied,
O'er nature's wounds and wrecks preside;
Whilst Vengeance in the lurid air
Lifts her red arm, exposed and bare,
On whom that ravening brood of fate,*
Who lap the blood of sorrow, wait;
Who, Fear, this ghastly train can see,
And look not madly wild like thee?

Epode

In earliest Greece to thee with partial choice
The grief-full Muse addressed her infant tongue;
The maids and matrons on her awful voice,
Silent and pale, in wild amazement hung.

Yet he,† the bard who first invoked thy name,
Disdained in Marathon its power to feel:[10]
For not alone he nursed the poet's flame,
But reached from Virtue's hand the patriot's steel.

But who is he whom later garlands grace,[11]
Who left awhile o'er Hybla's dews to rove,
With trembling eyes thy dreary steps to trace,
Where thou and Furies shared the baleful grove?[12]

Wrapped in thy cloudy veil the incestuous queen‡
Sighed the sad call her son and husband heard,

* Alluding to the Κυνας αφυκτους [inescapable dogs] of *Sophocles*. See the *Electra*.

† Aeschylus.

‡ Jocasta.

When once alone it broke the silent scene,
  And he, the wretch of Thebes, no more appeared.[13]

O Fear, I know thee by my throbbing heart,
  Thy withering power inspired each mournful line,
Though gentle Pity claim her mingled part,[14]
  Yet all the thunders of the scene are thine!

Antistrophe

Thou who such weary lengths hast passed,
Where wilt thou rest, mad nymph, at last?
Say, wilt thou shroud in haunted cell,
Where gloomy Rape and Murder dwell?
Or in some hollowed seat,
'Gainst which the big waves beat,
Hear drowning seamen's cries in tempests brought!
Dark power, with shuddering meek submitted thought
Be mine to read the visions old,
Which thy awakening bards have told:
And, lest thou meet my blasted view,
Hold each strange tale devoutly true;
Ne'er be I found, by thee o'erawed,
In that thrice-hallowed eve abroad,
When ghosts, as cottage-maids believe,
Their pebbled beds permitted leave,
And goblins haunt, from fire or fen
Or mine or flood, the walks of men!
  O thou whose spirit most possessed!
The sacred seat of Shakespeare's breast!
By all that from thy prophet broke,
In thy divine emotions spoke,
Hither again thy fury deal,
Teach me but once like him to feel:
His cypress wreath[15] my meed decree,
And I, O Fear, will dwell with thee!

3.6 Edmund Burke (1729–97), *A Philosophical Enquiry into the Origin of Our Ideas of the Sublime and Beautiful* (1757)

The basis of Burke's influential treatise is the contrast between the sublime and the beautiful. Not only are their effects unlike and opposite, but they are fundamentally differentiated by their origin in alternative 'final causes', or guiding principles. Beauty is linked to pleasure, society and the goal of reproduction. The sublime is linked to mingled pain and delight (as opposed to pleasure), to ideas of terror and danger, and to self-preservation. The following extracts come from four of the five divisions of the *Enquiry*. First, from Part I, where the distinctions just outlined are introduced. Second, from Part II, devoted to characterising the sublime; the sections on 'Terror', 'Obscurity' and 'Power' begin a series which also include 'Privation', 'Vastness', 'Infinity', 'Succession and Uniformity' and other effects of the sublime in architecture, poetry and nature, including specific colours, sounds and smells. The presentation of ideas in Part II has sometimes encouraged a 'checklist' approach in relating Burke's theory to works of Gothic fiction. The third extract, from Part III which focuses on the idea of beauty, reveals the gender binary implicit in Burke's comparison of the sublime and the beautiful. Part IV returns to the underlying argument about the social function of the sublime, and the final extract describes how artificial terror operates physiologically to maintain the health of the nervous system. The sublime is thereby given a providential justification.

Source: Edmund Burke (1987) *A Philosophical Enquiry into the Origin of our Ideas of the Sublime and Beautiful*, ed. Adam Phillips, Oxford: Oxford University Press, pp. 35–7, 53–5, 58–63, 103, 105, 121–3.

★

Of the passions which belong to SELF-PRESERVATION (I.vi)

Most of the ideas which are capable of making a powerful impression on the mind, whether simply of Pain or Pleasure, or of the modifications of those, may be reduced very nearly to these two heads, *self-preservation* and *society*; to the ends of one or the other of which all our passions are calculated to answer. The passions which concern self-preservation, turn mostly on *pain* or *danger*. The ideas of *pain*, *sickness*, and *death*, fill the mind with strong emotions of horror; but *life* and *health*, though they put us in a capacity of being affected with pleasure, they make no such impression by the simple enjoyment. The passions therefore which are conversant about the preservation of the individual, turn chiefly on *pain* and *danger*, and they are the most powerful of all the passions.

Of the SUBLIME (I.vii)

Whatever is fitted in any sort to excite the ideas of pain, and danger, that is to say, whatever is in any sort terrible, or is conversant about terrible objects, or operates in a manner analogous to terror, is a source of the *sublime*; that is, it is productive of the strongest emotion which the mind is capable. I say the strongest emotion, because I am satisfied the ideas of pain are much more powerful than those which enter on the part of pleasure. Without all doubt, the torments which we may be made to suffer, are much greater in their effect on the body and mind, than any pleasures which the most learned voluptuary could suggest, or than the liveliest imagination, and the most sound and exquisitely sensible body could enjoy. Nay I am in great doubt, whether any man could be found who would earn a life of the most perfect satisfaction, at the price of ending it in the torments, which justice inflected in a few hours on the late unfortunate regicide in France.[16] But as pain is stronger in its operation than pleasure, so death is in general a much more affecting idea than pain; because there are very few pains, however exquisite, which are not preferred to death; nay, what generally makes pain itself, if I may say so, more painful, is, that it is considered as an emissary of this king of terrors. When danger or pain press too nearly, they are incapable of giving any delight, and are simply terrible; but at certain distances, and with certain modifications, they may be, and they are delightful, as we every day experience. The cause of this I shall endeavour to investigate hereafter.

Of the passion caused by the SUBLIME (II.i)

The passion caused by the great and sublime in *nature*, when those causes operate most powerfully, is Astonishment; and astonishment is that state of the soul, in which all its motions are suspended, with some degree of horror. In this case the mind is so entirely filled with its object, that it cannot entertain any other, nor by consequence reason on that object which employs it. Hence arises the great power of the sublime, that far from being produced by them, it anticipates our reasonings, and hurries us on by an irresistible force. Astonishment, as I have said, is the effect of the sublime in its highest degree; the inferior effects are admiration, reverence and respect.

TERROR (II.ii)

No passion so effectually robs the mind of all its powers of acting and reasoning as fear. For fear being an apprehensions of pain or death, it operates in a manner that resembles actual pain. Whatever therefore is terrible, with regard to sight, is sublime too, whether this cause of terror, be endured with greatness of dimensions or not; for it is impossible to look on any thing as trifling, or contemptible, that may be dangerous. There are many animals, who though far from being large, are yet capable of raising ideas of the sublime, because they are considered as objects of terror. As serpents and poisonous animals of almost all kinds. And to things of great dimensions, if we annex an adventitious idea of terror, they become without comparison greater. A level plain of a vast extent on land, is certainly no mean idea; the prospect of such a plain may be as extensive as a prospect of the ocean; but can it ever fill the mind with any thing so great as the ocean itself? This is owing to several causes, but it is owing to none more than this, that the ocean is an object of no small terror. Indeed terror is in all cases whatsoever, either more openly or latently the ruling principle of the sublime. Several languages bear a strong testimony to the affinity of these ideas. They frequently use the same word, to signify indifferently the modes of astonishment or admiration and those of terror. Θάμβος is in greek, either fear or wonder; δεινός is terrible or respectable; αἰδέω, to reverence or to fear. *Vereor* in latin, is what αἰδέω is in greek. The Romans used the verb *stupeo*, a term which strongly marks the state of an astonished mind, to express the effect either of simple fear, or of astonishment; the word *attonitus*, (thunder-struck) is equally expressive of the alliance of these ideas; and do not the french *etonnement* and the english *astonishment* and *amazement*, point out as clearly the kindred emotions which attend fear and wonder? They who have a more general knowledge of languages, could produce, I make no doubt, many other and equally striking examples.

OBSCURITY (II.iii)

To make any thing very terrible, obscurity seems in general to be necessary. When we know the full extent of any danger, when we can accustom our eyes to it, a great deal of the apprehension vanishes. Every one will be sensible of this, who considers how greatly night adds to our dread, in all cases of danger, and how much the notions of ghosts and goblins, of which none can form clear ideas, affect minds, which give credit to the popular tales concerning such sorts of beings. Those despotic governments, which are founded on the passions of men, and principally upon the passion of fear, keep their chief as much as may be from the public eye. The policy has been the same in many cases of religion. Almost all the heathen temples were dark. Even in the barbarous temples of the Americans at this day, they keep their idol in a dark part of the hut, which is consecrated to his worship. For this purpose too the druids performed all their ceremonies in the bosom of the darkest woods, and in the shade of the oldest and most spreading oaks. No person seems better to have understood the secret of heightening, or of setting terrible things, if I may use the expression, in their strongest light by the force of a judicious obscurity, than Milton. His description of Death in the second book is admirably studied; it is astonishing with what a gloomy pomp, with what a significant and expressive uncertainty of strokes and colouring he has finished the portrait of the king of terrors.

> *The other shape,*
> *If shape it might be called that shape had none*
> *Distinguishable, in member, joint, or limb;*
> *Or substance might be called that shadow seemed,*
> *For each seemed either; black he stood as night;*
> *Fierce as ten furies; terrible as hell;*
> *And shook a deadly dart. What seemed his head*
> *The likeness of a kingly crown had on.*[17]

In this description all is dark, uncertain, confused, terrible, and sublime to the last degree.

Of the difference between CLEARNESS and OBSCURITY with regard to the passions (II.iv)

. . . I am sensible that this idea has met with opposition, and is likely still to be rejected by several. But let it be considered that hardly any thing can strike the mind with its greatness, which does not make some sort of approach towards infinity; which nothing can do whilst we are able to perceive its bounds; but to see an object distinctly, and to perceive its bounds, is one and the same thing. A clear idea is therefore another name for a little idea. There is a passage in the book of Job amazingly sublime, and this sublimity is principally due to the terrible uncertainty of the thing described. *In thoughts from the visions of the night, when deep sleep falleth upon men, fear came upon me and trembling, which made all my bones to shake. Then a spirit passed before my face. The hair of my flesh stood up. It stood still,* but I could not discern the form thereof; *an image was before mine eyes; there was silence; and I heard a voice, – Shall mortal man be more just than God?*[18] We are first prepared with the utmost solemnity for the vision; we are first terrified, before we are let even into the obscure cause of our emotion; but when this grand cause of terror makes its appearance, what is it? is it not, wrapt up in the shades of its own incomprehensible darkness, more aweful, more striking, more terrible, than the liveliest description, than the clearest painting could possibly represent it? When painters have attempted to give us clear representations of these very fanciful and terrible ideas, they have I think almost always failed; insomuch that I have been at a loss, in all the pictures I have seen of hell, whether the painter did not intend something ludicrous. Several painters have handled a subject of this kind, with a view of assembling as many horrid phantoms as their imagination could suggest; but all the designs I have chanced to meet of the temptations of St. Anthony, were rather a sort of odd wild grotesques, than any thing capable of producing a serious passion. In all these subjects poetry is very happy. Its apparitions, its chimeras, its harpies, its allegorical figures, are grand and affecting; and though Virgil's Fame, and Homer's Discord, are obscure, they are magnificent figures. These figures in painting would be clear enough, but I fear they might become ridiculous.

POWER (II.v)

Besides these things which *directly* suggest the idea of danger, and those which produce a similar effect from a mechanical cause, I know of nothing which is not some modification of power. And this branch rises as naturally as the other two branches, from terror, the common stock of every thing that is sublime. The idea of power at first view, seems of the class of these indifferent ones, which may equally belong to pain or to pleasure. But in reality, the affection arising from the idea of vast power, is extremely remote from that neutral character. For first, we must remember, that the idea of pain, in its highest degree, is much stronger than the highest degree of pleasure; and that it preserves the same superiority through all the subordinate gradations. From hence it is, that where the chances for equal degrees of suffering or enjoyment are in any sort equal, the idea of the suffering must always be prevalent. And indeed the ideas of pain, and above all of death, are so very affecting, that whilst we remain in the presence of whatever is supposed to have the power of inflicting either, it is impossible to be perfectly free from terror. Again, we know by experience, that for the enjoyment of pleasure, no great efforts of power are at all necessary; nay we know, that such efforts would go a great way towards destroying our satisfaction: for pleasure must be stolen, and not forced upon us; pleasure follows the will; and therefore we are generally affected with it by many things of a force greatly inferior to our own. But pain is always inflicted by a power in some way superior, because we never submit to pain willingly. So that strength, violence, pain and terror, are ideas that rush in upon the mind together. Look at a man, or any other animal of prodigious strength, and what is your idea before reflection? Is it that this strength will be subservient to you, to your ease, to your pleasure, to your interest in any sense? No; the emotion you feel is, lest this enormous strength should be employed to the purposes of rapine and destruction. That power derives all its sublimity from the terror with which it is generally accompanied, will appear evidently from its effect in the very few cases, in which it may be possible to strip a considerable degree of strength of its ability to hurt. When you do this, you spoil it of every thing sublime, and it immediately becomes contemptible. An ox is a creature of vast strength; but he is an innocent creature, extremely serviceable, and not at all dangerous; for which reason the idea of an ox is by no means grand. A bull is strong too; but his strength is of another kind; often very destructive, seldom (at least amongst us) of any use in our business; the idea of a bull is therefore great, and it has frequently a place in sublime descriptions, and elevating comparisons. Let us look at another strong animal in the two distinct lights in which we may consider him. The horse in the light of an useful beast, fit for the plough, the road, the draft, in every social useful light the horse has nothing of the sublime; but is it thus that we are affected with him, *whose neck is cloathed with thunder, the glory of whose nostrils is terrible, who swalloweth the ground with fierceness and rage, neither believeth that it is the sound of the trumpet?*[19] In this description the useful character of the horse entirely disappears, and the terrible and sublime blaze out together. We have continually about us animals of a strength that is considerable, but not pernicious. Amongst these we never look for the sublime: it comes upon us in the gloomy forest, and in the howling wilderness, in the form of the lion, the tiger, the panther, or rhinoceros. Whenever strength is only useful, and employed for our benefit or our pleasure, then it is never sublime; for nothing can act agreeably to us, that does not act in conformity to our will; but to act agreeably to our will, it must be subject to us; and therefore can never be the cause of a grand and commanding conception. The description of the wild ass, in Job, is worked up into no small sublimity, merely by insisting on his freedom, and his setting mankind at defiance; otherwise the description of such an animal could have had nothing noble in it. *Who hath loosed (says he) the bands of the wild ass? whose house I have made the wilderness, and the barren land his dwellings. He scorneth the multitude of the city, neither regardeth he the voice of the driver. The range of the mountains is his pasture.* The magnificent description of the unicorn and of leviathan in the same book, is full of the same heightening circumstances. *Will the unicorn be willing to serve thee? canst thou bind the unicorn with his band in the furrow? wilt thou trust him because his strength is great? – Canst thou draw out leviathan with an hook? will he make a covenant with thee? wilt thou take him for a servant for ever? shall not one be cast down even at the sight of him?* In short, wheresoever we find strength, and in what light soever we look upon power, we shall all along observe the sublime the concomitant of terror, and contempt the attendant on a strength that is subservient and innoxious. The race of dogs in many of their kinds, have generally a competent degree of strength and swiftness; and they exert these, and other valuable qualities which they possess, greatly to our convenience and pleasure. Dogs are indeed the most social, affectionate, and amiable animals of the whole brute creation; but love approaches must nearer to contempt than is commonly imagined; and accordingly, though we caress dogs, we borrow from them an appellation of the most despicable kind, when we employ terms of reproach; and this appellation is the common mark of the last vileness and contempt in every language. Wolves have not more strength than several species of dogs; but on account of their unmanageable fierceness, the idea of a wolf is not despicable; it is not excluded from grand descriptions and similitudes. Thus we are affected by strength, which is *natural* power. The power which arises from institution in kings and commanders, has the same connection with terror. Sovereigns are frequently addressed with the title of *dread majesty*. And it may be observed, that young persons little acquainted with the world, and who have not been used to approach men in power, are commonly struck with awe which takes away the free use of their faculties. *When I prepared my seat in the street (says Job) the young men saw me, and hid themselves.*[20] Indeed so natural is this timidity with regard to power, and so strongly does it inhere in our constitution, that very few are able to conquer it, but by mixing much in the business of the great world, or by using no small violence to their natural dispositions. I know some people are of opinion, that no awe, no degree of terror, accompanies the idea of power, and have hazarded to affirm, that we can contemplate the idea of God himself without any such emotion. I purposely avoided when I first considered this subject, to introduce the idea of that great and tremendous being, as an example in an argument so light as this; though it frequently occurred to me, not as an objection to, but as a strong confirmation of my notions in this matter. I hope, in what I am going to say, I shall avoid presumption, where it is almost impossible for any mortal to speak with strict propriety. I say then, that whilst we consider the Godhead merely as he is an object of the understanding, which forms a complex idea of power, wisdom, justice, goodness, all stretched to a degree far exceeding the bounds of our comprehension, whilst we consider the divinity in this refined and abstracted light, the imagination and passions are little or nothing affected. But because we are bound by the condition of our nature to ascend to these pure and intellectual ideas, through the medium of sensible images, and to judge of these divine qualities by their evident acts and exertions, it becomes extremely hard to disentangle our idea of the cause from the effect by which we are led to know it. Thus when we contemplate the Deity, his attributes and their operation coming united on the mind, form a sort of sensible image, and as such are capable of affecting the imagination. Now, though in a just idea of the Deity, perhaps none of his attributes are predominant, yet to our imagination, his power is by far the most striking. Some reflection, some comparing is necessary to satisfy us of his wisdom, his justice, and his goodness; to be struck with his power, it is only necessary that we should open our eyes. But whilst we contemplate so vast an object, under the arm, as it were, of almighty power, and invested upon every side with omnipresence, we shrink into the minuteness of our own nature, and are, in a manner, annihilated before him. And though a consideration of his other attributes may relieve in some measure our apprehensions; yet no conviction of the justice with which it is exercised, nor the mercy with which it is tempered, can wholly remove the terror that naturally arises from a force which nothing can withstand. If we rejoice, we rejoice with trembling; and even whilst we are receiving benefits, we cannot but shudder at a power which can confer benefits of such mighty importance. When the prophet David contemplated the wonders of wisdom and power, which are displayed in the oeconomy of man, he seems to be struck with a sort of divine horror, and cries out, *fearfully and wonderfully am I made!*[21] . . .

Beautiful objects small (III.xiii)

. . . There is a wide difference between admiration and love. The sublime, which is the cause of the former, always dwells on great objects, and terrible; the latter on small ones, and pleasing; we submit to what we admire, but we love what submits to us; in one case we are forced, in the other we are flattered into compliance. In short, the ideas of the sublime and the beautiful stand on foundations so different, that it is hard, I had almost said impossible, to think of reconciling them in the same subject, without considerably lessening the effect of the one or the other upon the passions. So that attending to their quantity, beautiful objects are comparatively small.

Gradual VARIATION (III.xv)

. . . Observe that part of a beautiful woman where she is perhaps the most beautiful, about the neck and breasts; the smoothness; the softness; the easy and insensible swell; the variety of the surface, which is never for the smallest space the same; the deceitful maze, through which the unsteady eye slides giddily, without knowing where to fix, or whither it is carried. Is not this a demonstration of that change of surface continual and yet hardly perceptible at any point which forms one of the great constituents of beauty? . . .

How the Sublime is produced (IV.v)

Having considered terror as producing an unnatural tension and certain violent emotions of the nerves; it easily follows, from what we have just said, that whatever is fitted to produce such a tension, must be productive of a passion similar to terror, and consequently must be a source of the sublime, though it should have no idea of danger connected with it. So that little remains towards shewing the cause of the sublime, but to shew that the instances we have given of it in the second part, relate to such things, as are fitted by nature to produce this sort of tension, either by the primary operation of the mind or the body. With regard to such things as affect by the associated idea of danger, there can be no doubt but that they produce terror, and act by some modification of that passion; and that terror, when sufficiently violent, raises the emotions of the body just mentioned, can as little be doubted. But if the sublime is built on terror, or some passion like it, which has pain for its object; it is previously proper to enquire how any species of delight can be derived from a cause so apparently contrary to it. I say, *delight*, because, as I have often remarked, it is very evidently different in its cause, and in its own nature, from actual and positive pleasure.

How pain can be a cause of delight (IV.vi)

Providence has so ordered it, that a state of rest and inaction, however it may flatter our indolence, should be productive of many inconveniences; that it should generate such disorders, as may force us to have recourse to some labour, as a thing absolutely requisite to make us pass our lives with tolerable satisfaction; for the nature of rest is to suffer all the parts of our bodies to fall into a relaxation, that not only disables the members from performing their functions, but takes away the vigorous tone of fibre which is requisite for carrying on the natural and necessary secretions. At the same time, that in this languid inactive state, the nerves are more liable to the most horrid convulsions, than when they are sufficiently braced and strengthened. Melancholy, dejection, despair, and often self-murder, is the consequence of the gloomy view we take of things in this relaxed state of body. The best remedy for all these evils is exercise or *labour*; and labour is a surmounting of *difficulties*, an exertion of the contracting power of the muscles; and as such resembles pain, which consists in tension or contraction, in every thing but degree. Labour is not only requisite to preserve the coarser organs in a state fit for their functions, but it is equally necessary to these finer and more delicate organs, on which, and by which, the imagination, and perhaps the other mental powers act. Since it is probable, that not only the inferior parts of the soul, as the passions are called, but the understanding itself makes use of some fine corporeal instruments in its operation; though what they are, and where they are, may be somewhat hard to settle: but that it does make use of such, appears from hence; that a long exercise of the mental powers induces a remarkable lassitude of the whole body; and on the other hand, that great bodily labour, or pain, weakens, and sometimes actually destroys the mental faculties. Now, as a due exercise is essential to the coarse muscular parts of the constitution, and that without this rousing they would become languid, and diseased, the very same rule holds with regard to those finer parts we have mentioned; to have them in proper order, they must be shaken and worked to a proper degree.

EXERCISE necessary for the finer organs (IV.vii)

As common labour, which is a mode of pain, is the exercise of the grosser, a mode of terror is the exercise of the finer parts of the system; and if a certain mode of pain be of such a nature as to act upon the eye or the ear, as they are the most delicate organs, the affection approaches more nearly to that which has a mental cause. In all these cases, if the pain and terror are so modified as not to be actually noxious; if the pain is not carried to violence, and the terror is not conversant about the present destruction of the person, as these emotions clear the parts, whether fine, or gross, of a dangerous and troublesome incumbrance, they are capable of producing delight; not pleasure, but a sort of delightful terror, a sort of tranquillity tinged with terror; which as it belongs to self-preservation is one of the strongest of all the passions. Its object is the sublime. Its highest degree I call *astonishment*; the subordinate degrees are awe, reverence, and respect, which by the very etymology of the words shew from what source they are derived, and how they stand distinguished from positive pleasure.

3.7 Originality

3.7a Edward Young (1683–1765), *Conjectures on Original Composition* (1759)

Young's treatise rejected the neo-classical rules with unprecedented boldness in favour of sublime inspiration. He nevertheless supported his argument with the authority of Longinus, Shakespeare and Pindar, whose odes had an important influence on the poetry of Collins, among others (see 3.5).

Source: [Edward Young] (1759), *Conjectures on Original Composition, in a Letter to the Author of Sir Charles Grandison*, London: Millar and Dodsley, pp. 11–13.

★

. . . An *Imitator* shares his crown, if he has one, with the chosen Object of his Imitation; an *Original* enjoys an undivided applause. An *Original* may be said to be of a *vegetable* nature; it rises spontaneously from the vital root of Genius; it *grows*, it is not *made*: *Imitations* are often a sort of *Manufacture* wrought up by those *Mechanics*, *Art*, and *Labour*, out of preexistent materials not their own.

Again: We read *Imitation* with somewhat of his langour, who listens to a twice-told tale; Our spirits rouze at an *Original*; that is a perfect stranger, and all throng to learn what news from a foreign land: And tho' it comes, like an *Indian* Prince, adorned with feathers only, having little of weight; yet of our attention it will rob the more Solid if not equally New: Thus every Telescope is lifted at a new-discovered star; it makes a hundred Astronomers in a moment, and denies equal notice to the sun. But if an *Original*, by being as excellent, as new, adds admiration to surprize, then are we at the Writer's mercy; on the strong wing of his Imagination, we are snatched from *Britain* to *Italy*, from Climate to Climate, from Pleasure to Pleasure; we have no Home, no Thought, of our own; till the Magician drops his Pen: And then falling down into ourselves, we awake to flat Realities, lamenting the change, like the Beggar who dreamt himself a Prince. . . .

3.7b Horace Walpole (1717–97), Preface to the second edition of *The Castle of Otranto* (1765)

In the Preface to the first edition of the novel, Walpole evaded potential criticism of the story's improbability by passing it off as a translation of a fourteenth-century manuscript. In this second Preface, he acknowledged authorship and attempted to excuse its wildness on other, aesthetic grounds. His first claim is to originality: departing from the examples of past and present romance in order to liberate imagination, and create a new literary domain. His second is of faithfulness to the example of Shakespeare. This might seem paradoxical, but eighteenth-century aesthetic theory was so attached to the authority of precedent that even originality required a model. Walpole extends his defence of Shakespeare into an attack on Voltaire's recent strictures on the English dramatist; this section has not been included here, but for a note on the context see the headnote to 1.8b.

Source: Horace Walpole (1996), *The Castle of Otranto: A Gothic Story*, revd. edn, Oxford and New York: Oxford University Press, pp. 9–14.

★

The favourable manner in which this little piece has been received by the public, calls upon the author to explain the grounds on which he composed it. But before he opens those motives, it is fit that he should ask pardon of his readers for having offered his work to them under the borrowed personage of a translator. As diffidence of his own abilities, and the novelty of the attempt were his sole inducements to assume that disguise, he flatters himself he shall appear excusable. He resigned his performance to the impartial judgement of the public; determined to let it perish in obscurity, if disapproved; nor meaning to avow such a trifle, unless better judges should pronounce that he might own it without a blush.

It was an attempt to blend the two kinds of romance, the ancient and the modern. In the former all was imagination and improbability: in the latter, nature is always intended to be, and sometimes has been, copied with success. Invention has not been wanting; but the great resources of fancy have been dammed up, by a strict adherence to common life. But if in the latter species Nature has cramped imagination, she did but take her revenge, having been totally excluded from old romances. The actions, sentiments, conversations, of the heroes and heroines of ancient days are as unnatural as the machines employed to put them in motion.

The author of the following pages thought it possible to reconcile the two kinds. Desirous of leaving the powers of fancy at liberty to expatiate through the boundless realms of invention, and thence of creating more interesting situations, he wished to conduct the mortal agents in his drama according to the rules of probability; in short, to make them think, speak and act, as it might be supposed mere men and women would do in extraordinary positions. He had observed, that in all inspired writings, the personages under the dispensation of miracles, and witnesses to the most stupendous phenomena, never lose sight of their human character: whereas in the productions of romantic story, an improbable event never fails to be attended by an absurd dialogue. The actors seem to lose their senses the moment the laws of nature have lost their tone. As the public have applauded the attempt, the author must not say he was entirely unequal to the task he had undertaken: yet if the new route he has struck out shall have paved a road for men of brighter talents, he shall own with pleasure and modesty, that he was sensible the plan was capable of receiving greater embellishments than his imagination or conduct of the passions could bestow on it.

With regard to the deportment of the domestics, on which I have touched in the former preface, I will beg leave to add a few words. The simplicity of their behaviour, almost tending to excite smiles, which at first seem not consonant to the serious cast of the work, appeared to me not only not improper, but was marked designedly in that manner. My rule was nature. However grave, important, or even melancholy, the sensations of princes and heroes may be, they do not stamp the same affections on their domestics: at least the latter do not, or should not be made to express their passions in the same dignified tone. In my humble opinion, the contrast between the sublime of the one, and the *naïveté* of the other, sets the pathetic of the former in a stronger light. The very impatience which a reader feels, while delayed by the coarse pleasantries of vulgar actors from arriving at the knowledge of the important catastrophe he expects, perhaps heightens, certainly proves that he has been artfully interested in, the depending event. But I had higher authority than my own opinion for this conduct. That great master of nature, Shakespeare, was the model I copied. Let me ask if his tragedies of Hamlet and Julius Caesar would not lose a considerable share of the spirit and wonderful beauties, if the humour of the grave diggers, the fooleries of Polonius, and the clumsy jests of the Roman citizens were omitted, or vested in heroics? Is not the eloquence of Antony, the nobler and affectedly unaffected oration of Brutus, artificially exalted by the rude bursts of nature from the mouths of their auditors? These touches remind one of the Grecian sculptor, who, to convey the idea of a Colossus within the dimensions of a seal, inserted a little boy measuring his thumb . . .

[Walpole goes on to defend Shakespeare from the criticisms of Voltaire, and examines the latter's comments in some detail].

The result of all I have said is to shelter my own daring under the cannon of the brightest genius this country, at least, has produced. I might have pleaded, that having created a new species of romance, I was at liberty to lay down what rules I though fit for the conduct of it: but I should be more proud of having imitated, however faintly, weakly, and at a distance, so masterly a pattern, than to enjoy the entire merit of invention, unless I could have marked my work with genius as well as with originality. Such as it is, the public have honoured it sufficiently, whatever rank their suffrages allot to it.

3.7c William Duff (1732–1815), *An Essay on Original Genius and its Various Modes of Exertion in Philosophy and the Fine Arts, Particularly in Poetry* (1767)

The confident and expansive style of Duff's treatise is a measure of the progress made against the rules of neo-classicism. Duff was a Scottish clergyman and active participant in the 'Aberdonian Enlightenment'; he was writing in the aftermath of the 'discovery' of Ossian (see Hugh Blair, 2.8), and the Celtic Homer is enlisted with pride within the ranks of true 'Original Genius'. In addition to the predictable, polemical elevation of invention over imitation, irregularity over order, enthusiasm over reason, there is the historical dimension typical of the Scottish school of aesthetic theory. Ultimately, the outlook for genius is bleak, for it is 'displayed in utmost vigour in early and uncultivated periods of society' (289), and the modern era is characterised by a luxury and refinement which is inimical to the poetic imagination.

Source: William Duff (1767), *An Essay on Original Genius and Its Various Modes of Exertion in Philosophy and the Fine Arts, Particularly in Poetry*, London: Dilly, pp. 89–90; 138–43.

★

Book 2, section I. Of that Degree of Genius which is Properly Denominated Original

. . . Original Genius is distinguished from every other degree of this quality, by a more vivid and a more comprehensive Imagination, which enables it both to take in a greater number of objects, and to conceive them more distinctly; at the same time that it can express its ideas in the strongest colours, and represent them in the most striking light. It is likewise distinguished by the superior quickness, as well as justness and extent, of the associating faculty; so that with surprising readiness it combines at once every homogeneous and corresponding idea, in such a manner as to present a complete portrait of the object it attempts to describe. But, above all, it is distinguished by an inventive and plastic Imagination, by which it sketches out a creation of its own, discloses truths that were formerly unknown, and exhibits a succession of scenes and events which were never before contemplated or conceived. In a word, it is the peculiar character of original Genius to strike out a path for itself whatever sphere it attempts to occupy; to start new sentiments, and throw out new light on every subject it treats. It delights in every species of fiction, and sometimes discovers itself in the more severe investigations of causes and effects. It is distinguished by the most uncommon, as well as the most surprising combinations of ideas; by the novelty, and not unfrequently by the sublimity and boldness of its imagery in composition. . . .

Book 2, section III. Of Original Genius in Poetry

. . . The third and last sort of characters, in which, above all others, an original Genius will most remarkably display his invention, is of that kind which we called PRAETERNATURAL, and is altogether different from mere HUMAN characters. Witches, Ghosts, Fairies, and such other unknown visionary beings, are included in the species of which we are speaking. Of the manner of existence, nature and employment of these wonderful beings, we have no certain or determinate ideas. It should seem that our notions of them, vague and indistinct as they are, are derived from tradition and popular opinion; or are the children of Fancy, Superstition, and Fear. These causes concurring with, as well as operating upon, the natural credulity of mankind, have given birth to prodigies and fables concerning 'Gorgons, and Hydras, and chimeras dire'; which have been always eagerly swallowed by the vulgar, though they may have been justly rejected by the wise. However averse the latter may be to think with the former on subjects of this kind, it is certain, that their ideas of Ghosts, Witches, Daemons, and such like apparitions, must be very much the same with theirs, since they draw them from the same source, that of traditionary relation; and, how reluctant soever the Judgment may be to yield its assent, the Imagination catches and retains the impression, whether we will or not. It is true, the ideas of those beings, which are common to all, are very general and obscure; there is therefore great scope afforded for the flights of Fancy in this boundless region. Much may be invented, and many new ideas of their nature and offices may be acquired. The wildest and most exuberant imagination will succeed best in excursions of this kind, 'beyond the visible diurnal sphere,' and will make the most stupendous discoveries in its aerial tour. In this region of fiction and fable, original Genius will indulge its adventurous flight without restraint: it will dart a beam upon the dark scenes of futurity, draw the veil from the invisible world, and expose to our astonished view 'that undiscovered country, from whose bourne no traveller returns.'

Shakespear, with whose words we concluded the last sentence, is the only *English* writer, who with amazing boldness has ventured to burst the barriers of a separate state, and disclose the land of Apparitions, Shadows, and Dreams; and he has nobly succeeded in his daring attempt. His very peculiar excellence in this respect will be more properly illustrated in another part of our Essay. In the mean time we may observe, that it will be hazardous for any one to pursue the track which he has marked out; and that none but a Genius uncommonly original, can hope for success in the pursuit.

Should such a Genius arise, he could not desire a nobler field for the display of an exuberant Imagination, than what the spiritual world, with its strange inhabitants, will present to him. In describing the nature and employment of those visionary beings, whose existence is fixed in a future state, or of those who exist in the present, or may be supposed to inhabit the 'midway air,' but are possessed of certain powers and faculties, very different from what are possessed by mankind, he is not, as in describing human characters, restricted to exact probability, much less to truth: for we are in most instances utterly ignorant of the powers of different or superior beings; and, consequently, are very incompetent judges of the probability or improbability of the particular influence, or actions attributed to them. All that we require of a Poet therefore, who pretends to exhibit characters of this kind, is, that the incidents, in effectuating which they are supposed to be concerned, be possible, and consonant to the general analogy of their nature; an analogy, founded not upon truth or strict probability, but upon common tradition or popular opinion. It is evident therefore that the Poet, who would give us a glimpse of the other world, and an idea of the nature, employment, and manner of existence of those who inhabit it, or of those other imaginary beings, who are in some respects similar to, but in others totally different from mankind, and are supposed to dwell on or about this earth, has abundant scope for the exercise of the most fertile Invention. This ideal region is indeed the proper sphere of Fancy, in which she may range with a loose rein, without suffering restraint from the severe checks of Judgment; for Judgment has very little jurisdiction in this province of Fable. The invention of the supernatural characters above-mentioned, and the exhibition of them, with their proper attributes and offices, are the highest efforts and the most pregnant proofs of truly ORIGINAL GENIUS. . . .

3.8 John Aikin and Anna Laetitia Aikin (later Barbauld) (1747–1822 and 1743–1825), 'On the Pleasure Derived from Objects of Terror; with Sir Bertrand, A Fragment' (1773)

Lucy Aikin, the niece of the authors, attributed the essay to Anna Laetitia Aikin and the fictional fragment to her brother John (cited by Levy, 1996, p. 163). Together the essay which investigates the taste for fictional terrors and the accompanying experimental fragment represent the first serious attempt to theorise and build on Walpole's innovation. 'Sir Bertrand' became celebrated in its own right, receiving unqualified approval from Walpole and Nathan Drake. Other essays in the collection *Miscellaneous Pieces* dealt with romance, monastic institutions, dreams, and 'those kinds of distress which excite agreeable sensations'.

Source: John and Anna Laetitia Aikin (1773), *Miscellaneous Pieces in Prose*, London: Joseph Johnson, pp. 119–37.

That the exercise of our benevolent feelings, as called forth by the view of human afflictions, should be a source of pleasure, cannot appear wonderful to one who considers that relation between the moral and natural system of man, which has connected a degree of satisfaction with every action or emotion productive of the general welfare. The painful sensation immediately arising from a scene of misery, is so much softened and alleviated by the reflex sense of self-approbation attending virtuous sympathy, that we find, on the whole, a very exquisite and refined pleasure remaining, which makes us desirous of again being witnesses to such scenes, instead of flying from them with disgust and horror. It is obvious how greatly such a provision must conduce to the ends of mutual support and assistance. But the apparent delight with which we dwell upon objects of pure terror, where our moral feelings are not in the least concerned, and no passion seems to be excited but the depressing one of fear, is a paradox of the heart, much more difficult of solution.

The reality of this source of pleasure seems evident from daily observation. The greediness with which the tales of ghosts and goblins, of murders, earthquakes, fires, shipwrecks, and all the most terrible disasters attending human life, are devoured by every ear, must have been generally remarked. Tragedy, the most favourite work of fiction, has taken a full share of those scenes; 'it has supt full with horrors' – and has, perhaps, been more indebted to them for public admiration than to its tender and pathetic parts. The ghost of Hamlet, Macbeth descending into the witches' cave, and the tent scene in Richard, command as forcibly the attention of our souls as the parting of Jaffeir and Belvedira, the fall of Wolsey, or the death of Shore.[22] The inspiration of *terror* was by the antient critics assigned as the peculiar province of tragedy; and the Greek and Roman tragedians have introduced some extraordinary personages for this purpose: not only the shades of the dead, but the furies, and other fabulous inhabitants of the infernal regions. Collins, in his most poetical ode to Fear [see 3.5], has finely enforced this idea.

> Tho' gentle Pity claim her mingled part,
> Yet all the thunders of the scene are thine.

The old Gothic romance and the Eastern tale, with their genii, giants, enchantments, and transformations, however a refined critic may censure them as absurd and extravagant, will ever retain a most powerful influence on the mind, and interest the reader independently of all peculiarity of taste. Thus the great Milton, who had a strong bias to these wildnesses of the imagination, has with striking effect made the stories 'of forests and enchantments drear,' a favourite subject with his *Penseroso*; and had undoubtably their awakening images strong upon his mind when he breaks out,

> Call up him that left half-told
> The story of Cambuscan bold; &c.
> (II. 109–10)

How are we then to account for the pleasure derived from such objects? I have often been led to imagine that there is a deception in these cases; and that the avidity with which we attend is not proof of our receiving real pleasure. The pain of suspense, and the irresistible desire of satisfying curiosity, when once raised, will account for our eagerness to go quite through an adventure, though we suffer actual pain during the whole course of it. We rather chuse to suffer the smart pang of a violent emotion than the uneasy craving of an unsatisfied desire. That this principle, in many instances, may involuntarily carry us through what we dislike, I am convinced from experience. This is the impulse which renders the poorest and most insipid narrative interesting when once we get fairly into it; and I have frequently felt it with regard to our modern novels, which, if lying on my table, and taken up in an idle hour, have led me through the most tedious and disgusting pages, while, like Pistol eating his leek,[23] I have swallowed and execrated to the end. And it will not only force us through dullness, but through actual torture – through the relation of a Damien's execution,[24] or an inquisitor's act of faith. When children, therefore, listen with pale and mute attention to the frightful stories of apparitions, we are not, perhaps, to imagine that they are in a state of enjoyment, any more than the poor bird which is dropping into the mouth of the rattlesnake – they are chained by the ears, and fascinated by curiosity. This solution, however, does not satisfy me with respect to the well-wrought scenes of artificial terror which are formed by a sublime and vigorous imagination. Here, though we know before-hand what to expect, we enter into them with eagerness, in quest of a pleasure already experienced. This is the pleasure constantly attached to the excitement of surprise from new and wonderful objects. A strange and unexpected event awakens the mind, and keeps in on the stretch; and where the agency of invisible beings is introduced, of 'forms unseen, and mightier far than we,' our imagination, darting forth, explores with rapture the new world which is laid open to its view, and rejoices in the expansion of its powers. Passion and fancy co-operating elevate the soul to its highest pitch; and the pain of terror is lost in amazement.

Hence, the more wild, fanciful, and extraordinary are the circumstances of a scene of horror, the more pleasure we receive from it; and where they are too near common nature, though violently borne by curiosity through the adventure, we cannot repeat it or reflect on it, without an over-balance of pain. In the *Arabian nights* are many most striking examples of the terrible joined with the marvellous: the story of Aladdin and the travels of Sinbad are particularly excellent. The *Castle of Otranto* is a very spirited modern attempt upon the same plan of mixed terror, adapted to the model of Gothic romance. The best conceived, the most strongly worked-up scene of mere natural horror that I recollect, is in Smollett's *Ferdinand count Fathom*; where the hero, entertained in a lone house in a forest, finds a corpse just slaughtered in the room where he is sent to sleep, and the door of which is locked upon him. It may be amusing for the reader to compare his feelings upon these, and from thence form his opinion of the justness of my theory. The following fragment, in which both these manners are attempted to be in some degree united, is offered to entertain a solitary winter's evening.

★★★

—After this adventure, Sir Bertrand turned his steed towards the woulds, hoping to cross these dreary moors before the curfew. But ere he had proceeded half his journey, he was bewildered by the different tracks, and not being able, as far as the eye could reach, to espy any object but the brown heath surrounding him, he was at length quite uncertain which way he should direct his course. Night overtook him in this situation. It was one of those nights when the moon gives a faint glimmering of light through the thick black clouds of a lowering sky. Now and then she suddenly emerged in full splendor from her veil; and then instantly retired behind it, having just served to give the forlorn Sir Bertrand a wide extended prospect over the desolate waste. Hope and native courage a while urged him to push forwards, but at length the increasing darkness and fatigue of body and mind overcame him; he dreaded moving from the ground he stood on, for fear of unknown pits and bogs, and alighting from his horse in despair, he threw himself on the ground. He had not long continued in that posture when the sullen toll of a distant bell struck his ears – he started up, and turning towards the sound discerned a dim twinkling light. Instantly he seized the horse's bridle, and with cautious steps advanced towards it. After a painful march he was stopt by a moated ditch surrounding the place from whence the light proceeded; and by a momentary glimpse of moon-light he had a full view of a large antique mansion, with turrets at the corners, and an ample porch in the centre. The injuries of time were strongly marked on every thing about it. The roof in various places was fallen in, the battlements were half demolished, and the windows broken and dismantled. A draw-bridge, with a ruinous gate-way at each end, led to the court before the building – He entered, and instantly the light, which proceeded from a window in one of the turrets, glided along and vanished; at the same moment the moon sunk beneath a black cloud, and the night was darker than ever. All was silent – Sir Bertrand fastened his steed under a shed, and approaching the house traversed its whole front with light and slow footsteps – All was still as death – He looked in at the lower windows, but could not distinguish a single object through the impenetrable gloom. After a short parley with himself, he entered the porch, and seizing a massy iron knocker at the gate, lifted it up, and hesitating, at length struck a loud stroke. The noise resounded through the whole mansion with hollow echoes. All was still again – He repeated the strokes more boldly and louder – another interval of silence ensued – A third time he knocked, and a third time still. He then fell back to some distance that he might discern whether any light could be seen in the whole front – It again appeared in the same place and quickly glided away as before – at the same instant a deep sullen toll sounded from the turret. Sir Bertrand's heart made a fearful stop – He was a while motionless; then terror impelled him to make some hasty steps towards his steed – but shame stopt his flight; and urged by honour, and a resistless desire of finishing the adventure, he returned to the porch;

and working up his soul to a full readiness of resolution, he drew forth his sword with one hand, and with the other lifted up the latch of the gate. The heavy door, creaking upon its hinges, reluctantly yielded to his hand – he applied his shoulder to it and forced it open – he quitted it and stept forward – the door instantly shut with a thundering clap. Sir Bertrand's blood was chilled – he turned back to find the door, and it was long ere his trembling hands could seize it – but his utmost strength could not open it again. After several ineffectual attempts, he looked behind him, and beheld, across a hall, upon a large staircase, a pale bluish flame which cast a dismal gleam of light around. He again summoned forth his courage and advanced towards it – It retired. He came to the foot of the stairs, and after a moment's deliberation ascended. He went slowly up, the flame retiring before him, till he came to a wide gallery – The flame proceeded along it, and he followed in silent horror, treading lightly, for the echoes of his footsteps startled him. It led him to the foot of another staircase, and then vanished – At the same instant another toll sounded from the turret – Sir Bertrand felt it strike upon his heart. He was now in total darkness, and with his arms extended began to ascend the second stair-case. A dead cold hand met his left hand and firmly grasped it, drawing him forcibly forwards – he endeavoured to disengage himself, but could not – he made a furious blow with his sword, and instantly a loud shriek pierced his ears, and the dead hand was left powerless in his – He dropt it, and rushed forwards with a desperate valour. The stairs were narrow and winding, and interrupted by frequent breaches, and loose fragments of stone. The stair-case grew narrower and narrower, and at length terminated in a low iron grate. Sir Bertrand pushed it open – it led to an intricate winding passage, just large enough to admit a person on his hands and knees. A faint glimmering of light served to show the nature of the place. Sir Bertrand entered – A deep hollow groan resounded from a distance through the vault – He went forwards and proceeding beyond the first turning, he discerned the same blue flame which had before conducted him. He followed it. The vault, at length, suddenly opened into a lofty gallery, in the midst of which a figure appeared, compleatly armed, thrusting forwards the bloody stump of an arm, with a terrible frown and menacing gesture, and brandishing a sword in his hand. Sir Bertrand undauntedly sprung forwards; and aiming a fierce blow at the figure, it instantly vanished, letting fall a massy iron key. The flame now rested upon a pair of ample folding doors at the end of the gallery. Sir Bertrand went up to it, and applied the key to a brazen lock – with difficulty he turned the bolt – instantly the doors flew open, and discovered a large apartment, at the end of which was a coffin rested upon a bier, with a taper burning on each side of it. Along the room on both sides were gigantic statues of black marble, attired in the Moorish habit, and holding enormous sabres in their right hands. Each of them reared his arm, and advanced one leg forwards, as the knight entered; at the same moment the lid of the coffin flew open, and the bell tolled. The flame still glided forwards, and Sir Bertrand resolutely followed, till he arrived within six paces of the coffin. Suddenly, a lady in a shrowd and black veil rose up in it, and stretched out her arms towards him – at the same time the statues clashed their sabres and advanced. Sir Bertrand flew to the lady and clasped her in his arms – she threw up her veil and kissed his lips; and instantly the whole building shook as with an earthquake, and fell asunder with a horrible crash. Sir Bertrand was thrown into a sudden trance, and on recovering, found himself seated on a velvet sofa, in the most magnificent room he had ever seen, lighted with innumerable tapers, in lustres of pure crystal. A sumptuous banquet was set in the middle. The doors opening to soft music, a lady of incomparable beauty, attired with amazing splendor entered, surrounded by a troop of gay nymphs more fair than the Graces – She advanced to the knight, and falling on her knees thanked him as her deliverer. The nymphs placed a garland of laurel upon his head, and the lady led him by the hand to the banquet, and sat beside him. The nymphs placed themselves at the table, and a numerous train of servants entering, served up the feast; delicious music playing all the time. Sir Bertrand could not speak for astonishment – he could only return their honours by courteous looks and gestures. After the banquet was finished, all retired but the lady, who leading back the knight to the sofa, addressed him in these words:—

3.9 Clara Reeve (1729–1807), Preface to *The Old English Baron: A Gothic Story* (1778)

The first edition was published in 1777, with the title *The Champion of Virtue: A Gothic Story*. Reeve in the Preface to her novel makes clear that she is deliberately following Walpole's lead. She uses the subtitle 'A Gothic Story' as Walpole did in his second edition of *The Castle of Otranto*. However she also announces some modifications; the marvellous, in her tale, will be brought, 'within the utmost *verge* of possibility', and the moral tendency will be made more explicit. This was an attempt to reconcile Gothic romance with the demands of contemporary criticism, and proved to be very successful. Walpole's response in letters to friends was, however, scathing: 'Have you seen *The Old English Baron*, a Gothic story, professedly written in imitation of *Otranto*, but reduced to reason and probability! It is so probable, that any trial for murder at the old Bailey would make a more interesting story.'

Source: Clara Reeve (1967), *The Old English Baron: A Gothic Story*, Oxford: Oxford University Press, pp. 1–6.

★

As this Story is of a species which, tho' not new, is out of the common track, it has been thought necessary to point out some circumstances to the reader, which will elucidate the design, and it is hoped, will induce him to form a favourable, as well as a right judgment of the work before him.

This Story is the literary offspring of the Castle of Otranto, written upon the same plan, with a design to unite the most attractive and interesting circumstances of the ancient Romance and modern Novel, at the same time it assumes a character and manner of its own, that differed from both; it is distinguished by the appellation of a Gothic Story, being a picture of Gothic times and manners. Fictitious Stories have been the delight of all times and all countries, by oral tradition in barbarous, by writing in more civilized ones; and altho' some persons of wit and learning have condemned them indiscriminately, I would venture to affirm, that even those who so much affect to despise them under one form, will receive and embrace them under another.

Thus, for instance, a man shall admire and almost adore the Epic poems of the Ancients, and yet despise and execrate the ancient Romances, which are only Epics in prose.

History represents human nature as it is in real life; – alas, too often a melancholy retrospect! – Romance displays only the amiable side of the picture; it shews the pleasing features, and throws a veil over the blemishes: Mankind are naturally pleased with what gratifies their vanity; and vanity, like all other passions of the human heart, may be rendered subservient to good and useful purposes.

I confess that it may be abused, and become an instrument to corrupt the manners and morals of mankind; so may poetry, so may plays, so may every kind of composition; but that will prove nothing more than the old saying lately revived by the philosophers the most in fashion, 'that every earthly thing has two handles.'

The business of Romance is, first, to excite the attention; and, secondly, to direct it to some useful, or at least innocent, end; Happy the writer who attains both these points, like Richardson! and not unfortunate, or undeserving praise, he who gains only the latter, and furnishes out an entertainment for the reader!

Having, in some degree, opened by design, I beg leave to conduct my reader back again, till he comes within view of the Castle of Otranto; a work which, as already has been observed, is an attempt to unite the verious merits and graces of the ancient Romance and modern Novel. To attain this end, there is required a sufficient degree of the marvellous, to excite the attention; enough of the manners of real life, to give an air of probability to the work; and enough of the pathetic, to engage the heart in its behalf.

The book we have mentioned is excellent in the two last points, but has a redundancy in the first; the opening excites the attention very strongly; the conduct of the story is artful and judicious; the characters are admirably drawn and supported; the diction polished and elegant; yet, with all these brilliant advantages, it palls upon the mind (though it does not upon the ear); and the reason is obvious, the machinery is so violent, that it destroys the effect it is intended to excite. Had the story been kept within the utmost *verge* of probability, the effect had been preserved, without losing the least circumstance that excites or detains attention.

For instance; we can conceive, and allow of, the appearance of a ghost; we can even dispense with an enchanted sword and helmet; but then they must keep within limits of credibility: A sword so large as to require an hundred men to lift it; a helmet that by its own weight forces a passage through a court-yard into an arched vault, big enough for a man to go through; a picture that walks out of its frame; a skeleton ghost in a hermit's cowl: – When your expectation is wound up to the highest pitch, these circumstances take it down with a witness, destroy the work of imagination, and, instead of attention, excite laughter. I was both surprised and vexed to find the enchantment dissolved, which I wished might continue to the end of the book; and several of its readers have confessed the same disappointment to me: The beauties are so numerous, that we cannot bear the defects, but want it to be perfect in all respects.

In the course of my observations upon this singular book, it seemed to me that it was possible to compose a work upon the same plan, wherein these defects might be avoided; and the *keeping*, as in *painting*, might be preserved.

But then I began to fear it might happen to me as to certain translators, and imitators of Shakespeare; the unities may be preserved, while the spirit is evaporated. However, I ventured to attempt it; I read the beginning to a circle of friends of approved judgment, and by their approbation was encouraged to proceed, and to finish it.

By the advice of the same friends I printed the first Edition in the country, where it circulated chiefly, very few copies being sent to London, and being thus encouraged, I have determined to offer a second Edition to that public which has so often rewarded the efforts of those, who have endeavoured to contribute to its entertainment.

The work has lately undergone a revision and correction, the former Edition being very incorrect; and by the earnest solicitation of several friends, for whose judgment I have the greatest deference, I have consented to a change of the title from the *Champion of Virtue* to the *Old English Baron*: – as that character is thought to be the principal one in the story.

I have also been prevailed upon, though with extreme reluctance, to suffer my name to appear in the title-page; and I do now, with the utmost respect and diffidence, submit the whole to the candour of the Public.

3.10 Henry Mackenzie (1745–1831), 'Account of the German theatre' (1790)

Die Räuber (1781) by Johann Christoph Friedrich von Schiller, was one of the key texts to emerge from the 'Sturm und Drang' ('Storm and Stress') movement in German literature, to which Goethe and Herder also contributed from the 1770s. Mackenzie's is probably the earliest British response, and his account of the play's impact on young minds was confirmed when an English translation, *The Robbers*, appeared in 1792. Coleridge, then a student at Cambridge, wrote in a letter:

> My God! Southey! Who is this Schiller? This Convulsor of the Heart? Did he write his Tragedy amid the yelling of Fiends? – I should not like to [be] able to describe such Characters – I tremble like an Aspen Leaf – Upon my Soul, I write to you because I am frightened . . . Why have we ever called Milton sublime?

A rash of translations from the German in the early 1790s, including Schiller's novella *The Ghost-Seer* (first published 1789, translated 1795), had a decisive impact on the development of Gothic fiction in Britain. Its perceived political influence can also be measured by the appearance of a burlesque in *The Anti-Jacobin Review* (see 5.11).

Source: Henry Mackenzie (1790), *Transactions of the Royal Society of Edinburgh*, vol. II, pp. 191–2.

★

. . . I have ventured this long and particular account of the tragedy in question, because it appears to me one of the most uncommon productions of untutored genius that modern times can boast. Confessedly irregular and faulty, both in plan and conduct, it were needless, and perhaps unfair, to offer any remarks on its defects. But its power over the heart and the imagination must be acknowledged. Every body has heard the anecdote of its effects on the scholars at the school of *Fribourg*, where it was represented soon after its first appearance. They were so struck and captivated with the grandeur of the character of its hero *Moor*, that they agreed to form a band like his in the forests of Bohemia, had elected a young nobleman for their chief, and had pitched on a beautiful young lady for his *Amelia*, whom they were to carry off from her parents house, to accompany their flight. To the accomplishment of this design, they had bound themselves by the most solemn and tremendous oaths; but the conspiracy was discovered by an accident, and its execution prevented.

The energy of this tragedy's effect is not to be wondered at, especially on young minds, whose imaginations are readily inflamed by the enthusiasm of gigantic enterprise and desperate valour, whose sensibility is easily excited by the sufferings of a great unhappy mind, and who feel a sort of dignity and pride in leaving the beaten road of worldly prudence, though the path by which they leave it may sometimes deviate from moral rectitude. But hence, to some parts of an audience, the danger of a drama such as this. It covers the natural deformity of criminal actions with the veil of high sentiment and virtuous feeling, and thus separates (if I may be pardoned the expression) the *moral sense* from that morality which it ought to produce. This the author has, since its first publication, been candid enough to acknowledge, and reprobates, in terms perhaps more strong that it deserves, his own production as of a very pernicious tendency. He has left his native country, *Wirtemberg*, from which I believe indeed some consequences of the publication of this tragedy had driven him, and now lives at *Manheim*, where he publishes a periodical work, and has written one or two other tragedies, which have a high reputation. If his genius can accommodate itself to better subjects, and to a more regular conduct of the drama, no modern poet seems to possess powers so capable of bending the mind before him, of rousing its feelings by the elevation of his sentiments, or of thrilling them with the terrors of his imagination. . . .

3.11 Odes and the taste for terror

By the 1790s, the idea that terror, and specifically superstitious terror, could form the basis for a work of literature or art was familiar, if not universally accepted. The tentative arguments put forward in the odes of Joseph Warton and Collins (3.5) were made superfluous by the overwhelming strength of public demand. The poems in this section show a move towards gratuitous and unapologetic indulgence in emotion. They are, however, notably derivative in their catalogue of horrors. The interest lies in slight deviations from the tropes established by pre-romantic poets, as a register of response to political and cultural changes that together seemed to constitute a general reign of terror. It is only rarely that 'terror', 'horror' and 'fear' were distinguished and separately defined. Dennis at the beginning of the century (3.2) and Radcliffe at the end (3.14) are notable exceptions.

3.11a Robert Southey (1774–1843), 'To Horror' (1791)

Source: Robert Southey (1843), *The Poetical Works of Robert Southey*, 10 vols, London: Longman, Brown, Green and Longman, vol. II, pp. 129–31.

Τὶν γὰϱ ποτα εἴσομαι
  τὰν ϰαὶ σϰύλιϰες τϱομέσντι
Ἐϱχομέναν νεϰύων ἀγά τ' ὴϱιά, ϰαι μέλαν αἶμα.
Theocritus

Dark Horror! hear my call!
Stern Genius, hear from thy retreat
On some old sepulchre's moss-canker'd seat,
Beneath the Abbey's ivied wall
That trembles o'er its shade;
There wrapt in midnight gloom, alone,
Thou lovest to lie and hear
The roar of waters near,
And listen to the deep dull groan
Of some perturbed sprite
Borne fitful on the heavy gales of night.

Or whether o'er some wide waste hill
Thou see'st the traveller stray,
Bewilder'd on his lonely way,
When, loud and keen and chill,
The evening winds of winter blow,
Drifting deep the dismal snow
Or if thou followest now on Greenland's shore,
With all thy terrors, on the lonely way
Of some wreck'd mariner, where to the roar
Of herded bears, the floating ice-hills round
Return their echoing sound,
And by the dim drear Boreal light
Givest half his dangers to the wretch's sight.

Or if thy fury form,
When o'er the midnight deep
The dark-wing'd tempests sweep,
Beholds from some high cliff the increasing storm,
Watching with strange delight,
As the black billows to the thunder rave,
When by the lightning's light
Thou see'st the tall ship sink beneath the wave.

Bear me in spirit where the field of fight
Scatters contagion on the tainted gale,
When, to the Moon's faint beam,
On many a carcase shine the dews of night,
And a dead silence stills the vale,
Save when at times is heard the glutted Raven's scream.

Where some wreck'd army from the Conqueror's might
Speed their disastrous flight,
With thee, fierce Genius! let me trace their way,
And hear at times the deep heart-groan
Of some poor sufferer left to die alone;
And we will pause, where, on the wild,
The mother to her breast,
On the heap'd snows reclining, clasps her child,
Not to be pitied now, for both are now at rest.

Black HORROR! speed we to the bed of Death,
Where one who wide and far
Hath sent abroad the myriad plagues of war
Struggles with his last breath;
Then to his wildly-starting eyes
The spectres of the slaughter'd rise;
Then on his phrensied ear
Their calls for vengeance and the Demons' yell
In one heart-maddening chorus swell;
Cold on his brow convulsing stands the dew,
And night eternal darkens on his view.

HORROR! I call thee yet once more!
Bear me to that accursed shore,
Where on the stake the Negro writhes.
Assume thy sacred terrors then! dispense
The gales of Pestilence!
Arouse the opprest; teach them to know their power;
Lead them to vengeance! and in that dread hour
When ruin rages wide,
I will behold and smile by MERCY's side.

3.11b Stephen Hole (1746–1803), 'Ode to Terror' (1792)

Source: Rev. Richard Polwhele, ed. (1792), *Poems, Chiefly By Gentlemen of Devonshire and Cornwall*, Bath: Cadell et al., pp. 95–100.

★

Around me night and silence reign –
My beating breast
Seems with some huge weight opprest,
And strives to shake it off in vain.
Oh, let me close my orbs of sight,
And in my bosom check the panting breath!
Encircled by the shades of night,
Let me here unnotic'd rest!
And yet, as if the hand of death
Lay heavy on me, moisture cold bedews
My shivering limbs: and fancy views
Scenes of unknown terrors rise.
Advancing footsteps strike my ear;
Low-murmurs in the forest sound:
The rustling leaves are strew'd around.
Reluctant, yet compell'd by fear,
I ope my anxious eyes.

Now wildly through the extended plain,
With the moon's mild light array'd,
I gaze – yet all dismay'd,
Would fain, but dare not close their lids again.
See through the path in yonder grove,
Silent and slow a phantom move!
Pale grief is on his brow imprest,
And darkly down his snow-white vest
From his gor'd bosom sanguine streams descend.
He stops, he turns, on me he bends his view,
His course unknown he waves me to pursue –
Oh, let me hence my tottering footsteps bend!
Alas! in vain I seek to fly,
My powerless limbs their aid deny;
And fear, that gave the spectre birth,
Rivets me motionless to earth.

Let me shake off this causeless dread:
Let me my fortitude resume!

In vain – for at this awful hour,
Bursting the cearments of the tomb,
Ascend the spirits of the dead,
And roam thro' night compell'd by magic's wond'rous power.
This is the time, when o'er the corse
Festering in death, with accents hoarse
The raven croaks, or beats with ominous wings
The murderer's window – at the sound
Trembling he starts, he glares around,
And feels the thrilling pangs of guilt's infixed stings.

This is the time, waiting their destin'd prey,
And shunning day's detecting eye,
In covert hid unpitying ruffians lie.
To his lov'd home the traveller bends his way,
That home he never more shall view!
At once up starts the savage crew;
By earthly fiends inclos'd he stands:
For mercy at their feet he bends;
He lifts his pleading eyes;
In anguish clasps his hands;
Conjures them by his dear domestic ties –
But lo! the ruthless sword descends:
Cold in his breast he feels
The deadly point: he feebly reels
Forth bursts the vital stream, he gasps, he dies.

Hark, loudly-echoing through the glade,
Shrieks of distress my ears invade:
Nearer and nearer rolls the sound –
Like thee, poor wretch, 'twill soon be mine,
This transient being to resign:
I feel, I feel the life-bereaving wound.
My soul within me sinks dismay'd!
My pity, hapless man! was thine,
But oh, I could not, durst not give thee aid!

Illusions fly! the peaceful power
Of silence reigns o'er hills, o'er dale, and bower:
An awful stillness that my soul affrights –
For now on yon drear heath,
Hags profane, and hell-born sprights,
Plan schemes of future woe, and scenes of death.

Muttering slowly spells profound,
In mystic circle round and round
The necromantic fire they go,
Kindled from the realms below.
Now dusky flames ascend the skies,
As 'mid the blaze they charms unhallow'd throw.

Now they vanish from my sight –
Mingling with the shades of night,
On yonder sable cloud they fly,
And urge the wrathful tempest through the sky.
They bid its wings of darkness sweep
The surging billows – wide around
They foam, they roar; the rocks rebound.
The anxious Pilot's art is vain:
Down to the unfathom'd deep
The vessel sinks, and o'er it boils the main.
Now, horror-proof, with deadly aim,
While the moon, trembling at the sight,
Veils her silver front in night,
They wing the lightning's shafts of flame
Through sable clouds disparting wide;
Spread ruin through the peaceful plains,
And fire the cots of lowly swains;
And sink to dust the castle's towering pride.
Protect me, save me! whence was driven
That beam which shot athwart the heaven? –
It gave a dreadful light –
Ah whence proceeds this sudden gloom,
Dark as the mansions of the tomb,
That clothes the brow of night?
My faultering tongue amazement chains,
And ice seems creeping through my veins.

Alas! ideal terrors have disjoin'd
My powers of reason, and unhing'd my mind.
'Twas but a Meteor's sudden glance: again
The moon, yon blackening cloud withdrawn,
Streams radiance o'er the dewy lawn,
And skirts the wood with light, and gild the distant plain.

Fell spectre of the haggard eye,
Wild gesture, and erected hair,
Quick from my presence fly!
Ease, ease awhile my heart opprest,

Lest, lost and woe-begone, Despair
Should seal me for her own,
And Reason, banish'd from her throne,
To Madness should resign my tortur'd breast.

Author's note: Some apology, possibly, ought to be made for the Dithyrambic measure adopted in these Odes. If the desultory nature of their subject, and abrupt transitions of the sentiment, (for each is supposed to be written under the immediate influence of the imagination) will not excuse it, no other plea, I fear, can be offered.

3.11c Nathaniel Howard (dates unknown), 'To Horror' (1804)

Source: Nathaniel Howard (1804), *Bickleigh Vale, With Other Poems*, London: Murray and Longman; York: Wilson & Spence, pp. 110–14.

★

Horror, tyrant of the throbbing breast.
Gray.[26]

Dread power! in realms of darkness nurst
'Midst shrieks of guilt, and groans accurst,
Where grins Despair in ghastly pain,
And rapturous Madness clanks his chain, . . .
THEE, I invoke! . . . Gay bowers, adieu!
Where Pleasure leads her bounding crew,
Blithe Health, and frolic Youth that roves
Thro' gardens and ambrosial groves,
Brisk Mirth, whose bright-expanding bloom
Ne'er felt the damp of Sorrow's gloom,
Adieu! the surly evening sheds
Deep shadows o'er the mountain-heads:
Low groan the refted mountain-heads:
Low groan the refted woodlands bleak,
The spirits of the cataract shriek! . . .
Horror! with strange, delightful fear
Lead my fit soul to deserts drear;
To church-yards, where hyenas roam,
And tear the body from the tomb;
To vast savannas full of dread;
Or, where vex'd Midnight never sleeps
Mid torrents hoarse and howling steeps!

Or, where the hoary ANDES shroud
Their stormy cliffs in many a cloud,
Which Danger, heedless of alarms,
Upclimbs with lightning-blasted arms!

To damp dark dungeons let me stray
Where the lone captive pines away;
Where no warm sun, no summer gale
Sheds freshness on his visage pale:
There see him raise his wither'd head,
Deep groaning o'er his flinty bed,
Whilst ever-hopeless Silence lowers,
And, slow, slow lag the gloomy hours.

Stern, awful HORROR! thou canst tell
What pangs the mother's bosom swell,
When bare on distant rocks outcast
Her child's corse blisters to the blast,
Alone, unnotic'd; – while the surge
Hoarse-heaving, moans the mournful dirge!

In sullen silence thou hast sought
Black groves, with dark collected thought,
Where erst the Druids met thy view,
And human victims grimly slew!
Thou heard'st their death-denouncing cries,
They bled beneath thy savage eyes.

Oh! lay me oft at gloom of night
Where hags perform their direful rite;
And, wrapt in terrors, flash on high
Their livid lightning thwart the sky;
Or, on some victim's hated form
Dart the full fury of their storm!
. . . For lightnings shoot, and thunders roll,
Dear, and congenial to my soul.

3.11d Henry Kirke White (1785–1806), 'Ode to H. Fuseli, Esq., R.A., On Seeing Engravings from his Designs' (1807)

The poem was first published in 1807 in a posthumous collection of White's writings edited by his mentor, Robert Southey. Henry Fuseli (1741–1825), born in Switzerland but resident for many years in London, created a sensation in 1781 with his painting *The Nightmare,* and went on to illustrate many of the more macabre or awe-inspiring scenes from Shakespeare and Milton.

Source: Henry Kirke White [1907] *Poems, Letters and Prose Fragments of Kirke White,* ed. John Drinkwater, London: Routledge, pp. 64–7.

★

Mighty magician! who on Torneo's brow,
When sullen tempests wrap the throne of night,
Art wont to sit and catch the gleam of light,
That shoots athwart the gloom opaque below;
And listen to the distant death-shriek long
From lonely mariner foundering in the deep,
Which rises slowly up the rocky steep,
While the weird sisters weave the horrid song:
Or when along the liquid sky
Serenely chaunt the orbs on high,
Dost love to sit in musing trance,
And mark the northern meteor's dance,
(While far below the fitful oar
Flings its faint pauses on the steepy shore,)
And list the music of the breeze,
That sweeps by fits the bending seas;
And often bears with sudden swell
The shipwreck'd sailor's funeral knell,
By the spirits sung, who keep
Their night-watch on the treacherous deep,
And guide the wakeful helms-man's eye
To Helicé in northern sky:
And there upon the rock inclined
With mighty visions fill'st the mind,
Such as bound in magic spell
Him* who grasp'd the gates of Hell,
And bursting Pluto's dark domain,
Held to the day the terrors of his reign.

Genius of Horror and romantic awe,
Whose eye explores the secrets of the deep,
Whose power can bid the rebel fluids creep,
Can force the inmost soul to own its law;
Who shall now, sublimest spirit,
Who shall now thy wand inherit,

* Dante.

From him* thy darling child who best
Thy shuddering images exprest?
Sullen of soul, and stern and proud,
His gloomy spirit spurn'd the crowd,
And now he lays his aching head
In the dark mansion of the silent dead.

Mighty magician! long thy wand has lain
Buried beneath the unfathomable deep;
And oh! forever must its efforts sleep,
May none the mystic sceptre e'er regain?
Oh yes, 'tis his! – Thy other son;
He throws thy dark-wrought tunic on,
Fuesslin waves thy wand, – again they rise,
Again thy wildering forms salute our ravish'd eyes,
Him didst thou cradle on the dizzy steep
Where round his head the volley'd lightnings flung,
And the loud winds that round his pillow rung,
Wooed the stern infant to the arms of sleep.
Or on the highest top of Teneriffe
Seated the fearless boy, and bade him look
Where far below the weather-beaten skiff
On the gulf bottom of the ocean strook.
Thou mark'dst him drink with ruthless ear
The death-sob, and, disdaining rest,
Thou saw'st how danger fired his breast,
And in his young hand couch'd the visionary spear.
Then, Superstition, at thy call,
She bore the boy to Odin's Hall,
And set before his awe-struck sight
The savage feast and spectred fight;
And summon'd from his mountain tomb
The ghastly warrior son of gloom,
His fabled Runic rhymes to sing,
While fierce Hresvelger flapp'd his wing;
Thou show'dst the trains the shepherd sees,
Laid on the stormy Hebrides,
Which on the mists of evening gleam,
Or crowd the foaming desert stream;
Lastly her storied hand she waves,
And lays him in Florentian caves;
There milder fables, lovelier themes,
Enwrap his soul in heavenly dreams,

* Ibid.

There Pity's lute arrests his ear,
And draws the half-reluctant tear;
And now at noon of night he roves
Along the embowering moonlight groves,
And as from many a cavern'd dell
The hollow wind is heard to swell,
He thinks some troubled spirit sighs;
And as upon the turf he lies
Where sleeps the silent beam of night,
He sees below the gliding sprite,
And hears in Fancy's organs sound
Aërial music warbling round.

Taste lastly comes and smooths the whole,
And breathes her polish o'er his soul;
Glowing with wild, yet chasten'd heat,
The wonderous work is now complete.

The Poet dreams: – The shadow flies,
And fainting fast its image dies.
But lo! the Painter's magic force
Arrests the phantom's fleeting course;
It lives – it lives – the canvass glows,
And tenfold vigour o'er it flows.
The Bard beholds the work achieved,
And as he sees the shadow rise,
Sublime before his wondering eyes,
Starts at the image his own mind conceived.

3.12 Gottfried August Bürger (1747–94), *Lenore* (1796)

Bürger took his inspiration from the ballad tradition of the ghostly lover returned to redeem a love vow; 'Sweet William's Ghost' from Percy's *Reliques* is an obvious precursor (see Ehrenpreis, 1966, 67 and 1.4). However, like 'Alonzo the Brave and the Fair Imogine' which appeared in Lewis's *The Monk* in the same year, *Lenore* exceeded the effects of the old ballads with its gruesome detail, driving rhythm and sensational climax. British readers received it with wild enthusiasm as something wholly original and extraordinary. No fewer than five translations appeared in 1796, and this rivalry helped to ensure that the poem was constantly discussed. The version included here, by William Taylor of Norwich (1765–1836), was written in 1790 under the title 'Lenora' (later changed to 'Ellenore') and had circulated for some time in manuscript. It was the first to appear and was generally agreed to be the finest: Charles Lamb wrote of it to Coleridge, 'Have you read a ballad called "Leonora" in the second number of the "Monthly Magazine"? If you have!!!!!!!!!!!!!!' The young Walter Scott was among the translators, despite knowing very little German. His version, 'William and Helen', was produced in one night in a white heat of enthusiasm. It was to be his first publication, and was later included in 'Monk' Lewis's anthology *Tales of Wonder* (1801).

Source: Anne Henry Ehrenpreis, ed. (1966), *The Literary Ballad*, London: Edward Arnold, pp. 67–76.

At break of day from frightful dreams
  Upstarted Ellenore:
My William, art thou slayn, she sayde,
  Or dost thou love no more?

He went abroade with Richard's host[27]
  The paynim[28] foes to quell;
But he no word to her had writt,
  An[29] he were sick or well.

With blore[30] of trump and thump of drum
  His fellow-soldyers come,
Their helms bedeckt with oaken boughs,
  They seeke their long'd-for home.

And evry road and evry lane
  Was full of old and young
To gaze at the rejoycing band,
  To haile with gladsom toung.

'Thank God!' their wives and children sayde,
  'Welcome!' the brides did saye;
But grief or kiss gave Ellenore
  To none upon that daye.

And when the soldyers all were bye,
  She tore her raven hair,
And cast herself upon the growne,
  In furious despair.

Her mother ran and lyfte her up,
  And clasped her in her arm,
'My child, my child, what dost thou ail?
  God shield thy life from harm!'

'Oh mother, mother! William's gone
  What's all besyde to me?
There is no mercie, sure, above!
  All, all were spar'd but he!'

'Kneele downe, thy paternoster saye,
  'T will calm thy troubled spright:
The Lord is wise, the Lord is good;
  What He hath done is right.'

'O mother, mother! saye no so;
  Most cruel is my fate:
I prayde, and prayde; but watte avaylde?
  'T is now, alas! too late.'

'Our Heavenly Father, if we praye,
  Will help a suffring child:
Go take the holy sacrament;
  So shall thy grief grow mild.'

'O mother, what I feele within,
  No sacrament can staye;
No sacrament can teche the dead
  To bear the sight of daye.'

'May-be, among the heathen folk
  Thy William false doth prove,
And put away his faith and troth,
  And take another love.

'Then wherefor sorrowe for his loss?
  Thy moans are all in vain:
But when his soul and body parte,
  His falsehoode brings him pain.'

'Oh mother, mother! gone is gone:
  My hope is all forlorn;
The grave my only safeguard is –
  O had I ne'er been born!

'Go out, go out, my lamp of life;
  In grizely darkness die:
There is no mercie, sure, above.
  Forever let me lie.'

'Almighty God! O do not judge
  My poor unhappy child;
She knows not what her lips pronounce,
  Her anguish makes her wild.

'My girl, forget thine earthly woe,
  And think on God and bliss;
For so, at least shall not thy soul
  Its heavenly bridegroom miss.'

'O mother, mother! what is bliss,
  And what the fiendis cell?
With him 'tis heaven any where,
  Without my William, hell.

'Go out, go out, my lamp of life,
  In endless darkeness die:
Without him I must loathe the earth,
  Without him scorn the skie.'

And so despair did rave and rage
  Athwarte her boiling veins;
Against the Providence of God
  She hurlde her impious strains.

She bet her breast, and wrung her hands,
  And rollde her tearless eye,
From rise of morn, til the pale stars
  Again orespread the skye.

When harke! abroade she herde the tramp
  Of nimble-hoofed steed;
She herde a knight with clank alighte,
  And climbe the stair in speed.

And soon she herde a tinkling hand,
  That twirled at the pin;[31]
And thro her door, that opened not,
  These words were breathed in.

'What ho! what ho! thy door undo;
  Art watching or asleepe?
My love, dost yet remember me,
  And dost thou laugh or weepe?'

'Ah! William here so late at night!
  Oh! I have wachte and wak'd:
Whense art thou come? For thy return
  My heart has sorely ak'd.'

'At midnight only we may ride;
  I come ore land and see:
I mounted late, but soone I go;
  Aryse, and come with mee.'

'O William, enter first my bowre,
  And give me one embrace:
The blasts athwarte the hawthorn hiss;
  Awayte a little space.'

'Tho blasts athwarte the hawthorn hiss,
  I may not harbour here;
My spurs are sett, my courser pawes,
  My hour of flight is nere.

'All as thou lyest upon thy couch,
  Aryse, and mount behinde;
To-night we'le ride a thousand miles,
  The bridal bed to finde.'

'How, ride to-night a thousand miles?
  Thy love dost bemock:
Eleven is the stroke that still
  Rings on within the clock.'

'Looke up; the moon is bright, and we
  Outstride the earthly men:
I'le take thee to the bridal bed,
  And night shall end but then.'

'And where is then thy house, and home,
  And bridal bed so meet?'
''Tis narrow, silent, chilly, low,
  Six planks, one shrouding sheet.'

'And is there any room for me,
  Wherein that I may creepe?'
'There's room enough for thee and me,
  Wherein that we may sleepe.

'All as thou lyest upon thy couch,
  Aryse, no longer stop;
The wedding-guests thy coming wayte,
  The chamber-door is ope.'

All in her sarke,[32] as there she lay,
  Upon his horse she sprung;
And with her lily hands so pale
  About her William clung.

And hurry-skurry off they go,
  Unheeding wet or dry;
And horse and rider snort and blow,
  And sparkling pebbles fly.

How swift the flood, the mead, the wood,
  Aright, aleft, are gone!
The bridges thunder as they pass,
  But earthly sowne[33] is none.

Tramp, tramp, across the land they speede;
  Splash, splash, across the see:
'Hurrah! the dead can ride apace;
  Dost fear to ride with me?

'The moon is bright, and blue the night;
  Dost quake the blast to stem?
Dost shudder, mayd, to seeke the dead?'
  'No, no, but what of them?'

Now glumly sownes yon dirgy song!
  Night-ravens flappe the wing.
What knell doth slowly tolle ding dong?
  The psalms of death who sing?

Forth creeps a swarthy funeral train,
  A corse is on the biere;
Like croke of todes from lonely moores,
  The chauntings meete the eere.

'Go, beare her corse when midnight's past,
  With song, and tear, and wail;
I've gott my wife, I take her home,
  My hour of wedlock hail!

'Leade forth, O clark, the chaunting quire,
  To swell our spousal-song:
Come, preest, and reade the blessing soone;
  For our dark bed we long.'

The bier is gon, the dirges hush;
  His bidding all obaye,
And headlong rush thro briar and bush,
  Beside his speedy waye.

Halloo! halloo! how swift they go,
  Unheeding wet or dry;
And horse and rider snort and blow,
  And sparkling pebbles fly.

How swift the hill, how swift the dale,
  Aright, aleft, are gon!
By hedge and tree, by thorp[34] and town,
  They gallop, gallop on.

Tramp, tramp, across the land they speede;
  Splash, splash, across the see:
'Hurrah! the dead can ride apace;
  Dost feare to ride with mee?

'Look up, look up, an airy crew
  In roundel dances reele:
The moon is bright, and blue the night,
  Mayst dimly see them wheele.

'Come to, come to, ye ghostly crew,
  Come to, and follow me,
And daunce for us the wedding daunce,
  When we in bed shall be.'

And brush, brush, brush, the ghostly crew,
  Came wheeling ore their heads,
All rustling like the witherd leaves
  That wide the whirlwind spreads.

Halloo! halloo! away they go,
  Unheeding wet or dry;
And horse and rider snort and blow,
  And sparkling pebbles fly.

And all that in the moonshyne lay,
  Behind them fled afar;
And backward scudded overhead
  The skie and every star.

Tramp, tramp, across the land they speede;
  Splash, splash, across the see:
'Hurrah! the dead can ride apace;
  Dost fear to ride with mee?

'I weene the cock prepares to crowe;
  The sand will soone be run:
I snuffe the early morning air;
  Downe, downe! our work is done.

'The dead, the dead can ride apace:
  Our wed-bed here is fit:
Our race is ridde, our journey ore,
  Our endless union knit.'

And lo! an yron-grated gate
  Soon biggens[35] to their view:
He crackde his whyppe; the locks, the bolts,
  Cling, clang! asunder flew.

They passe, and 'twas on graves they trodde;
  ''Tis hither we are bound:'
And many a tombstone ghastly white
  Lay in the moonshyne round.

And when he from his steed alytte,
  His armure, black as cinder,
Did moulder, moulder all awaye,
  As were it made of tinder.

His head became a naked skull;
  Nor hair nor eyne[36] had he:
His body grew a skeleton,
  Whilome[37] so blithe of ble.[38]

And at his dry and boney heel
  No spur was left to bee;
And in his witherd hand you might
  The scythe and hour-glass see.

And lo! his steed did thin to smoke,
  And charnel-fires outbreathe;
And pal'd, and bleachde, then vanishde quite
  The mayd from underneathe.

And hollow howlings hung in air,
  And shrekes from vaults arose:
Then knewe the mayd she might no more
  Her living eyes unclose.

But onward to the judgment-seat,
  Thro' mist and moonlight dreare,
The ghostly crew their flight persewe,
  And hollowe in her eare:

'Be patient; tho thyne heart should breke,
  Arrayne not Heaven's decree;
Thou nowe art of thy bodie reft,
  Thy soul forgiven bee!'

3.13 Nathan Drake (1766–1836), essays 'On Gothic Superstition' and 'On Objects of Terror' (1798)

Drake followed the Aikins (3.8) in producing a miscellany of literary criticism accompanied by experimental fragments. Like them, he is particularly interested in the role of emotion in literature, discussing its relation to imagination, poetic genius and the response of the reader. In an essay, 'On the Government of the Imagination; on the Frenzy of Tasso and Collins', Drake regrets that the tendency towards passionate enthusiasm that characterises genius sometimes in the past led to insanity, but sees no danger in contemporary Gothic writing:

> In the present century, when science and literature have spread so extensively, the heavy clouds of superstition have been dispersed, and have assumed a lighter and less formidable hue; for though the tales of Walpole, Reeve and Radcliffe, or the poetry of Wieland, Bürger and Lewis, still powerfully arrest attention, and keep and ardent curiosity alive, yet is their machinery, by no means, an object of popular belief, nor can it, I should

> hope, now lead to dangerous credulity, as when in the times of Tasso, Shakespeare, and even Milton, witches and wizards, spectres and fairies, were nearly as important subjects of faith as the most serious doctines of religion.

Drake is interesting as a pioneering commentator on the modern movement in terror fiction. In the two essays reproduced here, he develops the Aikins' distinction between effects of natural and supernatural terror, and reinforces the genealogy of 'enthusiastic' writers which had been evolving through the eighteenth century.

Source: Nathan Drake (1970), *Literary Hours, or Sketches Critical and Narrative,* 2 vols, facsimile of 2nd revd edn, 1800, New York: Garland, vol. II, pp. 137–49, 353–62.

★

No. VIII. On Gothic Superstition

> *There would he dream of graves, and corses pale;*
> *And ghosts, that to the charnel-dungeon throng,*
> *And drag a length of clanking chain, and wail,*
> *Till silenc'd by the owl's terrific song,*
> *Or blasts that shriek by fits the shuddering isles along. –*
>
> *Anon in view a portal's blazon'd arch*
> *Arose; the trumpet bids the valves unfold;*
> *And forth an host of little warriors march,*
> *Grasping the diamond lance, and targe of gold:*
> *Their look was gentle, their demeanor bold,*
> *And green their helms, and green their silk attire;*
> *And here and there, right venerably old,*
> *The long rob'd minstrels wake the warbling wire,*
> *And some with mellow breath the martial pipe inspire.*
>
> BEATTIE.[39]

Of the various kinds of superstition which have in any age influenced the human mind, none appear to have operated with so much effect as what has been termed the Gothic. Even in the present polished period of society, there are thousands who are yet alive to all the horrors of witchcraft, to all the solemn and terrible graces of the appalling spectre. The most enlightened mind, the mind free from all taint of superstition, involuntarily acknowledges the power of gothic agency; and the late favourable reception which two or three publications in this style have met with, is a convincing proof of the assertion. The enchanted forest of Tasso, the spectre of Camöens, and the apparitions of Shakspeare, are to this day highly pleasing, striking, and sublime features in these delightful compositions. –

And although this kind of superstition be able to arrest every faculty of the human mind, and to shake, as it were, all nature with horror, yet does it also delight in the most sportive and elegant imagery. The traditionary tales of elves and fairies still convey to a warm imagination an inexhausted source of invention, supplying all those wild, romantic, and varied ideas with which a wayward fancy loves to sport. The Provençal bards, and the neglected Chaucer and Spenser, are the originals from whence this exquisite species of fabling has been drawn, improved, and applied with so much inventive elegance by Shakspeare. The flower and the leaf of Chaucer is replete with the most luxuriant description of these praeternatural beings. –

The vulgar gothic therefore, an epithet here adopted to distinguish it from the regular mythology of the Edda,[40] turns chiefly on the awful ministrations of the spectre, or the innocent gambols of the Fairy, the former, perhaps, partly derived from Platonic Christianity, the latter from the fictions of the East, as imported into Europe during the period of the Crusades; but whatever be its derivation, it is certainly a mode of superstition so assimilated with the universal apprehension of superior agency, that few minds have been altogether able to shake it off. Even to Philosophy admitting of the doctrine of immaterialism, it becomes no easy task consistently to deny the possibility of such an interference. Whilst it therefore gives considerable latitude to the imagination, it seems to possess more rationality than almost any other species of fabling; for confined by no adherence to any regular mythological system, but depending merely upon the possible, and to some highly probable, visitation of immaterial agents, it has even in the present metaphysical period still retained such a degree of credit as yet to render it an important and impressive machine beneath the guidance of genuine poesy. It to those who have paid the most subtile attention to the existence and relative action of matter and spirit, it becomes a subject of doubt to deny the visible operation of spirit, surely in the bosom of the million it must still preserve some portion of influence, and as, if such an agency exist, its laws and direction must be to us altogether unknown, it furnishes, if not the probable, at least the possible, at all times a sufficient basis, for the airy structure of the poet. –

It is remote from every wish of the Author to encourage any superstition that may render his fellow creatures alive to unnecessary and puerile terror, but allowing the existence and occasionally the visible exertion of spirit upon matter, with the wise and with the good no painful emotion can arise, and if one more pang be added to the struggles of conscious guilt, the world, he should imagine, would be no sufferer; but it is here only as furnishing fit materials for poetical composition that a wish for preserving such a source of imagery is expressed. When well conducted, a grateful astonishment, a welcome sensation of fear, will alike creep through the bosom of the Sage and the Savage, and it is, perhaps, to the introduction of such well-imagined agency, or when not introduced upon the scene, to a very frequent allusion to it, that Shakspeare, beyond any other poet, owes the capability of raising the most awful, yet the most delightful species of terror. No poet, adopting a machinery of a similar kind, has wielded it with equal effect. Among the Italians it is too frequently addressed solely to the imagination, Ariosto in general, and Tasso sometimes, descending to all the extravaganza of oriental fiction; conducted, as by Shakspeare, it powerfully moves the strongest passions of the heart. –

Next to the Gothic in point of sublimity and imagination comes the Celtic, which, if the superstition of the Lowlands be esteemed a part of it, may with equal propriety, be divided into the terrible and the sportive; the former, as displayed in the poems of Ossian; the latter, in the songs and ballads of the Low Country. This superstition, like the gothic, has the same happy facility of blending its ideas with the common apprehensions of mankind; it does not, like most mythological systems, involve every species of absurdity, but, floating loose upon the mind, founds its imagery upon a metaphysical possibility, upon the apppearance of superior, or departed beings. Ossian has, however, opened a new field for invention, he has given fresh colouring to his supernatural agents, he has given them employments new to gothic fiction: his ghosts are not the ghosts of Shakspeare, yet are they equally solemn and striking. The abrupt and rapid fervour of imagination, the vivid touches of enthusiasm, mark his composition, and his spectres rush upon the eye with all the stupendous vigour of wild and momentary creation. So deep and uniform a melancholy pervades the poetry of this author, that, whether from natural disposition, or the pressure of misfortune, from the face of the country which he inhabited, or the insulated state of society, he seems ever to have avoided imagery of a light and airy kind; otherwise, from the originality of his genius, much in this way might have been expected. As to the superstition of the Lowlands, it differs so little from the lighter gothic, that I am not warranted in drawing any distinction between them. It is not, however, peculiar to this district of Scotland, the Highlanders in many parts, especially in their beautiful little vales, being still enthusiastic in their belief of it. –

And here may I be pardoned if I offer a few strictures upon the dress which the British Ossian has assumed. Greatly as I admire the pathos and sublime imagery of this Bard of other times, I cannot but regret the style in which Mr. Macpherson has chosen to clothe him. A stiffness the most rigid, a monotony the most tedious, are its general characteristics, and were it not for the very powerful appeals to the heart and imagination few readers would be tempted to a second perusal. That Dr. Blair, however, a Critic of acknowledged taste and judgment,[41] that he should approve of this mode of composition, nay, should prefer it to any species of versification, is, to me, still more extraordinary; nor can I any way account for such a remarkable, and as I should hope almost insulated, opinion, for in other instances, the perfect judge of melody and rhythm in english poetry, is apparent. How had the pathos and sublimity of Ossian been heightened, how mingled with every variety of harmony and rhythmical cadence, had the versification of Cowper and Milton been adopted. Mr. Macpherson has termed his translation a literal one, but if really built upon oral tradition, upon a species of legendary poesy sang and set to music in a manner calculated to assist the memory, how monstrously must it have deviated from the original; had it been his wish to have given us a faithful copy of these interesting fictions, the ballad stanza would, perhaps have afforded the choicest vehicle, but if ambitious of founding a structure of his own on these tales, the boundless variety of blank verse would surely have done more justice to his conceptions; they certainly merit a better style, and when this desideratum is obtained I shall not hesitate in placing Ossian (whether of ancient or modern production is to me perfectly indifferent) on the same shelf with Homer, Shakspeare, and Milton. –

But to return. – These are then (the vulgar gothic and the Celtic) the only two species of superstition which are still likely to retain their ground; founded chiefly on the casual interference of immaterial beings, and therefore easily combining with the common feelings of humanity, they may yet with propriety decorate the pages of the poet, when the full-formed system of mythology, will be rejected as involving too much fiction. Some attempts, however, have been lately made to revive the Scandinavian or Islandic mythology, and the sublime effusions of Gray and Sayers have thrown a magic lustre round the daring creations of the Edda. That they will ever become popular must, I should imagine, be a matter of considerable doubt, but these authors have written for the few, for the lovers of genuine poetry, and with their suffrage they will certainly be contented.

It has been however too much the fashion among critical writers to condemn the introduction of any kind of supernatural agency although perfectly consonant with the common feelings of mankind; and the simple, yet powerful superstitions recommended to the poet in this paper, seem to bid fair for sharing the fate of more complex systems: but whilst they are thus formed to influence the people, to surprise, elevate, and delight, with a willing admiration, every faculty of the human mind, how shall criticism with impunity dare to expunge them? Genius has ever had a predilection for such imagery, and I may venture, I think, to predict, that if at any time these romantic legends be totally laid aside, our national poetry will degenerate into mere morality, criticism, and satire; and that the sublime, the terrible, and the fanciful in poetry, will no longer exist. The recent publication of Mr. Hole's Arthur has, indeed, called the attention of the public to many of these fertile sources of invention, but although the work has great merit, it is confessedly built too much upon the Italian mode of fabling; the machinery is not sufficiently aweful to excite eager attention, and throughout the whole poem, perhaps, the heart is too little engaged. Imagery of this kind should not only awaken surprise, but, to leave a lasting impression, both pity and terror. Should Arthur, however, in a future edition be enlarged, and what enlargement may not a work of pure imagination admit of, a more frequent introduction of the pathetic would, most probably, seal it for immortality, for it is nevertheless

In scenes like these, which daring to depart
From sober truth, are still to nature true,
And call forth fresh delight to Fancy's view,
Th'heroic muse employ'd her Tasso's art!
How have I sat, when pip'd the pensive wind,
To hear his harp, by British Fairfax strung,
Prevailing poet, whose undoubting mind
Believ'd the magic wonders which he sung!
Hence at each sound imagination glows;
Hence his warm lay with softest sweetness flows;
Melting, it flows, pure, num'rous, strong and clear,
And fills th' impassion'd heart, and wins th' harmonious ear.
COLLINS[42]

Although so great a disparity evidently obtains between the two species of Gothic superstition, the terrible and the sportive; yet no author, that I am acquainted with, has, for narrative machinery, availed himself of this circumstance, and thrown them into immediate contrast. The beautiful fragment lately published by Mrs. Barbauld, under the title of Sir Bertrand, the transition is immediately from the deep Gothic to the Arabic or Saracenic superstition; which, although calculated to surprise, would have given more pleasure, perhaps, and would have rendered the preceding scenes of horror more striking, had it been of a light and contrasted kind. Struck, therefore, with the propriety of the attempt, and the exquisite beauty that would probably result from such an opposition of imagery, I have determined to devote a few papers to this design, and in the following Ode and Tale,[43] which are solely amenable to the tribunal of Fancy, much of both species of the vulgar gothic superstition is introduced. Entirely relinquished to the guidance of imagination the author has not only employed the possibilities of immaterial agency, but the more obsolete and preternatural terrors of witchcraft, and enchantment; the latter are, perhaps, except in some secluded parts of the country, nearly banished from the popular creed, but at the supposed period of our story, and for two centuries afterwards Witches were thought really to exist, and Spenser most probably drew from nature, having actually seen such a shed, the reputed abode of a witch, when he penned the following descriptive lines:

There in a gloomy hollowe glen she found
A little cottage build of stickes and reedes,
In homely wise, and wall'd with sods around,
In which a witch did dwell, in loathly weedes,
And wilfull want, all carelesse of her needes.
B.iii.cant.7.st.6.

At all events it was thought necessary to acquaint the reader with the machinery of the succeeding ode and tale, that provided he choose not to venture among their horrors, he may pass forward to scenes of a more tranquil nature.

No. XVII. On Terror

Objects of terror may with propriety be divided into those which owe their origin to the agency of super-human beings, and form a part of every system of mythology, and into those which depend upon natural causes and events for their production. In the essay on gothic superstition the former species has been noticed, and a tale presented to the reader whose chief circumstances are brought about through the influence of preternatural power; on the latter we shall now deliver a few observations, and terminate them with a fragment in which terror is attempted to be excited by the interference of simple material causation.[44]

Terror thus produced requires no small degree of skill and arrangement to prevent its operating more pain than pleasure. Unaccompanied by those mysterious incidents which indicate the ministration of beings mightier far than we, and which induce that thrilling sensation of mingled astonishment, apprehension and delight so irresistably captivating to the generality of mankind, it will be apt to create rather horror and disgust than the grateful emotion intended. To obviate this result, it is necessary either to interpose pictoresque description, or sublime and pathetic sentiment, or so to stimulate curiosity by the artful texture of the fable, or by the uncertain and suspended fate of an interesting personage, that the mind shall receive such a degree of artificial pleasure as may mitigate and subdue what, if naked of decoration and skilful accompaniment, would shock and appal every feeling heart.

A poem, a novel, or a picture may however, notwithstanding its accurate imitation of nature, and beauty of execution, unfold a scene so horrid, or so cruel, that the art of the painter or the poet is unable to render it communicative of the smallest pleasurable emotion. He who could fix, for instance, upon the following event as a fit subject for the canvas, was surely unaquainted with the chief purport of his art. 'A robber who had broken into a repository of the dead, in order to plunder a corse of some rich ornaments, is said to have been so affected with the hideous spectacle of mortality which presented itself when he opened the coffin, that he slunk away, trembling and weeping, without being able to execute his purpose.' 'I have met,' says Dr. Beattie, 'with an excellent print upon this subject; but was never able to look at it for half a minute together.'* In a collection of scotish ballads, pubished by Mr. Pinkerton, there is one termed *Edward*, which displays a scene which no poet, however great his talents, could render tolerable to any person of sensibility. A young man, his sword reeking with blood, rushes into the presence of his mother at whose suggestion he had the moment before destroyed his father. A short dialogue ensues which terminates by the son pouring upon this female fiend the curses of hell.† The *Mysterious Mother* also, a tragedy by the late celebrated Lord Orford[45] labours under an insuperable defect of this kind, The plot turns upon a mother's premeditated incest with her own son, a catastrophe productive only of horror and aversion, and for which the many well-written scenes introductory to this monstrous event cannot atone.

No efforts of genius on the other hand are so truly great as those which approaching the brink of horror, have yet, by the art of the poet or painter, by adjunctive and pictoresque embellishment, by pathetic, or sublime emotion, been rendered powerful in creating the most delightful and fascinating sensation. Shakspeare, if we dismiss what is now generally allowed not to be his, the wretched play of Titus Andronicus, has seldom, if ever, exceeded the bounds of salutary and grateful terror. Many strong instances of emotion of this kind unmingled with the wild fictions of superstition, yet productive of the highest interest, might, had we room for the insertion, be quoted from his drama, but perhaps the first specimen in the records of poetry is to be found in the works of an elder poet, in the *Inferno* of *Dante*.

A whole family perishing from hunger in a gloomy dungeon, would appear to partake too much of the *terrible* for either poetry or painting, yet has Dante, by the introduction of various pathetic touches rendered such a description the most striking, original and affecting scene perhaps in the world,[46] and *Sir Joshua Reynolds* by his celebrated picture of Ugolino, has shewn that, through the medium of exalted genius, it is equally adapted to the canvas. *Michael Angelo* too, an enthusiastic disciple of Dante, and possessing similar powers, has likewise executed a Bas-Relief on the subject . . .

* Beattie on Poetry and Music, p. 115.

† Select Scotish Ballads, vol. 1 p. 80.

[Drake cites at length Joseph Warton's translation of the scene from Dante in his 'Essay' on Pope.]

In the productions of Mrs. Radcliffe, the Shakspeare of Romance Writers, and who to the wild landscape of Salvator Rosa has added the softer graces of a Claude, may be found many scenes truly terrific in their conception, yet so softened down, and the mind so much relieved, by the intermixture of beautiful description, or pathetic incident, that the impression of the whole never becomes too strong, never degenerates into horror, but pleasurable emotion is ever the predominating result. In her last piece, termed *The Italian*, the attempt of Schedoni to assassinate the amiable and innocent Ellena whilst confined with Banditti in a lone house on the sea shore, is wrought up in so masterly a manner that every nerve vibrates with pity and terror, especially at the moment when about to plunge a dagger into her bosom he discovers her to be his daughter: every word, every action of the shocked and self-accusing Confessor, whose character is marked with traits almost superhuman, appal yet delight the reader, and it is difficult to ascertain whether ardent curiosity, intense commiseration, or apprehension that suspends almost the faculty of breathing, be, in the progress of this well-written story, most powerfully excited.

Smollet too, notwithstanding his peculiar propensity for burlesque and broad humour, has in his *Ferdinand Count Fathom*, painted a scene of natural terror with astonishing effect; with such vigour of imagination indeed, and minuteness of detail, that the blood runs cold, and the hair stands erect from the impression. The whole turns upon the Count, who is admitted during a tremendous storm, into a solitary cottage in a forest, discovering a body just murdered in the room where he is going to sleep, and the door of which, on endeavouring to escape, he finds fastened upon him.

The sublime Collins likewise, in his lyric pieces, exhibits much admirable imagery which forcibly calls forth the emotions of fear as arising from natural causes; the concluding lines of the following description of Danger make the reader absolutely shudder, and present a picture at once true to nature and full of originality.

> Danger, whose limbs of giant mold
> What mortal eye can fix'd behold?
> Who stalks his round, an hideous form!
> Howling amidst the midnight storm
> *Or throws him on the ridgy steep*
> *Of some loose hanging rock to sleep.**

The exquisite scotch ballad of *Hardyknute*, so happily compleated by Mr. Pinkerton, may be also mentioned as including several incidents which for genuine pathos, and for that species of terror now under consideration,

* Ode to Fear [see 3.5].

cannot easily be surpassed. The close of the first, and commencement of the second part are particularly striking. . . .

3.14 Ann Radcliffe (1764–1823), 'On the Supernatural in Poetry' (1826)

Radcliffe's final work of fiction, *Gaston de Blondeville*, was published posthumously in 1826. It had a framing prologue involving two contemporary travellers on their way by horseback to Kenilworth, who reveal in their conversation widely contrasting views on literature and imagination. This was first published separately in the *New Monthly Magazine*, as an independent essay in aesthetic theory. It suggests the continuing importance of Shakespeare, and contemporary methods of staging his plays, as an example for modern writers employing effects of terror, specifically the supernatural. There are also pointed remarks on Burke's definition of the sublime, which throw interesting light on Radcliffe's fictional techniques.

Source: *New Monthly Magazine*, vol. 16 (1), (January 1926), pp. 145–52.

★

One of our travellers began a grave dissertation on the illusions of the imagination. 'And not only on frivolous occasions,' said he, 'but in the most important pursuits of life, an object often flatters and charms at a distance, which vanishes into nothing as we approach it; and 'tis well if it leave only disappointment in our hearts. Sometimes a severer monitor is left there.'

These truisms, delivered with an air of discovery by Mr. S——, who seldom troubled himself to think upon any subject, except that of a good dinner, were lost upon his companion, who, pursuing the airy conjectures which the present scene, however humbled, had called up, was following Shakspeare into unknown regions. 'Where is now the undying spirit,' said he, 'that could so exquisitely perceive and feel? that could inspire itself with the various characters of this world, and create worlds of its own; to which the grand and the beautiful, the gloomy and the sublime of visible Nature, up-called not only corresponding feelings, but passions; which seemed to perceive a soul in every thing: and thus, in the secret workings of its own characters, and in the combinations of its incidents, kept the elements and local scenery always in unison with them, heightening their effect. So the conspirators at Rome pass under the fiery showers and sheeted lightning of the thunder-storm, to meet, at midnight, in the porch of Pompey's theatre. The streets being then deserted by the affrighted multitude, that place, open as it was, was convenient for their council; and, as to the storm, they felt it not; it was not more terrible to them than their own passions, nor so terrible to others as the dauntless spirit that makes them, almost unconsciously, brave its fury. These appalling circumstances, with others of supernatural import, attended the fall of the conqueror of the world – a man, whose power Cassius represents to be dreadful as this night, when the sheeted dead were seen in the lightning to glide along the streets of Rome.[47] How much does the sublimity of these attendant circumstances heighten our idea of the power of Caesar, of the terrific grandeur of his character, and prepare and interest us for his fate. The whole soul is roused and fixed, in the full energy of attention, upon the progress of the conspiracy against him; and, had not Shakspeare wisely withdrawn him from our view, there would have been no balance of our passions.' – 'Caesar was a tyrant,' said Mr. S——. W—— looked at him for a moment, and smiled, and then silently resumed the course of his own thoughts. No master ever knew how to touch the accordant springs of sympathy by small circumstances like our own Shakspeare. In Cymbeline, for instance, how finely such circumstances are made use of, to awaken, at once, solemn expectation and tenderness, and, by recalling the softened remembrance of a sorrow long past, to prepare the mind to melt at one that was approaching, mingling at the same time, by means of a mysterious occurrence, a slight tremour of awe with our pity. Thus, when Belarius and Arviragus return to the cave where they had left the unhappy and worn-out Imogen to repose, while they are yet standing before it, and Arviragus, speaking of her with tenderest pity, as 'the poor sick Fidele,' goes out to enquire for her, – solemn music is heard from the cave, sounded by that harp of which Guiderius says, '*Since the death of my dearest mother, it did not speak before*. All solemn things should answer solemn accidents.' Immediately Arviragus enters with Fidele senseless in his arms:

> 'The bird is dead, that we have made so much of.
> – How found you him?
> Stark, as you see, thus smiling.
> – I though he slept, and put
> My clouted brogues from off my feet, whose rudeness
> Answered my steps too loud.' – 'Why he but sleeps!'
>
> 'With fairest flowers
> While summer lasts, AND I LIVE HERE, FIDELE,
> I'll sweeten thy sad grave –.'[48]

Tears alone can speak the touching simplicity of the whole scene. Macbeth shows, by many instances, how much Shakspeare delighted to heighten the effect of his characters and his story by correspondent scenery: there the desolate heath, the troubled elements, assist the mis-chief of his malignant beings. But who, after hearing Macbeth's thrilling question –

—What are these,
So withered and so wild in their attire,
That look not like the inhabitants o' the earth,
And yet are on't?[49]—

who would have thought of reducing them to mere human beings, by attiring them not only like the inhabitants of the earth, but in the dress of a particular country, and making them downright Scotch-women? thus not only contradicting the very words of Macbeth, but withdrawing from these cruel agents of the passions all that strange and supernatural air which had made them so affecting to the imagination, and which was entirely suitable to the solemn and important events they were foretelling and accomplishing. Another *improvement* on Shakspeare is the introducing a crowd of witches thus arrayed, instead of the three beings 'so withered and so wild in their attire.'

About the latter part of this sentence, W——, as he was apt to do, thought aloud, and Mr. S—— said, '*I*, now, have sometimes considered, that it was quite sensible to make Scotch witches on the stage, appear like Scotch women. You must recollect that, in the superstition concerning witches, they lived familiarly upon the earth, mortal sorcerers, and were not always known from mere old women; consequently they must have appeared in the dress of the country where they happened to live, or they would have been more than suspected of witchcraft, which we find was not always the case.'

'You are speaking of old women, and not of witches,' said W—— laughing, 'and I must more than suspect you of crediting that obsolete superstition which destroyed so many wretched, yet guiltless persons, if I allow your argument to have any force. I am speaking of the only real witch – the witch of the poet; and all our notions and feelings connected with terror accord with his. The wild attire, the look *not of this earth*, are essential traits of supernatural agents, working evil in the darkness of mystery. Whenever the poet's witch condescends, according to the vulgar notion, to mingle mere ordinary mischief with her malignity, and to become familiar, she is ludicrous, and loses her power over the imagination; the illusion vanishes. So vexatious is the effect of the stage-witches upon my mind, that I should probably have left the theatre when they appeared, had not the fascination of Mrs. Siddons's[50] influence so spread itself over the whole play, as to overcome my disgust, and to make me forget even Shakspeare himself; while all consciousness of fiction was lost, and his thoughts lived and breathed before me in the very form of truth. Mrs. Siddons, like Shakspeare, always disappears in the character she represents, and throws an illusion over the whole scene around her, that conceals many defects in the arrangements of the theatre. I should suppose she would be the finest Hamlet that ever appeared, excelling even her own brother in that character; she would more fully preserve the tender and refined melancholy, the deep sensibility, which are the peculiar charm of

Hamlet, and which appear not only in the ardour, but in the occasional irresolution and weakness of his character – the secret spring that reconciles all his inconsistencies. A sensibility so profound can with difficulty be justly imagined, and therefore can very rarely be assumed. Her brother's firmness, incapable of being always subdued, does not so fully enhance, as her tenderness would, this part of the character. The strong light which shows the mountains of a landscape in all their greatness, and with all their rugged sharpness, gives them nothing of the interest with which a more gloomy tint would invest their grandeur; dignifying, though it softens, and magnifying, while it obscures.'

'I still think,' said Mr. S——, without attending to these remarks, 'that, in a popular superstition, it is right to go with the popular notions, and dress your witches like the old women of the place where they are supposed to have appeared.'

'As far as these notions prepare us for the awe which the poet designs to excite, I agree with you that he is right in availing himself of them; but, for this purpose, every thing familiar and common should be carefully avoided. In nothing has Shakspeare been more successful than in this; and in another case somewhat more difficult – that of selecting circumstances of manners and appearance for his supernatural beings, which, though wild and remote, in the highest degree, from common apprehension, never shock the understanding by incompatibility with themselves – never compel us, for an instant, to recollect that he has a licence for extravagance. Above every ideal being is the ghost of Hamlet, with all its attendant incidents of time and place. The dark watch upon the remote platform, the dreary aspect of the night, the very expression of the office on guard, "the air bites shrewdly; it is very cold;" the recollection of a star, an unknown world, are all circumstances which excite forlorn, melancholy, and solemn feelings, and dispose us to welcome, with trembling curiosity, the awful being that draws near; and to indulge in that strange mixture of horror, pity, and indignation, produced by the tale it reveals. Every minute circumstance of the scene between those watching on the platform, and of that between them and Horatio, preceding the entrance of the apparition, contributes to excite some feeling of dreariness, or melancholy, or solemnity, or expectation, in unison with, and leading on toward that high curiosity and thrilling awe with which we witness the conclusion of the scene. So the first question of Bernardo, and the words in reply, "Stand and unfold yourself." But there is not a single circumstance in either dialogue, not even in this short one, with which the play opens, that does not take its secret effect upon the imagination. It ends with Bernardo desiring his brother-officer, after having asked whether he has had "quiet watch," to hasten the guard, if he should chance to meet them; and we immediately feel ourselves alone on this dreary ground.

'When Horatio enters, the challenge – the dignified answers, "Friends to this ground, and liegemen to the Dane," – the question of Horatio to

Bernardo, touching the apparition – the unfolding of the reason why "Horatio has consented to watch with them the minutes of this night" – the sitting down together, while Bernardo relates the particulars of what they had seen for two nights; and, above all, the few lines with which he begins his story, "Last night of all," and the distinguishing, by the situation of "yon same star," the very point of time when the spirit had appeared – the abruptness with which he breaks off, "the bell then beating one" – the instant appearance of the ghost, as though ratifying the story for the very truth itself – all these are circumstances which the deepest sensibility only could have suggested, and which, if you read them a thousand times, still continue affect you almost as much as the first. I thrill with delighted awe, even while I recollect and mention them, as instances of the exquisite art of the poet.'

'Certainly you must be very superstitious,' said Mr. S——, 'or such things could not interest you thus.'

'There are few people less so than I am,' replied W——, 'or I understand myself and the meaning of superstition very ill.'

'That is quite paradoxical.'

'It appears so, but so it is not. If I cannot explain this, take it as a mystery of the human mind.'

'If it were possible for me to believe the appearance of ghosts at all,' replied Mr. S——, 'it would certainly be the ghost of Hamlet; but I never can suppose such things; they are out of all reason and probability.'

'You would believe the immortality of the soul,' said W——, with solemnity, 'even without the aid of revelation; yet our confined faculties cannot comprehend *how* the soul may exist after separation from the body. I do not absolutely know that spirits are permitted to become visible to us on earth; yet that they may be permitted to appear for very rare and important purposes, such as could scarcely have been accomplished without an equal suspension, or a momentary change, of the laws prescribed to what we call *Nature* – that is, without one more exercise of the same CREATIVE POWER of which we must acknowledge so many millions of existing instances, and by which alone we ourselves at this moment breathe, think, or disquisite at all, cannot be impossible, and, I think, is probable. Now, probability is enough for the poet's justification, the ghost being supposed to have come for an important purpose. Oh, I should never be weary of dwelling on the perfection of Shakspeare, in his management of every scene connected with that most solemn and mysterious being, which takes such entire possession of the imagination, that we hardly seem conscious we are beings of this world while we contemplate "the extravagant and erring spirit." The spectre departs, accompanied by natural circumstances as touching as those with which he had approached. It is by the strange light of the glow-worm, which " 'gins to pale his ineffectual fire"; it is at the first scent of the morning air – the living breath, that the apparition retires. There is, however, no little vexation in seeing the ghost of Hamlet *played*. The finest imagination is requisite to give the due colouring to such a character on the stage; and yet almost any actor is thought capable of performing it. In the scene where Horatio breaks his secret to Hamlet, Shakspeare, still true to the touch of circumstances, makes the time evening, and marks it by the very words of Hamlet, "Good even, sir," which Hammer and Warburton changed, without any reason, to "good morning," thus making Horatio relate his most interesting and solemn story by the clear light of the cheerfullest part of the day; when busy sounds are stirring, and the sun itself seems to contradict every doubtful tale, and lessen every feeling of terror. The discord of this must immediately be understood by those who have bowed the willing soul to the poet.'

'How happens it then,' said Mr. S——, 'that objects of terror sometimes strike us very forcibly, when introduced into scenes of gaiety and splendour, as, for instance, in the Banquet scene in Macbeth?'

'They strike, then, chiefly by the force of contrast,' said W——; 'but the effect, though sudden and strong, is also transient; it is the thrill of horror and surprise, which they then communicate, rather than the deep and solemn feelings excited under more accordant circumstances, and left long upon the mind. Who ever suffered for the ghost of Banquo, the gloomy and sublime kind of terror, which that of Hamlet calls forth? though the appearance of Banquo, at the high festival of Macbeth, not only tells us that he is murdered, but recalls to our minds the fate of the gracious Duncan, laid in silence and death by those who, in this very scene, are revelling in his spoils. There, though deep pity mingles with our surprise and horror, we experience a far less degree of interest, and that interest too of an inferior kind. The union of grandeur and obscurity, which Mr. Burke describes as a sort of tranquillity tinged with terror, and which causes the sublime, is to be found only in Hamlet; or in scenes where circumstances of the same kind prevail.'

'That may be,' said Mr. S——, 'and I perceive you are not one of those who contend that obscurity does not make any part of the sublime.' 'They must be men of very cold imaginations,' said W——, 'with whom certainty is more terrible than surmise. Terror and horror are so far opposite, that the first expands the soul, and awakens the faculties to a high degree of life; the other contracts, freezes, and nearly annihilates them. I apprehend, that neither Shakspeare nor Milton by their fictions, nor Mr. Burke by his reasoning, anywhere looked to positive horror as a source of the sublime, though they all agree that terror is a very high one; and where lies the great difference between horror and terror, but in the uncertainty and obscurity, that accompany the first, respecting the dreaded evil?'

'But what say you to Milton's image – "On his brow sat horror plumed."'[51]

'As an image, it certainly is sublime; it fills the mind with an idea of power, but it does not follow that Milton intended to declare the feeling of horror to be sublime; and after all, his image imparts more of terror than of horror; for it is not distinctly pictured forth, but is seen in glimpses through obscuring shades, the great outlines only appearing, which excite the imagination to complete the rest; he only says, "sat horror plumed"; you will observe, that the look of horror and the other characteristics are left to the imagination of the reader; and according to the strength of that, he will feel Milton's image to be either sublime or otherwise. Milton, when he sketched it, probably felt, that not even his art could fill up the outline, and present to other eyes the countenance which his "mind's eye" gave to him. Now, if obscurity has so much effect on fiction, what must it have in real life, when to ascertain the object of our terror, is frequently to acquire the means of escaping it. You will observe, that this image, though indistinct or obscure, is not confused.'

'How can any thing be indistinct and not confused?' said Mr. S——.

'Ay, that question is from the new school,' replied W.; 'but recollect, that obscurity, or indistinctness, is only a negative, which leaves the imagination to act upon the few hints that truth reveals to it; confusion is a thing as positive as distinctness, though not necessarily so palpable; and it may, by mingling and confounding one image with another, absolutely counteract the imagination, instead of exciting it. Obscurity leaves something for the imagination to exaggerate; confusion, by blurring one image into another, leaves only a chaos in which the mind can find nothing to be magnificent, nothing to nourish its fears or doubts, or to act upon in any way; yet confusion and obscurity are terms used indiscriminately by those, who would prove, that Shakspeare and Milton were wrong when they employed obscurity as a cause of the sublime, that Mr. Burke was equally mistaken in his reasoning upon the subject, and that mankind have been equally in error, as to the nature of their own feelings, when they were acted upon by the illusions of those great masters of the imagination, at whose so potent bidding, the passions have been awakened from their sleep, and by whose magic a crowded Theatre has been changed to a lonely shore, to a witch's cave, to an enchanted island, to a murderer's castle, to the ramparts of an usurper, to the battle, to the midnight carousal of the camp or the tavern, to every various scene of the living world.'

'Yet there are poets, and great ones too,' said Mr. S——, 'whose minds do not appear to have been very susceptible of those circumstances of time and space – of what you, perhaps, would call the picturesque in feeling – which you seem to think so necessary to the attainment of any powerful effect on the imagination. What say you to Dryden?'

'That he had a very strong imagination, a fertile wit, a mind well prepared by education, and great promptness of feeling; but he had not – at least not in good proportion to his other qualifications – that delicacy of feeling, which we call taste; moreover, that his genius was overpowered by the prevailing taste of the court, and by an intercourse with the world, too often humiliating to his morals, and destructive of his sensibility. Milton's better morals protected his genius, and his imagination was not lowered by the world.'

'Then you seem to think there may be great poets, without a full perception of the picturesque; I mean by picturesque, the beautiful and grand in nature and art – and with little susceptibility to what you would call the accordant circumstances, the harmony of which is essential to any powerful effect upon your feelings.'

'No; I cannot allow that. Such men may have high talents, wit, genius, judgment, but not the soul of poetry, which is the spirit of all these, and also something wonderfully higher – something too fine for definition. It certainly includes an instantaneous perception, and an exquisite love of whatever is graceful, grand, and sublime, with the power of seizing and combining such circumstances of them, as to strike and interest a reader by the representation, even more than a general view of the real scene itself could do. Whatever this may be called, which crowns the mind of a poet, and distinguishes it from every other mind, our whole heart instantly acknowledges it in Shakspeare, Milton, Gray, Collins, Beattie, and a very few others, not excepting Thomson, to whose powers the sudden tear of delight and admiration bears at once both testimony and tribute. How deficient Dryden was of a poet's feelings in the fine province of the beautiful and the graceful, is apparent from his alteration of the Tempest, by which he has not only lessened the interest by incumbering the plot, but has absolutely disfigured the character of Miranda, whose simplicity, whose tenderness and innocent affections, might, to use Shakspeare's own words in another play, "be shrined in crystal." A love of moral beauty is as essential in the mind of a poet, as a love of picturesque beauty. There is as much difference between the tone of Dryden's moral feelings and those of Milton, as there is between their perceptions of the grand and the beautiful in nature. Yet, when I recollect the "Alexander's Feast," I am astonished at the powers of Dryden, and at my own daring opinions upon them; and should be ready to unsay much that I have said, did I not consider this particular instance of the power of music upon Dryden's mind, to be as wonderful as any instance he has exhibited of the effect of that enchanting art in his sublime ode. I cannot, however, allow it to be the finest ode in the English language, so long as I remember Gray's Bard, and Collins's Ode on the Passions. – But, to return to Shakspeare, I have sometimes thought, as I walked in the deep shade of the North Terrace of Windsor Castle, when the moon shone on all beyond, that the scene must have been present in Shakspeare's mind, when he drew the night-scenes in Hamlet; and, as I have stood on the platform, which there projects over the precipice, and have heard only the measured step of a sentinel or the clink of his arms, and have seen his shadow passing by moonlight, at the foot of the high Eastern tower, I have almost expected to see the royal shade armed cap-a-pee standing still on the lonely platform before me. The very star – "yon same star that's westward from the pole" – seemed to watch over the Western towers of the Terrace, whose high dark lines marked themselves upon the heavens. All has been so still and shadowy, so great and solemn, that the scene appeared fit for "no mortal business nor any sounds that the earth owns." Did you ever observe the fine effect of the Eastern tower, when you stand near the Western end of the North terrace, and its tall profile rears itself upon the sky, from nearly the base to the battled top, the lowness of the parapet permitting this? It is most striking at night, when the stars appear, at different heights, upon its tall dark line, and when the sentinel on watch moves a shadowy figure at its foot.'

Notes

1 Swedenborg notes in his edition, 'Among those who so objected were Davenant in his preface to *Gondibert* and Hobbes in his answer to Davenant.'
2 In *Leviathan*, 3.34.
3 University scholar.
4 Longinus, *On the Sublime*, section 9.
5 Cf. Joseph Addison, *The Spectator*, no. 418 (30 June 1712): 'When we look on such hideous objects, we are not a little pleased to think we are in no Danger of them. We consider them at the same time, as dreadful and harmless; so that the more frightful appearance they make, the greater is the Pleasure we receive from the sense of our own safety.'
6 Horace, *Epistles*, 2.2.140: 'A most pleasant delusion'.
7 Dryden refers to 'that fairy kind of writing, which depends only upon the Force of Imagination' in the Dedication of *King Arthur* (1691).
8 Horace, *Ars Poetica*, 244–6:

> A Satyr that comes staring from the Woods,
> Must not at first speak like an Orator:
> But, tho' his Language should not be refin'd,
> It must not be Obscene, and Impudent.

Trans. Earl of Roscommon, 1709.
9 *The Rehearsal* (1672), attributed to George Villiers, Duke of Buckingham; V.i.
10 Aeschylus (525–456 BC), who fought in the Athenian army at Marathon.
11 Sophocles (496–406 BC).
12 The setting of Sophocles' *Oedipus Coloneus*.
13 The stanza refers to a scene from *Oedipus Tyrannus* by Sophocles; in the original footnote, Collins quotes in Greek lines 1622–5.
14 Pity and terror are linked in Aristotle's theory of tragic catharsis in *Poetics*.
15 The cypress was traditionally associated with melancholy.
16 Robert Francis Damiens was publicly tortured and executed on 28 March 1757, for the attempted assassination of Louis XV.
17 *Paradise Lost*, 2.666–73 (misquoted).
18 Job, 4.13–17.
19 Job, 39 – the following two quotations are from 39 and (on leviathan) 41.

20 Job, 29.
21 Psalms, 149 (misquoted).
22 In addition to *Hamlet* and *Macbeth*, the references are to Shakespeare's *Richard III*, Otway's *Venice Preserv'd* and Rowe's *Jane Shore*.
23 A scene from Shakespeare's *Henry V*.
24 See note 16 above.
25 'For what shall I chant . . . to her at whom dogs shudder / As she [Hecate] moves among the tombs of the dead and the black blood.' *Idylls*, 2.11–13.
26 Thomas Gray, *The Bard: A Pindaric Ode*, l. 130.
27 Richard I's crusade.
28 pagan.
29 if.
30 blast.
31 rattled the latch.
32 shift.
33 sound.
34 hamlet.
35 increases in size.
36 eyes.
37 some time ago.
38 complexion.
39 See 2.9; James Beattie, *The Minstrel, or, The Progress of Genius*, Book 1, ll. 284–8 and 298–306.
40 Two ancient collections of Scandinavian mythology.
41 Hugh Blair; see 2.6.
42 See 1.9; William Collins, *Ode on the Popular Superstitions of the Highlands of Scotland* (1749–50), ll. 188–92 and 196–203.
43 The essay is followed by an 'Ode to Superstition' and a tale entitled in some editions 'Henry Fitzowen', which have not been included here.
44 The latter, titled 'Montmorency', is not included here.
45 The title inherited by Horace Walpole; *The Mysterious Mother* was a tragic drama published in a limited edition in 1768 but never performed.
46 Ugolino della Gheradesca (d. 1289) was leader of the Guelph faction in Pisa, imprisoned and starved to death by his enemies, along with four of his sons and grandsons. Dante relates the story in the *Inferno* (32.124–33), and it was also a favourite theme of artists.
47 See *Julius Caesar*, I.iii, II.i and II.ii.
48 *Cymbeline*, IV.ii.197–8, 209–10, 213–15, 218–20.
49 *Macbeth*, I.iii.39–42.
50 Sarah Siddons (1755–1831) and her brother John Philip Kemble (1757–1823) were the most celebrated tragic actors of the day, and Lady Macbeth was considered Siddons's best role.
51 *Paradise Lost*, 4.988–9; 'brow' substituted for 'crest'.

4 Anti-Gothic

4.1 Horace (65–8 BC), *Ars Poetica* (trans. 1709)

Just as Longinus was frequently cited in order to justify originality and flights of the imagination in literature, so other classical authors provided a basis for condemning the 'Gothic' writings of Walpole and his heirs. Plato excluded poets from the ideal republic on the grounds that their pleasing fictions encouraged irrational impulses, and could play no useful part in moral or political education. Critics of the eighteenth century tended to make a distinction between useful literature, which illustrated moral truths and did so in a rational and plausible manner, and illegitimate writing, which failed to do either of these things. Aristotle's *Poetics* furnished some of the 'rules' of drama, which were sometimes loosely applied to criticism of the new genre of the novel (see 3.1, and Walpole's boast that *Otranto* obeys the three unities of time, place and action, 3.7b). But Horace's *Ars Poetica* was by far the most frequent resort of opponents of Gothic fiction and drama. In particular, the phrase '*incredulus odi*' (from line 188), 'What I cannot for a moment believe, I cannot for a moment behold with interest or anxiety' in Samuel Johnson's paraphrase, echoes and re-echoes as a motto for the assaults of anti-Gothic criticism; the point being that probability, literary decorum, is the vital condition for the ethical usefulness of literature.

Source: Horace ([*c.* 12–8 BC] 1709), *Of the Art of Poetry: A Poem*, trans. the Earl of Roscommon, London: H. Hills, pp. 3–4, 7, 8–9.

★

If in a Picture (Piso) you should see
A Handsome Woman with a Fishes Tail,
Or a Man's Head upon a Horse's Neck,
Or Limbs of Beasts of the most different Kinds,
Cover'd with Feathers of all sorts of Birds,
Wou'd you not laugh, and think the Painter mad?
Trust me, that Book is as ridiculous,

Whose incoherent Stile (like sick Mens Dreams)
Varies all shapes, and mixes all Extreams.
Painters and Poets have been still allow'd,
Their Pencils, and their Fancies unconfin'd.
This Priviledge we freely give and take;
But Nature, and the Common Laws of Sense,
Forbid to reconcile *Antipathies*,
Or make a Snake engender with a Dove,
And hungry Tygers court the tender Lambs:
Some that at first have promis'd mighty things,
Applaud themselves when a few florid Lines
Shine through the insipid Dulness of the rest:
Here they describe a Temple, or a Wood,
Or Streams that through delightful Meadows run,
And there the Rainbow, or the rapid *Rhine*;
But they misplace them all, and crowd them in,
And are as much to seek in other things,
As he that only can design a Tree,
Would be to draw a Shipwreck, or a Storm;
When you begin with so much Pomp and Show,
Why is the End so little and so low?
Be what you will, so you be still the same.
Most Poets fall into the grossest Faults,
Deluded by a seeming Excellence:
By striving to be short, they grow obscure,
And when they would write smoothly, they want Strength,
Their Spirits sink; while others, that affect
A lofty Stile, swell to a Tympany;
Some timerous Wretches start at every blast,
And fearing a Tempest, dare not leave the Shore;
Others in Love with wild Variety,
Draw Boars in Waves, and Dolphins in a Wood.
Thus fear of Erring, join'd with want of Skill,
Is a most certain way of Erring still. . . .

If your bold Muse dare tread unbeaten Paths,
And bring new Characters upon the Stage,
Be sure you keep them up to their first Height.
New Subjects are not easily explain'd,
And you had better chuse a well-known theam,
Than trust to an Invention of your own;
For what originally others writ,
May be so well disguis'd, and so improv'd,
That with some Justice it may pass for yours:
But then you must not copy trivial things,

Nor Word for Word too faithfully translate,
Nor (as some servile Imitators do)
Prescribe at first such strict uneasy Rules,
As they must ever slavishely observe,
Or all the Laws of Decency renounce. . . .

Some things are acted, others only told;
But what we hear, moves less that what we see:
Spectators only have their Eyes to trust,
But Auditors must trust their Ears and you;
Yet there are things improper for a Scene,
Which Men of Judgment only will relate.
Medea must not draw her Murdering Knife,
And spill her Childrens Blood upon the Stage,
Nor *Atreus* there his horrid Feast prepare,
Cadmus's and *Progene*'s *Metamorphosis*,
(She to a Swallow turn'd he to a Snake)
And whatsoever contradicts my Sense,
I hate to see, and never can believe.[1] . . .

4.2 Novel versus romance

4.2a Samuel Johnson (1709–84), *The Rambler*, No. 4 (1750)

This influential essay implicitly opposes the works of Fielding and Smollett in favour of the open didacticism of Richardson's novels. In doing so, it also sets some of the terms by which Gothic fiction would later be condemned, with the assertion that romance and its improbabilities belong to the past, while the writers of the present are (and *should* be) concerned only with real life; that the depiction of heroic villains has a damaging effect on the morality of readers; and that 'what we cannot credit we shall never imitate'. Above all, Johnson puts forward the general principle that fictional narratives should serve the role of instruction, offering an ideal version of the world by which the minds of 'the young, the ignorant, and the idle' could be guided.

Source: *The* Rambler, no. 4 (31 March 1750). Quoted from *Yale Edition of the Works of Samuel Johnson* (1969) eds W. J. Bate and Albrecht B. Strauss, New Haven and London: Yale University Press, vol. 3, pp. 19–25.

★

Simul et jucunda et idonea dicere vitae.
Horace, ARS POETICA, 1.334

And join both profit and delight in one.
Creech.

The works of fiction, with which the present generation seems more particularly delighted, are such as exhibit life in its true state, diversified only by accidents that daily happen in the world, and influenced by passions and qualities which are really to be found in conversing with mankind.

This kind of writing may be termed not improperly the comedy of romance, and is to be conducted nearly by the rules of comic poetry. Its province is to bring about natural events by easy means, and to keep up curiosity without the help of wonder: it is therefore precluded from the machines[2] and expedients of the heroic romance, and can neither employ giants to snatch away a lady from the nuptial rites, nor knights to bring her back from captivity; it can neither bewilder its personages in desarts, nor lodge them in imaginary castles.

I remember a remark made by Scaliger upon Pontanus,[3] that all his writings are filled with the same images; and that if you take from him his lillies and his roses, his satyrs and his dryads, he will have nothing left that can be called poetry. In like manner, almost all the fictions of the last age will vanish, if you deprive them of a hermit and a wood, a battle and a shipwreck.

Why this wild strain of imagination found reception so long, in polite and learned ages, it is not easy to conceive; but we cannot wonder that, while readers could be procured, the authors were willing to continue it: for when a man had by practice gained some fluency of language, he had no further care than to retire to his closet, let loose his invention, and heat his mind with incredibilities; a book was thus produced without fear of criticism, without the toil of study, without knowledge of nature, or acquaintance with life.

The task of our present writers is very different; it requires, together with that learning which is to be gained from books, that experience which can never be attained by solitary diligence, but must arise from general converse, and accurate observation of the living world. Their performances have, as Horace expresses it, *plus oneris quantum veniae minus*,[4] little indulgence, and therefore more difficulty. They are engaged in portraits of which every one knows the original, and can detect any deviation from exactness of resemblance. Other writings are safe, except from the malice of learning, but these are in danger from every common reader; as the slipper ill executed was censured by a shoemaker who happened to stop on his way at the Venus of Apelles.[5]

But the fear of not being approved as just copyers of human manners, is not the most important concern that an author of this sort ought to have before him. These books are written chiefly to the young, the ignorant, and the idle, to whom they serve as lectures of conduct, and introductions into life. They are the entertainment of minds unfurnished with ideas, and therefore easily susceptible of impressions; not fixed by principles, and therefore easily following the current of fancy; not informed by experience, and consequently open to every false suggestion and partial account.

That the highest degree of reverence should be paid to youth, and that nothing indecent should be suffered to approach their eyes or ears; are precepts extorted by sense and virtue from an ancient writer, by no means eminent for chastity of thought.[6] The same kind, tho' not the same degree of caution, is required in every thing which is laid before them, to secure them from unjust prejudices, perverse opinions, and incongruous combinations of images.

In the romances formerly written, every transaction and sentiment was so remote from all that passes among men, that the reader was in very little danger of making any applications to himself; the virtues and crimes were equally beyond his sphere of activity; and he amused himself with heroes and with traitors, deliverers and persecutors, as with beings of another species, whose actions were regulated upon motives of their own, and who had neither faults nor excellencies in common with himself.

But when an adventurer is levelled with the rest of the world, and acts in such scenes of the universal drama, as may be the lot of any other man; young spectators fix their eyes upon him with closer attention, and hope by observing his behaviour and success to regulate their own practices, when they shall be engaged in the like part.

For this reason these familiar histories may perhaps be made of greater use than the solemnities of professed morality, and convey the knowledge of vice and virtue with more efficacy than axioms and definitions. But if the power of example is so great, as to take possession of the memory by a kind of violence, and produce effects almost without the intervention of the will, care ought to be taken that, when the choice is unrestrained, the best examples only should be exhibited; and that which is likely to operate so strongly, should not be mischievous or uncertain in its effects.

The chief advantage which these fictions have over real life is, that their authors are at liberty, tho' not to invent, yet to select objects, and to cull from the mass of mankind, those individuals upon which the attention ought most to be employ'd; as a diamond, though it cannot be made, may be polished by art, and placed in such a situation, as to display that lustre which before was buried among common stones.

It is justly considered as the greatest excellency of art, to imitate nature; but it is necessary to distinguish those parts of nature, which are most proper for imitation: greater care is still required in representing life, which is so often discoloured by passion, or deformed by wickedness. If the world be promiscuously described, I cannot see of what use it can be to read the account; or why it may not be as safe to turn the eye immediately upon mankind, as upon a mirror which shows all that presents itself without discrimination.

It is therefore not a sufficient vindication of a character, that it is drawn as it appears, for many characters ought never to be drawn; nor of a narrative, that the train of events is agreeable to observation and experience, for that observation which is called knowledge of the world, will be found much more frequently to make men cunning than good. The purpose of these writings is surely not only to show mankind, but to provide that they may be seen hereafter with less hazard; to teach the means of avoiding the snares which are laid by Treachery for Innocence, without infusing any wish for that superiority with which the betrayer flatters his vanity; to give the power of counteracting fraud, without the temptation to practise it; to initiate youth by mock encounters in the art of necessary defence, and to increase prudence without impairing virtue.

Many writers, for the sake of following nature, so mingle good and bad qualities in their principle personages, that they are both equally conspicuous; and as we accompany them through their adventures with delight, and are led by degrees to interest ourselves in their favour, we lose the abhorrence of their faults, because they do not hinder our pleasure, or, perhaps, regard them with some kindness for being united with so much merit.

There have been men indeed splendidly wicked, whose endowments threw a brightness on their crimes, and whom scarce any villainy made perfectly detestable, because they never could be wholly divested of their excellencies; but such have been in all ages the great corrupters of the world, and their resemblance ought no more to be preserved, than the art of murdering without pain.

Some have advanced, without due attention to the consequences of this notion, that certain virtues have their correspondent faults, and therefore that to exhibit either apart is to deviate from probability. Thus men are observed by Swift to be 'grateful in the same degree as they are resentful.'[7] This principle, with others of the same kind, supposes man to act from a brute impulse, and persue a certain degree of inclination, without any choice of the object; for, otherwise, though it should be allowed that gratitude and resentment arise from the same constitution of the passions, it follows not that they will be equally indulged when reason is consulted; yet unless that consequence be admitted, this sagacious maxim becomes an empty sound, without any relation to practice or to life.

Nor is it evident, that even the first motions to these effects are always in the same proportion. For pride, which produces quickness of resentment, will obstruct gratitude, by unwillingness to admit that inferiority which obligation implies; and it is very unlikely, that he who cannot think he receives a favour will acknowledge or repay it.

It is of the utmost importance to mankind, that positions of this tendency should be laid open and confuted; for while men consider good and evil as springing from the same root, they will spare the one for the sake of the other, and in judging, if not of others at least of themselves, will be apt to estimate their virtues by their vices. To this fatal error all those will contribute, who confound the colours of right and wrong, and instead of helping to settle their boundaries, mix them with so much art, that no common mind is able to disunite them.

In narratives, where historical veracity has no place, I cannot discover why there should not be exhibited the most perfect idea of virtue; of virtue not angelical, nor above probability, for what we cannot credit we shall never imitate, but the highest and purest that humanity can reach, which, exercised in such trials as the various revolutions of things shall bring upon it, may, by conquering some calamities, and enduring others, teach us what we may hope, and what we can perform. Vice, for vice is necessary to be shewn, should always disgust; nor should the graces of gaiety, or the dignity of courage, be so united with it, as to reconcile it to the mind. Wherever it appears, it should raise hatred by the malignity of its practices, and contempt by the meanness of its stratagems; for while it is supported by either parts or spirit, it will be seldom heartily abhorred. The Roman tyrant was content to be hated, if he was but feared; and there are thousands of the readers of romances willing to be thought wicked, if they may be allowed to be wits. It is therefore to be steadily inculcated, that virtue is the highest proof of understanding, and the only solid basis of greatness; and that vice is the natural consequence of narrow thoughts, that it begins in mistake, and ends in ignominy.

4.2b Clara Reeve (1729–1807), *The Progress of Romance, Through Times, Countries, and Manners* (1785)

Reeve, like Johnson, draws an absolute distinction between novels and romances, and suggests that the latter are obsolete. In her later review of examples of modern fiction, she includes *The Castle of Otranto* (and by implication her own *The Old English Baron*) in the category of 'Novels and Stories Original and Uncommon'. In fact, as Walpole's second Preface suggests (3.7b), Gothic fictions were a hybrid form, confounding existing generic definitions. Their ability to combine 'what never happened nor is likely to happen' with genuinely moving representations of 'the joys and distress, of the persons in the story' was a source of perplexity for many critics.

Source: Clara Reeve (1785), *The Progress of Romance, Through Times, Countries, and Manners; With Remarks On the Good and Bad Effects of It, On Them Respectively*, 2 vols, Colchester: W. Keymer, vol. I, p. 111.

★

The Romance is an heroic fable, which treats of fabulous persons and things. – The Novel is a picture of real life and manners, and of the times it was written. The Romance in lofty and elevated language, describes what never happened nor is likely to happen. – The Novel gives a familiar relation of such things, as pass every day before our eyes, such as may happen to our friend, or to ourselves; and the perfection of it, is to represent every scene, in so easy and natural a manner, and to make them appear so probable, as to deceive us into a persuasion (at least while we are reading) that all is real, until we are affected by the joys or distresses, of the persons in the story, as if they were our own.

4.3 Tampering with history: the response to Sophia Lee's *The Recess* (1785)

Sophia Lee's novel, which relates the adventures of two invented daughters of Mary, Queen of Scots, provoked some unease concerning the mingling of fiction and recorded history. As Ernest Baker has pointed out (Baker, 1934, vol. 5, pp. 179, n. 2, 181–2), Lee took her inspiration from the French writer Prévost d'Exiles, whose *Life and Adventures of Mr Cleveland* (translated into English in 1734) professed to be a secret history of the illegitimate son of Cromwell.

4.3a Sophia Lee (1750–1824), 'Advertisement' to *The Recess* (1785)

Source: Sophia Lee (1785), *The Recess; or, A Tale of Other Times*, 3 vols, London: T. Cadell.

★

Not being permitted to publish the means which enriched me with the obsolete manuscript from whence the following tale is extracted, its simplicity alone can authenticate it. – I make no apology for altering the language to that of the present age, since the author's would be frequently unintelligible. – A wonderful coincidence of events stamps the narration at least with probability, and the reign of Elizabeth was that of romance. If this lady was not the child of fancy, her fate can hardly be paralleled; and the line of which she came has been marked by an eminent historian, as one distinguished alike by splendor and misery.

The characters interwoven in this story agree, in the outline, with history; and if love, or friendship, veil a fault, or irradiate a virtue, it is but reasonable to allow of a weakness all feel in some particular instance. History, like painting, only perpetuates the striking features of the mind; whereas the best and worst actions of princes often proceed from partialities and prejudices, which live in their hearts, and are buried with them.

The depredations of time have left chasms in the story, which sometimes only heightens the pathetic. An inviolable respect for truth would not permit me to attempt connecting these, even where they appeared faulty.

To the hearts of both sexes nature has enriched with sensibility, and experience with refinement, this tale is humbly offered; in the persuasion such will find it worthy their patronage.

4.3b Review of *The Recess* (1786)

Source: *Gentleman's Magazine*, vol. 56, p. 327.

★

Two sisters, the fruit of a private marriage, supposed to have taken place between Mary, Queen of Scots and the Duke of Norfolk, are the heroines of this story. Our limits will not allow us to trace them through the wonderful series of their adventures. *Per varios casus et tot descrimina rerum.*[8] The language is animated, and, in general, correct: the story is managed with considerable art, ingenuity and judgement; and the various passions of the mind are pourtrayed in strong and lively colours. The writer seems well acquainted with the times she describes. The truth of character is rigidly preserved, for the peculiarities of Elizabeth and James are not delineated with more exactness in Hume or Robertson.[9] The imagination is indeed transported into other times, and we find ourselves in the midst of the court of Elizabeth: but, though Leicester, Essex, and Sidney must interest us more than those men of straw that flutter through our modern novels, we cannot entirely approve the custom of interweaving fictitious incident with historic truth; and, as the events related approach nearer the aera we live in, the impropriety increases; for the mind, preoccupied with the real fact, rejects, not without disgust, the embellishments of fable. – These volumes, however, are calculated to supply not only amusement but instruction; and we recommend them with pleasure to the attention of the publick.

4.3c Richard Graves (1715–1804), from the Introduction to *Plexippus* (1790)

Source: Richard Graves (1790) *Plexippus: or, The Aspiring Plebeian*, London: J. Dodsley, pp. viii–xii.

★

I take this opportunity of saying a word on what are called '*historical* romances': in which some ingenious writers (especially amongst the French) have often mixed truth with fiction in such a manner as must necessarily lead young minds into error, and introduce confusion into all history.

If our hero is the creature of our imagination, we may paint him as we please; with one eye, like Hannibal; or one leg shorter than the other, like Agesilaus; and may employ him, and keep him alive or put him to death, as best suits our purpose. And, though Virgil is blamed for bringing Dido and Aeneas together; yet in such remote fabulous ages, especially where the chronology is dubious, such a liberty is excusable.

But we should be cautious how we ascribe moral qualities, inconsistent with the character or action, not warranted by the history of great men, in more enlightened periods. Though pope Sixtus Quintus admired the character of our Elizabeth, and Christina of Sweden longed to see Cromwell; yet a novellist could not decently, or with much probability, *feign* an intrigue between his holiness and the virgin queen, or between the fanatical Cromwell and the amorous, though learned queen of Sweden.

The ingenious defence of Mary queen of Scots, being mentioned t'other night at a card-table, a maiden lady, who would pardon murder or sacrilege rather than any violation of the laws of chastity; and who

> Thinks the nation ne'er can thrive,
> Till prostitutes are *burnt alive*.
>
> Prior.[10]

cried out, 'Oh! she was an abandoned woman! don't defend her; she had two *bastards* (*natural children*, I suppose, you'll call them) by the duke of Norfolk.'

I said, I had never met with that circumstance, even in Buchanan, or any history of those times. 'Oh!' says she, 'it is very true: I have just been reading an entertaining *novel*, which is *founded* entirely upon *that fact*.'

I made no reply; but, as soon as I got home, added this Postcript.

4.4 Anon., 'Terrorist Novel Writing' (1798)

Satire of Gothic arises from the same premise as moral opposition: the genre's characteristic improbability. But in spite of this, satire has almost the reverse tendency. Whereas serious criticism holds that the fictions are dangerous, proposes their censorship and inadvertently promotes their consumption as 'forbidden fruit', squibs like 'Terrorist Novel Writing' depend on the easy availability of the target texts. Their humour is based on familiarity, with at most a vague intention to diminish the popularity of their object by ridicule. A side-effect of such satires was the role they played in confirming the existence of Gothic as a distinct sub-genre, or literary idiom. Although the label 'Gothic' was not yet used in a regular way, around 1797 a number of descriptive titles were invented, including 'modern Romance', 'the *terrible* school' and 'the *hobgoblin-romance*'. The following text takes the form of an aggrieved letter to a journal. In an added footnote, the editor launches a very pointed, pedantic but poorly spelt and ungrammatical, attack on Radcliffe; some have speculated that she gave up publishing in 1797 in response to abuse of this kind.

Source: *Spirit of the Public Journals for 1797*, vol. 1 (London, 1798), pp. 223–5.

★

Sir,*

I never complain of fashion, when it is confined to externals – to the form of a cap, or the cut of a lapelle; to the colour of a wig, or the tune of a ballad; but when I perceive that there is such a thing as fashion even in composing books, it is, perhaps, full time that some attempt should be made to recall writers to the old boundaries of common sense.

I allude, Sir, principally to the great quantity of novels with which our circulating libraries are filled, and our parlour tables covered, in which it has been the fashion to make *terror* the *order of the day*, by confining the heroes and heroines in old gloomy castles, full of spectres, apparitions, ghosts, and dead men's bones. This is now so common, that a Novelist blushes to bring about a marriage by ordinary means, but conducts the happy pair through long and dangerous galleries, where the light burns blue, the thunder rattles, and the great window at the end presents the hideous visage of a *murdered* man, *uttering* piercing groans, and developing shocking mysteries. If a curtain is withdrawn, there is a bleeding body behind it; if a chest is opened, it contains a skeleton; if a noise is heard, somebody is receiving a deadly blow; and if a candle goes out, its place is sure to be supplied by a flash of lightning. Cold hands

* [footnote added by the editor of the journal] It is easy to see that the satire of this letter is particularly levelled at a literary lady of considerable talents, who has presented the world with three novels, in which she hat found out the secret of making us 'fall in love with what we fear to look on.' – The *system of terror* which she is adopted is not the only reproach to which she is liable. Besides, the tedious monotony of her descriptions, she affects in the most disgusting manner a knowledge of languages, countries, customs, and objects of art of which she is lamentably ignorant. She suspends *tripods* from the cieling by chains, not knowing that a *tripod* is a utensil standing upon three feet. – She covers the kingdom of Naples with India figs because *St Pierre* has introduced these tropical plants in his tales, of which the scene is laid in Italy – and she makes a convent of monks a necessary appendage to a monastery of nuns. This shews how well a lady understands the wants of her sex. Whenever she introduces an Italian word it is sure to be a gross violation of language. Instead of making a nobleman's servant call him *Padrone*, or *Illustrissimo*, she makes him address him by the title of *Maestro*, which is Italian for a teacher. She converts the singular of *Lazzaroni* into Lazzaro, &c. &c. &c.

This lady's husband told a friend that he was going to Germany with his wife, the object of whose journey was to pick up materials for a novel. I think in that case, answered his friend, that you had better let her go alone!

grasp us in the dark, statues are seen to move, and suits of armour walk off their pegs, while the wind whistles louder than one of Handel's chorusses, and the still air is more melancholy than the dead march in Saul.

Such are the dresses and decorations of a modern novel, which, as Bayes says, is calculated to 'elevate and surprise'; but in doing so, carries the young reader's imagination into such a confusion of terrors, as must be hurtful. It is to great purpose, indeed, that we have forbidden our servants from telling the children stories of ghosts and hobgoblins, if we cannot put a novel into their hands which is not filled with monsters of the imagination, more frightful than are to be found in Glanvil,[11] the famous *bug-a-boo* of our forefathers.

A novel, if at all useful, ought to be a representation of human life and manners, with a view to direct the conduct in the most important duties of life, and to correct its follies. But what instruction is to be reaped from the distorted ideas of lunatics, I am at a loss to conceive. Are we come to such a pass, that the only commandment necessary to be repeated is, 'Thou shalt do no murder?' Are the duties of life so changed, that all the instructions necessary for a young person is to learn to walk at night upon the battlements of an old castle, to creep hands and feet along a narrow passage, and meet the devil at the end of it? Is the corporeal frame of the female sex so masculine and hardy, that it must be softened down by the touch of dead bodies, clay-cold hands, and damp sweats? Can a young lady be taught nothing more necessary in life, than to sleep in a dungeon with venomous reptiles, walk through a ward [wood] with assassins, and carry bloody daggers in their pockets, instead of pin-cushions and needle-books?

Every absurdity has an end, and as I observe that almost all novels are of the terrific cast, I hope the insipid repetition of the same bugbears will at length work a cure. In the mean time, should any of your female readers be desirous of catching the season of terrors, she may compose two or three very pretty volumes from the following recipe:

Take – An old castle, half of it ruinous.
A long gallery, with a great many doors, some secret ones.
Three murdered bodies, quite fresh.
As many skeletons, in chests and presses.
An old woman hanging by the neck; with her throat cut.
Assassins and desperadoes '*quant suff.*'
Noise, whispers, and groans, threescore at least.

Mix them together, in the form of three volumes to be taken at any of the watering places, before going to bed.

PROBATUM EST.

4.5 The *Monk* affair

Matthew Gregory Lewis wrote *The Monk* at the age of nineteen, inspired, as he explained in a letter to his mother, by Ann Radcliffe's *The Mysteries of Udolpho*. The novel, with its spectacular supernaturalism accompanied by scenes of rampant sexuality and horrible cruelty and suffering, was like nothing ever seen before, and certainly very different from Radcliffe. It was instantly successful, quickly going through three editions. But it was not long before a critical reaction set in, heightened by the discovery that the author was now a Member of Parliament. Coleridge's review was the most measured of the negative critical responses. Once Mathias had (anonymously) posed what amounted to a legal challenge for blasphemy in *The Pursuits of Literature*, attacks were narrowed to Lewis's supposed irreligion, suggested by a passage in which Elvira is praised by the narrator for bowdlerising her young daughter's copy of the Bible (cited by Coleridge in the first extract). Lewis, clearly rattled, amended it in the fourth edition.

4.5a Samuel Taylor Coleridge (1772–1834), review of *The Monk* (1797)

Source: *Critical Review*, vol. 19 (February 1797), pp. 194–200.

The horrible and the preternatural have usually seized on the popular taste, at the rise and decline of literature. Most powerful stimulants, they can never be required except by the torpor of an unawakened, or the langour of an exhausted, appetite. The same phaenomenon, therefore, which we hail as a favourable omen in the belles lettres of Germany, impresses a degree of gloom in the compositions of our countrymen. We trust, however, that satiety will banish what good sense should have prevented; and that, wearied with fiends, incomprehensible characters, with shrieks, murders, and subterraneous dungeons, the public will learn, by the multitude of the manufacturers, with how little expense of thought or imagination this species of composition is manufactured. But, cheaply as we estimate romances in general, we acknowledge, in the work before us, the offspring of no common genius. The tale is similar to that of Santon Barsista in the Guardian.[12] Ambrosio, a monk, surnamed the Man of Holiness, proud of his own undeviating rectitude, and severe to the faults of others, is successfully assailed by the tempter of mankind, and seduced to the perpetration of rape and murder, and finally precipitated into a contract in which he consigns his soul to everlasting perdition.

The larger part of the three volumes is occupied by the underplot, which, however, is skilfully and closely connected with the main story, and is subservient to its development. The tale of the bleeding nun is truly terrific; and we could not easily recollect a bolder or more happy conception that that of the burning cross on the forehead of the wandering Jew (a mysterious character, which, though copied as to its more prominent features from Schiller's incomprehensible Armenian,[13] does, nevertheless, display great vigour of fancy). But the character of Matilda, the chief agent in the seduction of Antonio [*sic* for Ambrosio], appears to us to be the author's master-piece. It is, indeed, exquisitely imagined, and as exquisitely supported. The whole work is distinguished by the variety and impressiveness of its incidents; and the author everywhere discovers an imagination rich, powerful, and fervid. Such are the excellencies; – the errors and defects are more numerous, and (we are sorry to add) of greater importance.

All events are levelled into one common mass, and become almost equally probable, where the order of nature may be changed whenever the author's purposes demand it. No address is requisite to the accomplishment of any design; and no pleasure therefore can be received from the perception of *difficulty surmounted*. The writer may make us wonder, but he cannot surprise us. For the same reasons a romance is incapable of exemplifying a moral truth. No proud man, for instance, will be made less proud by being told that Lucifer once seduced a presumptuous monk. *Incredulus odit.*[14] Or even if, believing the story, he should deem his virtue less secure, he would yet acquire no lessons of prudence, no feelings of humility. Human prudence can oppose no sufficient shield to the power and cunning of supernatural beings; and the privilege of being proud might be fairly conceded to him who could rise superior to all earthly temptations, and whom the strength of the spiritual world alone would be adequate to overwhelm. So falling, he would fall with glory, and might reasonably welcome his defeat with the haughty emotions of a conqueror. As far, therefore, as the story is concerned, the praise which a romance can claim, is simply that of having given pleasure during its perusal; and so many are the calamities of life, that he who has done this, has not written uselessly. The children of sickness and solitude thank him. – To this praise, however, our author has not entitled himself. The sufferings which he describes are so frightful and intolerable, that we break with abruptness from the delusion, and indignantly suspect the man of a species of brutality, who could find a pleasure in wantonly imagining them; and the abominations which he pourtrays with no hurrying pencil, are such as the observation of character by no means demanded, such as 'no observation of character can justify, because no good man would willingly suffer them to pass, however transiently, through his own mind.' The merit of a novellist is in proportion (not simply to the effect, but) to the *pleasurable* effect which he produces. Situations of torment, and images of naked horror, are easily conceived; and a writer in whose works they abound, deserves our gratitude almost equally with him who should drag us by way of sport through a military hospital, or force us to sit at the dissecting-table of a natural philosopher. To trace the nice boundaries, beyond which terror and sympathy are deserted by the pleasurable emotions, – to reach those limits, yet never to pass them, – *hic labor, hic opus est.*[15] Figures that shock the imagination, and narratives that mangle the feelings, rarely discover *genius*, and always betray a low and vulgar *taste*. Nor has our author indicated less ignorance of the human heart in the management of the principal character. The wisdom and goodness of providence have ordered that the tendency of vicious actions to deprave the heart of the perpetrator, should diminish in proportion to the greatness of his temptations. Now, in addition to constitutional warmth and irresistible opportunity, the monk is impelled to incontinence by friendship, by compassion, by gratitude, by all that is amiable, and all that is estimable; yet in a few weeks after his first frailty, the man who had been described as possessing much general humanity, a keen and vigorous understanding, with habits of the most exalted piety, degenerates into an uglier fiend than the gloomy imagination of Dante would have ventured to picture. Again, the monk is described as feeling and acting under the influence of an appetite which could not co-exist with his other emotions. The romance-writer possesses an unlimited power over situations; but he must scrupulously make his characters act in congruity with them. Let him work *physical* wonders only, and we will be content to *dream* with him for a while; but the first *moral* miracle which he attempts, he disgusts and awakens us. Thus our judgment remains unoffended, when, announced by thunders and earthquakes, the spirit appears to Ambrosio involved in blue fires that increase the cold of the cavern; and we acquiesce in the power of the silver myrtle which made gates and doors fly open at its touch, and charmed every eye into sleep. But when a mortal, fresh from the impression of that terrible appearance, and in the act of evincing for the first time the witching force of this myrtle, is represented as being at the same moment agitated by so fleeting an appetite as that of lust, our own feelings convince us that this is not improbable, but impossible; not preternatural, but contrary to nature. The extent of the powers that may exist, we can never ascertain; and therefore we feel no great difficulty in yielding a temporary belief to any, the strangest, situation of *things*. But that situation once conceived, how beings like ourselves would feel and act in it, our own feelings sufficiently instruct us; and we instantly reject the clumsy fiction that does not harmonise with them. These are the two *principal* mistakes in *judgment*, which the author has fallen into; but we cannot wholly pass over the frequent incongruity of his style with his subjects. It is gaudy where it should have been severely simple; and too often the mind is offended by phrases the most trite and colloquial, where it demands and had expected a sternness and solemnity of diction.

A more grievous fault remains, – a fault for which no literary excellence can atone, – a fault which all other excellence does but aggravate, as adding subtlety to a poison by the elegance of its preparation. Mildness of censure would here be criminally misplaced, and silence would make us accomplices. Not without reluctance then, but in full conviction that we are performing a duty, we declare it to be our opinion, that the Monk is a romance, which if a parent saw in the hands of a son or daughter, he might reasonably turn pale. The temptations of Ambrosio are described with a libidinous minuteness, which, we sincerely hope, will receive its best and only adequate censure from the offended conscience of the author himself. The shameless harlotry of Matilda, and the trembling innocence of Antonia, are seized with equal avidity, as vehicles of the most voluptuous images; and though the tale is indeed a tale of horror, yet the most painful impression which the work left on our minds was that of great acquirements and splendid genius employed to furnish a *mormo*[16] for children, a poison for youth, and a provocative for the debauchee. Tales of enchantments and witchcraft can never be *useful*: our author has contrived to make them *pernicious*, by blending, with an irreverent negligence, all that is most awfully true in religion with all that is most ridiculously absurd in superstition. He takes frequent occasion, indeed, to manifest his sovereign contempt for the latter, both in his own person, and (most incongruously) in that of his principal characters; and that his respect for the *former* is not excessive, we are forced to conclude from the treatment which its inspired writings receive from him. Ambrosio discovers Antonia reading –

'He examined the book which she had been reading, and had now placed upon the table. It was the Bible.

'"How!" said the friar to himself, "Antonia reads the Bible, and is still so ignorant?"

'But, upon a further inspection, he found that Elvira had made exactly the same remark. That prudent mother, while she admired the beauties of sacred writings, was convinced that, unrestricted, no reading more improper could be permitted a young woman. Many of the narratives can only tend to excite ideas the worst calculated for a female breast: every thing is called plainly and roundly by its name; and the *annals of a brothel would scarcely furnish a greater choice of indecent expressions*. Yet this is the book which young women are recommended to study, which is put into the hands of children, able to comprehend little more than those passages of which they had better remain ignorant, and which but too *frequently inculcates the first rudiments of vice*, and gives the first alarm to the still sleeping passions. Of this was Elvira so fully convinced, that she would have preferred putting into her daughter's hands "Amadis de Gaul," or "The Valiant Champion Tirante the White"; and *would sooner have authorised her studying the lewd exploits of Don Galaor, or the lascivious jokes of the Damsel Plazer di mi vida*.' Vol.II, p. 247.

The impiety of this falsehood can be equalled only by its impudence. This is indeed as if a Corinthian harlot, clad from head to foot in the transparent thinness of the Cöan vest, should affect to view with prudish horror the naked knee of a Spartan matron! If it be possible that the author of these blasphemies is a Christian, should he not have reflected that the only passage in the scriptures,* which could give a *shadow* of plausibility to the *weakest* of these expressions, is represented as being spoken by the Almighty himself? But if he be an infidel, he has acted consistently enough with that character, in his endeavours first to influence the fleshly appetites, and then to pour contempt on the only book which would be adequate to the task of recalming them. We believe it not absolutely impossible that a mind may be so deeply depraved by the habit of reading lewd and voluptuous tales, as to use even the Bible in conjuring up the spirit of uncleanness. The most innocent expressions might become the first link in the chain of association, when a man's soul had been so poisoned; and we believe it not absolutely impossible that he might extract pollution from the word of purity, and, in a literal sense, *turn the grace of God into wantonness*.

4.5b Thomas Mathias (1754?–1835), *The Pursuits of Literature* (1798)

This extract is from the Preface to the Fourth (and last) Dialogue of the poem. In the original it is annotated with several long and tortuous footnotes, typical of Mathias's style, quoting the offending passage from *The Monk* (in vol. 2, chapter 4) and citing numerous comparable instances in which authors or publishers had been successfully prosecuted for obscene and blasphemous books.

Source: Thomas Mathias (1803), *The Pursuits of Literature: A Satirical Poem in Four Dialogues*, 12th edn, London: T. Becket, Dialogue IV, pp. 244–50.

★

. . . In my Preface to the Third Dialogue, feeling the importance of my subject in its various branches, I asserted that,

> LITERATURE, *well or ill conducted*, IS THE GREAT ENGINE *by which* ALL CIVILIZED STATES *must ultimately be supported or overthrown*

I am now more and more deeply impressed with this truth, if we consider the nature, variety, and extent of the word Literature.

* Ezekiel, chap. xxiii.

We are no longer in an age of ignorance; and information is not partially distributed according to the ranks, and orders, and functions, and dignities of social life. All learning has an index, and every science its abridgment. I am scarcely able to name any man whom I consider as wholly ignorant. We no longer look exclusively for learned authors in the usual place, in the retreats of academic erudition, and in the seats of religion. Our peasantry now read the *Rights of Man* on mountains, and moors, and by the way side; and shepherds make the analogy between their occupation and that of their governors. Happy indeed had they been taught to make no other comparison. Our *unsexed* female writers now instruct, or confuse, us and themselves in the labyrinth of politics, or turn us wild with Gallic frenzy.

But there is a publication of the time too peculiar, and too important to be passed over in a general reprehension. There is nothing with which it may be compared. A legislator in our own parliament, a member of the House of Commons of Great Britain, and elected guardian and defender of the laws, the religion, and the good manners of the country, has neither scrupled nor blushed to depict, and to publish to the world, the arts of lewd and systematic seduction, and to thrust upon the nation the most open and unqualified blasphemy against the very code and volume of our religion. And all this, with his name, style and title, prefixed to the novel or romance called 'THE MONK'. And one of our public theatres has allured the public attention still more to this novel, by a scenic representation of an Episode in it. 'O Proceres Censore opus est, an Haruspice nobis?'* I consider this as a new species of legislative or state-parricide.

What is it to the kingdom at large, or what is it to all those whose office it is to maintain truth, and to instruct the rising abilities and hope of England, that the author of THE MONK is *a very young man*? That forsooth he is a man of genius and fancy? So much the worse. That there are very poetical descriptions of castles and abbies in this novel? So much the worse again, the novel is more alluring on that account. Is this a time to poison the waters of our land in their springs and fountains? Are we to add incitement to incitement, and corruption to corruption, till there neither is, nor can be, a return to virtuous action and to regulated life? Who knows *the age* of this author? I presume very few. Who does *not know*, that he is a Member of Parliament? He has told us all so himself.

I pretend not to know, (Sir John Scott knows, and practises too, whatever is honourable, and virtuous, and dignified in learning and professional ability[17]) I pretend not, I say, to know whether this be an object of parliamentary animadversion. But we can feel that it is an object of moral and of national reprehension, when a Senator openly and daringly violates his first duty to his country. There are wounds and obstructions, and diseases

* Juv[enal] Sat[ires] 2: 'O ye chiefs of the land, does this require a censor to publish it, or an augur to explain the prodigy? Do ye call for the arm of the law, or the lustration of religion?'

in the political, as well as the natural, body, for which the removal of the part affected is alone efficacious. At an hour like this, are we to stand in consultation on the remedy, when not only the disease is ascertained, but the very stage of the disease, and its specific symptoms? Are we to spare the sharpest instruments of authority and of censure, when public establishments are gangrened in the life-organs?

I fear, if our legislators are wholly regardless of *such* writings, and of such principles, *among their own members*, it may be said to them, as the Roman Satirist said to the patricians of the empire, for offences slight indeed, when compared to these;

> At vos Trojugenae vobis ignoscitis, et quae
> Turpia cerdoni Volesos Brutosque decebunt.*

There is surely something peculiar in these days; something wholly unknown to our ancestors. But men, however dignified in their political station, or gifted with genius and fortune, and accomplishments, may at least be made ashamed, or alarmed, or convicted before the tribunal of public opinion. Before that tribunal, and to the law of reputation, and every binding and powerful sanction by which that law is enforced, is Mr. LEWIS this day called to answer.

4.5c 'A Friend to Genius', 'An Apology for The Monk' (1797)

This letter defends *The Monk* against a number of charges, including those brought specifically by Coleridge and Mathias. There is a rare assertion, of more general interest, that 'incredible fiction' can be made 'a proper vehicle for moral instruction'.

Source: *Monthly Mirror*, vol. 3 (April 1797), pp. 210–15.

★

Mr. Editor,

It is with no inconsiderable pain that I have remarked the numerous attacks which have been made by the host of critics on the ingenious author of the MONK, for the supposed vicious tendency of that excellent romance. The author is universally allowed to be endowed with nature's best gift, genius, and in the work before us is generally acknowledged to discover throughout an imagination, rich, powerful, and fervid. This able writer, is, however, attacked on a point which, I am sure, must

* Juv. Sat. 8.v.181: 'But ye, who boast yourself of *Trojan* ancestry, find excuses for one another; and such actions, as would disgrace the meanest mechanic, are esteemed honourable in men of rank and dignity.'

make him feel little satisfaction in the applause which his genius commands. It is asserted by almost all the critics who have sat in judgment on this admirable performance, that its *tendency* is to deprave the heart, to vitiate the understanding, and to enlist the passions in the cause of vice. Differing as I do with these censors, as to this and other objections, I wish, through the medium of your impartial publication, to rescue his production from this undeserved obliquy. I have not the pleasure of Mr. Lewis's acquaintance, and I know not how this apology may be received on his part, but the defence of genius is the common cause of all men of the least pretensions to literature; and every person who can enjoy works of taste, has the right of rescuing them from unmerited attacks. I should, as little as the critics, wish to be the apologist of vice, or the defender of lasciviousness; but justice requires that error, and error of such magnitude, as it regards Mr. Lewis's character, should be detected and exposed.

The error of the principal objection to this romance, viz. that of its vicious *tendency*, appears to me entirely to arise from inaccuracy of observation of the author's work, of the human heart, and of the meaning of the word tendency. It is not a temporary effect, produced upon the imagination or the passions, by particular passages, which can fairly be cited as the tendency of the work; we must examine what are the probable general results from the whole, and not judge from these partial and fleeting effects.

In this view, I maintain, this beautiful romance is well calculated to support the cause of virtue, and to teach her lessons to man. I am not old enough to have my heart steeled against the effects of the strongest of the human passions, nor young enough to riot in lascivious description, or wanton in the regions of obscene imagery. I can feel as disgusted as the critics with such defects; but I entreat these *grey bearded* gentleman to consider again whether there are any such images in the work before us. The lessons of virtue which I see in the Monk, are striking and impressive. In the character of Ambrosio we see a man delineated of strong passions, which have been for a long period subdued by as strong resolution; of a natural disposition to virtue, but, like all other men, with some portion of vice, which has been fostered by the situation into which his fate had thrown him; he is haughty, vindictive, and austere. The greatest error of which he is guilty, is too great a confidence in his own virtue, too great a reliance on his own hatred of vice. We are taught by his conduct that this unbounded confidence, by blinding the mind as to the real consequences which result, lays the foundation for, vice, and opens an easy road to great excesses. We have again a very forcible illustration in Ambrosio, a man of the strongest understanding and the highest powers of reason, of the danger of receding even in the least from the path of virtue, or giving way in the slightest degree to the insidious approaches of vice. *C'est le premier pas qui coute*,[18] is a truth long established, and is well illustrated in the present instance. We see and feel strongly this danger, and the lesson is the more forcible, in proportion to the strength of understanding which is shown in the Monk. We learn that when once a man ventures into the pool of vice, that he plunges deeper and deeper till he is completely overwhelmed. These are striking and impressive lessons.

There are many other moral lessons which are inculcated by the work in the strongest manner; the tendency, therefore, i.e. the general effect likely to result, is favourable to the cause of virtue and morality. We are however told, that 'the temptations of Ambrosio are described with a libidinous minuteness, which leaves the painful impression of great acquirements and splendid genius, employed to furnish poison for youth, and a provocative for the debauchee' [*Critical Review*, for February, 1797]. If this were the case, I must give up my author in part, though still the tendency of the whole would be good. But I deny the fact. I request that the character and circumstances of Ambrosio may be seriously considered. To a man of strong understanding, austerity of manners, and great self command, strong temptations must be offered. If the author had made the Monk sink under a slight temptation, he would have offended against the laws of probability, and shocked the reason of his readers. I ask if it be possible to describe such temptations as were calculated to seduce such a man, with greater delicacy and decorum than our author has done: and I will take for example the strongest instances – the conclusion of chapter 2. vol. 1. p. 253 of vol. 2 and his attack on Antonia in p. 36 and 37 of vol. 3. The answer, I am persuaded, must be – No! Highly coloured as these passages are, I maintain that no heart but one already depraved, could rise from them, if the preceding part of the work had been perused, with the least impurity. The mind that could draw food for vicious appetites from this work, must have made no little progress in the paths of profligacy and debauchery; so strong are the entrenchments erected before the heart, by the *general tendency* of the work.

The previous part is calculated to prevent all the evil which may arise from warmth of description, by the interest we take in observing the gradual progress of vice in Ambrosio's bosom, and the hatred we of course must feel for this insidious adversary. The work can be read only by three descriptions of persons; either those whose minds, by habitual vice, are prepared to turn even the least hint to the purposes of food for their depraved appetites, or as incitements to their dormant desires, which require stimulants; or those who are wavering between vice and virtue, whose minds may be led to either, by interesting their passions strongly for one or the other; or else, young, innocent, and undepraved persons. The first deserve not notice: purity itself would be poison to their hearts, and the modestest allusion whould excite depraved ideas. The passions of the second will be, I contend, excited more strongly to virtue than to vice by the Monk, because the horrors consequent on his vicious conduct are so strongly portrayed, as to destroy the momentary effect, if any were produced, of the passages which are rather warm in description. The last, from the very supposition of their being yet innocent and unpolluted, and in consequence ignorant, can not have improper ideas excited, or their passions roused to vice; as, in the first place, they will not be able to understand as much as our *knowing* critics, nor can the confused notions of felicity which may be excited destroy the purity of their minds, or the effect of the moral lessons inculcated. The writer of this paper felt not a single loose idea excited by the warmest passages, so perfectly had he imbibed the moral lessons which the author has so forcibly brought forward.

The critics themselves seem aware of this tendency of the work, and therefore endeavour to deprive the author of the defence, by roundly asserting that 'a romance is incapable of exemplifying moral truth; and that he who could rise superior to all earthly temptation, and whom the strength of the spiritual world alone would be adequate to overwhelm, might reasonably be proud, and would fall with glory.' As applied to the Monk, there are two errors in this assertion. The reader of this romance has no reason to imagine, till the greater part of the mischief has been done, that any but earthly temptations are used against the hero. The fall of Ambrosio is precisely that which would happen to any man of a similar character, assailed as he was by the fascinating arts of a woman, skilled in exciting the strongest passions, and endowed with the most attractive charms. We see the gradual progress she makes in undermining his virtue by merely human means. His feeling, his gratitude, and finally the strong desires of human nature are all combined to ensure his fall. But still the temptations appear to be no more than human. We see where a man of truly virtuous principles would have commenced resistance; we observe and lament his first deviation from the path of virtue; and cannot withold our wishes that he may remain firm when the first disposition to yield manifests itself. Matilda appears to be merely a woman, though a woman of the greatest charms, and of an extraordinary character; but still there is nothing improbable or unnatural in the means of temptation, nothing that a man of a strong mind and pure virtue would not have resisted. The lesson therefore is taught and deeply imbibed before the discovery of supernatural agency is made, and that discovery does not and cannot eradicate the morality before inculcated.

Nor is it true in general that moral truth cannot be conveyed in romance. The general sense of mankind is against the critics in this assertion. From the earliest ages fiction, and incredible fiction, has been thought a proper vehicle for moral instruction, for the fables of Aesop, to the tales, allegories, and visions of modern days. The religion itself which these gentlemen profess inculcates the notion that Lucifer is the author of all our vicious propensities, and that he is the continual seducer of man. An allegorical representation of this being visibly interfering is no more therefore than adopting popular belief, and turning it to the purposes of instruction. It is no more improbable, on the notion of this great tempter, that a man should yield to his agency, when he himself assumes the human figure, than when he is supposed, as he is, to inhabit the bodies of all the vicious, and supply the crafty and artful with the means of operating on inferior minds. We do not the less blame Eve, because we are told that she yielded to the temptation of the serpent.

As to the minor objections made to the conduct of parts of the story, and defects of style and description, I feel not myself called on to defend, my object not being to establish the literary but moral excellence of the work. The only remaining objection which I shall attempt to answer is that 'our author has contrived to make his romance pernicious, by blending, with an irreverent negligence, all that is most awfully true in religion, with all that is most ridiculously absurd in superstition. He takes frequent occasion, indeed, to manifest his sovereign contempt for the latter, both in his own person and in that of his principal characters; and that his respect for the former is not excessive we are forced to conclude from the treatment which its inspired writers receive from him.'

In support of this observation we have a garbled passage quoted by the critics, in which the author has noticed with too much warmth, we must confess, some of the passages of the bible, which are undoubtedly improper for the eye of a young female. It is not fair to quote this passage without adding the eulogiums which the author has passed on the morality of the sacred writings, both in that passage and others in the work. Whether the author be or be not a Christian, is not the inquiry, but whether there be any foundation for the observation made on the indecency of some parts of our religious code; this the critics are obliged to allow is the case in one instance, viz. Ezekiel chap. 23. There are also other examples which must be in the eye of every man who has read these writings with attention. The indiscriminate perusal of such passages as occur, in which every thing is called by its vulgar name, in which the most luxuriant images are described, as in Solomon's Song, must certainly be improper for young females. So fully aware were the Jews of this truth, that they prohibited the reading of Solomon's Song, till a certain age, when the passions are in subjection. The warmth of expression is too great, but we may pardon this, since we see a desire of preventing the mischievous effects of even the most generally excellent production. – The author, so far from deserving to be stigmatized as an enemy to Christianity, appears to me to be acting as one of its best friends, when he endeavours to prevent the mischief which may ensue from mixing what may be improper for young minds, with the rest of a work so generally excellent in its morality, so pure in its doctrines.

The mischief which might be produced would be the greater, because of the reverence with which young persons are generally taught to regard the sacred writings. The impression of such images as are blamed, would be the more deeply engraven on the mind, as they believe that nothing can be learned there but purity and innocence. I should have thought that these critics might have overlooked an error into which they themselves have fallen to a still greater excess: for they cannot allow the moral tendency of the romance to plead the pardon of two or three passages, which appear to them to be too luxuriant, and too replete with wanton imagery.

I have thus, Sir, endeavoured to shew that the attacks made on Mr. Lewis are unfounded, and that when the critic stares and trembles to find the author of the Monk a legislator, his horror is not reasonable; and that with propriety we may apply to those men who can drink vice at the fountain of the Monk, the expression of this very critic: 'The most innocent expressions may become the first link in the chain of association, when a man's soul has been poisoned and depraved by the habit of reading lewd and voluptuous tales; and we believe it not absolutely impossible that he might extract pollution from the word of purity, and turn the grace of God into wantonness.'

I hope I have succeeded in showing, that 'the author has not endeavoured to inflame the fleshy appetites, and then to pour contempt on the only book which would be adequate to the task of reclaiming them.' If I have not failed in this object, I shall feel a satisfaction in having employed a leisure hour in a task so delightful as rescuing from disgrace, in my opinion unmerited, a man of such talents, taste, and brilliancy of imagination, as the author of the Monk. I hope this attempt will not be displeasing to him who is the most concerned, nor fail of its effect on the public mind. My motives are, however, pure; I know I am as great an enemy to licentiousness as the critics themselves, and I trust I have shewn myself

A FRIEND TO GENIUS

4.6 Gothic drama

In spite of the praise lavished on Shakespeare's scenes of supernatural terror, and their popularity with audiences, there was strong critical opposition to the introduction of the marvellous into contemporary dramatic writing. Dramatic adaptations of the best-known Gothic novels were produced by specialists like Robert Jephson and James Boaden, but in each case any hint of the supernatural was removed. The overt reason for the double standard was that since dramatic fictions are visible, the inclusion of imaginary beings would represent an added affront to reason. Another unspoken reason might lie in the difference between public and private representation and consumption; the more socially heterogeneous and volatile nature of theatre audiences, for instance, seems to have inclined writers, critics and theatre managers against experimentation. Only M. G. Lewis had both the audacity to include a 'real ghost' in his cast of characters, and the influence – on the strength of the *The Monk* – to get it staged.

4.6a Reviews of Harriet Lee, *The Mysterious Marriage* (1798)

Harriet Lee (1757–1851) was the younger sister of Sophia Lee, author of *The Recess* (see 4.3). Her own writing career began with a novel, *The Errors of Innocence* (1786), and a comedy drama, *The New Peerage*, produced in 1787. The failure of *The Mysterious Marriage* was a setback, but the collection of stories she wrote with Sophia, *Canterbury Tales* (5 vols, 1797–1805), had a better reception, in particular Harriet's tale of psychological torment, 'Kruitzner', often cited as a source for Byron's 'Manfred'.

★

Analytical Review, vol. 27 (1798), pp. 295–6

We are led to suspect, from the querulous strain of an advertisement, which is prefixed to this play, that miss Lee has made some unsuccessful endeavour to procure its performance: 'the difficulty, that *during the present management of the theatres*, attends producing any piece to advantage upon the stage, has hitherto inclined the author to consign hers to obscurity.' One or two more passages of similar import betray disappointment. We must confess, that had the managers of Drury-lane or Covent-garden offered the manuscript of this drama for our opinion of its merits, and probability of it's success, we dare scarcely have advised a representation of it: the characters are not supported with sufficient spirit, and, of course, the dialogue is feeble and undignified. The ghost of a murdered female is introduced into the 'Mysterious Marriage,' and as the play was written some years ago, miss Lee puts in her claim to originality of idea in conjuring up the spectre, though, as she justly observes, the charm of novelty may now be lost.

We are really sorry, that any merit should be claimed for perverting the simplicity of the drama by the introduction of visionary and phantastic beings: supernatural agency is the taste of a barbarous age, and ought to be banished from our theatres at once. Miss Lee will hardly plead a precedent in Shakspeare or Ben Jonson; her own good sense, surely, will suggest the impropriety of an attempt to revive the exploded superstitions of a former age, and the impossibility that the same effect should be produced by a representation of them now, which attended them at the time when Shakspeare and Ben Jonson lived. No, no; let ghosts and hobgoblins people the pages of a romance, but never let their forms be seen to glide across the stage.

British Critic, vol. 12 (1798), p. 73

In the advertisement prefixed, the author asserts her claim to 'originality of idea', in conjuring up a *female spectre*; and she proves it, by the circumstance of her play having been read, more than two years since, by Mr. Colman and other literary gentlemen. To us, the originality appears not worth contending for. We would interdict the production of any *new* spectre on the stage. *This* 'reign of terror' is over: 'incredulus odi'. In a *modern* play, ghosts cannot be tolerated: they are generally mere substitutes for good sense and good writing. We acknowledge, however, that in this play there are several passages written with taste and feeling; and this is the sort of praise to which the author seems principally to aspire. But as a whole, *we* cannot warmly commend it. The plot is of ordinary construction; and the principal characters are mere common-place personages; some angelical, others diabolical. The appearance of the spectre, for a moment, contributes nothing to the catastrophe; which is brought about chiefly by an incident always at hand, the stroke of a dagger. The *verses* are the worst part of the performance.

4.6b Matthew Gregory Lewis (1775–1818), Postscript to *The Castle Spectre* (1798)

Source: Matthew Gregory Lewis (1798), *The Castle Spectre: A Drama,* London: J. Bell, pp. 102–3.

★

... Against *my Spectre* many objections have been urged: one of them I think rather curious. She ought not to appear, because the belief in Ghosts no longer exists! In my opinion, this is the very reason why she *may* be produced without danger; for there is now no fear of increasing the influence of superstition, or strengthening the prejudices of the weak-minded. I confess I cannot see any reason why Apparitions may not be as well permitted to stalk in a tragedy, as Fairies be suffered to fly in a pantomime, or Heathen Gods and Goddesses to cut capers in a grand ballet, and I should rather imagine that *Oberon* and *Bacchus* now find as little credit to the full as the *Cock-lane Ghost,*[19] or the Spectre of *Mrs. Veal.*[20]

Never was any poor soul so ill-used as *Evelina's*, previous to her presenting herself before the audience. The Friends to whom I read my Drama, the Managers to whom I presented it, the Actors who were to perform in it – all combined to persecute by *Spectre*, and requested me to confine my Ghost to the Green-Room. Aware that without her my catastrophe would closely resemble that of the *Grecian Daughter*,[21] I persisted in retaining her. The event justified my obstinacy: *The Spectre* was as well treated before the curtain as she had been ill-used behind it; and as she continues to make her appearance nightly with increased applause, I think myself under great obligations both to her and her representative.

4.6c 'Academicus', 'On the Absurdities of the Modern Stage' (1800)

Source: *Monthly Mirror*, vol. 10 (1800), pp. 180–2.

★

somnia, terrores magicos, miracula, sagas,
Nocturnos lemures, portentaque, Thessala rides,
Horace[22]

This is the very coinage of your brain
This bodiless creation, ecstasy,
Is very cunning in. [*Hamlet*, III.iv.139–41]

If charnel houses, and our graves, must send
Those that we bury back, our monuments
Shall be the maws of kites. [*Macbeth*, III.iv.70–2]

Rest, rest, perturbed spirit, rest, I say. [*Hamlet*, I.v.190]
Shakspere

Mr. Editor,

The subject of the following, needs no preface. It will be sufficient to observe, that its object is, like Prospero's wand, to cause the ghostly spirits of dramatic poesy, the terrific, wild, and numerous apparitions that haunt Old Drury and Covent Garden, 'to vanish into thin air, and, like the baseless fabric of a vision, leave not a wreck behind' [*The Tempest*, IV.i.150–1, 156, misquoted]. Happy shall I be, and I shall have gained the object I had in view, if I can but dissolve the spell, and convince my readers, that the fairy tales; the Cock Lane Ghost; *Mother Bunch*'s romances; or even the mighty magician of *Udolpho*, *Aladdin* and the *Wonderful Lamp*, or the *Castle Spectre*, are very well in the nursery, will please children, when the *coral*[23] will not, but are not to be endured by men of sense and judgment, or who have ceased to think or act *like* children. Cannot these inspired writers, 'these fickle pensioners of Morpheus' train,' cannot they let the dead be at peace? Must they be ever raking their ashes to conjure up 'shadowy forms' and ideal mockeries, and horrible spectres? And cannot they indulge fancy's fire, without diving into mysteries more sacred than the Eleusinian, or pretending to search beyond the grave? They are the offspring, the undoubted progeny of Cerberus and Midnight; nay more, instead of shooting folly as it flies, they are the warmest patrons and guardians of it; they are either fools, or think every one of their countrymen so. – Are we to have prodigies and monstrous omens, horrid shapes, and the fruits of brooding darkness forced on us at a place to which we resort to be instructed and amused? Are we to expect to meet fiction instead of reality, on the stage? Cannot sober melancholy be pourtrayed without the aid of turrets and gloomy Gothic corridors haunted by ghosts? Better, should honest John Bull, from the one shilling gallery, call out for Rule Britannia, in the heart of the representation. – Atque ursum et pugiles media inter carmina noscat.[24] I would rather the gods, noisy and vociferous as they are in their mirth, would put to flight the souls of the departed, than that they should make their appearance to the disgrace of the good sense of a British audience.

That on the stage, where every action of life is, in general, understood to be faithfully represented, where nature should be displayed simple, pure, and unaffected, and most certainly should be the chief object, the primum mobile of the dramatist; where a due regard to truth is of the first moment, that improbability of the most extravagant kind, that unnatural absurdity, and ridiculous deviations from common sense and common experience, should be tolerated, nay, encouraged, by the applause of a numerous and trifling herd of *soi-disant* critics and pretended amateurs of the art, is a matter of astonishment, and calls for serious observation. Surely there is sufficient latitude for the pen of the dramatic poet; there is food for his contemplation; there are human follies, Mr. Editor, which might assuredly provoke laughter from the most rigid of the sect of Heraclitus, and there are also objects of compassion, which might force tears from Democritus himself, were he living.[25] Have we not dashing Goldfinches presented daily before our eyes?[26] So we not see them continually at watering places? Do we not meet them in the streets of London displaying their fashionable persons, dress, and equipage, to the gaze of vulgar admiration? Do we not hear of the misfortunes of a Beverley,[27] which would draw tears from the most obdurate stoic? Have we eyes, and see not; reason, and yet cannot understand? A family plunged into distress by a fashionable folly; a wife lamenting the death of a man who might have been an ornament to the society he has disgraced; a helpless assemblage of innocent children loudly and ineffectually demanding their father, who has lately fallen a victim to the infernal vice of gaming, destructive as it is contagious and universal? – Are not these subjects worthy the attention of those who write for the stage? Can the fate of such men as these be too well known or drawn in too strong and vivid colours to be shunned? Can the quicksands of gaming be too well guarded against? Do we stand in need of examples for villainy? How many men of fashionable gallantry are there, who have debauched their benefactors' wives, wounded their feeling in the most tender point, and embittered their lives for ever in return for the favours they have received? Are we not every where infested with men of honour, who suffer their tradesmen to starve? Let the author bring forth these characters to public view, execration, and infamy.

> Respicere exemplar vitae morumque jubebo
> Doctum imitatorem et *veras* hinc ducere voces.[28]

Does he seek for variety of character? Have we not *intriguing* duchesses, *superannuated* and *noble* rakes, *pedantic* females, whether of the refined Della Crusca,[29] or the more grave and moral Blue Stocking Academy, gentlemanly blacklegs,[30] youth who burn with a desire of being distinguished for their eccentric and prodigal conduct, *amorous* old maids, *clerical* bucks, *political* quidnuncs,[31] servile imitators of the vices of great and *exalted* personages, opulent men starving for want, and pennyless Lackland *bloods* of the *first* water? These are subjects at which satire might shoot her darts with impunity, nay, with the applause of every well-wisher of society. So true it is, that *totus mundus agit histrionam* – or, as Shakspere has it, *All the World's a stage*. These, and these only, I maintain, are the characters to be hunted down, or to be brought forward on the boards of a public theatre, unless the dramatic writer is daring enough to pourtray a virtuous character, such as a faithful friend, an affectionate father, a loving husband, and, lastly, that *rara avis*,[32] an honest man.

Yours, &c.

ACADEMICUS

4.7 Parodies

It was the fiction of Ann Radcliffe and her imitators that tended to be most often parodied, perhaps because Lewis and the more extreme German horror novelists already verged on self-parody. Admittedly, alongside the lacklustre *The New Monk* (1798) there were a number of burlesques of Lewis's 'Alonzo the Brave and the Fair Imogene'; but Lewis himself wrote the best of them, 'Giles Jollup the Grave and Brown Sally Green', which he included in the fourth edition of *The Monk* alongside the original. The collection of verse narratives *Tales of Wonder* (1800), which he produced with Walter Scott, gave rise to the famous cartoon by Gillray, as well as a parodic *Tales of Terror* (1801). The following extracts take Radcliffe as their target; specifically the mannerisms of her sentimental but highly inquisitive heroines. They might be compared with Jane Austen's famous spoof of her heroine's Gothic fantasies in *Northanger Abbey*, once considered a damning dismissal of an inferior and now forgotten species of fiction, today more likely to be described as an oblique commentary on the reality of women's social oppression.

4.7a William Beckford (1759–1844), *Azemia* (1797)

Beckford was the author of the orientalist Gothic tale *Vathek* (1786), which was compared to the *Arabian Nights* on its first appearance. In the following extracts from *Azemia*, written under the frilly pseudonym Jaquetta Agneta Mariana Jenks, he effectively imitates Radcliffe's elaborate method of picturesque description and her sentimental idiom, also poking fun at her pretentious and sometimes inaccurate use of foreign terms. His opposition to her device of the 'explained supernatural' was remarkably insistent throughout *Azemia* and another burlesque fiction, *Modern Novel-writing* (1796). The fact that he included a seriously frightening tale of terror involving a real ghost elsewhere in *Azemia* suggests that he felt an important aesthetic principle was at stake.

Source: [William Beckford] (1797), *Azemia: A Descriptive and Sentimental Novel. Interspersed with Pieces of Poetry by Jaquetta Agneta Mariana Jenks*, 2 vols, London: Sampson Low, vol. I, pp. 39–41, 50–4.

The weather was extremely warm; and Azemia, who had been in habits of enjoying the cool air of the fountained quadrangles of the haram, overshadowed with the palm of the cedar, and *deciduous cypress*, also larches and poplars, now languished for a little fresh air, and determined to attempt finding her way to the garden, as a scene *interesting to her imagination*. Having *wound down* the only staircase (which was rather narrow), and entered a passage rather old (of which the white-wash had fallen from the walls), she found herself in a narrow passage, terminated by two large bucking-tubs, and a broken queen's-ware bason of uncommon dimensions. The garden, or rather court, then appeared: she descended three steps, and entered a walk, formed of native earth, but bordered with ossifications of sheep, and shells of cockle and oyster, which gave this eastern part of the inclosure *rather a marine appearance*; while the more elevated borders enclosed an old oil-jar, in which had once grown a root of Angelica, but it was now no longer verdant. To the west, however, were scattered several small tufts of turnips, intermingled with mint and marjoram: nor was ornament wholly neglected; for in a more remote quarter grew a flourishing plant of the Canterbury bell. – The view beyond the garden was crowned with the awful summits of the neighbouring cheminées,* and beyond, through a wicket in the wall, *the eye caught* a part of the wild shores of the Thames, with wharfs and ozier grounds, the whole terminating in a remote prospect of the gloomy remains of two fresh-water pirates suspended some years before at Cuckhold's Point . . .

* *Chemineés*. Some little variation of spelling may be allowed where dignity is to be given to a subject – Chemineés is certainly better than chimney's, as being more like Pyrenées.

By this time evening came on; and when the vague sensations that had fluttered in the innocent breast of Azemia had a little subsided, she went in a pensive way into a neighbouring lumber room: it was old, spacious, and dark. Azemia imagined that her cat, now dearer to her than ever, had kittened there; and in the present moment it offered something like a solace to her mind, to reflect on the tender offices she might engage in, in nursing the infant progeny. She advanced therefore into the lumber-room; and slowly, and with difficulty, making her way among old sea chests, hammocks, and tables, coils of rope, remnants of carpets, and damaged pictures (for the immediate ancestor of Mrs. Periwinkle had been a broker), she at length reached the west side of this gloomy apartment.

There was a dreary solemnity about it; it was silent and solitary – the setting sun had almost sunk beneath the horizon, and his oblique rays, obscured by the neighbouring warehouse of an eminent dry salter, were almost entirely obfuscated by the succedaneums, placed in the dilapidated casements, which consisted of a piece of a mariner's check habiliment, and a wad of faded plaid that had composed the phillibeg of a Highlander in the year 1745. Azemia, who had never during her early youth been in so *queer* a place, looked round her somewhat dismayed, and for a moment her fears suspended her benevolent purpose. At length, recollecting the helpless family of her cat, she sighed, and began to search for them: she listened, but nothing was heard, save only the wind, that whispered in the waving of a harrateen bed, suspended to a dyer's pole on the adjoining roof. It was terrific! – Azemia shuddered – and as no gentle purring, no soft salutation of feline solicitation saluted her ear, and the wind howled with redoubled violence, moving the Scotch plaid to and fro, she found her resolution unequal to a further progress in this forlorn building; and was retreating, when a closet door creaking on its hinges slowly opened, and at the same moment some loose boards, on which she stood, *cracked*: Azemia started – she looked up, and beheld the figure of an old man, bald and squalid, sitting in a long dark robe reaching to his feet: his beard was as white as snow – his throat bare and wrinkled – and his withered hands, with long nails, appeared beneath the cuffs of his garment. Azemia looked at him with terror and astonishment: he nodded to her; yet there was something of an air about him that interested her, and a paralytic tremor agitated his head – but he did not speak. Azemia had never heard of a ghost* (in Turkey they are but little in use;) but terror, of she knew not what, possessed her; still she could not move from the spot. The figure nodded again and Azemia, in extreme apprehension, hastened back to her

* Lest another opportunity should not offer to explain in the sequel of my widely-wandering history, this ghastly and terrific appearance, I let my readers understand, that it was *not a real ghost*, or even a *wax-work figure*, but a large Chinese Mandarin, damaged in its voyage to Europe, and which had nodded ever since in the museum of Mrs. Periwinkle.[33]

apartment, and shut the lumber-room door, by placing a joint stool against it. For the present, the excessive agitation of her spirits banished the idea both of her fond lover and her favourite animal.

4.7b Eaton Stannard Barrett (1786–1820), *The Heroine* (1813)

In Barrett's *The Heroine* the romance-reading Cherry Wilkinson (alias Cherubina de Willoughby) is ultimately returned to her senses by the aid of a stalwart suitor and a strict diet of serious books, but the delirious silliness of her earlier adventures sits uneasily with this didacticism. The first extract is from a spoof novel within the novel, 'Il Castello di Grimgothico, or Memoirs of Lady Hysterica Belamour', purportedly the history of Cherubina's long-lost 'mother'; in fact, part of a hoax designed to play upon the heroine's belief in her noble parentage, a wild burlesque of the sensationalist fictions which had originally perverted her mind.

Source: Eaton Stannard Barrett, *The Heroine, or Adventures of Cherubina*, intr. Michael Sadleir, London: Matthews & Marrot, 1927. Although this is based on the third edition published in 1815, it includes the section 'Il Castello di Grimgothico' from the first edition of 1813, pp. 211–14, 349–51.

★

Chapter III

Be thou a spirit of health, or goblin damn'd?
Shakespeare

FRESH EMBARRASSMENTS. – AN INSULT FROM A SPECTRE. – GRAND DISCOVERIES. – A SHRIEK. – A TEAR. – A SIGH. – A BLUSH. – A SWOON.

It is a remark founded upon the nature of man, and universally credited by the thinking part of the world, that to suffer is an attribute of mortality.

Impressed with a due conviction of this important precept, our heroine but smiled as she heard Stiletto lock her door. It was now midnight, and she took up her lamp to examine the chamber. Rusty daggers, mouldering bones, and ragged palls, lay scattered in all the profusion of feudal plenty.

Several horrors now made their appearance; but the most uncommon was a winged eyeball that fluttered before her face. 'Say, little, foolish, fluttering thing?'[34]

She began shrieking and adjusting her hair at a mirror, when lo! she beheld the reflection of a ghastly visage peeping over her shoulder!

Much disconcerted, the trembling girl approached the bed. An impertinent apparition, with a peculiar nose, stood there, and made faces at her. She felt offended at the freedom, to say nothing of her being half dead with fright.

'Is it not enough,' thought she, 'to be harassed by beings of this world, but those of the next too must think proper to interfere? I am sure,' said she, as she raised her voice in a taunting manner, '*En verité*, I have no desire to meddle with *their* affairs. *Sur ma vie*, I have no taste for brimstone. So let me just advise a *certain* inhabitant of a *certain* world (not the *best*, I believe,) to think less of *my* concerns, and more of *his own*.'

Having thus asserted her dignity, without being too personal, she walked to the casement in tears, and sang these simple lines, which she graced with intermittent sobs.

SONG

Alas, well-a-day, woe to me,
  Singing willow, willow, willow;
My lover is far, far at sea
  On a billow, billow, billow.
Ah, Theodore, would thou could'st be
  On my pillow, pillow, pillow!

Here she heaved a deep sigh, when, to her utter astonishment, a voice, as if from a chamber underneath took up the tune with these words:

SONG

Alas, well-a-day, woe to me,
  Singing sorrow, sorrow, sorrow;
A ducat would soon make me free,
  Could I borrow, borrow, borrow;
And then I would pillow with thee,
  To-morrow, morrow, morrow!

Was it? – It was! – Yes, it *was* the voice of her love, her life, her long-lost Theodore de Willoughby!!! How should she reach him? Forty times she ran round and round her chamber, with agitated eyes and distracted tresses . . .

At length Hysterica found a sliding pannel. She likewise found a moth-eaten parchment, which she sat down to peruse. But, gentle reader, imagine her emotions, on decyphering these wonderful words.

MANUSCRIPT

— Six tedious years — — and all for what? — — — — — — No sun, no moon. — — Murd — — Adul — — because I am the wife of Lord

Belamour. — — then tore me from him, and my little Hysterica — — — — — Cruel Stiletto! — — He confesses that he put the sleeping babe into a basket — — sent her to the Baroness de Violenci — — oaken cross — — Chalk — — bruised gooseberry — — — — — — I am poisoned — — a great pain across my back — — I — j — k — — Oh! — Ah! — Oh! — — — —

Fascinante Peggina Belamour

This then was the mother of our heroine; and the MS. elucidated beyond dispute, the mysteries which had hitherto hung over the birth of that unfortunate orphan.

We need not add that she fainted, recovered, passed through the pannel, discovered the dungeon of her Theodore; and having asked him how he did, 'Comment vous portez vous' fell into unsophisticated hysterics.

Letter XL

I have now so far recovered by bodily health, that I am no longer confined to my room; while the good Stuart, by his lively advice and witty reasoning, more complimentary than reproachful, and more insinuated than expressed, is perfecting my mental reformation.

He had lately put Don Quixote into my hands; and on my returning it to him, with a confession of the benefit which I derived from it, the conversation naturally ran upon romances in general. He thus delivered his sentiments.

'I do not protest against the perusal of fictitious biography altogether; for many works of this kind may be read without injury, and some with advantage. Novels such as the Vicar of Wakefield, Cecilia, O'Donnel, The Fashionable Tales, and Coelebs, which draw man as he is, imperfect, instead of man as he cannot be, superhuman, are both instructive and entertaining. Romances, such as the Mysteries of Udolpho, the Italian, and the Bravo of Venice, which address the imagination alone, are often captivating, and seldom detrimental. But unfortunately, so seductive is the latter class of composition, that people are apt to become too fond of it, and to neglect more useful books. This, however, is not the only evil. Romances, indulged in extreme, act upon the mind like inebriating stimulants; first elevate, and at last enervate it. They accustom it to admire ideal scenes of transport and distraction; and to feel disgusted with the vulgarities of living misery. They likewise incapacitate it from encountering the turmoils of active life; and teach it erroneous notions of the world, by relating adventures too improbable to happen, and depicting characters too perfect to exist . . .'

4.8 E.A., 'On the Good Effects of Bad Novels' (1798)

The writer of this letter argues paradoxically that the worse the novel (and it is suggested that Gothic novels are the very worst), the more it furthers the cause of general enlightenment. Although the terms of the discussion are much the same as those of more straightforward opponents – including the assumption that the audience for novels was largely female – this utilitarian twist is singular.

Source: *Lady's Monthly Museum*, vol. 1 (1798), pp. 258–9.

★

I am one of those persons, peculiarly adapted for *things as they are*, who discover in every evil the seeds of immediate or remote advantage.

I believe that every evil is perpetually employed in destroying itself; while every good is unceasingly strengthening and expanding; and that to this purpose even evil is subservient. Consequently, I believe that 'Whatever *is*, is right.'[35]

But, to enjoy this optimism thoroughly, it is necessary that the mind should possess very diffusive philanthropy: how, otherwise, shall we contemplate with calmness the ruin of the greater part of the present, and immediately succeeding generations, merely because their misfortunes will produce the happiness of posterity! Yet thus it is with novels – I mean *bad* novels; – they are universally read, and universally mischievous; but they are daily bringing themselves into contempt, and daily producing advantages very different from their apparent tendency: meantime, thousands are hourly corrupted by them, in their tastes, their morals, and their hearts.

How fortunate, then, is it for me, that I can look upon the best side of this picture! You shall read in what manner I console myself.

If we look at the female part of mankind, and speak of it as one individual, we shall perceive that it is just emerging from infancy. If, however, we separate the particles of this composition, we shall find that the appearance of refinement, which had induced us to suppose this *emerging*, is not produced by an equal improvement in the whole; but rather, that many enlightened, and some splendid, individuals among them serve to illumine the features of the rest; while the greater part are, in themselves, buried in the profoundest night. Now, I contend that, if this period of female mental infancy be compared with that of the male, the ladies will suffer nothing in the comparison: so that we may reasonably hope, and, indeed, particular examples assure us, that their maturity may hereafter vie with our own.

Have we forgotten that, when *we* first began to cultivate our understandings, *we* had our Monkish legends, our crusades, and our hobgoblins;

our witchings, and our conundrums? Have we forgotten these things, that we look so haughtily upon the fair who now admire them?

Let us observe the utility of these compositions which the greater part of our novels imitate so well.

They induce persons to read, who, but for these, would never read at all.

It is the *Spectator*, I think, that remarks that, in order to allure persons to a habit of reading, it is only necessary that they should read, a little, frequently; and that, if they do this, he cares not whether the subject be 'Tom Thumb,' or 'Thomas Aquinas,' – gross nonesense, or profound argument. Not that considerable preference is wanting; but he is persuaded that those who read the first attentively, will soon wish to study the second.

The truth is – our understanding is progressively fitted for the growth of knowledge; precisely as a rock becomes capable of vegetable treasure.

It may seem a very odd comparison, when I oppose the literature for which our *circulating libraries* are *most* famous, to the family of plants called mosses: I go on, nevertheless, to shew their affinity.

Nature has provided this class of vegetables for the most useful purposes. We suppose a bare and rugged rock: hither the birds, the winds, or even the waters, convey the smallest and most imperceptible species of moss. These form resting places for the accumulation of earth; and even themselves, dying away, increase the stock. Meantime the seeds of larger kinds successively take root, and afford food and lodgment to the smaller insects, who die, and with the mosses add to the embankment. There is now earth sufficient for the *stone-crop*, the *house-leek*, and other species of moss; and as these decay, the *wall-flower* and the *pellitory* find nourishment, and deck the spot with sweetness and with beauty.

So, in the mind, idle tales first cling to its barren surface: they make, however, a little soil, in which better things may grow. That soil, or judgment, becomes deeper. More weighty and extensive matters may now strike into it. And see! – where first was barrenness, – then glittering moss, without solidity, – now the fair flowers of fancy blow, and their fragrance is enjoyed! The judgment has gained quantity and fertility; and now the charms of poetic taste have place. Thus, then, to these *lichen-like-novels* we owe the foundation of real improvement.

The progress of science does not end here. On the rock we have supposed the flowers decay, and the earth increases: odoriferous and flowering shrubs take root, and by chance some cocoa comes floating to the place, or some winged pine feed is blown thither. Then lofty and storm-defying trees adorn the formerly grey stone: birds and beasts enjoy their existence beneath its shades, and support theirselves with its fruits. Carry on the thought through countless ages – and you shall see this rock supporting pastures, and forests; rivers, and cities: – thus, where the flowers of fancy flourish, elegance and vigour of understanding shall soon be seen;

and some 'glorious, golden opportunity' present objects to the mind as useful as the cocoa, as magnificent as the cedar: creation enjoys the improvement, and mankind itself revels in the comforts and luxuries of its produce. Yet nothing had grown there, had it not first been clothed with moss. Mark how anxious *Nature* is for the perfection of the natural and the moral world: every unsightly object is covered with moss and with ivy; and our girls flock to the circulating libraries!

All hail, then, those fortunate authors to whose labours we are indebted for such signal blessings! Some there are to whom the sage listens with holy admiration; to whom the philosopher resorts for information, and the man of taste for reiterated pleasure: but what praise is due to such, when compared with those who can stop the giddy in their way, and teach those to feel the charms of letters who never felt them before;-can make the idle assiduous, and the listless thoughtful.

Let me see a girl take up an absurd novel; if she is pleased with it, I will pronounce that it is perfectly fitted for her capacity: as methodism is the most proper religion for those whose minds are weak and depraved enough to applaud it. In ninety-nine instances these predilections will produce the misery of the admirer; but in the hundredth a strong understanding will learn, from the very lessons, to despise the instructor. A good taste will spring from the detestation of bad; and thus, spreading itself to myriads of mankind, in luxuriant branches from the well nourished root, will have ample vengeance for the ninety-nine who have been destroyed.

We will enquire, too, whether, of those that perished none ultimately contributed to the general weal of the world? *I* can suppose, that she who owes her misery to these books will be very solicitous, in the thoughtfulness of misfortune, to teach her child behaviour directly opposite to that which they encourage: *I* can suppose that she who has passed 'From loveless youth, to unrespected age',[36] will be careful to warn her children that they do not throw away their lives upon that which produces no benefit: or, to take ordinary cases, I can suppose that the girl who now becomes acquainted with the contents of bad novels, will use no small degree of precaution to prevent her children from perusing them. You see how I console myself!

Bad novels, then, are most excellent things: and the worse they are written, so much the better for society: they will gain the greatest number of those who have, hitherto never read – for such cannot understand any part of a book that is tolerably put together; – and what is best of all, they will, at the same time, have the fewest admirers: because the more glaring the absurdity is, the greater will be the number of those who discover it! Moreover, I do really, and not jocularly, wish to see very stupid stories written (and thanks to *circulating libraries*, I shall not wish in vain); because they attract readers. These, having tasted books, commonly seek for others and it is hard, indeed, if some of the latter are not moderately good; and the reader is by this time prepared to comprehend them. Now something like argument or inference will sometimes be drawn from the actions related; and the reader, having been thus cheated into half a page of logic, finds that it has nothing in it quite so dreadful as was apprehended: thus the very novel reader is seduced into a philosopher; and all those good things, haply, follow, with a perspective of which I indulged myself in a former part of my letter.

My hypothesis, as will be perceived, is founded upon an opinion, that many have learned to despise novels by reading them; and have acquired sense by studying nonsense. These, notwithstanding, are by no means the most favourable methods of attaining understanding. Some would teach us to *hate* vice by exhibiting its features: for my own part, I would rather inculcate the love of virtue by displaying goodness. I think precisely the same of taste. I cannot allow the study of what is good can be really benefited by the contrast of what is bad: yet I readily acknowledge, that these two modes of instruction are adapted for different persons; and that mine is, perhaps, more useful to preserve the refinement of such as already possess it, than to impart it to those who are unacquainted with its nature.

Go on, therefore, you who write vile novels! Croud absurdity upon absurdity; patch deformity with deformity; caricature the works of Providence; mar the outlines of his wisdom, till its form is rendered doubtful, and its beauty denied; twist the paths of virtue till their end and object are lost; strew those of vice so thick with flowers, that their characteristics may become equivocal, and their waymarks uncertain; draw fantastick characters; paint their countenances woful; and then tell your readers, that *you are almost inclined to doubt the goodness of God for making them so*!* – if, indeed, you mean *their maker*, *their creator*, I doubt with you! Go on: – do these things; and my earnest wishes attend you! – And you, fair Ladies, read on; gather together all the novels that you can find; read them till – till you have acquired sense enough to see their worthlessness!

4.9 W.W., 'On Novels and Romances' (1802)

The prose style of this essay is particularly convoluted, but worth overcoming for its full explanation of why female readers are more susceptible to fiction than males, and the detailed objections to *The Mysteries of Udolpho* and *The Monk*.

Source: *Scots Magazine*, vol. 64 (1802), pp. 470–4, 545–8.

★

* Expression in an admired Novel.

Few works, in the present day, meet with greater encouragement, than those of imagination. But, whether this encouragement has encreased in a more than corresponding degree, beyond that, which has been afforded to other works, will, at least, be doubted. Former ages have likewise their romances and their tales: and, although there were less delicacy of manners, and refinement of language displayed, they possessed what could not fail to render them more acceptable to the age in which they were wrote: they contained an account of feudatory contentions and courtesies, or extolled the exploits and adventures of chivalrous knights; and sometimes related events, often extraordinary and marvellous indeed, but which had been accomplished, it was believed, by the intervention of supernatural agency.

And if we were to go back to the days of the Troubadours, we would find, that without the aid of printing, such writings were circulated and read with avidity. War and love, to which these heroes dedicated so much of their time, were, together with religion, the themes on which they dwelt; and from them it is easy to discover the character and manners of the people of the 12th century.

The pictures of life, however, which are given in our days, by no means deserve to be nor are they, so universally countenanced. Flat and insipid – they substitute whining weakness for passion; and, in place of character and manners agreable to the present *costume*, they speak of these which never had any existence, or which, in the revolutions of time, have long since disappeared. What then, it must be asked, will be the opinion of other ages, when they come to form their opinion of the present, from our writings?

Did we not know, that it is principally to the female sex, the authors of such romances are indebted for the favourable reception their works meet with; it might be a matter of some suprise, they are so much encouraged. But without wishing to insinuate, that the minds of the fair are naturally more light and unstable than our own, it must be observed, they are the principal support of writings of this kind; and that it is the encouragement they afford, which has given confidence to many a young author, not a few of whom, are indeed, females, to thrust their literary bantlings into the world, in the belief, that they would amuse, and inform, the idle and uninitiated.

It will not, however, be denied, that no small degree of encouragement is likewise given to those works of fancy by some men, whose education and habits, have rendered them incapable of relishing or understanding works of a higher character; and, that it is not improbable, a still greater degree of favour would be shewn by such persons to writings of this kind, were the means they possess of engaging in the affairs and amusements of the world, circumscribed to the limits which society has marked to the other sex. But the many opportunities which men have, of entering into the bustle of life, present to many of them, pleasures and enjoyments, far superior, in their apprehensions, to what reading or solitude can afford.

Without waiting to settle precisely, the degree of encouragement which is really given by one class of readers above another, he may, at least, venture to assert, that the female mind is more readily affected by the *tendency* of such works: and that the justice of this remark, it is presumed, will be acknowedged, when their habits of life, sensibility of mind, and their quickness and delicacy of sensation are considered. When to the perusal, therefore, of the endless variety of love-stories, which the authors of these works detail, many hours, even those allotted to sleep, are sacrificed, the consequences, as they are inevitable, ought greatly to be deprecated; as from thence arise, it will be seen, the false estimate of human life, and of human enjoyments, with which the minds of those are endued, who devote so much of their time to entertainments of this kind. They return with palled senses, to the world's concerns, after revelling in the luxurious and voluptuous descriptions, which appear in the pages of a novel – scenes on which their readers' enraptured fancy is ever found to dwell with inexpressible delight; but which, at last, irresistibly impel the tender and too susceptible heart, to yield to the delusive sensations of bliss, with which the bosom is filled.

Besides generating imbecility of mind, the sensibility of readers of novels, it will likewise be observed, is easily awakened, and the tear of sympathy quickly afforded, to an imaginary tale of woe, while, it is probable, to a scene of real distress, if it comes not attended with circumstances similar to those related in a romance, pity is denied as they know not how to compassionate what appears to them, to be vulgar sufferings! Such is the effect of these false representations of life produce on weak and youthful minds.

If any thing further were required, in support of what is here said to be the consequences which result from an indiscriminate perusal of such books, the opinions of an author of a medical treatise lately published, might be referred to. While attending to the influence which the affections and passions of the mind are found to have on our system, he does not hesitate to say, that among the mournful passions, must be included, an extravagant degree of love, and into which he says, young females particularly, are precipitated, merely, by reading improper novels. After detailing a melancholy catalogue of diseases, to which this passion gives rise, he adds, 'That in the houses appropriated to the unhappy victims of insanity, he generally meets with three classes: the first consist of men deprived of their understandings by pride; the second of girls by love; and the third of women by jealousy.'

With these reflections on the dangerous effects which arise from novels, and after offering a few observations on the general features of such works, we shall proceed to remark, more particularly, on the merits of some of those, which have obtained more than ordinary notice on account of the reputation of their authors, or the possession of some peculiarity of subject.

To raise novels to estimation, it will not be found necessary, it is presumed, that they should possess any real superiority, or intrinsic worth. A stranger, indeed, to the merits of works, which engage the attention of so many readers, in every rank of life, would be ready to imagine that they stood recommended by the possession of almost every excellence; or, at least, that some great moral would be found forcibly inculcated, in a style, where both beauty and correctness appeared; that in those volumes written avowedly for the purpose of beguiling a tedious hour, he would be certain of finding some pleasing tale, detailed with simplicity and chasteness – where the characters were maintained with consistency, and exhibited agreeably to nature; and that the various feelings and passions which these characters were made to possess, should be found expressed in a language suitable to each, but alas! works so formed and executed, would require powers far beyond those which the generality of novel-writers are known to possess. Instead of a judicious arrangement of incident, and of the just delineation of manners and character, we meet only, for the most part, with an incongruous fiction where perfection is studied, or the very *acmé* of vice represented, in direct opposition to nature, it will be perceived, as well as to the opinion of almost every critic. We are told by no contemptible authority,* that imperfect characters interest us more than perfect ones; 'that we are doubly instructed when we see, in one and the same example, what we ought to follow and what we ought to avoid.' What advantage then can be expected to arise from works where perfection is aimed at, and where crimes are familiarly mentioned which had, or can have, any existence in this world, but in the distempered fancy of an author who has bewildered himself in beating about for an untrodden path.

These feeble performances, recommended only by the readiness of authors to avail themselves of the corrupt taste of readers, are always founded on some story of gallantry, in which we meet only with crude conceptions, and wild reveries, expressed in florid terms, and with insipid triteness. To complete the tale, there is generally interwoven, indeed, but not in the most ingenuous manner, some marvellous tale, relating to a castle – a man in armour – and probably a ghost.† Such literary abortions, are, it is true, soon forgotten, but it is a matter of suprise, they should ever have been brought forward to public view. . . .

* Dr Wilkie.

† A late writer has happily characterised the turn of mind, perceived in such authors. – 'The novelist,' he observes, 'breaking loose from society, wild, into forests and deserts, in search of caves and uninhabited castles; where, forgetting every law of nature, and even every feature of the human countenance, he paints men and women, such as were never in existence; and there, amidst the shades of night and horror, rattles his chains, and conjures up his ghosts, till having frightened his readers out of their wits, he vainly supposes, he has charmed them into applause.'

[Discussion of *Rinaldo* by Mr Ireland, criticising the over-elaborate language.]

In some novels, a number of events of a marvellous nature are detailed, so as to induce a belief, that they are the effect of supernatural causes; but, by a subsequent developement of the hidden springs of action, which, it may be supposed, time only could discover, all of them are, at the end of the volume, reconciled with probability: thus shewing, how easy it is to impose on weak and superstitious minds, when the effect only is exposed to view. – The late Horace Walpole, although he has shocked credulity itself, in a romance of his own, speaks of the interest which may be excited in works judiciously managed throughout, on this plan.[37] But it requires no small share of ability to conduct readers, without allowing them to become languid, through a number of volumes, amid such extraordinary and apparently miraculous occurrences. We have, indeed, many romances, where the author appears to found a claim to attention on a recital only of the most wonderful incidents and marvellous events – a love of which, it is well known, has, in every age, characterized the greatest part of mankind. But the imagination will not allow of being always on the stretch; as we expect to see, the different occurrences in narration, stated clearly, and with openness, as they naturally rise one from the other, we cannot but feel dissatisfied, when we perceive any part concealed for the purpose of holding the mind in suspense, or reserved, in order, that some other circumstance may bewilder and astonish us the more. Among other novels, to which those observations will apply, may be mentioned the 'Mysteries of Udolpho,' by Mrs Radcliffe – a work, in which many passages occur, that cannot but strike the most superficial reader, as being particularly objectionable. In one volume, after being informed of the injunctions, which Emily received from her dying father, to burn some manuscript papers, which were deposited underneath a board in one of the rooms of his chateau, we are, in the following, entertained with the struggle which took place between duty and that curiosity which is said to be so natural to the sex; but not one word is mentioned of those sentences, over which she *happened* to glance her eye, that produced such surprise, and excited such a tumult in her breast. In another passage, we are informed at some length, of Emily's having descended into a vault of the castle of Udolpho, and of the horror with which her mind was filled, on seeing some object in a niche, from which she had withdrawn a curtain; but it is not, until the conclusion, we are informed, that it was a skeleton, which then appeared to be made of wax, that alarmed and terrified her so much.[38]

Such a method of relating incidents, in any other book than a novel, would justly render it contemptible. It may be necessary, however, for some writers of novels, to reserve the explanation of some circumstances until the end, for the purpose of facilitating a reconciliation of the numerous contradictions they run into. But for an author of ordinary capacity, the power which every writer of such works possesses to render such an expedient unnecessary, might be thought sufficient. As life and death are in their hands, the denouements could always, and readily, it might be supposed, be made agreeable to their fancy. The usual way to close a work is, as in a modern comedy, when the curtain drops, to bring all the persons into view, when reformation of manners and marriages at once take place – all are made happy, that will admit of being so; and the incorrigible, either consigned to the punishment of their own conscience, or *killed off*.

[Part II begins with discussion of *Caroline of Litchfield*, a translation from the German, with 'love in every page'.]

The effect produced by works of this kind, however, are trifling, it may be said, when compared to the mischief which is occasioned by the perusal of some others. The silly unmeaning fictions relating to love may, indeed, fill the mind with romantic notions, and give a distaste for the affairs of life, as has already been mentioned; but they will seldom, it is believed, vitiate the morals, or corrupt the heart. This is reserved for works of another character: works in which these stories of gallantry and of love are attempted to be enlivened by a language the most indecent and improper, and where the purpose of the author seems evidently to be, to cherish into a flame passions which Nature, of herself, is sufficiently able, at all times, to keep alive without the aid of such meretricious arts. The authors of volumes of this nature will, it is apprehended, be found among those worn-out debauchees, who love to contemplate scenes they are no longer capable of sharing in; but it is greatly to be regretted that so many of the young and innocent of both sexes, should be so readily exposed to the evil tendency of lucubrations proceeding from so polluted a source.

It will hardly be necessary to enumerate those which are thus distinguished by their dangerous and baneful principles. A well known volume of memoirs, and its author, a Mr Cleland, cannot, however, be overlooked.[39] This work, it may confidently be said, has hardly ever been surpassed in the wickedness and profligacy of its views: and the contrition of its author, who resided in the west of England, was no less remarkable; for, during the last years of his life, according to the newpapers of that time, he suffered the deepest mental affliction arising from a conviction of the irreparable and incalculable injury he had done to society.

Among the number just mentioned, we may likewise be allowed to place the production of '*The Monk*' by Mr Lewis, M.P. and on which a few strictures will now be offered.

Two stories, related in alternate chapters, but conjoined in some degree at the close of the volumes, form what is called 'The Monk'. That only, however, which properly comes under the title of the work, it will be necessary to consider; and, of it we may be allowed first to observe, that it is a story which cannot find place among those that are known to possess a *negative* merit; wherein, if little be found to admire, nothing appears, at the same time, to call for serious blame; neither can it be numbered with those of which the intentions of the author are equivocal; where, amidst many improper allusions, we find some great example of justice exercised, or something of a moral discovered, although detailed in language the most indelicate. So far removed from these, or any of a similar nature, is the work in question, that after allowing something of merit in point of style, we may, without the imputation of prejudice, venture to assert, that all the faults and immoralities ascribed to novels will be found realized in the Monk: murders, incest, and all the horrid and aggravated crimes which it is possible to conceive, appear in every chapter, and are dwelt on with seeming complacency, without any apparent intention of advantage to the reader from such a recital.

The truth of these observations, will, it is presumed, appear by attending to the fundamental parts of the story. – The hero of the tale, brought up in a cell, and early inured to the rigid discipline of the monastery, is a stranger to every vice, and never knew of an unlawful indulgence of passion. Formed in this school, he distinguishes himself by the zealous fulfilment of every religious duty; and renders himself remarkable, at the same time, for the strictness and severity of his moral conduct. His sanctity, his knowledge, and his eloquence, become so conspicuous, that he is elected superior of the order, and at length is the object of the admiration of all Madrid. Such was the youthful Ambrosia [*sic*, for Ambrosio], when every temptation, every allurement, is unavailingly presented by the devil, in human form, who had become envious of the popularity which his eloquent harangues had gained him among all ranks of people. But it required Virtue herself to shake his well regulated mind: his latent passions could only be blown into a flame by first yielding to the gratification of the most pleasing and honourable feelings that can fill the human breast – gratitude to the preserver of his life, and a wish to save, in his turn, the life of one who is about to fall a sacrifice for his sake: motives that cannot fail powerfully to second desires which Nature never meant should be eradicated. To these incitements are likewise superadded, the reiterated importunities made by the silent eloquence of love, aided by beauty, and the irresistible fascinations of female excellence. All these concurring, it will not be wondered a dereliction from virtue is induced: a dereliction that led to all the crimes which followed.

If we can at all understand the author, he means to hold up the character of Ambrosia to the abhorrence of his readers; to excite a fixed disgust for the crimes which are committed; and likewise to exemplify, that neither the most unfeigned piety, nor the most stern virtue, are sufficient to exempt from temptations, or that their possessor will be enabled to resist such temptation. But surely these views cannot be effected, or even promoted, by the present story. As has already been remarked, an example can only be useful which has a mixture of good and ill, and is of such a nature, at the same time, that we can make an easy approach to it, by conceiving that we ourselves are exposed to such causes as lead into a similar situation; no benefit can, therefore, be derived from the contemplation of characters that are either super-human, or are so distorted, as scarcely to preserve a human feature: And, as a triumph in this case, when assailed by such powerful and irresistible incentives to vice, would be more than human, so pity, and not exultation, is demanded at the punishment for crimes, which all the energy and strength we are capable of exerting, could not enable us to oppose successfully. Where then is the moral, or the useful lesson, held up in this work? None such, it is believed, will be found. On the contrary, it has a tendency to familiarise the imagination with crimes the most hideous and unnatural, and to discourage the practice of virtue, by lessening the confidence which every man ought to entertain of his own strength of mind.

Of the character of Ambrosia the same may be said as of the Oedipus of Sophocles. When a man is precipitated, not by any fault of his own, into the greatest misery – When he is led, by a blind fatality, to the commission of the most horrid deeds, a recital of them will seldom awaken virtuous feelings, or give rise to a tender sympathy in our breasts for the sufferer.

But to conclude – It is no less difficult to speak with temper and moderation of the production in question, than to discover the author's motives for laying before the public a story so indelicate and improper – so improbable and abhorrent. Besides, no degree of unity appears; on the contrary, the whole seems to be a mass of the most extravagant and horrible conceptions, from the time when the devil, under the semblence of a young and beautiful female, completes the seduction of Ambrosia, until he flies away with him from the prison of the inquisition, and afterwards, by fixing his claws in the bare scalp of the poor deluded monk, dashes him against a rock! Throughout the whole of this loathsome story the author dwells with seeming pleasure on the horrid and monstrous catalogue of supernatural crimes and enormities which his two heroes, Ambrosia, and the devil his loving coadjutor, enter into the commission of, and which it is utterly impossible for a reader, we would believe, of the smallest share of sensibility, to contemplate for a moment without sickening – What then would be our surprise, were we to understand, that this work has been read by a young and beautiful female, on whose every feature, sit modesty and virtue? We could easily believe, that the lips which seemed destined only to give utterance to the dictates of a heart, pure as the pious vestal's, would enquire of others, if they had read the Monk? It is surely to be regretted, that youth should be exposed to the baneful influence of such works – works which these valuable repositories, circulating libraries, disseminate with unceasing industry.

Without mentioning the productions of a Sterne, a Mackenzie, or a Goldsmith; a Smollet, or a Fielding, – there are some volumes, however, that must be rescued from the contempt which the rational mind is disposed to bestow on works of fancy; and which will, on the other other hand, always be read with pleasure, and with no inconsiderable share of advantage to many readers. At the head of these, we may be allowed to place the works of Richardson, D'Arblay, &c. – Authors, who possess so much merit, as to entitle them to be mentioned with respect, but not with such adulatory praise as to admit that they possess, above all others, the best knowledge of the human heart; or that their writings contain so many virtuous principles, as to sanction their being made the theme of pulpit eloquence.

4.10 'Rimelli', 'Novels and Romances' (1802)

The letter reiterates some of the standard criticisms, but singles out Radcliffe's fiction for its praiseworthy morality without alluding to its improbability, and, like the writer of 4.8, proposes that any form of reading is better than none.

Source: *Monthly Mirror*, vol. 14 (July 1802), pp. 81–2.

★

Mr. Editor,

It has been proposed as a question, whether the reading of romances and novels *only* (to the exclusion of all *other* books) or whether no reading of any kind whatever would be productive of the worst consequences. I have considered this question over and over again, and maturely weighed every pro and con that occurred to me on the subject. It is urged by the 'anti-novelists' that romances and novels serve only to estrange the minds of youth (especially of females) from their own affairs, and transmit them to those of which they read: so that, while totally absorbed in lamenting and condoling with the melancholy situation of a Julia, an Emily, or a Matilda, or lost in the admiration of the glorious deeds of some *all-perfect* novel hero, they neglect both their own interest, and the several duties which they owe to parent, friend, or brother. That such is but too often the case, I am sorry to be obliged to confess. Yet, though a great part of our modern novels are flimsy productions, without either good writing or good sense, others mere catchpenny trash, and *some* immoral and even impious; though the press teems with 'Midnight Bells,', 'Black Castles,' 'Haunted Towers,' 'Mysterious Monks,' &c. &c. with a long train of ghost, phantoms, &c. yet I am inclined to think that many excellent precepts and morals are inculcated in by far the greatest part of them; and that the rest are to be censured rather as being *absurd*, *improbable*, *and illwritten*, than tending to corrupt the mind. (I except some few, such as the 'Monk' by Mr. Lewis, which is not only immoral, but blasphemous, cum paucis aliis.) For example those written by the ingenious and amiable Mrs. Anne [*sic*] Radcliffe, and Dr. Moore's 'Edward,' 'Zeluco,' &c. which are not only commendable, but thank-worthy; possess, in my opinion, the powers of pleasing and instructing at the same time: a rare coalition! The latter *particularly* paints life in accurate colours, and from the various actions and opinions of the characters, deduces morals the most wholesome and unexceptionable. I might mention several others of hardly inferior merits, but let these suffice. Such productions as these are doubly excellent; because, while they inculcate the best morals, they give the readers an accurate knowledge of life and manners; of which it is highly proper young people should have a correct idea. For a young unsophisticated person just entering upon life, imbibes with eagerness whatever principles he first becomes acquainted with; and if these should happen to have a bad tendency, what would become of him, if his mind had not been guarded against them, by some previous insight into the sophistry and fallacy of the world, which are duly exposed in the works beforementioned? But if we consider the other side of the question, and suppose a person, who, having never looked into a book, consequently can have no taste for reading, what a plodding, insensible, and worldly-minded mortal do we behold! Such a person may, possibly, make his way through the world with tolerable success, but can never have any pretensions to the character of a *gentleman*. He may meet with the applause of those of his own stamp (among the 'common herd'); but by the sensible and discerning his education will be considered as an everlasting monument of his own and his parents' folly. I am, Mr. Editor, yours, as I hope I ever shall be, with all due respect.

Rimelli

4.11 John Dunlop, *The History of Fiction* (1814)

Dunlop's magisterial history deals briefly with English Gothic fiction. The extracts include his general comments on the genre, bracketing a survey of works by Walpole, Reeve and Radcliffe. The tone is belittling, yet dispassionate; the novels serve the purpose of recreation, even if their morality is simplistic and their plots are absurd.

Source: John Dunlop (1845), *The History of Fiction: Being a critical account of the most celebrated prose works of fiction from the earliest Greek romances to the novels of the present age*, 4th edn, London: Longmans, Brown, Green, & Longmans, pp. 413, 418.

★

. . . Although, as has been already mentioned, it is not my design to enter into a minute consideration of English novels, an analysis of which would require some volumes, it would not be proper altogether to overlook a *Romantic* species of novel, which seems in a great measure peculiar to the English, which differs in some degree from any fiction of which I have yet given an account, and which has recommended itself to a numerous class of readers by exciting powerful emotions of terror.

'There exists,' says an elegant writer, 'in every breast at all susceptible of the influence of imagination, the germ of a certain superstitious dread of the world unknown, which easily suggests the ideas of commerce with it. Solitude – darkness – low-whispered sounds – obscure glimpses of objects, tend to raise in the mind that thrilling mysterious terror, which has for its object "the powers unseen, and mightier far than we."'

It is perhaps singular, that emotions so powerful and universal should not have been excited by fiction at an earlier period; for this species of composition cannot be traced higher than the Castle of Otranto, by Horace Walpole. . . .

. . . On the whole, the species of composition which we have just been considering, though neither very instructive in its nature, nor so fitted, as some other kinds of fictitious writing, to leave agreeable impressions on the mind, is not without its value. To persons who are occupied with very severe and serious studies, romances of this kind afford perhaps a better relaxation than those which approach more nearly to the common business of life. The general tendency, too, of all these terrific works is virtuous. The wicked marquis or the villainous monk, meet at length the punishment they deserve, while the happy heroine, undisturbed by hobgoblins, or the illusions created by the creaking of doors, sobbing of the wind, or partial gleams of light, discovers at length that the terrific castle, or mouldering abbey, in which she had been alarmed or tormented, is a part of her own domain, and enjoys in connubial happiness the extensive property of which she had unjustly been deprived. All this may be very absurd, but life perhaps has few things better than sitting at the chimney-corner in a winter evening, after a well-spent day, and reading such absurdities. . . .

Notes

1 References to a number of Greek legends: Medea murdered her two children in revenge when her husband Jason abaondoned her (events depicted in Euripides' play *Medea*); Atreus, king of Argos, revenged himself on the brother, who had seduced his wife, by serving him the flesh of his own children at a banquet; to avoid the persecutions of the Hera, the hero Cadmus and his wife Harmonia asked for help from the gods and were turned into serpents; Procne, wronged by her husband Tereus, murdered their son, and when Tereus threatened to kill her was turned into a swallow.

2 A literary contrivance of an improbable kind, involving for instance the intervention of a supernatural being, as in the expression *deus ex machina*.
3 Julius Caesar Scaliger (1484–1558) wrote a treatise on poetics.
4 *Epistles*, 2.1.170.
5 See Pliny, *Natural History*, 35.
6 See Juvenal, 14.
7 In fact a remark by Pope, from the Swift–Pope *Miscellanies*, vol. 2 (1727), pp. 354.
8 'Through various changes and so many dangers', Virgil, *Aeneid*, 1.204.
9 David Hume and William Robertson, the two most celebrated historians of the period.
10 Matthew Prior, 'Paolo Purganti and His Wife: an honest, but simple pair', ll. 45–6 (adapted).
11 Joseph Glanvill (1636–80) was a scholar and clergyman, who wrote *Saducismus Triumphatus* (1681) in defence of the belief in witchcraft.
12 'Santon Barsisa' in *Guardian*, No. 148, 31 August 1713; Lewis mentions it as a source in the 'Advertisement' to his novel.
13 A character in *The Ghostseer*.
14 'To disbelieve is to dislike'; Horace, *Ars Poetica*, 1.188.
15 'This is the effort, this is the work.' Source unidentified.
16 Bugbear.
17 Sir John Scott was Attorney-General at the time, responsible for prosecutions for libel, and for state and treason trials. Lewis was never in fact charged.
18 Literally, 'It's the first step which costs'.
19 See 1.6.
20 See 1.1.
21 Arthur Murphy, *The Grecian Daughter* (1772).
22 'Dreams, terrors of magic, marvels, witches, ghosts of the night, Thessalian portents – you laugh at these.' *Epistles*, 2.2.209.
23 A child's toy made of coral.
24 Misquote of Horace, *Epistles*, 2.1.185–6: if 'noscat' is corrected to 'poscat', it would translate as 'He asks for the bear and boxers in the middle of the poetry', i.e. he doesn't like arty plays, and want entertainment (particular thanks to Matthew Steggle for this note).
25 Heraclitus was known as the 'weeping philosopher' for his melancholy outlook, Democritus as the 'laughing philosopher'.
26 A character in Thomas Holcroft's comic drama *The Road to Ruin* (1792).
27 Probably a reference to the main character in Edward Moore's *The Gamester: A Tragedy* (1753), a role taken by Garrick at Drury Lane.
28 'I would bid the skilful imitator to study examples of life and of manners, and thence to evolve faithful descriptions', Horace, *Ars Poetica*, 317.
29 A school of English poetry, fashionable in the 1790s, in which female authors, notably Hester Thrale Piozzi, Mary Robinson and Hannah Cowley, were prominent.
30 Swindlers.
31 Busybodies.
32 Rare bird.
33 There is a reference here to the episode of the black veil in Radcliffe's *The Mysteries of Udolpho*; the reader is kept waiting through half the novel to learn – in a notorious anti-climax – that a wax effigy is hidden behind it.

34 A line from 'Ballad Singers' Medley Duets' included in William Thomas Thomas's *An Original Collection of Songs.*
35 Pope, *An Essay on Man,* 4.394.
36 Pope, 'Epistle to a Lady' (1743), l. 125.
37 See 3.7b.
38 Cf. 4.7a, n. ii.
39 John Cleland, *Fanny Hill: Memoirs of a Woman of Pleasure* (1748–9).

5 Gothic and revolution

5.1 'Demophilius', *The Genuine Principles of the Ancient Saxons, or English Constitution* (1776)

Published in Philadelphia on the eve of the American Revolution, this anonymous collection makes clear how central a Saxon/Gothic genealogy was to revolutionary politics. J. G. A. Pocock notes that 'Thomas Jefferson wanted to place Hengist and Horsa on the Great Seal of the United States, and he argued in *The Rights of British America* (1775) that American settlers held their lands by conquest like the Angles and Saxons, and therefore held them allodially, under no allegiance to the king' (1987, p. 377).

Much of the following extract is reproduced from the anonymous *An Historical Essay on the English Constitution* (1771) which is 'commonly regarded as marking an epoch in the revival of Saxonism' (Smith 1987, p. 100).[1] An uncompromising insistence on the democratic nature of the ancient constitution is its most notable feature.

Source: Demophilius, *The Genuine Principles of the Ancient Saxons, or English Constitution: Carefully Collected from the Best Authorities*, Philadelphia: Robert Bell, 1776, pp. 4–8.

★

. . . A Convention being soon to sit in Philadelphia; I have thought it my duty to collect some sentiments from a certain, very scarce book entitled an *Historical Essay on the English Constitution* and publish them, with whatever improving observations our different circumstances may suggest, for the perusal of the gentlemen concerned in the arduous task of framing a constitution.[2]

'That beautiful system formed, (as Montesquieu says,) in the German woods, was introduced into England about the year four hundred and fifty.'[3] The peculiar excellence of this system consisted in its incorporating small parcels of the people into little communities by themselves. These petty states *held parliaments often*; for whatever concerned them in common, they met together and debated in common; and after due consideration of the matter, they called a vote and decided the question by a majority of voices. In these councils every man had a voice, who had a residence of his own in the tithing, (or township) and paid his tax and performed his share of the public duties. This salutary institution, our honorable Conference of Committees has again revived at their late sitting.

To avoid the tumult; which always must attend the hearing and determining civil and criminal cases, by a popular tribunal, they had their executive courts in every township; and still kept the legislative and executive departments separate, in all cases whatsoever.

Among these people we find the origin of the inestimable trial by juries; and I am much mistaken if our present Justices of the Peace, may not also trace their derivation from the same salubrious source. However that may be, one thing is certain, that[4] 'they founded their government on the common rights of mankind. They made the elective power of the people the first principle of the constitution and delegated that power to such men as they could best confide in. But they were curiously cautious in that respect, knowing well the degenerating principles of mankind; that power makes a vast difference in the temper and behaviour of men, and often converts a good man in private life to a tyrant in office. For this reason they never gave up their natural liberty or delegated their power for making laws, to any man for a longer time than one year.

'The object upon which our elective power acts is remarkably different from that of the Romans. Theirs was directed to operate in the election of their chief officers, and particularly their consuls; or those who were vested with the executive authority whom they changed annually. But the senate where the principal power in their state was lodged, was a more fixed body of men and not subject to the elective power of the people.

'Our Saxon forefathers almost reversed this principle; for they made their witenagemot or parliament, where the principal power was lodged, annually moveable and entirely subject to the elective power of the people; and gave a more fixed state to the executive authority. This last they confined within a certain sphere of action, prescribed by law; so that it could not operate to the injury of any individual either in his person or property; and was controllable in all acts of state by the elective power which they vested annually in their witenagemot, or parliament.

'The annual exercise of the elective power, was the quintessence, the life and soul of the constitution; and the basis of the whole fabric of their government, from the internal police of the minutest part of the county, to the administration the government of the whole kingdom. This Saxon institution formed a perfect model of government; where the natural rights of mankind were preserved, in their full exercise, pure and perfect, as far as the nature of society will admit of.

'It would be something very surprising to find the people of England continually disputing about the principles and powers, vested in the constituent parts of their government; did we not know that at this day it consists of a mixture of the old, or first establishment, and that which took place at (and since) what is commonly called the conquest, by William the First. These two forms of government, the first founded upon the principles of liberty, and the latter upon the principles of slavery, it is no wonder they are continually at war, one with the other. For the first is grounded upon the natural rights of mankind, in the constant annual exercise of their elective power, and the latter upon the despotic rule of one man. Hence our disputants, drawing their arguments from two principles, widely different, must of course differ in their conclusions.

'Our Saxon forefathers established their government in Britain, before the transactions of mankind were recorded in writing; at least among the northern nations. They therefore handed down to posterity, the principles of their government, by the actual exercise of their rights; which became the ancient usage and custom of the people, and the law of the land. And hence it came to pass, that when this ancient custom and usage ceased to act, the remembrance of the custom ceased with it. We may add to this, that, since the conquest, our arbitrary kings and men of arbitrary principles, have endeavoured to destroy the few remaining records, and historical facts that might keep in remembrance a form of government so kind, friendly and hospitable to the human Species. It is for these reasons that we have such a scarcity of historical evidence, concerning the principles and manner of conducting the first establishment of our mode of government in this kingdom.

'However, notwithstanding these difficulties, there are many customs, forms, principles and doctrines, that have been handed down to us by tradition; which will serve as so many landmarks, to guide our steps to the foundation of this ancient structure, which, is only buried under the rubbish collected by time, and new establishments. *Whatever is of Saxon establishment is truly constitutional; but whatever is Norman is heterogeneous to it, and partakes of a tyrannical spirit.*[5]

'From these sources it is, that I would endeavor to draw the outlines of this ancient model of government, established in this kingdom by our Saxon forefathers; where it continued to grow and flourish; for six hundred years; till it was overwhelmed and destroyed by William the first, commonly called the Conqueror, and lay buried under a load of tyranny for one hundred and forty seven years. When it arose again, like a phoenix from its own ashes in the reign of Henry the Third, by the assistance of many current causes, but principally by the bravery of the English people, under the conduct and intrepidity of our ancient and immortal barons, who restored it, in part, once more to this Isle. And tho' much impaired, maimed, and disfigured, it has stood the admiration of many ages; and still remains *the most noble and ancient monument of Gothic antiquity*.' . . .[6]

5.2 Report of the Committee of the Revolution Society (1789)

This report represents the minutes of the meeting at the London Tavern on 4 November 1789 at which Richard Price delivered his sermon celebrating the French Revolution which provoked Edmund Burke to write his *Reflections*. As the minutes make clear, radical opinion interpreted the events of 1789 in terms of the Glorious Revolution of 1688. For many historically minded commentators a key aspect of Gothic writing was the mirroring of the Glorious and French Revolutions where the balance of similarities and differences found itself repeatedly disturbed by stubborn anxieties concerning illegitimacy and usurpation. Maurice Levy's comment is typical: '"Gothic", I believe, was the historically dated response of the English psyche to what was happening on the far side of the channel. It was, I think, a regression to a safe revolution (safe, because it had already taken place and was a thing of the past) as well as the defense and illustration of the 1688 principles of controlled political power and religious *via media*' (Smith and Sage, 1994, p. 2).

Source: Richard Price (1789), *A Discourse on the Love of Our Country, Delivered at the Revolution Society on 4 November 1789, with an Appendix Containing the Report of the Committee of the Revolution Society*, London: T. Cadell.

★

A Report from the Committee was brought up, from which the following is an extract:

'Your Committee are persuaded, that by the union of the friends of freedom, their rights are ascertained and established; and trusting that it will be highly honourable to avow ourselves, in the most explicit manner, advocates for the pure and genuine principles of civil and religious liberty, they have with this view prepared a book, in which those gentlemen who are inclined to let their names be transmitted to posterity, as the friends of the great and glorious Revolution of 1688, may insert them after the following preamble, and a declaration of assent to the three following propositions.

PREAMBLE

'This Society, sensible of the important advantages arising to this country by its deliverance from popery and arbitrary power, and conscious that, under God, we owe that signal blessing to the Revolution, which seated our deliverer King William the Third upon the throne; do hereby declare our firm attachment to the civil and religious principles which were recognized and established by that glorious event, and which has preserved the succession in the prostestant line; and our determined resolution to maintain, and, to the utmost of our power, to perpetuate, those blessings to the latest posterity.

'Three Propositions containing the fundamental principles of the Society:

1. That all civil and political authority is derived from the people.
2. That the abuse of power justifies resistance.
3. That the right of private judgment, liberty of conscience, trial by jury, the freedom of the press, and the freedom of election, ought ever to be held sacred and inviolable.

'The Committee farther resolved,

That in order to cause the principles of the Revolution to be well understood, extensively propagated, and firmly maintained; and to preserve the glorious fabric of the British Constitution; and to transmit the invaluable blessings of public freedom to posterity, unimpaired and improved, it becomes the people to establish societies throughout the kingdom upon Revolution principles, to maintain a correspondence with each other, and to form that grand concentrated union of the true friends of public liberty, which may be necessary to maintain its existence.

'The Committee concluded their Report with congratulating members of the Society, as Britons, and citizens of the world, upon their noble spirit of civil and religious liberty which had, since the last meeting, so conspicuously shone forth on the continent, more especially on the glorious success of the French Revolution; and with expressing their ardent wishes that the influence of so glorious an example may be felt by all mankind, until tyranny and despotism shall be swept from the face of the globe, and universal liberty and happiness prevail.'

Dr. Price then moved, and it was unanimously resolved, that the following Congratulatory address to the National Assembly of France, be transmitted to them, signed by the Chairman:

'The Society for commemorating the Revolution in Great Britain, disdaining national partialities, and rejoicing in every triumph of liberty and justice over arbitrary power, offer to the National Assembly of France their congratulations on the Revolution in that country, and on the prospect it gives to the two first kingdoms in the world, of a common participation in the blessings of civil and religious liberty.

'They cannot help adding their ardent wishes of an happy settlement of so important a Revolution, and at the same time expressing the particular satisfaction, with which they reflect the tendency of the glorious example given in France to encourage other nations to assert the unalienable rights of mankind, and thereby to introduce a general reformation in the governments of Europe, and to make the world free and happy.'

Stanhope, Chairman.

5.3 Edmund Burke (1729–97), *Reflections on the Revolution in France* (1790)

Burke had been a leading politician on the liberal wing of the Whig party since 1766. In the 1770s he had joined Richard Price, among others, in criticising government policy towards the American colonies. The shock of the *Reflections* was therefore so much the greater; Burke's impassioned condemnation of the French Revolution was widely regarded by liberals in Britain as a betrayal, and it inspired equally fervent responses.

Reflections was itself a response, formally addressed to M. De Pont, a 'very young gentleman at Paris', who had invited Burke's opinion, as a well-known champion of liberty, on the recent developments in France. It is also framed as a response to Richard Price's *A Discourse on the Love of our Country* (compare 5.2); the first of the following extracts is part of a detailed refutation of Price's comparison of the revolution of 1688 with that of 1789. Burke rejects forcefully the notion that either event was legitimated by an ancient constitution which gave the nation the right to choose or overturn its ruler. In doing so, he appropriates the Gothic past to the conservative cause, in a way which was to have far-reaching effects. The radical orator John Thelwall testified to Burke's role in reshaping the terms of political debate. After reading the *Reflections,* he could no longer believe in the Whig slogan of 'the glorious and happy constitution'. Burke had written,

> the most raving and fantastical, sublime, and scurrilous, paltry and magnificent, and in every way most astonishing book ever sent into the world. A book, I will venture to say, which has made more democrats, among the thinking part of mankind, than all the works ever written in answer to it.
> (*The Tribune*, 1795–6, 3 vols, II, p. 220)

The *Reflections* helped to polarise opinion, encouraging the pro-revolutionary faction to break away from the language of precedent and antiquity in favour of 'pure' reason and natural right, while providing conservatism with a new, emotive rhetoric of organic nationhood.

The second passage given here includes the famous set-piece on the plight of Marie Antoinette, which illustrates another aspect of Burke's Gothicism. Burke had, of course, first entered the public stage as the author of *A Philosophical Enquiry into our Ideas of the Sublime and the Beautiful* (1757; 3.7), a study in belles lettres roughly contemporary with Hurd's *Letters on Chivalry and Romance* (1762; 2.6) In the *Reflections,* he takes the idea of chivalry as an agent of social cohesion, an idea which had been evolving in scholarly dissertations on the romance form, and turns it into a political philosophy of pressing relevance. The transcendent beauty of the French queen, the venerable system of rank based on landed inheritance, feudal notions of allegiance and 'proud submission', are all rolled together into a radiant vision of the status quo. 'One's country ought to be lovely': for Burke, this is not a factitious or accidental loveliness but a matter of inherent qualities growing out of the nation's deepest, historical nature. A subject possessing imagination and sensibility will chivalrously submit himself to the nation, dedicated to the preservation of its values, mores, manners and institutions.

Throughout the *Reflections*, Burke pursues an aesthetic strategy which his adversaries considered to be, in quite precise ways, Gothic. There is no attempt to follow a neo-classical model of argumentation, with the stress on dispassionate logic, system and clarity of ideas. Instead, Burke tends to derive the authority of his statements from feeling and experience. The long sentences with their multiple sub-clauses give the impression of an outpouring of emotion. The language constantly shifts back and forth from concrete to abstract, from the abstruse to the almost demotic. There is a rich flow of metaphor, a rhetorical device commonly associated with irrational leaps of the imagination, primitive culture and original genius. Gothic imagery is used to evoke the immanence of the past within the present, for instance in the description of the French constitution as a ruined castle, or of the state 'grasped as in a kind of mortmain for ever' (partially literalising the ghoulish legal tenet of 'dead hand', transference of property to a corporation in perpetuity).

Source: Edmund Burke, *Reflections on the Revolution in France and on the Proceedings in Certain Societies in London Relative to that Event: In a Letter Intended to Have Been Sent to a Gentleman in Paris* (1790). Quoted from Edmund Burke (1968), *Reflections on the Revolution in France*, ed. Conor Cruise O'Brien, Harmondsworth, Middlesex: Penguin, pp. 98–9, 119–22, 169–75.

★

. . . There is ground enough for the opinion that all the kingdoms of Europe were, at a remote period, elective, with more or fewer limitations in the objects of choice; but whatever kings might have been here or elsewhere, a thousand years ago, or in whatever manner the ruling dynasties of England or France may have begun, the King of Great Britain is at this day king by a fixed rule of succession, according to the laws of his country; and whilst the legal conditions of the compact of sovereignty are performed by him (as they are performed) he holds his crown in contempt of the choice of the Revolution Society, who have not a single vote for a king amongst them, either individually or collectively; though I make no doubt they would soon erect themselves into an electoral college, if things were ripe to give effect to their claim. His majesty's heirs and successors, each in his own time and order, will come to the crown with the same contempt of their choice with which his majesty has succeeded to that he wears.

Whatever may be the success of evasion in explaining away the gross error of *fact*, which supposes that his majesty (though he holds it in concurrence with the wishes) owes his crown to the choice of his people, yet nothing can evade their full explicit declaration, concerning the principle of a right in the people to choose, which right is directly maintained, and tenaciously adhered to. All the oblique insinuations concerning election bottom in this proposition, and are referable to it. Lest the foundation of the king's exclusive legal title should pass for a mere rant of adulatory freedom, the political Divine[7] proceeds dogmatically to assert,* that by the principles of the Revolution the people of England have acquired three fundamental rights, all which, with him, compose one system and lie together in one short sentence; namely, that we have acquired a right

1. 'To choose our own governors.'
2. 'To cashier them for misconduct.'
3. 'To frame a government for ourselves.'

This new, and hitherto unheard-of bill of rights, though made in the name of the whole people, belongs to those gentlemen and their faction only. The body of the people of England have no share in it. They utterly disclaim it. They will resist the practical assertion of it with their lives and fortunes. They are bound to do so by the laws of their country, made at the time of that very Revolution, which is appealed to in favour of the fictitious rights claimed by the society which abuses its name. . . .

You will observe, that from Magna Charta to the Declaration of Right, it has been the uniform policy of our constitution to claim and assert our liberties, as an *entailed inheritance* derived to us from our forefathers, and to be transmitted to our posterity; as an estate specially belonging to the people of this kingdom without any reference whatever to any other more general or prior right. By this means our constitution preserves an unity in so great a diversity of its parts. We have an inheritable crown; an inheritable peerage; and an house of commons and a people inheriting privileges, franchises, and liberties, from a long line of ancestors.

This policy appears to me to be the result of profound reflection; or rather the happy effect of following nature, which is wisdom without reflection, and above it. A spirit of innovation is generally the result of a selfish temper and confined views. People will not look forward to posterity, who never look backward to their ancestors. Besides, the people of England well know, that the idea of inheritance furnishes a sure principle of conservation, and a sure principle of transmission; without at all excluding a principle of improvement. It leaves acquisition free; but it secures what it acquires. Whatever advantages are obtained by a state proceeding on these maxims, are locked fast as in a sort of family settlement; grasped as in a kind of mortmain for ever. By a constitutional policy, working after the pattern of nature, we receive, we hold, we

* P. 34, *Discourse on the Love of our Country*, by Dr. Price.

transmit our government and our privileges, in the same manner in which we enjoy and transmit our property and our lives. The institutions of policy, the goods of fortune, the gifts of Providence, are handed down, to us and from us, in the same course and order. Our political system is placed in a just correspondence and symmetry with the order of the world, and with the mode of existence decreed to a permanent body composed of transitory parts; wherein, by the disposition of a stupendous wisdom, moulding together the great mysterious incorporation of the human race, the whole, at one time, is never old, or middle-aged, or young, but in a condition of unchangeable constancy, moves on through the varied tenour of perpetual decay, fall, renovation, and progression. Thus, by preserving the method of nature in the conduct of the state, in what we improve we are never wholly new; in what we retain we are never wholly obsolete. By adhering in the manner and on those principles to our forefathers, we are guided not by the superstition of antiquaries, but by the spirit of philosophic analogy. In this choice of inheritance we have given to our frame of polity the image of a relation in blood; binding up the constitution of our country with our dearest domestic ties; adopting our fundamental laws into the bosom of our family affections; keeping inseparable, and cherishing with the warmth of all their combined and mutually reflected charities, our state, our hearths, our sepulchres, and our altars.

Through the same plan of a conformity to nature in our artificial institutions, and by calling in the aid of her unerring and powerful instincts, to fortify the fallible and feeble contrivances of our reason, we have derived several other, and those no small benefits, from considering our liberties in the light of an inheritance. Always acting as if in the presence of canonized forefathers, the spirit of freedom, leading in itself to misrule and excess, is tempered with an awful gravity. This idea of a liberal descent inspires us with a sense of habitual native dignity, which prevents that upstart insolence almost inevitably adhering to and disgracing those who are the first acquirers of any distinction. By this means our liberty becomes a noble freedom. It carries an imposing and majestic aspect. It has a pedigree and illustrating ancestors. It has its bearings and its ensigns armorial. It has its gallery of portraits; its monumental inscriptions; its records, evidences, and titles. We procure reverence to our civil institution on the principle upon which nature teaches us to revere individual men; on account of their age; and on account of those from whom they are descended. All your sophisters cannot produce any thing better adapted to preserve a rational and manly freedom than the course that we have pursued, who have chosen our nature rather than our speculations, our breasts rather than our inventions, for the great conservatories and magazines of our rights and privileges.

You might, if you pleased, have profited by our example, and have given to your recovered freedom a correspondent dignity. Your privileges, though discontinued, were not lost to memory. Your constitution, it is true, whilst you were out of possession, suffered waste and dilapidation; you possessed in some parts the walls, and in all the foundations of a noble and venerable castle. You might have repaired those walls; you might have built on those foundations. Your constitution was suspended before it was perfected; but you had the elements of a constitution very nearly as good as could be wished. . . .

It is now sixteen or seventeen years since I saw the queen of France, then the dauphiness, at Versailles; and surely never lighted on this orb, which she hardly seemed to touch, a more delightful vision. I saw her just above the horizon, decorating and cheering the elevated sphere she just began to move in, – glittering like the morningstar, full of life, and splendour, and joy. Oh! what a revolution! and what a heart must I have to contemplate without emotion that elevation and that fall! Little did I dream when she added titles of veneration to those of enthusiastic, distant, respectful love, that she should ever be obliged to carry the sharp antidote against disgrace concealed in that bosom; little did I dream that I should have lived to see such disasters fallen upon her in a nation of gallant men, in a nation of men of honour, and of cavaliers. I thought ten thousand swords must have leaped from their scabbards to avenge even a look that threatened her with insult. But the age of chivalry is gone. That of sophisters, economists, and calculators, has succeeded; and the glory of Europe is extinguished for ever. Never, never more shall we behold that generous loyalty to rank and sex, that proud submission, that dignified obedience, that subordination of the heart, which kept alive, even in servitude itself, the spirit of an exalted freedom. The unbought grace of life, the cheap defence of nations, the nurse of manly sentiment and heroic enterprise, is gone! It is gone, that sensibility of principle, that chastity of honour, which felt a stain like a wound, which inspired courage whilst it mitigated ferocity, which ennobled whatever it touched, and under which vice itself lost half its evil, by losing all its grossness.

This mixed system of opinion and sentiment had its origin in the ancient chivalry; and the principle, though varied in its appearance by the varying state of human affairs, subsisted and influenced through a long succession of generations, even to the time we live in. If it should ever be totally extinguished, the loss I fear will be great. It is this which has given its character to modern Europe. It is this which has distinguished it under all its forms of government, and distinguished it to its advantage, from the states of Asia, and possibly from those states which flourished in the most brilliant periods of the antique world. It was this, which, without confounding ranks, had produced a noble equality, and handed it down through all the gradations of social life. It was this opinion which mitigated kings into companions, and raised private men to be fellows with kings. Without force or opposition, it subdued the fierceness of pride and power; it obliged sovereigns to submit to the soft collar of social esteem, compelled stern authority to submit to elegance, and gave a dominating vanquisher of laws to be subdued by manners.

But now all is to be changed. All the pleasing illusions, which made power gentle and obedience liberal, which harmonized the different shades of life, and which, by a bland assimilation, incorporated into politics the sentiments which beautify and soften private society, are to be dissolved by this new conquering empire of light and reason. All the decent drapery of life is to be rudely torn off. All the superadded ideas, furnished from the wardrobe of a moral imagination, which the heart owns, and the understanding ratifies, as necessary to cover the defects of our naked, shivering nature, and to raise it to dignity in our own estimation, are to be exploded as a ridiculous, absurd, and antiquated fashion.

On this scheme of things, a king is but a man, a queen is but a woman; a woman is but an animal, and an animal not of the highest order. All homage paid to the sex in general as such, and without distinct views, is to be regarded as romance and folly. Regicide, and parricide, and sacrilege, are but fictions of superstition, corrupting jurisprudence by destroying its simplicity. The murder of a king, or a queen, or a bishop, or a father, are only common homicide; and if the people are by any chance, or in any way, gainers by it, a sort of homicide much the most pardonable, and into which we ought not to make too severe a scrutiny.

On the scheme of this barbarous philosophy, which is the offspring of cold hearts and muddy understandings, and which is as void of solid wisdom as it is destitute of all taste and elegance, laws are to be supported only by their own terrors, and by the concern which each individual may find in them from his own private speculations, or can spare to them from his own private interests. In the groves of their academy, at the end of every vista, you see nothing but the gallows. Nothing is left which engages the affections on the part of the commonwealth. On the principles of this mechanic philosophy, our institutions can never be embodied, if I may use the expression, in persons; so as to create in us love, veneration, admiration, or attachment. But that sort of reason which banishes the affections is incapable of filling their place. These public affections, combined with manners, are required sometimes as supplements, sometimes as correctives, always as aids to law. The precept given by a wise man, as well as a great critic, for the construction of poems, is equally true as to states: *Non satis est pulcra esse poemata, dulcia sunto.*[8] There ought to be a system of manners in every nation, which a well-formed mind would be disposed to relish. To make us love our country, our country ought to be lovely.

But power, of some kind or other, will survive the shock in which manners and opinions perish; and it will find other and worse means for its support. The usurpation which in order to subvert ancient institutions, has destroyed ancient principles, will hold power by arts similar to those by which it has acquired it. When the old feudal and chivalrous spirit of fealty, which, by freeing kings from fear, freed both kings and subjects from the precautions of tyranny, shall be extinct in the minds of men, plots and assassinations will be anticipated by preventive murder and preventive confiscation, and that long roll of grim and bloody maxims, which form the political code of all power, not standing on its own honour, and the honour of those who are to obey it. Kings will be tyrants from policy, when subjects are rebels from principle.

When ancient opinions and rules of life are taken away, the loss cannot possibly be estimated. From that moment we have no compass to govern us; nor can we know distinctly to what port we steer. Europe, undoubtedly, taken in a mass, was in a flourishing condition the day on which your revolution was completed. How much of that prosperous state was owing to the spirit of our old manners and opinions is not easy to say; but as such causes cannot be indifferent in their operation, we must presume, that, on the whole, their operation was beneficial.

We are but too apt to consider things in the state in which we find them, without sufficiently adverting to the causes by which they have been produced, and possibly may be upheld. Nothing is more certain, than that our manners, our civilization, and all the good things which are connected with manners and with civilization, have, in this European world of ours, depended for ages upon two principles; and were indeed the result of both combined; I mean the spirit of a gentleman, and the spirit of religion. The nobility and the clergy, the one by profession, the other by patronage, kept learning in existence, even in the midst of arms and confusions, and whilst governments were rather in their causes, than formed. Learning paid back what it received to nobility and to priesthood; and paid it with usury, by enlarging their ideas, and by furnishing their minds. Happy if they had all continued to know their indissoluble union, and their proper place! Happy if learning, not debauched by ambition, had been satisfied to continue the instructor, and not aspired to be the master! Along with its natural protectors and guardians, learning will be cast into the mire, and trodden down under the hoofs of a swinish multitude.

If, as I suspect, modern letters owe more than they are always willing to own to ancient manners, so do other interests which we value full as much as they are worth. Even commerce, and trade, and manufacture, the gods of our economical politicians, are themselves perhaps but creatures; are themselves but effects, which, as first causes, we choose to worship. They certainly grew under the same shade in which learning flourished. They too may decay with their natural protecting principles. With you, for the present at least, they all threaten to disappear together. Where trade and manufactures are wanting to a people, and the spirit of nobility and religion remains, sentiment supplies, and not always ill supplies, their place; but if commerce and the arts should be lost in an experiment to try how well a state may stand without these old fundamental principles, what sort of a thing must be a nation of gross, stupid, ferocious, and, at the same time, poor and sordid, barbarians, destitute of religion, honour, or manly pride, possessing nothing at present, and hoping for nothing hereafter?

I wish you may not be going fast, and by the shortest cut, to that horrible and disgustful situation. Already there appears a poverty of conception, a coarseness and vulgarity, in all the proceedings of the Assembly and of all their instructors. Their liberty is not liberal. Their science is presumptuous ignorance. Their humanity is savage and brutal.

It is not clear, whether in England we learned those grand and decorous principles and manners, of which considerable traces yet remain, from you, or whether you took them from us. But to you, I think, we trace them best. You seem to me to be – *gentis incunabula nostrae.*[9] France has always more or less influenced manners in England; and when your fountain is choked up and polluted, the stream will not run long, or not run clear, with us, or perhaps with any nation. This gives all Europe, in my opinion, but too close and connected a concern in what is done in France. Excuse me, therefore, if I have dwelt too long on the atrocious spectacle of the 6th of October, 1789, or have given too much scope to the reflections which have arisen in my mind on occasion of the most important of all revolutions, which may be dated from that day, I mean a revolution in sentiments, manners, and moral opinions. As things now stand, with everything respectable destroyed without us, and an attempt to destroy within us every principle of respect, one is almost forced to apologize for harbouring the common feelings of men. . . .

5.4 Ann Radcliffe (1764–1823), *A Sicilian Romance* (1790)

Radcliffe's husband was editor and proprietor of the Whig newspaper, the *English Chronicle*, which enthusiastically welcomed the French Revolution, while her own family had links with the same Dissenting culture that included Priestley and Price.[10] The following passage from her second novel, welcoming the enlightenment dawning over Gothic institutions, echoes the contemporary rhetoric of emancipation surrounding the French Revolution.

Source: Ann Radcliffe (1994), *A Sicilian Romance*, ed. Alison Milbank, Oxford: Oxford University Press, pp. 116–17.

★

The abbey of St Augustin was a large magnificent mass of Gothic architecture, whose gloomy battlements, and majestic towers arose in proud sublimity from amid the darkness of the surrounding shades. It was founded in the twelfth century, and stood a proud monument of monkish superstition and princely magnificence . . .

The view of this building revived in the mind of the beholder the memory of past ages. The manners and characters which distinguished them arose to his fancy, and through the long lapse of years he discriminated those customs and manners which formed so striking a contrast to the modes of his own times. The rude manners, the boisterous passions, the daring ambition, and the gross indulgences which formerly characterized the priest, the nobleman, and the sovereign, had now begun to yield to learning – the charms of refined conversation – political intrigue and private artifices. The dark clouds of prejudice break away before the sun of science, and gradually dissolving, leave the brightening hemisphere to the influence of his beams. But through the present scene appeared only a few scattered rays, which served to shew more forcibly the vast and heavy masses that concealed the forms of truth. Here prejudice, not reason, suspended the influence of the passions; and scholastic learning, mysterious philosophy, and crafty sanctity, supplied the place of wisdom, simplicity, and pure devotion.

5.5 Mary Wollstonecraft (1759–97), *A Vindication of the Rights of Men* (1790)

Mary Wollstonecraft was an important member of the circle that had the radical publisher Joseph Johnson at its centre. Although her *A Vindication of the Rights of Men* was only one of the numerous replies to Burke, it is particularly interesting for the way it strongly develops the view that Burke's *Reflections* are the product of an effeminate, decadent, Gothic mind. Her linking of primogeniture to outmoded feudal customs is of obvious relevance to the 1790s Gothic novel, as is her critique of sensibility and her attack on Burke's theories of the sublime and the beautiful.

Source: Mary Wollstonecraft (1790), *A Vindication of the Rights of Men, in a Letter to the Right Honourable Edmund Burke on the Revolution in France,* London: J. Johnson, pp. 9–10, 12, 42–5, 47–8, 50–1, 60–1, 93–5, 105–8, 143–5.

. . . I glow with indignation when I attempt, methodically, to unravel your slavish paradoxes, in which I can find no fixed first principle to refute; I shall not, therefore, condescend to shew where you affirm in one page what you deny in another; and how frequently you draw conclusions without any previous premises: – it would be something like cowardice to fight with a man who had never exercised the weapons which his opponent chose to combat with.

I know that you have a mortal antipathy to reason; but, if there is any thing like argument, or first principles, in your wild declamation, behold the result: – that we are to reverence the rust of antiquity, and term the unnatural customs, which ignorance and mistaken self-interest have consolidated, the sage fruit of experience: and that if we do discover some errors, our *feelings* should lead us to excuse, with blind love, or unprincipled filial affection, the venerable vestiges of ancient days. These are gothic notions of beauty – the ivy is beautiful though it insidiously destroys the trunk from which it receives support. . . .

In the infancy of society, confining our view to our own country, customs were established by the lawless power of an ambitious individual, or a weak prince was obliged to comply with every demand of the licentious barbarous insurgents, who disputed his authority with irrefragable arguments at the point of their swords, or the more specious requests of the Parliament, who only allowed him conditional supplies.

Are these the venerable pillars of our constitution? And is Magna Charta to rest for its chief support in a former grant, which reverts to another, till chaos becomes the base of the mighty structure – or we cannot tell what? – for coherence, without some pervading principle of order, is a solecism. . . .

Man has been termed, with strict propriety, a microcosm, a little world in himself. – He is so; – yet must, however, be reckoned an ephemera, or, to adopt your figure of rhetoric, a summer's fly. The perpetuation of property in our families is one of the privileges you most warmly contend for; but it would not be very difficult to prove that the mind must have a very limited range that thus confines its benevolence to such a narrow circle, which, with great propriety, may be included in the sordid calculations of blind self-love.

A brutal attachment to children has appeared most conspicuous in parents who have treated them like slaves, and demanded due homage for all the property they transferred to them, during their lives. It has led them to force their children to break the most sacred ties; to do violence to a natural impulse, and run into legal prostitution to increase wealth or shun poverty; and, still worse, the dread of a parental malediction has made many weak characters violate truth in the face of Heaven; and, to avoid a father's angry curse, the most sacred promises have been broken.

Who can recount all the unnatural crimes which the laudable, interesting desire of perpetuating a name has produced? The younger children have been sacrificed to the eldest son; sent into exile, or confined in convents, that they might not encroach on what was called, with shameful falsehood, the family estate. Will Mr. Burke call this parental affection reasonable or virtuous? – No; it is the spurious offspring of over-weening, mistaken pride – and not that first source of civilization, natural parental affection, that makes no difference between child and child, but what reason justifies by pointing out superior merit.

Another pernicious consequence which arises from this artificial affection is, the insuperable bar which it puts in the way of early marriages. It would be difficult to determine whether the minds or bodies of our youth are most injured by this impediment. Our young men become selfish coxcombs, and gallantry with modest women, and intrigues with those of another description, weaken both mind and body, before either has arrived at maturity. The character of a master of a family, a husband, and a father, forms the citizen imperceptibly, by producing a sober manliness of thought, and orderly behaviour; but, from the lax morals and depraved affections of the libertine, what results? – a finical man of taste, who is only anxious to secure his own private gratifications, and to maintain his rank in society. The same system has an equally pernicious effect on female morals. – Girls are sacrificed to family convenience, or else marry to settle themselves in a superior rank, and coquet without restraint with the fine gentleman whom I have already described. And to such lengths has this vanity, this desire of shining carried them, that it is not now necessary to guard girls against imprudent love matches; for if some widows did not now and then *fall* in love, Love and Hymen would seldom meet, unless at a country church. . . .[11]

Property, I do not scruple to aver it, should be fluctuating, or it is an everlasting rampart, a barbarous feudal institution, that enables the rich to overpower talents and depress virtue.

Besides, an unmanly servility, most inimical to true dignity of character is, by these means fostered in society. Men of some abilities play on the follies of the rich, and mounting to fortune as they degrade themselves, they stand in the way of men of superior talents, who cannot advance in such dirty steps, or wade through the filth *they* never boggle at. Pursuing their way straight forward, their spirit is either bent or broken by the rich man's contumelies, or the difficulties they have to encounter. . . .

. . . 'On this scheme of things a king *is* but a man;* a queen *is* but a woman; a woman *is* but an animal, and an animal not of the highest order.' – All true, Sir; if she is not more attentive to the duties of humanity than fashionable ladies and queens are in general. I will still further accede to the opinion you have so justly conceived of the spirit which begins to animate this age. – 'All homage paid to the sex in general, as such, and without distinct views, is to be regarded as *romance* and folly.' Undoubtedly; because such homage vitiates them, prevents their endeavouring to obtain solid personal merit; and, in short, makes those beings vain inconsiderate dolls, who ought to be prudent mothers and useful

* As you ironically observe.

members of society. 'Regicide and sacrilege are but fictions of superstition corrupting jurisprudence, by destroying its simplicity. The murder of a king, or a queen, or a bishop, are only common homicide.'[12] – Again I agree with you; but you perceive, Sir, that by leaving out the word *father*, I think the comparison invidious. . . .

. . . I now speak of the genuine enthusiasm of genius, which, perhaps, seldom appears, but in the infancy of Civilization; for as this advances reason clips the wing of fancy – the youth becomes a man.

Whether the glory of Europe is set, I shall not now enquire; but probably the spirit of romance and chivalry is in the wane; and reason will gain by its extinction.

From observing several cold romantic characters I have been led to confine the term romantic to one definition – false, or rather artificial, feelings. Works of genius are read with a prepossession in their favour, and sentiments imitated, because they were fashionable and pretty, and not because they were forcibly felt.

In modern poetry the understanding and memory often fabricate the pretended effusions of the heart, and romance destroys all simplicity; which, in works of taste, is but a synonymous word for truth. This romantic spirit has extended to our prose, and scattered artificial flowers over the most barren heath; or a mixture of verse and prose producing the strangest incongruities. The turgid bombast of some of your periods fully proves these assertions; for when the heart speaks we are seldom shocked by hyperbole, or dry raptures. . . .

If you had given the same advice to a young history painter of abilities, I should have admired your judgment, and re-echoed your sentiments. Study, you might have said, the noble models of antiquity, till your imagination is inflamed, and, rising above the vulgar practice of the hour, you may institute without copying those great originals. A glowing picture, or some interesting moment, would probably have been produced by these natural means; particularly if one little circumstance is not overlooked, that the painter had noble models to revert to, calculated to excite admiration and stimulate emulative exertions.

But, in settling a constitution that involved the happiness of millions, that stretch beyond the computation of science, it was, perhaps, necessary to brave a higher model in view than the *imagined* virtues of their forefathers, and wise to deduce their respect for themselves from the only legitimate source, respect for justice. Why was it a duty to repair an ancient castle, built in barbarous ages, of Gothic materials? why were they obliged to rake amongst heterogeneous ruins; or rebuild old walls, whose foundations could scarcely be explored, when a simple structure might be raised on the foundation of experience, the only valuable inheritance our forefathers can bequeath? . . .

Where is the dignity, the infallibility of sensibility, in the fair ladies, whom, if the voice of rumour is to be credited, the captive negroes curse in all the agony of bodily pain, for the unheard of tortures they invent? It is probable that some of them, after a flagellation, compose their ruffled spirits and exercise their tender feelings by the perusal of the last new novel. – How true these tears are to nature, I leave you to determine. But these ladies may have read your Enquiries concerning the origin of our ideas of the Sublime and Beautiful, and, convinced by your arguments, have laboured to be pretty, by counterfeiting weakness.

You may have convinced them that *littleness* and weakness are the very essence of beauty; and that the Supreme Being, in giving women beauty in the most supereminent degree, seemed to command them, by the powerful voice of Nature, not to cultivate the moral virtues that might chance to excite respect, and interfere with the pleasing sensations they were created to inspire. Confining thus truth, fortitude, and humanity, within the rigid pale of manly morals, they might justly argue, that to be loved, woman's high end and great distinction! they should 'learn to lisp, to totter in their walk,' and nick-name God's creatures. Never, they might repeat after you, was any man, much less a woman, rendered amiable by the force of those exalted qualities, fortitude, justice, wisdom, and truth; and thus forewarned of the sacrifice they must make to those austere, unnatural virtues, they would be authorised to turn all their attention to their persons, systematically neglecting morals to secure beauty. – Some rational old woman might chance to stumble at this doctrine, and hint, that in avoiding atheism you had not steered clear of the mussulman's creed; but you could readily exculpate yourself by turning the charge on Nature, who made our idea of beauty independent of reason. Nor would it be necessary for you to recollect, that if virtue has any other foundation than worldly utility, you have clearly proved that one half of the human species, at least, have not souls; and that Nature, by making women little, smooth, delicate, fair creatures, never designed that they would exercise their reason to acquire the virtues that produce opposite, if not contradictory, feelings. The affection produced by them, to be uniform and perfect, should not be tinctured with the respect moral virtues inspire, lest pain should be blended with pleasure, and admiration disturb the soft intimacy of love. This laxity of morals in the female world is certainly more captivating to a libertine imagination than the cold arguments of reason, that give no sex to virtue. If beautiful weakness was interwoven in a woman's frame, if the chief business of her life is to inspire love, and Nature has made an eternal distinction between the qualities that dignify a rational being and this animal perfection, her duty and happiness in this life must clash with any preparation for a more exalted state. So that Plato and Milton were grossly mistaken in asserting that human love led to heavenly, and was only an exaltation of the same affection; for the love of the Deity, which is mixed with the most profound reverence, must be love of perfection, and not compassion for weakness. . . .

Surveying civilized life, and seeing, with undazzled eye, the polished vices of the rich, their insincerity, want of natural affections, with all the specious train that luxury introduces, I have turned impatiently to the poor, to look for man undebauched by riches or power – but, alas! What did I see? A being scarcely above the brutes, over which it tyrannized; a broken spirit, worn-out body, and all those gross vices which the example of the rich, rudely copied, could produce. Envy built a wall of separation, that made the poor hate, whilst they bent to their superiors; who, on their part, stepped aside to avoid the loathsome sight of human misery.

What were the outrages of a day to these continual miseries? Let those sorrows hide their diminished head before the tremendous mountain of woe that thus defaces our globe! Man preys on man; and you mourn for the idle tapestry that decorated a gothic pile, and the dronish bell that summoned the fat priest to prayer. You mourn for the empty pageant of a name, when slavery flaps her wing, and the sick heart retires to die in lonely wilds, far from the abodes of man. Did the pangs you felt for insulted nobility, the anguish that rent your heart when the gorgeous robes were torn off the idol human weakness had set up, deserve to be compared with the long-drawn sigh of melancholy reflection, when misery and vice thus seem to haunt our steps, and swim on the top of every cheering prospect? Why is our fancy to be appalled by terrific perspectives of a hell beyond the grave? – Hell stalks abroad; – the lash resounds on the slave's naked sides; and the sick wretch, who can no longer earn the sour bread of unremitting labour, steals to a ditch to bid the world a long good night – or, neglected in some ostentatious hospital, breathes its last amidst the laugh of mercenary attendants.

Such misery demands more than tears – I pause to recollect myself; and smother the contempt I feel rising for your rhetorical flourishes and infantine sensibility.

5.6 Thomas Paine (1737–1809), *The Rights of Man* (1790–2)

The Rights of Man was the most celebrated and notorious of all the replies to Burke, and rapidly became the bible of radical ideas. Paine's battle was importantly carried out at the level of language and style of argumentation, as well as principle. In the first extract he ridicules Burke's rhetorical graces and attachment to chivalry in contrastingly blunt and 'commonsense' terms. In the second, he carries out a forensic scrutiny of the term 'constitution', in an attempt to shift the ground of political debate away from ancient precedent. Government must be guided by pure reason. At the trial of Paine *in absentia*, for writing the second part of *The Rights of Man*, the Attorney General took the opportunity to restate the fact that the constitution 'has been growing . . . from time almost eternal, – impossible to trace'; another opponent of Paine described his demolition of the Whig myth of the liberty-loving Goth as 'a revolution in language' (cited by Smith, 1984, 44–5).

Source: Thomas Paine (1984), *The Rights of Man*, Harmondsworth: Penguin, Part 1, pp. 49–50, 70–2, Part 2, p. 192.

★

I know a place in America called Point-no-Point; because as you proceed along the shore, gay and flowery as Mr Burke's language, it continually recedes and presents itself at a distance before you; but when you have got as far as you can go, there is no point at all. Just thus it is with Mr Burke's three hundred and fifty-six pages. It is therefore difficult to reply to him. But as the points he wishes to establish may be inferred from what he abuses, it is in his paradoxes that we must look for his arguments.

As the tragic paintings by which Mr Burke has outraged his own imagination and seeks to work upon that of his readers, they are very well calculated for theatrical representation, where facts are manufactured for the sake of show, and accommodated to produce, through the weakness of sympathy, a weeping effect. But Mr Burke should recollect that he is writing History, and not Plays; and that his readers will expect truth and not the spouting rant of high-toned exclamation.

When we see a man dramatically lamenting in a publication intended to be believed, that, '*The age of chivalry is gone!*' that '*The glory of Europe is extinguished for ever*!' that '*The unbought grace of life*' (if any one knows what it is), '*the cheap defences of nations, the nurse of manly sentiment and heroic enterprise, is gone*!'[13] and all this because the Quixote age of chivalry nonsense is gone, what opinion can we form of his judgement, or what regard can we pay to his facts? In the rhapsody of his imagination, he had discovered a world of windmills, and his sorrows are, that there are no Quixotes to attack them. But if the age of aristocracy, like that of chivalry, should fall, (and they had originally some connection), Mr Burke, the trumpeter of the Order, may continue his parody to the end, and finish with exclaiming, '*Othello's occupation's gone*!' . . .

To possess ourselves of a clear idea of what government ought to be, we must trace it to its origin. In doing this, we shall easily discover that governments must have arisen, either *out* of the people, or *over* the people. Mr Burke has made no distinction. He investigates nothing to its source, and therefore he confounds everything: but he has signified his intention of undertaking at some future opportunity, a comparison between the constitutions of England and France. As he thus renders it a subject of controversy by throwing the gauntlet, I take him up on his own ground. It is in high challenges that high truths have the right of appearing; and I accept it with the more readiness, because it affords me, at the same time, an opportunity of pursuing the subject with respect to governments arising our of society.

But it will be first necessary to define what is meant by a *constitution*. It is not sufficient that we adopt the word; we must fix also a standard signification to it.

A constitution is not a thing in name only, but in fact. It has not an ideal, but a real existence; and wherever it cannot be produced in a visible form, there is none. A constitution is a thing *antecedent* to a government, and a government is only the creature of a constitution. The constitution of a country is not the act of its government, but of the people constituting a government. It is the body of elements, to which you can refer, and quote article by article; and which contains the principles on which the government shall be established, the manner in which it shall be organized, the powers it shall have, the mode of elections, the duration of parliaments, or by what other name such bodies my be called; the powers which the executive part of the government shall have; and, in fine, everything that relates to the complete organization of a civil government, and the principles on which it shall act, and by which it shall be bound. A constitution, therefore, is to a government, what the laws made afterwards by that government are to a court of judicature. The court of judicature does not make the laws, neither can it alter them; it only acts in conformity to the laws made: and the government is in like manner governed by the constitution.

Can then Mr Burke produce the English Constitution? If he cannot, we may fairly conclude, that though it has been so much talked about, no such thing as a constitution exists, or ever did exist, and consequently that the people have yet a constitution to form.

Mr Burke will not, I presume, deny the position I have already advanced; namely, that governments arise, either *out* of the people, or *over* the people. The English government is one of those which arose out of a conquest, and not out of society, and, consequently it arose over the people; and though it has been much modified from the opportunity of circumstances since the time of William the Conqueror, the country has never yet regenerated itself, and is therefore without a constitution. . . .

If we begin with William of Normandy, we find that the government of England was originally a tyranny, founded on an invasion and conquest of the country. This being admitted, it will then appear, that the exertion of the nation, at different periods, to abate that tyranny, and render it less intolerable, has been credited for a constitution.

Magna Carta, as it was called, (it is now like an almanac of the same data), was no more than compelling the government to renounce a part of its assumptions . . .

5.7 Thomas Christie (1761–96), *Letters on the Revolution in France* (1791)

Christie was a friend of Mary Wollstonecraft, Joseph Priestley and Joseph Johnson. The first passage neatly expresses the objections of the English radicals to the 'Gothic' nature of Burke's rhetoric and arguments. In particular, radicals sought to overturn the values Burke had attached to a key scene in his *Reflections,* where chivalrous devotion to the queen, 'proud submission' to one's country and its constitution, and manliness are all identified. In their attacks Radicals sought to reverse Burke's values: chivalry is feudal, backward and effeminate; the queen, rather than lovely, is of dubious virtue; while submission appears as an abdication of manly pride and citizenship. The essential elements of this rhetoric are implicit in the preceding extracts from Wollstonecraft and Paine, and explicit in the excerpt from Joseph Priestley (5.8). Throughout their attacks, radicals sought to pin the charge of 'superstition' on Burke, one of the Catholic qualities English nationalism defined itself against.

Source: Thomas Christie (1791), *Letters on the Revolution in France,* London: J. Johnson, pp. 4–5, 36–7.

. . . Ancient learning never appeared to me valuable, because it taught the *art of words*, and the *finesses of style*; but I was wont to honour it, because I believed it infused manly sentiment *and heroic principle*; because I had not met with a man who truly understood it, whom 'ancient learning had not warmed into the enlightened love of ancient freedom.' But Mr. Burke is an exception. He is a proof, that a man may have studied the sentiments and history of the patriots of Greece and Rome, and yet be capable of cherishing in his mind the principles of gothic feudality, and of consecrating in his writings the unclassic jargon of lawyers, monks and sophists of the middle ages.

Eloquence, my friend, was designed by the all-wise Author of Nature, to be the companion of Wisdom, and the guardian of Truth. With these associated, she appears a blooming fair, whose charms captivate every beholder: but separated from these, she becomes a wandering prostitute; her beauty no longer dazzles the pure eye, her voice no more delights the virtuous ear, her charms no longer attract the well-regulated mind. Had the *principles* of Mr. Burke's book been as *just* as the *language* of it is *splendid* and *sublime*, it would have merited a place amongst the first productions of human genius. As the apologist of ancient prejudice, he is without a rival: in that bad eminence he has attained the first rank. But what avails his tuneful periods, that only cheat us into error and deception? What avail his brilliant colours, that only varnish the deformity of folly and oppression? With majestic grace, worthy of a nobler office, he conducts us to the Temple of Superstition, and the magic of his language soothes our hearts into holy reverence and sacred awe. But when we enter to the consecrated portal, and behold a miserable deformed gothic idol in the corner of the temple, set up as the god of our adoration – in place of prostrating ourselves before it, we spurn with indignation at the delusion: the gaudy ornaments of the place serve but to render it more shocking; we turn with disgust from the false splendour of the mansion of Idolatry, and hasten with chearful steps to the humble abode of unadorned Truth, to bow before her august presence, and receive from her the simple and salutary instructions of eternal wisdom. . . .

The fame of Mr. Burke's name occasioned his book to be much read in France; but it produced little effect there. The arguments of it were not new to the French. They had almost all appeared before in the aristocratic speeches and pamphlets.

Harmless as he thinks it, he has not persuaded one patriot that the Bastille should be rebuilt. Indeed it could not be expected that his eloquence would do much in France, where it must be read in a translation. *Logic* is translatable. *Reason* is the same in all languages; but who can transfer *mere declamation* into a foreign tongue, without losing the spirit and consequently the *effect* of the original. Who can translate '*the unbought grace of life*'? a phrase to which no clear idea can be affixed; or – 'proud submission'? an expression that contains a contradiction. A man may be *proud of submitting*, as he may be proud of disgrace, and glory in his shame; but the *act* of submission itself implies *humility*, and can have nothing in it of *pride*. After such *incongruous conjunctions*, such *uncoalescible coalitions* as these, if I did not know Mr. Burke's principles, I should suspect he had a design to lead us into farther paradoxes, and that on some future occasion we should hear him talking, like Bayle, of *square circles*, which might possibly exist in some of the planets, though we had none such in our globe. . . .

5.8 Joseph Priestley (1733–1804), 'Of the Nature of Government, and the Rights of Men and of Kings' (1791)

Joseph Priestley was a leading figure in radical Dissenting circles. He was one of the original members of the Unitarian Society (1791), along with Richard Price. Something of a polymath, Priestley did important work in chemistry, and wrote on many other subjects, including education, rhetoric, theology, psychology and government. Partly as a result of his attacks on Burke, Priestley's house was severely damaged by a Birmingham 'King and Church' mob on the anniversary of the fall of the Bastille in 1791.

Source: Joseph Priestley (1791), *Letters to the Right Hon. Edmund Burke, Occasioned by his Reflections on the Revolution in France*, Birmingham: T. Pearson, pp. 22–3.

. . . With the superstitious respect for kings, and the spirit of chivalry, which nothing but an age of extreme barbarism recommended, and which civilization has banished, you seem to think that every thing great and dignified has left us, 'Never, never more,' you say, p. 113, 'shall we behold . . . by losing all its grossness.'[14] This is perhaps the most admired passage in your whole performance; but it appears to me, that in a great pomp of *words*, it contains but few *ideas*, and some of them inconsistent and absurd. So different also are men's feelings, from the difference, no doubt, of our educations, and the different sentiments we voluntarily cherish through life, that a situation which gives you the idea of *pride*, give me that of *meanness*. You are proud of what, in my opinion, you ought to be ashamed, the idolatry of a fellow creature, and the abasement of yourself. It discovers a disposition from which no 'manly sentiment, or heroic enterprise' can be expected. I submit to a king, or to any other civil magistrate, because the good order of society requires it, but I feel no *pride* in that *submission*; the 'subordination of my heart,' I reserve for *character* only, not for *station*. As a citizen, the object of my respect is *the nation*, and *the laws*. The *magistrates*, by whatever name they are called, I respect only as the confidential servants of the nation, and the administrators of the laws.

These sentiments, just in themselves, and favouring no superstition, appear to me to become men, whom nature has made equal, and whose great object, when formed into societies, it should be to promote their common happiness. I am proud of feeling myself *a man among men*, and I leave it you, Sir, to be 'proud of your *obedience*, and to keep alive,' as well as you can, 'in servitude itself the spirit of an exalted freedom.' I think it much easier, at least, to be preserved *out* of a state of servitude than *in* it. You take much pains to gild over your chains, but they are still chains.

If, Sir, you possess this 'generous loyalty, this proud submission of the heart,' both to *rank and sex*, how concentrated and exalted must be the sentiment, where rank and sex are united! What an *exalted freedom* would you have felt, had you had the happiness of being a subject of the Empress of Russia; your sovereign, being then a *woman*? Fighting under her auspices, you would no doubt, have been the most puissant of knights errant, and her redoubted champion, against the whole Turkish empire, the sovereign of which is only a *man*. . . .[15]

5.9 David Hartley (1732–1813), *Argument on the French Revolution* (1794)

Thomas Paine may have dismissed the idea of an ancient constitution, but his references to the tradition of royal tyranny established by William the Conqueror – a 'French bastard landing with an armed banditti, and establishing himself king of England against the consent of the natives' (Paine, 1987, p. 76) – left some room for the continuance of popular Anglo-Saxonism. David Hartley (son of the philosopher Hartley, and a friend of Benjamin Franklin), returns to arguments from precedent, as opposed to natural right, when he condemns the French *ancien régime* in terms of the theory of the 'Norman Yoke'. E. P. Thompson has suggested that after 1793, with the exile of Paine and the banning of *The Rights of Man* as seditious libel, there was a revival of interest among English Jacobins in the idea of re-asserting Saxon liberties (1970, pp. 95–6). This line of debate was probably perceived as a relatively safe option, in the context of intensifying government persecution.

Source: David Hartley (1794), *Arguments on the French Revolution,* Bath: R. Crutwell, pp. 10–15, 43.

. . . That the principles of the late government of France, were inconsistent with the laws of God and the rights of man, has been equally acknowledged, by the Democrat, the Aristocrat, and the late unfortunate Monarch himself. Under the term of monarchy is included not only the prerogative persons of the Monarch, and of those of the royal blood, but in the next degree to them, an aristocratical and tyrannous nobility, supporting and supported by the throne; and jointly forming a combined system of despotism, to the debasement and destruction of all other ranks in human society.

The instruments of this tyranny have been –

An irresistible military standing force.

An absolute command of the public purse by royal edict of taxation, requiring not even the appearance of popular assent beyond the insulting claim of compulsive registration.

The unconditional patronage of all offices of public trust, honour, or emolument, military and civil, together with an unbounded list of secondary ministerial offices of oppression.

The immense patronage of ecclesiastical preferments, secular and regular.

Feudal superiorities, with monopolizing and all-grasping entails, possessed by an oppressive nobility, entrenched within their own impregnable castles and forest laws; and insolently exempt from the common burdens of the state in proportion to the extent of those feudal territorial monopolies.

The multitudinous and inferior ranks of society torn from their families and the little comforts of their humble estate; devoted to the slaughter of war, to become the victims of the ambition, peculation, extravagance, pride, and cruelty of that nobility, who disdained to consider then, as fellow-subjects, or even as fellow-creatures; while they were themselves monopolizing, in the monarch's court, all the rights of man, in the boundless expence of a civil list, more than adequate to the support of the national dignity, foreign and domestic.

All public roads infested with a *mare-chaussée*[16] and barriers of inquisition, who passes – from whence to what place – and for what reasons, public, private, or personal.

All correspondence of letters subject to the dominion of the posts.

All communication of thoughts by the press, whether moral, civil, political, or religious, equally enthralled by public examination and conditional Licence.

An inquisitorial police invading the secret recesses and domestic privacies of the most wretched and helpless indigents.

A monarchical distribution of pretended justice, under the hand of power, and through the instrumentality of dependent and venal judges, uncontrolled by the restrictive verdict of impartial juries.

A metropolis harrowed and subdued by the perpetual terrors and dungeons of a bastile, the horrid cemetery of the living; their only *Habeas Corpus*, either for life or death, being a *lettre de cachét*.

Revengeful and inhuman cruelties in criminal prosecutions by rack and torture – with ferocious public executions, more horrid even than any possible human crimes.

The French monarchy under the reign of despots has been the universal enemy of mankind, in whole centuries of foreign and desolating wars, excited by the ambition of conquest, for the purpose of ravaging the properties, and destroying the lives and liberties of mankind. Such has been hitherto the persevering system of the late government of France for some centuries past, and such have been the unexaggerated effects of it. This enormity of despotism, for 1400 years, has at length produced the total subversion of that intolerable constitution of tyranny, to which the principles of the American revolution (adopted for different and opposite views by the court, and by the nation of France), have marshalled the way. The Revolution of France is now become the most signal and important event in the history of mankind; and in its consequences will affect all future civil establishments among nations.

The nations of Europe who stand in immediate proximity to this event, are much more interested in the prudent, and peaceful conduct of this cause, than they can be in referring it to the furious and sanguinary tribunal of arms: because all civil and political principles of human society are founded upon the laws of God, and the rights of man; and therefore they ought to be decided by the temperate, reflected, and unimpassioned use of reason, as the viceregent of God on earth, and the unerring guide to man. . . .

To foreign sovereignties I would represent the progressive advancement of British freedom, as a decisive example – an argument of warning to them. The aboriginal principle of the political and civil liberties of the British constitution, derived to us even so far back as from our Saxon ancestors, has lain like the good seed in the ground. It has struggled against tares, and weeds, and malignant plants, in the first chaos of society: It has in its growth aspired to the celestial element of freedom, having overawed and subdued all the cankered roots of despotism.

5.10 Peter Will, Translator's Preface to Karl Grosse, *Horrid Mysteries* (1796)

Karl Grosse's *Horrid Mysteries* is one of the fashionable tales of terror Isabella Thorpe recommends to Catherine Morland in *Northanger Abbey*. It is also one of the most famous examples of the Gothic sub-genre dealing with the Illuminati, an infernal secret society with the avowed mission of transforming feudal Europe into a continent of benevolent republics. The sub-genre was partly fuelled by the Abbé de Barruel's paranoiac *Memoirs, Illustrating the History of Jacobinism* (London: T. Burton, 1797). According to John Robison's follow-up exposé, *Proofs of a Conspiracy Against All the Governments of Europe*, fifth edition (Dublin, 1798), the father of the Illuminati was Adam Weishaupt, who founded the secret society in 1775 in Ingolstadt where he was the Professor of Canon law until his dismissal in 1786. To set the tone of his piece, Barruel has the following passage from Weishaupt's *Discourse for the Mysteries* as his epigraph: 'Princes and Nations shall disappear from the face of the Earth . . . and this Revolution shall be the work of Secret Societies.' Barruel takes Weishaupt at his word, claiming that the French Revolution was primarily the work of the Illuminati, whom he numbers at three hundred thousand 'adepts', plus two million fellow-travellers. Barruel's work sets out to systematise the Illuminati in all their types and variety; but in the end he produces an ever proliferating, paranoid discourse that itself comes to resemble a Gothic fantasy. Barruel's work influenced both Percy B. Shelley and Thomas Love Peacock, albeit in different ways. Robison reports that Baron Knigge (mentioned in the following extract) was an influential Illuminati who distributed many tracts arguing that Christianity should be understood as a 'mere allegory'. According to Robison, the tenor of his work is 'to make man discontented with their condition of civil subordination, and the restraints of revealed religion' (93).

Peter Will made something of a career out of translating sensational German novels into English. For instance, he also translated Cajetan Tschink's *The Victim of Magical Delusion*, another anti-Illuminati novel.

Source: *Horrid Mysteries, The Northanger Set of Jane Austen Novels*, ed. Devendra Varma, London: Folio Press, 1968, pp. xv–xviii.

Secret societies have, at all times, and in all civilized countries, either held out private advantages, or pretended to aim at the welfare of whole nations, in order to encrease the number of their members. Amongst the former, the Rosycrucians, whose order was instituted in Germany in the latter end of the fifteenth century, and pretended to be in possession of the philosophers' stone, and of many more valuable arcana, were, by far, the most famous; and, among the latter, the association known under the name of the Secret Tribunal, acquired the greatest celebrity; if we except the order of the Freemasons, which, probably, was the head source whence all other secret associations derived their origin. However, all these associations, avowedly instituted for the improvement of mankind, either in piety, knowledge, or felicity, generally deceived the sanguine expectations of those that suffered themselves to be ensnared by the imposing veil of mysteriousness, which, at bottom, was nothing better than a cloak of their defects, and of the private selfish views of their founders. However good and noble the primary principles of some of these institutions may have been in the beginning, yet they all degenerated, sooner or later, in a most lamentable and glaring manner. The Secret Tribunal, for instance, was certainly originally instituted for the noble purpose of putting a stop to the numerous murders and robberies perpetrated by the predatory nobility, whom the German Emperors did not dare to punish for their disobedience to the existing laws on account of their own imbecility; but it soon degenerated into a sanguinary and despotic tribunal, that was deaf to the voice of humanity and justice, and became the terror, instead of being the guardian angel, of Germany.

The secret order of the Illuminators in Bavaria, founded by the celebrated Weishaupt, and dispersed about six years since, affords a modern proof of the same assertion. It was founded on masonic principles, and its chief members were freemasons of the strict observance. The original views of that secret association were to dispel the dark clouds of superstition and ignorance, which still obscure the horizon of that and many other Roman Catholic countries, to protect and to assist virtue and merit, to see the places of public trust occupied by persons of known and tried abilities and rectitude, and to destroy the baneful family influence which distributes posts of the highest consequence to subjects devoid of all merit, save what they derive from their noble parentage or the weight of their purse. The general blissful consequences such an association promised to produce, the alluring prospects of promotion, the veil of masonic mysteriousness the hope of attaining higher knowledge, held out by the secret agents of the society, were powerful allurements, by means of which they prevailed on many well-wishers of the general good, amongst whom several Princes were, to associate with them, and interested the ambitious and the enthusiast for their cause. The society soon counted a great number of members, and rapidly spread all over Germany. The first geniuses of our age, philosophers and statesmen, were eager to take an active share in the execution of their, apparently, philanthropic plans; and it cannot be denied that Bavaria, and some other Roman Catholic countries in Germany, where priestcraft depressed the energy of the human mind, and ignorance and superstition swayed with a powerful hand, experienced many happy effects of the united secret exertions of the numerous members of that Society. However, it underwent the same fate all secret confederations, that have a political tendency, and are unauthorized and unprotected by the government, whose defects they pretend to ameliorate, are liable to experience. A spirit of philosophical investigation began, indeed, to pervade the countries that were under its influence, and Bavaria in particular; many great geniuses were roused from the mental lethargy in which they had been kept by the priesthood; the hatred against Protestants abated, and gave room to more liberal sentiments: however, the promising hopes the unknown Superiors of the order had held out to their disciples soon were visibly shaken. Self-interest, vengeance, ambition, and numberless other baneful passions, began, by degrees, to guide the influence of the association, which, by the many injuries it committed against the innocent object of the hatred of individual members, and by the glaring abuses of its great power, threatened to become a curse to mankind, instead of promoting the happiness of the world, and was, at length, dispersed by the interference of the Bavarian government. One of its superiors (Baron de Knigge who is an honour to human society) said, after his secession from the association, of all secret societies in general, and of that of the Illuminators in particular, 'All these secret associations are useless with regard to their efficacy, because they generally lay too much stress on miserable trifles and absurd ceremonies;

speak an emblematical language, that admits of many different interpretations, act after ill-digested plans, are imprudent in the choice of their members, consequently soon degenerate; and although they could, in the beginning, have advantages before public Societies, yet, in the sequel, are infected by defects of which the world justly complains. Whoever is animated with a desire of performing something great and useful, finds, in civil and domestic life, many opportunities of doing it, which not *one* improves as he ought to do. It must first be proved that nothing remains to be done in a public manner, or that insurmountable obstacles are thrown into the way of the zealous promoter of the general good, before one has a right to create a secret and peculiar compass of activity that is not sanctioned by Government. Benevolence needs no mysterious veil; friendship must originate in a free choice; and sociability does not require being promoted by secret means.

'These secret associations also produce baneful consequences to the world. They are noxious to the public; because all secret transactions are justly liable to suspicion; because the executive power can, with justice, demand being informed of the purpose of every activity for which individuals associate; because dangerous plans, and noxious doctrines, may be concealed behind the veil of secrecy, as well as noble views and higher knowledge; because not all members are informed of such dangerous designs, which frequently are hidden by the most beautiful external appearance; because only inferior geniuses suffer themselves to be confined by these moral stays; whereas those that are endowed with superior gifts, either do not long continue in those societies, are spoiled, degenerate, are misguided, or rule over the rest at the expense of their fellow associates; because *unknown* Superiors frequently direct the whole institution by secret machinations; and it is beneath the dignity of an intelligent man to work after a plan which he cannot overlook, and for whose importance and goodness he has no other security but the authority of people whom he does not know, to whom he engages himself without their entering into reciprocal obligations, without knowing where to apply to if he finds himself disappointed in his expectations. They are dangerous and hurtful to the public, because perverse heads and rogues take advantage of the darkness in which he is enfolded, usurp the supreme power, and abuse the other members for the attainment of their private views; because every mortal has his passions, and of course, brings them along with him into the Society, where they have a more extensive scope to range than under the eyes of the Public, being sheltered by the mask of secrecy and concealment; because all these Societies degenerate, by degrees, through the ill-conducted choice of the members that gradually creep in; because they advocate useful citizens from serious civil occupations, misleading them to idleness, or to an *useless* activity; because they become the rendezvous of adventurers and idlers; favour all kinds of political, religious, and philosophical enthusiasm; and, finally, because they are, sooner or later, infected by a monastical *esprit du corps*, cause a great deal of mischief, and afford numberless occasions for cabals, quarrels, persecution, intolerance, and injustice.'

This is the confession of a man that was, many years, a warm advocate for Freemasonry, and a superior of the Illuminators. The author of the subsequent pages has had but too many opportunities of making a similar experience with Baron de Knigge, and also was a member of the Order of the Illuminators, which he left before its dissolution. He has been driven out of his native Country by the secret persecutions of his former brethren, whose intrigues he exposed; and now resides at Algeziras, in Spain, deploring that he has suffered himself to be made a dupe to the ambitious views of a set of men, who promised him the possession of higher knowledge, and a share in the reformation of mankind, while their sole intention was to make him subservient to their private interest; and lamenting that he has sacrificed the best time of his life in hunting after a deluding phantom.

The events related by Marquis Carlos de G—— constitute a great part of his own history, which ought to be a serious warning to all those that listen to the seducing voice of secret, corresponding, and other Societies of a similar nature, that pretend to reform the defects of government, while selfish views are concealed under the imposing outside of philanthropy and patriotism; and the seeds of disaffection to the existing laws and of rebellion, are disseminated under the pretext of applying an healing balsam to the bleeding wounds of the Country.

The subsequent pages are, indeed, no pattern of a perfect Romance; however, the defects they evidently have are overbalanced by so many beauties, that the translator flatters himself their appearance in an English garb will, nevertheless, meet with a kind reception. If we consider that the author intended to erect therein a grateful monument to his dearest friends, to give a gentle warning to his numerous enemies, and to exhibit a faithful picture of the formation of his principles and of his character, which has been traduced with the bitterest acrimony; if we consider all this, we cannot but make some allowance for several obvious imperfections the discerning reader may meet with in the course of his reading; for it is much easier to erect a perfect edifice, if we are at liberty to choose our materials at pleasure, than when we design to interweave parts that already exist, and cannot be altered. Finally, the Translator thinks it needful to observe, that if the mysterious events occurring in the subsequent volumes, are not elucidated with that tiresome minuteness which renders many of our modern novels rather tedious than interesting, he flatters himself that the judicious readers will not be displeased at his confidence in their own ingenuity, which sufficiently will be enabled, by the hints the author has dropped to that purpose, to dispel the mystic gloom which he has been prevented to remove by the truth of Voltaire's words: *Le Secret d'ennuyer est le secret de tout dire.*[17]

5.11 *The Rovers; or, The Double Arrangement* (1798)

The Anti-Jacobin; or, Weekly Examiner came into being in late 1797 and ran until July 1798 when it was reconstituted as the monthly *Anti-Jacobin Review and Magazine*. The new *Anti-Jacobin* had a different editor but the same mission of exposing radicalism wherever it was to be found. The first *Anti-Jacobin*, in which *The Rovers* appeared, had close links to William Pitt's government. In the words of its editor, William Gifford, it had its origin in 'a number of men of brilliant talents and high connection . . . having determined to establish a weekly paper, for the purpose of exposing to deserved ridicule and indignation the political agitators by whom the country was then inundated' (quoted by de Montluzin, pp. 21). Friedrich Schiller's *The Robbers* (*Die Räuber*, 1781) was an obvious target. One of the most influential plays of the period, it directly raised the question of the validity of rebellion against corrupt authority. The *Anti-Jacobin* deploys ridicule, xenophobia, scatalogical humour and a sharp wit to deflate the glamour of Schiller's play. Published anonymously, *The Rovers* was jointly written by William Gifford, John Hookham Frere, George Ellis and George Canning.

Source: *The Anti-Jacobin; or, Weekly Examiner*, no. 31 (11 June 1798), pp. 243–4.

★

Plot

Rogero, son of the late Minister of the Count of Saxe Weimar, having, while he was at College, fallen desperately in love with Matilda Pottingen, daughter of his tutor, Doctor Engelbertus Pottingen, professor of civil law, and Matilda evidently returning his passion, the Doctor, to prevent ill consequences, sends his daughter on a visit to her aunt in *Wetteravia*, where she becomes acquainted with Casimere, a Polish officer, who happens to be quartered near her aunt's, and has several children by him.

Roderic, Count of Saxe Weimar, a prince of a tyrannical and licentious disposition, has for his prime minister and favourite, Gaspar, a crafty villain, who had risen to his post by first ruining, and then putting to death, Rogero's father. – Gaspar apprehensive of the power and popularity which the young Rogero may enjoy at his return to Court, seizes the occasion of his intrigue with Matilda (of which he is apprised officially by Doctor Pottingen), to procure from his master an order for the recall of Rogero from College, and for committing him to the care of the Prior of the *Abbey* of *Quedlinburgh*, a priest, rapacious, savage, and sensual, and devoted to Gaspar's interests – sending at the same time, private orders to the Prior to confine him in a dungeon.

Here Rogero languishes many years. His daily sustenance is administered to him through a grated opening at the top of a cavern, by the landlady of the *Golden Eagle* at Weimar, with whom Gaspar contracts, in the prince's name, for his support – intending, and more than once endeavouring, to corrupt the Waiter to mingle poison with the food, in order that he may get rid of Rogero for ever.

In the mean time Casimere, having been called away from the neighbourhood of Matilda's residence to other quarters, becomes enamoured of and marries Cecilia by whom he has a family, and whom he likewise deserts, after a few years cohabitation, on presence of business which calls him to *Kamschatka*.

Doctor Pottingen, now grown old and infirm, and feeling the want of his daughter's society, sends young Pottingen in search of her with strict injunctions not to return without her; and to bring with her either her present lover Casimere, or, should that not be possible, Rogero himself, if he can find him – the Doctor haying set his heart upon seeing his children comfortably settled before his death. Matilda, about the same period, quits her aunt's in search of Casimere, and Cecilia having been advertised (by an anonymous letter) of the falsehood of his *Kamschatka* journey, sets out in the post-wagon on a similar pursuit.

It is at this point of time the Play opens, with the accidental meeting of Cecilia and Matilda at the inn at Weimar. Casimere arrives there soon after, and falls in, first with Matilda, and then with Cecilia. Successive *éclaircissements* take place, and an arrangement is finally made, by which the two ladies are to live jointly with Casimere.

Young Pottingen, wearied with a few weeks search, during which he has not been able to find either of the objects of it, resolves to stop at Weimar, and wait events there. It so happens that he takes up his lodgings in the same house with Puddingfield and Beefington, two English noblemen, whom the tyranny of King John has obliged to fly from their country, and who, after wandering about the continent for some time, have fixed their residence at Weimar.

The news of the signature of Magna Charta arriving, determines Puddingfield and Beefington to return to *England*. Young Pottingen opens his case to them, and entreats them to stay to assist him in the object of his search. – This they refuse; but, coming to the inn where they are to set off for *Hamburgh*, they meet Casimere, from whom they had both received many civilities in *Poland*.

Casimere, by this time, tired of his 'Double arrangement', and having learnt from the Waiter that Rogero is confined in the vaults of the neighboring Abbey *for love*, resolves to attempt his rescue, and to make over Matilda to him as the price of his deliverance. He communicates his scheme to Puddingfield and Beefington, who agree to assist him, as also does young Pottingen. The Waiter of the inn proving to be a *Knight Templar* in disguise, is appointed leader of the expedition. A band of Troubadours, who happen to be returning from the Crusades, and a company of Austrian and Prussian grenadiers returning from the Seven Years War, are engaged as troops.

The attack on the Abbey is made with great success. The Count of Weimar and Gaspar, who are feasting with the Prior, are seized and beheaded in the refectory. The Prior is thrown into the dungeon, from which Rogero is rescued. Matilda and Cecilia rush in. The former recognises Rogero, and agrees to live with him. The children are produced on all sides – and young Pottingen is commissioned to write to his father, the Doctor, to detail the joyful events which have taken place, and to invite him to Weimar to partake of the general felicity.

Prologue – In Character

Too long the triumphs of our early times,
With civil discord and with regal crimes,
Have stain'd these boards; while Shakespeare's pen has shown
Thoughts, manners, men, to modern days unknown.
Too long have Rome and Athens been the rage (Applause)
And classic buskins soil'd a British stage.
To-night our bard, who scorns pedantic rules,
His plot has borrow'd from the German schools;
The German schools – where no dull maxims bind
The bold expansion of th' electric mind.
Fix'd to no period, circled by no space,
He leaps the flaming bounds of time and place:
Round the dark confines of the forest raves,
With gentle Robbers* stocks his gloomy caves;
Tells how Prime Ministers† are shocking things,
And *reigning Dukes* as bad as tyrant Kings;
How to *two* swains‡ *one* nymph her vows may give,
And how two damsels with *one* lover live!
Delicious scenes! Such scenes *our* bard displays,
Which, crown'd with German, sue for British, praise.
Slow are the steeds, that through Germania's roads
With hempen rein the slumbering post-boy goads;

* See the 'Robbers,' a German tragedy, in which Robbery is put in so fascinating a light, that the whole of a German university went upon the highway in consequence of it.

† See 'Cabal and Love,' a German tragedy – very severe against Prime Ministers and reigning Dukes of Brunswick. – This admirable performance very judiciously reprobates the hire of German troops for the *American War* in the reign of Queen Elizabeth – a practice which would undoubtedly have been highly discreditable to that wise and patriotic Princess, not to say wholly unnecessary, there being no American war at that particular time.

‡ See the 'Stranger, or Reform'd Housekeeper,' in which the former of these morals is beautifully illustrated; and 'Stella,' a genteel German Comedy, which ends with placing a man *bodkin* between *two wives*, like *Thames* between his *two banks*, in the 'Critic'. Nothing can be more edifying that these two dramas. I am shocked to hear that there are some people who think them ridiculous.

Slow is the lumbering post-boy, who proceeds
Through deep sands floundering, on those tardy steeds;
More slow, more tedious, from his husky throat
Twangs through the twisted horn the struggling note.

These truths confess'd – oh! Yet, ye travell'd few,
Germania's *plays* with eyes unjaundic'd view!
View and approve! – though in each passage fine
The faint translation* mock the genuine line,
Though the nice ear the erring sight belie,
For U *twice dotted* pronounc'd like *I*; (Applause)
Yet oft the scene shall Nature's fire impart,
Warm *from* the breast, and glowing *to* the heart!
Ye travell'd few, attend! On you our Bard
Builds his fond hope! Do you his genius guard!

5.12 Anonymous review of W. H. Ireland, *Rimualdo; or, The Castle of Badajos: A Romance* (1801)

The *Monthly Review* was among the more liberal of the contemporary journals. W. H. Ireland (1777–1835) was the notorious Shakespeare forger, exposed by the great textual critic Edmond Malone (1741–1812). Following his disgrace Ireland made his career as a Gothic novelist. His most famous work is *The Abbess* (1799).

Source: *Monthly Review*, vol. 34 (1801), p. 203.

The title of romance still invigorates our spirits. Old as we are, it recalls to our recollection the stories in which our youth delighted, of wandering knights, tilts, tournaments, enchanted castles, formidable giants, sea monsters, distressed damsels, tremendous fights, and impossible valour. We forget, however, that 'the days of chivalry are gone';[18] and that, in *present-day romance*, we must expect little other amusement than the oglio[19] of the modern novel supplies: consisting of unnatural parents, – persecuted

* These are the warnings very properly given to readers, to beware how they judge of what they cannot understand. Thus, if the translation runs, '*lightning of my soul, fulguration of angels, sulphur of hell*,' we should recollect that this is not coarse or strange in the German language, when applied by a lover to his mistress; but the English has nothing precisely parallel to the original Muylychause Arch-Angelichen, which means rather *emanation of the archangelican nature* – or to smellymykern vankelper, which, if literally rendered, would signify *made of the stuff of the same odour whereof the Devil makes flambeaus*. See *Schüttenbrüch* on the German Idiom.

lovers, – murders, – haunted apartments, – winding sheets, and winding stair-cases, – subterraneous passages, – lamps that are dim and perverse, and that always go out when they should not, – monasteries, – caves, – monks, tall, thin, and withered, with lank abstemious cheeks, – dreams, – groans, and spectres.

Such is the outline of *modern* romance.

Notes

1 The full title is *An Historical Essay on the English Constitution: or, An Impartial Inquiry into the Executive Power of the First Establishment of the Saxons in this Kingdom* (London: Edward & Charles Dilley, 1771). According to the British Library catalogue, it is the work of Obadiah Hulme although sometimes attributed to Allen Ramsay. The preface helpfully explains the purpose of the work: 'The motive, which induces the author to lay these papers before the public, is, an honest desire to show the true course of that general discontent, which now distracts the British Empire; and, to point out the constitutional means of reconciliation, between Great Britain and her distant provinces' (p. iii).

2 A reference to the framing of the American constitution.

3 Cf. Montesquieu, 1878, I, p. 173.

4 From here until the end of the text the anonymous 'Demophilius' quotes from *An Historical Essay*, pp. 6–10.

5 Emphasis added by Demophilius.

6 Emphasis added by Demophilius.

7 Richard Price. See 5.2.

8 Horace, *De Arte Poetica*, 99. 'It is not enough for poems to be fine; they must charm' (Blakeney) (from Penguin edition, p. 385).

9 Virgil, *Aeneid*, 2.105: *gentis cunabula nostrae*: 'The cradle of our people' (Penguin edition, p. 386).

10 See Rictor Norton, *The Mistress of Udolpho: The Life of Ann Radcliffe* (Leicester: Leicester University Press, 1999), pp. 61–2, 67–8.

11 I.e. among upper-class urban sophisticates the only time marriage and romantic love coincide is in the fornication of widows; you have to look to the country for romantic marriages.

12 Wollstonecraft is selectively quoting, and misquoting, Burke's *Reflections*. See 5.3.

13 Paine is quoting Burke's *Reflections*. See 5.3.

14 See 5.3.

15 A reference to Catherine the Great, who supposedly had a nymphomaniacal appetite for guardsmen. Marie Antoinette's alleged sexual perversions (lesbianism and incest, in particular) were also a staple of radical rhetoric.

16 The *maréchaussée* were a constabulary force.

17 The secret of being boring is to say everything.

18 A quotation from Edmund Burke's *Reflections on the Revolution in France* (1790). See p. 232.

19 A hotchpotch, a medley of heterogeneous material.

6 Gothic renovations

6.1 William Godwin (1756–1836) on romance and novel

Godwin was one of the leading radical intellectuals of the Romantic era. His *The Adventures of Caleb Williams* (1794) took the Gothic in a new, philosophical direction. His next, *St Leon* (1799), was also a generic experiment. The present essay, on the relationship between history and fiction, derives from the intervening period, and was never published in Godwin's lifetime. Godwin may have lost interest in the work, or there may not have been a suitable occasion for its publication. However, its very area of concern suggests another possibility. The first half of the essay (here omitted) develops two main arguments. Godwin's first argument is that histories that consider mankind 'in the mass', especially those developmental histories associated with Montesquieu in France and the Scottish Enlightenment in Britain, are hopelessly general. His second argument favourably contrasts the genius of the ancients with the mediocrity of the moderns, which is where we pick up the essay, with Godwin inveighing against the crass meaninglessness of much British history. Up to the Glorious Revolution we encounter tales of sound and fury; afterwards, the bland corruption of 'regime Whiggery'. In opposition to conventional history's grand narratives, Godwin favours individual stories, detailed narratives capable of articulating the complex trains of thoughts and motives which characterise the historical agent in true depth. Godwin brings his two arguments together when he insinuates that the Ancients were strikingly free individuals precisely because they did not subscribe to 'mass history'. That is to say, collective or generalised history has the effect of robbing agents of belief in their powers of individual action, thus guaranteeing the very mediocrity which is its object. The essay's apparent polemical purpose is to argue for the superiority of 'fable' over history: in a nutshell, that in plumbing the depths of individual motivation fiction is a more complex and truer kind of narrative, than conventional history with its flimsy generalisations. But behind this argument there is the even more important contention that we are doomed to live the mediocre, collective histories we write. Collective histories poison and retard society through the subtle message that individuals cannot make an impression on history, which is also to say, the future. Godwin wants to rescue the individual agent, the 'genius' who imagines a better possibility, and realises it within his or her society. Fiction, which concentrates on the individual's struggles to realise his intentions, is not only a truer kind of narrative, in that it is more particular, and therefore more complex; it is also a healthier kind of history, for it restores to society a creative sense of possibility.

For Godwin, romance is implicitly a more radical genre than the novel, for it is less constrained in its representations. Although Godwin does not distinguish between 'novel' and 'romance', per se, it seems clear that the 'vicious style of writing' Godwin finds himself accused of equates with romance, while the 'usual road' into which he finds himself being coerced is best thought of as the probable and ordinary course of the novel.

6.1a William Godwin, 'On History and Romance' (1797)

Source: William Godwin (1988), Appendix 4 of *Things as They Are; or, The Adventures of Caleb Williams*, ed. Maurice Hindle, New York: Penguin, pp. 366–73.

★

. . . What sort of an object is the history of England? Till the extinction of the wars of York and Lancaster, it is one scene of barbarism and cruelty. Superstition rides triumphant upon the subject neck of princes and of people, intestine war of noble with noble, or of one pretender to the crown against another, is almost incessant. The gallant champion is no sooner ousted, than he is led without form of law to the scaffold, or massacred in cold blood upon the field. In all these mighty struggles, scarcely a trace is to be found of a sense of the rights of men. They are combinations among the oppressors against him that would usurp their tyranny, or they are the result of an infatuated predilection for one despotic monster in preference to another. The period of the Tudors is a period of base and universal slavery. The reign of Elizabeth is splendid, but its far-famed worthies are in reality supple and servile courtiers, treacherous, undermining and unprincipled. The period of the Stuarts is the only portion of our history interesting to the heart of man. Yet its noblest virtues are obscured by the vile jargon of fanaticism and hypocrisy. From that moment that the grand contest excited under the Stuarts was quieted by the Revolution, our history assumes its most insipid and insufferable form. It is the history of negotiations and tricks, it is the history of revenues and debts, it is the history of corruption and political profligacy, but it is not the history of genuine independent man.

Some persons, endowed with too much discernment and taste not to perceive the extreme disparity that subsists between the character of ancient and of modern times, have observed that ancient history carries no other impression to their minds than that of exaggeration and fable.

It is not necessary here to enter into a detail of the evidence upon which our belief of ancient history is founded. Let us take it for granted that it is a fable. Are all fables unworthy of regard? Ancient history, says Rousseau, is a tissue of such fables, as have a moral perfectly adapted to the human heart. I ask not, as a principal point whether it be true or false? My first enquiry is, 'Can I derive instruction from it? Is it a genuine praxis upon the nature of man? Is it pregnant with the most generous motives and the most fascinating examples?' If so, I had rather be profoundly versed in this fable; that in all the genuine histories that ever existed.

It must be admitted indeed that all history bears too near a resemblance to fable. Nothing is more uncertain, more contradictory, more unsatisfactory than the evidence of facts. If this be the case in courts or justice, where truth is sometimes sifted with tenacious perseverance how much more will it hold true of the historian? He can administer no oath, he cannot issue his precept, and summon his witnesses from distant provinces, he cannot arraign his personages and compel there to put in their answer. He must take what they choose to tell, the broken fragments, and the scattered ruins of evidence.

That history which comes nearest to truth, is the mere chronicle of facts, places and dates. But this is in reality no history. He that knows only on what day the Bastille was taken and on what spot Louis XVI perished, knows nothing. He professes the mere skeleton of history. The muscles, the articulations, every thing in which the life emphatically resides, is absent.

Read Sallust.[1] To every action he assigns a motive. Rarely an uncertainty diversifies his page. He describes his characters with preciseness and decision. He seems to enter into the hearts of his personages, and unfolds their secret thoughts. Considered as fable, nothing can be more perfect. But neither is this history. There is but one further mode of writing history, and this is the mode principally prevalent in modem times. In this mode, the narrator is sunk in the critic. The main body of the composition consists of a logical deduction and calculation of probabilities. This species of writing may be of use as a whetstone upon which to sharpen our faculty of discrimination, but it answers none of the legitimate purposes of history.

From these considerations it follows that the noblest and most excellent species of history, may be decided to be a composition in which, with a scanty substratum of facts and dates, the writer interweaves a number of happy, ingenious and instructive inventions, blending them into one continuous and indiscernible mass. It sufficiently corresponds with the denomination, under which Abbé Prévost acquired considerable applause, of historical romance. Abbé Prévost differs from Sallust, inasmuch as he made freer use of what may be styled, the *licentia historica*.[2]

If then history be little better than romance under a graver name, it may not be foreign to the subject here treated, to enquire into the credit due to that species of literature, which bears the express stamp of invention, and calls itself romance or novel.

This sort of writing has been exposed to more obloquy and censure than any other.

The principal cause of this obloquy is sufficiently humorous and singular.

Novels, as an object of trade among booksellers, are of a peculiar cast. There are few by which immense sums of money can be expected to be gained. There is scarcely one by which some money is not gained. A class of readers, consisting of women and boys, all which is considerably numerous, requires a continual supply of books of this sort. The circulating libraries therefore must be furnished while, in consequence of the discredit which has fallen ups romance, such works are rarely found to obtain a place in the collection of the gentleman or the scholar. An ingenious bookseller of the metropolis, speculating upon this circumstance, was accustomed to paste an advertisement in his window, to attract the eye of the curious passenger, and to fire his ambition, by informing him of a 'want of novels for the ensuing season'.

The critic and the moralist, in their estimate of romances, have borrowed the principle that regulates the speculations of trade. They have weighed novels by the great and taken into their view the whole scum and surcharge of the press. But surely this is not the way in which literature would teach us to consider the subject.

When we speak of poetry, we do not fear to commend this species of composition, regardless of the miserable trash that from month to month finds its way from the press under the appellation of poet. The like may be said of history, or of books of philosophy, natural and intellectual. There is no species of literature that would stand this ordeal.

If I would estimate truly any head of composition, nothing can be more unreasonable, than for me to take into account every pretender to literature that has started in it. In poetry I do not consider the persons who merely know how to count their syllables and tag a rhyme; still less those who print their effusion in the form of verse without being adequate to either of these. I recollect those authors only who are endowed with some of the essentials of poetry, with its imagery, its enthusiasm, or its empire over the soul of man. Just so in the cause before us, I should consider only those persons who had really written romance, not those who had vainly attempted it.

Romance then, strictly considered, may be pronounced to be one of the species of history. The difference between romance and what ordinarily bears the denomination history, is this. The historian is confined to individual incident and individual man, and must hang upon that his invention or conjecture as he can. The writer collects his materials from all sources, experience, report, and the records of human affairs; then generalises them; and finally selects, from their elements and the various combinations they afford, those instances which he is best qualified to portray, and which he judges most calculated to impress the heart and improve the faculties of his reader. In this point of view we should be apt to pronounce that romance was a bolder species of composition than history.

It has been affirmed by the critics that the species of composition which Abbé Prévost and others have attempted, and according to which, upon a slight substratum of fact, all the licence of romantic invention is to be engrafted, is contrary to the principles of a just taste. History is by this means debauched and corrupted. Real characters are wantonly misrepresented. The reader, who has been interested by a romance of this sort, scarcely knows how to dismiss it from his mind when he comes to consider the genuine annals of the period to which it relates. The reality and the fiction, like two substances of disagreeing natures, will never adequately blend with each other. The invention of the writer is much too wanton not to discolour and confound the facts with which he is concerned; while on the other hand, his imagination is fettered and checked at every turn by facts that will not wholly accommodate themselves to the colour of his piece, or the moral he would adduce from it.

These observations, which have been directed against the production of historical romance, will be found not wholly inapplicable to those which assume the graver and more authentic name of history. The reader will be miserably deluded if, while he reads history, he suffers himself to imagine that he is reading facts. Profound scholars are so well aware of this, that, when they would study the history of any country, they pass over the historians that have adorned and decorated the facts, and proceed at once to the naked and scattered materials, out of which the historian constructed his work. This they do, that they may investigate the story for themselves; or, more accurately speaking, that each man, instead of resting in the inventions of another, may invent his history for himself, and possess his creed as he possesses his property, single and incommunicable.

Philosophers, we are told, have been accustomed by old prescription to blunder in the dark; but there is perhaps no darkness, if we consider the case maturely, so complete as that of the historian. It is a trite observation, to say that the true history of a public transaction is never known till many years after the event. The places, the dates, those things which immediately meet the eye of the spectator, are indeed as well known as they are ever likely to be. But the comments of the actors come out afterwards; to what are we the wiser? Whitlock and Clarendon,[3] who lived upon the spot, differ as much in their view of the transactions, as Hume[4] and the Whig historians have since done. Yet all are probably honest. If you be a superficial thinker, you will take up with one or other of their representations, as best suit your prejudices. But, if you are a profound one, you will see so many incongruities and absurdities in all, as deeply to impress you with the scepticism of history.

The man of taste and discrimination, who has properly weighed these causes, will be apt to exclaim, 'Dismiss me from the falsehood and impossibility of history, and deliver me over to the reality of romance.'

The conjectures of the historian must be built upon a knowledge of the characters of his personages. But we never know any man's character. My most intimate and sagacious friend continually misapprehends my motives. He is in most cases a little worse judge of them than myself and I am perpetually mistaken. The materials are abundant for the history of Alexander, Caesar, Cicero and Queen Elizabeth. Yet how widely do the best informed persons differ respecting them? Perhaps by all their character is misrepresented. The conjectures therefore respecting their motives in each particular transaction must be eternally fallacious. The writer of romance stands in this respect upon higher ground. He must be permitted, we should naturally suppose, to understand the character which is the creature of his own fancy.

The writer of romance then is to be considered as the writer of real history; while he who was formerly called the historian, must be contented to step down into the place of his rival, with this disadvantage, that he is a romance writer, without the arduous, the enthusiastic and the sublime licence of imagination, that belong to that species of composition. True history consists in a delineation of consistent, human character, in a display of the manner in which such a character acts under successive circumstances, in showing how character increases and assimilates new substances to its own, and how it decays, together with the catastrophe into which by its own gravity it naturally declines.

There is however, after all, a deduction to be made from this eulogium of the romance writer. To write romance is a task too great for the powers of man, and under which he must be expected to totter. No man can hold the rod so even, but that it will tremble and vary from its course. To sketch a few bold outlines of character is no desperate undertaking; but to tell precisely how such a person would act in a given situation, requires a sagacity scarcely less than divine. We never conceive a situation, or those minute shades in a character that would modify its conduct. Naturalists tell us that a single grain of sand more or less on the surface of the earth, would have altered its motion, and, in process of ages, have diversified its events. We have no reason to suppose in this respect, that what is true in matter, is false in morals.

Here then the historian in some degree, though imperfectly, seems to recover his advantage upon the writer of romance. He indeed does not understand the character he exhibits, but the events are taken out of his hands and determined by the system of the universe, and therefore, as far as his information extends, must be true. The romance writer, on the other hand, is continually straining at a foresight to which his faculties are incompetent, and continually fails. This is ludicrously illustrated in those few romances which attempt to exhibit the fictitious history of nations. That principle only which holds the planets in their course, is competent to produce that majestic series of events which characterises flux, and successive multitudes.

The result of the whole, is that the sciences and the arts of man are alike imperfect, and almost infantine. He that will not examine the collections and the efforts of man, till absurdity and folly are extirpated from among them, must be contacted to remain in ignorance, and wait for the state, where he expects that faith will give plan to sight, and conjecture be swallowed up in knowledge.

6.1b William Godwin, Preface to *Fleetwood* (1805)

Source: William Godwin, *Fleetwood* (1805), London: Richard Phillips, pp. v–vii.

Yet another novel from the same pen, which has twice before claimed the patience of the public in this form. The unequivocal indulgence which has been extended to my two former attempts, renders me doubly solicitous not to forfeit the kindness I have experienced.

One caution I have particularly sought to exercise: 'not to repeat myself.' Caleb Williams was a story of very surprising and uncommon events, but which were supposed to be entirely within the laws and established course of nature, as she operates in the planet we inhabit. The story of St. Leon is of the miraculous class; and its design, to 'mix human feelings and passions with incredible situations, and thus render them impressive and interesting.'

Some of those fastidious readers – they may be classed among the best friends an author has, if their admonitions are judiciously considered – who are willing to discover those faults which do not offer themselves to every eye, have remarked, that both these tales are in a vicious style of writing; that Horace has long ago decided, that the story we cannot believe, we are by all the laws of criticism called upon to hate;[5] and that even the adventures of the honest secretary,[6] who was first heard of ten years ago, are so much out of the usual road, that not one reader in a million can ever fear they will happen to himself.

Gentlemen critics, I thank you. In the present volumes I have served you with a dish agreeable to your own receipt, though I cannot say with any sanguine hope of obtaining your approbation.

6.2 Hugh Murray (1779–1846), *Morality of Fiction* (1805)

Hugh Murray's arguments on the value of fiction reflect an eighteenth-century tradition, perhaps best exemplified by Lord Kames's influential *The Elements of Criticism* (1762). Like Kames, Murray steers a middle course between outright condemnation and enthusiastic acceptance. He warns against 'philosophical romances', such as those by Godwin, which support 'some very ill-founded and dangerous principles' (p. 8). At the same time he argues that we have an innate appetite for improving stories: pleasure in stories is part of the 'consummate wisdom' of the 'human constitution' (p. 1).

Source: Hugh Murray (1805), *Morality of Fiction; or, An Inquiry into the Tendency of Fictitious Narratives, With Observations of Some of the Most Eminent*, Edinburgh: Mundell & Son, pp. 38–41.

In the case of political and historical fictions, it may be inquired, whether they ought to be altogether imaginary or founded in part upon real events. The last method may certainly assist that impression of reality, which is so necessary in order to give interest to the narrative. Yet there are circumstances, which may, perhaps, be found to overbalance this advantage. It must prove a severe restraint on the fancy of the writer, who will often find it no easy task to prevent his story from clashing with the history or tradition on which it is founded. The engrafted fiction also tends to give false impressions in regard to the history. Sometimes even, as will appear in the sequel, it throws over it an obscurity which is never removed. It seems, therefore, to be for the mutual advantage both of truth and fiction, that they should be kept altogether distinct; or, if a foundation must be laid in some real events, that they should be as few, and as remote, as possible, in point of time and place.

Is it proper, that narratives formed with this design should be crowded with surprising and improbable incidents? This has been long assumed by the writers of fiction as an indisputable privilege. Events, that in real life appear altogether incredible, are there quite in the common order of things. To conduct their hero through all the mazes of adventure; to involve him in difficulties apparently inextricable; to keep the reader perpetually on the rack of suspense and anxiety, are, in general, the objects chiefly aimed at by the authors of such performances. The more improbable an incident is, the more unlike common life, the better is it supposed fitted for their purpose. The origin of this mode of writing is easily accounted for. The invention of printing, and consequent diffusion of books, has given birth to a multitude of readers, who seek only for amusement, and wish to find it without trouble or thought. Works thus conducted, supply them with one which is level to the lowest capacities. How well they are adapted to the taste of this description of readers appears plainly from the extraordinary avidity with which they are devoured.

No good effect seems likely to result from such a kind of reading besides the mere childish pleasure it affords. It tends to give false views of human life; to inspire fantastic and visionary expectations; discontent with the uniformity of common life; and a disposition to choose the plan of conduct which leads to extraordinary adventures, rather than that which true wisdom points out. A crowd of incidents will leave little room for the display of character and sentiment, or any higher beauties, of which this kind of writing is susceptible. Even supposing them to exist there, the attention of the reader is likely to be too much occupied to admit of his receiving from them any deep impression. . . .

6.3 Review of Walter Scott's *The Lay of the Last Minstrel* (1805)

The Lay of the Last Minstrel (1805) was the first of Scott's 'metrical romances'. A series of works followed, including *Marmion* (1808), *Rokeby* and *The Bridal of Triermain* (both 1813). Scott scored a great popular success with his poetical romances, and together with the Waverley novels (see 6.6), helped bring chivalry back into vogue. The following review neatly articulates the poetic logic of Scott's project. Perhaps its most interesting feature is the reviewer's ability to rehearse eighteenth-century arguments on this matter (compare the extracts from Walpole, Blair or Beattie) while claiming novelty for it.

Source: *The Edinburgh Review*, vol. 9 (April 1805), pp. 1–2, 10.

★

We consider this poem as an attempt to transfer the refinements of modern poetry to the matter and the manner of the antient metrical romance. The author, enamoured of the lofty visions of chivalry, and partial to the strains in which they were formerly embodied, seems to have employed all the resources of his genius in endeavouring to recall them to the favour and admiration of the public, and in adapting to the taste of modern readers, a species of poetry which was once the delight of the courtly, but has long ceased to gladden any other eyes than those of the scholar and the antiquary. This is a romance, therefore, composed by a minstrel of the present day; of such a romance as we may suppose would have been written in modern times, if that style of composition had continued to be cultivated, and partaken consequently of the improvements which every branch of literature has received since the time of its desertion.

Upon this supposition, it was evidently Mr. Scott's business to retain all that was good, and to reject all that was bad in the models upon which he was to form himself; adding, at the same time, all the interest and the beauty which could possibly by assimilated to the manner and spirit of his original. It was his duty, therefore, to reform the rambling, obscure, and interminable narratives of the ancient romances, – to moderate their digressions, – to abridge or retrench their unmerciful or needless descriptions, – and to expunge altogether those feeble and prosaic passages, the rude stupidity of which is so apt to excite the derision of a modern reader; at the same time he has to rival, if he could, the force and vivacity of their minute and varied representations – the characteristic simplicity of their pictures of manners – the energy and conciseness with which they frequently describe great events – and the lively colouring and accurate drawing by which they give the effect of reality to every scene they undertake to delineate. In executing this arduous task, he was permitted to avail himself of all that variety of style and manner which had been sanctioned by the ancient practice, and bound to embellish his performance with all the graces of diction and verification of the minstrel's song. . . .

The ancient romance owes much of its interest to the lively picture which it affords of the times of chivalry, and of those usages, manners and institutions which we have been accustomed to associate in our minds, with a certain combination of magnificence with simplicity, and ferocity with romantic honour. The representations contained in those performances, however, are for the most part too rude and naked to give complete satisfaction. The execution is always extremely unequal; and though the writer sometimes touches upon the appropriate feeling with great effect and felicity, still this appears to be done more by accident than design; and he wanders away immediately into all sorts of ludicrous or uninteresting details, without any apparent consciousness of incongruity. These defects Mr. Scott has corrected with admirable address and judgment in the greater part of the work now before us: and while he has exhibited a very striking and impressive picture of the old feudal usages and institutions, he has shewn still greater talent in engrafting upon those descriptions all the tender or magnanimous emotions to which the circumstances of the story naturally give rise. Without impairing the antique air of the whole piece, or violating the simplicity of the ballad style, he has contrived, in this way, to impart a much greater dignity, and more powerful interest to his production, than could ever be attained by the unskilful and unsteady delineations of the old romancers.

6.4 Anna Laetitia Barbauld (1743–1824), 'On the Origin and Progress of Novel Writing' (1810)

Anna Laetitia Barbauld, *née* Aikin, was a radical Dissenter, and an important figure in the history of Gothic writing (see 3.8). In the introduction to her fifty-volume edition of the British novelists, Barbauld looks back to James Beattie's *On Fable and Romance* (2.10) and Clara Reeve's *The Progress of Romance* (4.2b), framing the history of the novel in evolutionary terms. As polite society advances, so, too, does narrative, from romance to novel, from 'tales of magic and enchantment' (p. 7) to probable depictions of modern life. But whereas they acknowledge the inevitability of fiction – Beattie grudgingly, Reeve defensively – Barbauld is frank in her approval: 'For my own part, I scruple not to confess that, when I take up a novel, my end and object is entertainment' (p. 44). As she says a little later, the 'unpardonable sin in a novel is dullness' (p. 45). The general censure directed towards the novel moves Barbauld to mount a defence by rebutting the most common criticism: novels 'have had a very strong effect in infusing principles and moral feelings. It is impossible to deny that the most glowing and impressive sentiments of virtue are to be found in many of these compositions, and have been deeply imbibed by their youthful readers' (p. 46).

Barbauld gamely defends the pedagogic value of novels, but her real interest in supporting them is more evident in her apparently casual assertion that 'Reading is the cheapest of pleasures: it is a domestic pleasure' (p. 44). Circulating libraries hold no terrors for liberals such as Barbauld: on the contrary, they have a democratising function (of a moderate kind) in bringing reading, and therefore knowledge, to the populace. Barbauld's preface is a wide-ranging essay on the origin and development of European fiction. The limits of her inclusive ardour, for instance in refusing to support the German school of Gothic fiction, may be taken as a measure of the public opprobrium attached to it.

Source: Originally published 1810. Quoted from Mrs. Barbauld (1820), 'On the Origin and Progress of Novel Writing', introduction to *The British Novelists, with an Essay, and Prefaces Biographical and Critical*, London: Rivington, pp. 1–3, 29–31.

★

A collection of Novels has a better chance of giving pleasure than of commanding respect. Books of this description are condemned by the grave, and despised by the fastidious; but their leaves are seldom found unopened, and they occupy the parlour and the dressing-room while productions of higher name are often gathering dust upon the shelf. It might not perhaps be difficult to show that this species of composition is entitled to a higher rank than has been generally assigned it. Fictitious adventures, in one form or other, have made a part of the polite literature of every age and nation. These have been grafted upon the actions of their heroes; they have been interwoven with their mythology; they have been moulded upon the manners of the age, – and, in return, have influenced the manners of the succeeding generation by the sentiments they have infused and the sensibilities they have excited.

Adorned with the embellishments of Poetry, they produce the epic; more concentrated in the story, and exchanging narrative for action, they become dramatic. When allied with some great moral end, as in the *Telemaque* of Fenelon and Marmontel's *Belisaire*, they may be termed didactic. They are often made the vehicles of satire, as in Swift's *Gulliver's Travels*, and the *Candide* and *Babouc* of Voltaire. They take a tincture from the learning and politics of the times, and are made use of successfully to attack or recommend the prevailing systems of the day. When the range of this kind of writing is so extensive, and its effects so great, it seems evident that it ought to hold a respectable place among the productions of genius; nor is it easy to say, why the poet, who deals in one kind of fiction, should have so high a place allotted him in the temple of fame; and the romance-writer so low a one as in the general estimation he is confined to. To measure the dignity of a writer by the pleasure he affords his readers is not perhaps using an accurate criterion; but the invention of a story, the choice of proper incidents, the ordonnance of the plan, occasional beauties of description, and above all, the power exercised over the reader's heart by filling it with the successive emotions of love, pity, joy, anguish, transport, or indignation, together with the grave impressive moral resulting from the whole, imply talents of the highest order, and ought to be appreciated accordingly. A good novel is an epic in prose with more of character and less (indeed in modern novels nothing) of the supernatural machinery.

If we look for the origin of fictitious tales and adventures, we shall be obliged to go to the earliest accounts of the literature of every age and country. The Eastern nations have always been fond of this species of mental gratification. The East is emphatically the country of invention. . . .

The Germans, formerly remarkable for the laborious heaviness and patient research of their literary labours, have, within this last century, cultivated with great success the field of polite literature. Plays, tales, and novels of all kinds, many of them by their most celebrated authors, were at first received with avidity in this country, and even made the study of their language popular. The tide has turned, and they are now as much depreciated.[7] The *Sorrows of Werter*, by Goethe, was the first of these with which we were familiarized in this country: we received it through the medium of a French translation. It is highly pathetic, but its tendency has been severely, perhaps justly, censured; yet the author might plead that he has given warning of the probable consequences of illicit and uncontrolled passions by the awful catastrophe. It is certain, however, that the impression made is of more importance than the moral deduced; and if Schiller's fine play of *The Robbers* has had, as we are assured was the case, the effect of leading some well-educated young gentlemen to commit depredations on the public,[8] allured by the splendour of the principal character, we may well suppose that Werther's delirium of passion will not be less seducing. Goethe has written another novel, much esteemed, it is said, by the Germans, which contains, amongst other things, criticisms on the drama. The celebrated Wieland has composed a great number of works of fiction; the scene of most of them laid in ancient Greece. His powers are great, his invention fertile, but his designs insidious. He and some others of the German writers of philosophical romances have used them as a frame to attack received opinions, both in religion and in morals. Two at least of his performances have been translated, *Agathon* and *Peregrine Proteus*. The former is beautifully written, but its tendency is seductive. The latter has taken for its basis a historical character; its tendency is also obvious. Klinger is an author who deals in the horrid. He subsists on murders and atrocities of all sorts, and introduces devils and evil spirits among his personages; he is said to have powers, but to labour under a total want of taste. In contrast to this writer and those of his class, may be mentioned *The Ghost Seer*, by Schiller, and *The Sorcerer* by another hand. These were written to expose the artifices of the Italian adepts of the school of Cagliostro.[9] It is well known that these were spreading superstition and enthusiasm on the German part of the continent to an alarming degree, and had so worked upon the mind of the late king of Prussia, that he was made to believe he possessed the power of rendering himself invisible, and was wonderfully pleased when one of his courtiers (who, by the way, understood his trade) ran against and jostled him, pretending not to see his Majesty. . . .

6.5 Charles R. Maturin (1782–1824), Preface to *The Milesian Chief* (1812)

Educated at Trinity College, Dublin, where he took orders, Maturin was the most significant of the late Gothic romancers. Indeed, his *Melmoth the Wanderer* (1820) has often been used as the terminal date of the first wave of Gothic writing. As he makes clear in the following 'preface', Maturin was acutely aware of his belated status as a writer persisting in a style that 'was out' when he was a boy. Despite his protestations to the contrary in the preface to *Women; or, Pour et Contre*, he continued to sneak Gothic romances into the public domain, despite the hostile reaction of such commentators as *The Quarterly Review*. Founded by John Murray in 1809, the *Quarterly* was a self-consciously Tory rival to the Whig *Edinburgh Review*.

In the words of the *Oxford Companion to English Literature*, the 'journal stood, politically, for the defence of the established order, Church, and Crown' (p. 802). As such, it is not surprising that the *Quarterly* did not warm to romances 'representing those struggles of passion when the soul trembles on the verge of the unlawful and the unhallowed'.

Source: Charles R. Maturin, *The Milesian Chief* (1812), London: Henry Colburn, pp. i–vi.

★

Dedication. To The Quarterly Reviewers

Gentlemen,

You have been pleased to notice the Romance of 'Montorio,'[10] and I am grateful for the notice. This is my motive for dedicating the following pages to you.

In so doing we are perfectly *quit*. It is obviously the purpose of modern Reviewers to give you not the slightest idea of the work they profess to notice, but their own sentiments: they merely assume the *title* of the work as a motto for a political, theological, or belles-lettre Essay, (as the case may be), and then – 'They write – good Gods! how they do write!'

The present Dedication shall *en suite* be entirely devoted to talking of myself.

I have written two Romances. The first I cannot help thinking exhibits some power of imagination and description, but unfortunately they are exhausted on a subject so much beyond the reach of life, or the tone and compass of ordinary feeling, that I might as well have given a map of *terra icognita*, and expected the reader to swear to its boundaries, or live on its productions.

Solicitous about the public feeling (as all who write must be), I consulted the Reviewers: and what did they tell me? – that they were profound judges, but would pronounce no decision; that they were consummate critics, but would give no advice.

Seriously I read the Reviews for information, and information I could get none – about myself. All I learned was that I was a bad writer, but why, or how, or in what manner I was to become better, they graciously left to myself.

These men abuse the public much; that some of them possess talent is undoubted; but why not exercise it in their *own right*, without borrowing a pretext from an office they do not discharge? Why not become *writers, instead of soi-disant* Reviewers?

If I posses any talent, it is that of darkening the gloomy, and of deepening the sad; of painting life in extremes, and representing those struggles of passion when the soul trembles on the verge of the unlawful and the unhallowed.

On the following pages I have tried to apply these powers to the scenes of actual life; and I have chosen my own country for the scene, because I believe it the only country on earth, where, from the strange existing opposition of religion, politics, and manners, the extremes of refinement and barbarism are united, and the most wild and incredible situations of romantic story are hourly passing before modern eyes.

In my first work I attempted to explore the ground forbidden to man; the sources of visionary terror; the 'formless and the void': in my present I have tried the equally obscure recesses of the human heart. If I fail in both, I shall – write again.

I am, Gentlemen,
With more respect for your talents, than gratitude for your information,
&c. &c.
The Author of Montorio
Dublin, Dec. 12th, 1811.

6.6 Walter Scott (1771–1832), 'Chapter 1: Introductory,' *Waverley* (1814)

Scott made his reputation as a writer of 'metrical romances' (see 6.3). In 1814 Scott changed the direction of his career with the publication of *Waverley*, a work which set the terms of his most significant contribution to literary history: the establishment of the historical novel (Shaw 1996, pp. 1–18). In his introduction Scott makes it clear that he is interested in charting a middle path between the modern novel of manners and the old fashioned, unfeasible romance of the Radcliffe school. His ostensible argument is that 'sixty years since' is the appropriate fictional middle ground, being sufficiently remote from the present to create scope for romance, without being so distant as to take us into the rude supernaturalisms of the Gothic period. However, beneath this aesthetic argument other motives are clearly at work, for 'sixty years since' the apparent time of indicting the work takes us to 1745, the eve of the Jacobite rebellion, arguably the most significant event in the recent shaping of contemporary Britain.[11]

Source: Sir Walter Scott (1986), *Waverley, or 'Tis Sixty Years Since*, ed. Claire Lamont, Oxford: Oxford University Press, pp. 3–5.

★

The title of this work has not been chosen without the grave and solid deliberation which matters of importance demand from the prudent. Even its first, or general denomination, was the result of no common research or selection, although, according to the example of my predecessors,

I had only to seize upon the most sounding and euphonic surname that English history or topography affords, and elect it at once as the title of my work, and the name of my hero. But, alas! what could my readers have expected from the chivalrous epithets of Howard, Mordaunt, Mortimer, or Stanley, or from the softer and more sentimental sounds of Belmour, Belville, Belfield and Belgrave, but pages of inanity, similar to those which have been so christened for half a century past? I must modestly admit I am too diffident of my own merit to place it in unnecessary opposition to preconceived associations: I have therefore, like a maiden knight with his white shield, assumed for my hero, WAVERLEY, an uncontaminated name, bearing with its sound little of good or evil, excepting what the reader shall be hereafter pleased to affix to it. But my second or supplemental title was a matter of much more difficult election, since that, short as it is, may be held as pledging the author to some special mode of laying his scene, drawing his characters, and managing his adventures. Had I, for example, announced in my frontispiece, 'Waverley, a Tale of other Days,' must not every novel-reader have anticipated a castle scarce less than that of Udolpho, of which the eastern wing had been long uninhabited, and the keys either lost or consigned to the care of some aged butler or housekeeper, whose trembling steps, about the middle of the second volume, were doomed to guide the hero, or heroine, to the ruinous precincts? Would not the owl have shrieked and the cricket cried in my very title-page? and could it have been possible for me, with a moderate attention to decorum, to introduce any scene more lively than might be produced by the jocularity of a clownish but faithful valet, or the garrulous narrative of the heroine's fille-de-chambre, when rehearsing the stories of blood and horror which she had heard in the servants' hall? Again, had my title borne, 'Waverley, a Romance from the German,' what head so obtuse as not to image forth a profligate abbot, an oppressive duke, a secret and mysterious association of Rosycrucians and illuminati, with all their properties of black cowls, caverns, daggers, electrical machines, trap-doors, and dark lanterns? Or if I had rather chosen to call my work a 'Sentimental Tale,' would it not have been a sufficient presage of a heroine with a profusion of auburn hair, and a harp, the soft solace of her solitary hours, which she fortunately finds always the means of transporting from castle to cottage, although she be sometimes obliged to jump out of a two-pair-of-stairs window, and is more than once bewildered on her journey, alone and on foot, without any guide but a blowzy peasant girl, whose jargon she hardly can understand? Or again, if my Waverley had been entitled 'A Tale of the Times,' wouldst thou not, gentle reader, have demanded from me a dashing sketch of the fashionable world, a few anecdotes of private scandal thinly veiled, and if lusciously painted so much the better; a heroine from Grosvenor Square, and a hero from the Barouche Club or the Four-in-Hand, with a set of subordinate characters from the elegantes of Queen

Anne Street East, or the dashing heroes of the Bow-Street Office? I could proceed in proving the importance of a title-page, and displaying at the same time my own intimate knowledge of the particular ingredients necessary to the composition of romances and novels of various descriptions. But it is enough, and I scorn to tyrannize longer over the impatience of my reader, who is doubtless already anxious to know the choice made by an author so profoundly versed in the different branches of his art.

By fixing then the date of my story Sixty Years before this present 1st November, 1805, I would have my readers understand that they will meet in the following pages neither a romance of chivalry, nor a tale of modern manners; that my hero will neither have iron on his shoulders, as of yore, nor on the heels of his boots, as is the present fashion of Bond Street; and that my damsels will neither be clothed 'in purple and in pall,' like the Lady Alice of an old ballad, nor reduced to the primitive nakedness of a modern fashionable at a route. From this my choice of an æra the understanding critic may farther presage, that the object of my tale is more a description of men than manners. A tale of manners, to be interesting, must either refer to antiquity so great as to have become venerable, or it must bear a vivid reflection of those scenes which are passing daily before our eyes, and are interesting from their novelty. Thus the coat of mail of our ancestors, and the triple-furred pelisse of our modern beaux, may, though for very different reasons, be equally fit for the array of a fictitious character; but who, meaning the costume of his hero to be impressive, would willingly attire him in the court dress of George the Second's reign, with its no collar, large sleeves, and low pocket-holes? The same may be urged, with equal truth, of the Gothic hall, which, with its darkened and tinted windows, its elevated and gloomy roof, and massive oaken table garnished with boar's-head and rosemary, pheasants and peacocks, cranes and cygnets, has an excellent effect in fictitious description. Much may also be gained by a lively display of a modern fete, such as we have daily recorded in that part of a newspaper entitled the Mirror of Fashion. But if we contrast these, or either of them, with the splendid formality of an entertainment given sixty Years since, it will be readily seen how much the painter of antique or of fashionable manners gains over him who delineates those of the last generation.

Considering the disadvantages inseparable from this part of my subject, I must be understood to have resolved to avoid them as much as possible, by throwing the force of my narrative upon the characters and passions of the actors; – those passions common to men in all stages of society, and which have alike agitated the human heart, whether it throbbed under the steel corslet of the fifteenth century, the brocaded coat of the eighteenth, or the blue frock and white dimity waistcoat of the present day. Upon these passions it is no doubt true that the state of manners and laws casts a necessary colouring; but the bearings, to use the language of heraldry, remain the same, though the tincture may be not only different, but opposed in strong contradistinction. The wrath of our ancestors, for example, was coloured *gules*; it broke forth in acts of open and sanguinary violence against the objects of its fury: our malignant feelings, which must seek gratification through more indirect channels, and undermine the obstacles which they cannot openly bear down, may be rather said to be tinctured sable. But the deep ruling impulse is the same in both cases; and the proud peer, who can now only ruin his neighbour according to law, by protracted suits, is the genuine descendant of the baron who wrapped the castle of his competitor in flames, and knocked him on the head as he endeavoured to escape from the conflagration. It is from the great book of Nature, the same through a thousand editions, whether of black letter or wire-wove and hot-pressed, that I have venturously essayed to read a chapter to the public. Some favourable opportunities of contrast have been afforded me, by the state of society in the northern part of the island at the period of my history, and may serve at once to vary and to illustrate the moral lessons which I would willingly consider as the most important part of my plan, although I am sensible how short these will fall of their aim, if I shall be found unable to mix them with amusement, – a task not quite so easy in this critical generation as it was 'Sixty Years since.'

6.7 Samuel Taylor Coleridge (1772–1834), *Biographia Literaria* (1817)

Coleridge began writing *Biographia Literaria* in 1814 as a preface to *Sibylline Leaves*, but it soon grew into an eccentrically structured account of Coleridge's intellectual development. The following is one of Coleridge's lengthy footnotes from *Biographia Literaria* expounding on the evils of light reading. For Coleridge, the supernatural, or phantasmal, has become a debased leisure commodity.

Source: S. T. Coleridge (1975), *Biographia Literaria*, London: J. M. Dent, p. 28.

For as to the devotees of the circulating libraries, I dare not compliment their pass-time, or rather kill-time, with the name of reading. Call it rather a sort of beggarly day-dreaming during which the mind of the dreamer furnishes for itself nothing but laziness and a little mawkish sensibility; while the whole *materiel* and imagery of the doze is supplied *ab extra* by a sort of mental *camera obscura* manufactured at the printing office, which *pro tempore* fixes, reflects and transmits the moving phantasms of one man's delirium, so as to people the barrenness of an hundred other brains afflicted with the same trance or suspension of all common sense and all definite purpose. We should therefore transfer this species of amusement (if indeed those can be said to retire *a musis*, who were never in their company, or relaxation be attributable to those whose bows are never bent) from the genus, reading, to that comprehensive class characterized by the power of reconciling the two contrary yet co-existing propensities of human nature, namely indulgence of sloth and hatred of vacancy. In addition to novels and tales of chivalry in prose or rhyme, (by which last I mean neither rhythm nor metre) this genus comprises as its species, gaming, swinging or swaying on a chair or gate; spitting over a bridge; smoking; snuff-taking: tête-à-tête quarrels after dinner between husband and wife; conning word by word all the advertisements of the Daily Advertizer in a public house on a rainy day, etc. etc. etc.

6.8 The supernaturalism of everyday life

The following two essays both employ the rhetorical device of assenting to the platitudes of scientific rationalism, with its sceptical refutation of the supernatural, before going on to undermine it. Both argue ultimately for the involuntary and universal nature of superstitious fears. This may seem to offer us a bland acceptance of the unknown, but both essays contain a hidden edge, for such an avowal of the supernatural implicitly denies the cultural inheritance of the Enlightenment.

6.8a Charles Lamb (1775–1834), 'Witches and Other Night Fears' (1821)

Source: Originally published in *London Magazine* (Oct. 1821). Quoted from Charles Lamb, *Selected Prose*, ed. Adam Phillips, Harmondsworth: Penguin, pp. 123–6.

. . . I was dreadfully alive to nervous terrors. The night-time solitude, and the dark, were my hell. The sufferings I endured in this nature would justify the expression. I never laid my head on my pillow, I suppose, from the fourth to the seventh or eighth year of my life – so far as memory serves in things so long ago – without an assurance, which realized its own prophecy, of seeing some frightful spectre. Be old Stackhouse then acquitted in part, if I say, that to his picture of the Witch raising up Samuel – (O that old man covered with a mantle!) I owe – not my midnight terrors, the hell of my infancy – but the shape and manner of their visitation. It was he who dressed up for me a hag that nightly sate upon my pillow – a sure bed-fellow, when my aunt or my maid was far from me. All day long, while the book was permitted me, I dreamed waking over his delineation, and at night (if I may use so bold an expression) awoke into sleep, and found the vision true. I durst not, even in the day-light, once enter the chamber where I slept, without my face turned to the window, aversely from the bed where my witch-ridden pillow was. – Parents do not know what they do when they leave tender babes alone to go to sleep in the dark. The feeling about for a friendly arm – the hoping for a familiar voice – when they wake screaming – and find none to soothe them – what a terrible shaking it is to their poor nerves! The keeping them up till midnight, through candle-light and the unwholesome hours, as they are called, – would, I am satisfied, in a medical point of view, prove the better caution. – That detestable picture, as I have said, gave the fashion to my dreams – if dreams they were – for the scene of them was invariably the room in which I lay. Had I never met with the picture, the fears would have come self-pictured in some shape or other – 'Headless bear, black man, or ape' – but, as it was, my imaginations took that form. – It is not book, or picture, or the stories of foolish servants, which create these terrors in children. They can at most but give them a direction. Dear little T. H.[12] who of all children has been brought up with the most scrupulous exclusion of every taint of superstition – who was never allowed to hear of goblin or apparition, or scarcely to be told of bad men, or to read or hear of any distressing story – finds all this world of fear, from which he has been so rigidly excluded *ab extra,* in his own 'thick-coming fancies'; and from his little midnight pillow, this nurse-child of optimism will start at shapes, unborrowed of tradition, in sweats to which the reveries of the cell-damned murderer are tranquillity.

Gorgons, and Hydras, and Chimaeras – dire stories of Celaeno and the Harpies may reproduce themselves in the brain of superstition – but they were there before. They are transcripts, types – the archetypes are in us, and eternal. How else should the recital of that, which we know in a waking sense to be false, come to affect us at all? – or

> – Names, whose sense we see not,
> Fray us with things that be not?

Is it that we naturally conceive terror from such objects, considered in their capacity of being able to inflict upon us bodily injury? – O, least of all! These terrors are of older standing. They date beyond body – or, without the body, they would have been the same. All the cruel, tormenting, defined devils in Dante – tearing, mangling, choking, stifling, scorching demons – are they one half so fearful to the spirit of a man, as the simple idea of a spirit unembodied following him –

> Like one that on a lonesome road
> Doth walk in fear and dread,
> And having once turn'd round, walks on,

And turns no more his head;
Because he knows a frightful fiend
Doth close behind him tread.*

That the kind of fear here treated of is purely spiritual – that it is strong in proportion as it is objectless upon earth – that it predominates in the period of sinless infancy – are difficulties, the solution of which might afford some probable insight into our ante-mundane condition, and a peep at least into the shadow-land of pre-existence.

My night-fancies have long ceased to be afflictive. I confess an occasional night-mare; but I do not, as in early youth, keep a stud of them. Fiendish faces, with the extinguished taper will come and look at me; but I know them for mockeries, even while I cannot elude their presence, and I fight and grapple with them. For the credit of my imagination, I am almost ashamed to say how tame and prosaic my dreams are grown. They are never romantic, seldom even rural. They are of architecture and of buildings – cities abroad, which I have never seen, and hardly have hope to see. I have traversed, for the seeming length of a natural day, Rome, Amsterdam, Paris, Lisbon – their churches, palaces, squares, market-places, shops, suburbs, ruins, with an inexpressible sense of delight – a map-like distinctness of trace – and a day-light vividness of vision, that was all but being awake. – I have formerly travelled among the Westmoreland fells – my highest Alps, – but they are objects too mighty for the grasp of my dreaming recognition; and I have again and again awoke with ineffectual struggles of the inner eye, to make out a shape in any way whatever, of Helvellyn. Methought I was in that country, but the mountains were gone. The poverty of my dreams mortifies me. There is Coleridge, at his will can conjure up icy domes, and pleasure-houses for Kubla Khan, and Abyssinian maids, and songs of Abara, and caverns, 'Where Alph, the sacred river runs', to solace his night solitudes – when I cannot muster a fiddle. Barry Cornwall[13] has his tritons and his nereids gamboling before him in nocturnal visions, and proclaiming sons born to Neptune – when my stretch of imaginative activity can hardly, in the night season, raise up the ghost of a fish-wife. To set my failures in somewhat a mortifying light – it was after reading the noble Dream of this poet, that my fancy ran strong upon these marine spectra; and the poor plastic power, such as it is, within me set to work, to humour my folly in a sort of dream that very night. Methought I was upon the ocean billows at some sea nuptials, riding and mounted high, with the customary train sounding their conchs before me, (I myself, you may be sure, the *leading god*,) and jollily we went careering over the main, till just where Ino Leucothea[14] should have greeted me (I think it was Ino) with a white embrace, the billows gradually subsiding, fell from a sea-roughness to a sea-calm, and

* Mr. Coleridge's Ancient Mariner.

thence to a river-motion, and that river (as happens in the familiarization of dreams) was no other than the gentle Thames, which landed me, in the wafture of a placid wave or two, alone, safe and inglorious, somewhere at the foot of Lambeth palace.

The degree of the soul's creativeness in sleep might furnish no whimsical criterion of the quantum of poetical faculty resident in the same soul waking. An old gentleman, a friend of mine, and a humorist, used to carry this notion so far, that when he saw any stripling of his acquaintance ambitious of becoming a poet, his first question would be, – 'Young man, what sort of dreams have you?' I have so much faith in my old friend's theory, that when I feel that idle vein returning upon me, I presently subside into my proper element of prose, remembering those eluding nereids, and that inauspicious inland landing.

6.8b Mary Shelley (1797–1851), 'On Ghosts' (1824)

Source: *London Magazine* vol. 9 (March 1824), pp. 253–6.

> I look for ghosts – but none will force
> Their way to me; 'tis falsely said
> That there was ever intercourse
> Between the living and the dead. – *Wordsworth*.

What a different earth do we inhabit from that on which our forefathers dwelt! The antediluvian world, strode over by mammoths, preyed upon by the megatherion, and peopled by the offspring of the Sons of God, is a better type of the earth of Homer, Herodotus, and Plato, than the hedged-in cornfields and measured hills of the present day. The globe was then encircled by a wall which paled in the bodies of men, whilst their feathered thoughts soared over the boundary; it had a brink, and in the deep profound which it overhung, men's imaginations, eagle-winged, dived and flew, and brought home strange tales to their believing auditors. Deep caverns harboured giants; cloudlike birds cast their shadows upon the plains; while far out at sea lay islands of bliss, the fair paradise of Atlantis or El Dorado sparkling with untold jewels. Where are they now? The Fortunate Isles have lost the glory that spread a halo round them; for who deems himself nearer to the golden age, because he touches at the Canaries on his voyage to India? Our only riddle is the rise of the Niger; the interior of New Holland, our only terra incognita; and our sole mare incognitum, the north-west passage. But these are tame wonders, lions in leash; we do not invest Mungo Park, or the Captain of the Hecla,[15] with divine attributes; no one fancies that the waters of the unknown river bubble up from hell's fountains, no strange and weird power is supposed to guide the ice-berg, nor do we fable that a stray pick-pocket from Botany

Bay has found the gardens of the Hesperides within the circuit of the Blue Mountains. What have we left to dream about? The clouds are no longer the charioted servants of the sun, nor does he any more bathe his glowing brow in the bath of Thetis;[16] the rainbow has ceased to be the messenger of the Gods, and thunder is no longer their awful voice, warning man of that which is to come. We have the sun which has been weighed and measured; but not understood; we have the assemblage of the planets, the congregation of the stars, and the yet unshackled ministration of the winds: – such is the list of our ignorance.

Nor is the empire of the imagination less bounded in its own proper creations, than in those which were bestowed on it by the poor blind eyes of our ancestors. What has become of enchantresses with their palaces of crystal and dungeons of palpable darkness? What of fairies and their wands? What of witches and their familiars? and, last, what of ghosts, with beckoning hands and fleeting shapes, which quelled the soldier's brave heart, and made the murderer disclose to the astonished noon the veiled work of midnight? These which were realities to our forefathers, in our wiser age –

> —Characterless are grated
> To dusty nothing.[17]

Yet is it true that we do not believe in ghosts? There used to be several traditionary tales repeated, with their authorities, enough to stagger us when we consigned them to that place where that is which 'is as though it had never been'.[18] But these are gone out of fashion. Brutus's dream has become a deception of his over-heated brain, Lord Lyttleton's vision is called a cheat; and one by one these inhabitants of deserted houses, moonlight glades, misty mountain tops, and midnight church-yards, have been ejected from their immemorial seats, and small thrill is felt when the dead majesty of Denmark blanches the cheek and unsettles the reason of his philosophic son.

But do none of us believe in ghosts? If this question be read at noon-day when –

> Every little corner, nook, and hole,
> Is penetrated with the insolent light –[19]

at such a time derision is seated on the features of my reader. But let it be twelve at night in a lone house; take up, I beseech you, the story of the Bleeding Nun; or of the Statue, to which the bridegroom gave the wedding ring, and she came in the dead of night to claim him, tall, white, and cold; or of the Grandsire, who with shadowy form and breathless lips stood over the couch and kissed the foreheads of his sleeping grand-children, and thus doomed them to their fated death;[20] and let all these details be assisted by solitude, flapping curtains, rushing wind, a long and dusky passage, an half open door – O, then truly, another answer may be given, and many will request leave to sleep upon it, before they decide whether there be such a thing as a ghost in the world, or out of the world, if that phraseology be more spiritual. What is the meaning of this feeling?

For my own part, I never saw a ghost except once in a dream. I feared it in my sleep; I awoke trembling, and lights and the speech of others could hardly dissipate my fear. Some years ago I lost a friend, and a few months afterwards visited the house where I had last seen him. It was deserted, and though in the midst of a city, its vast halls and spacious apartments occasioned the same sense of loneliness as if it had been situated on an uninhabited heath. I walked through the vacant chambers by twilight, and none save I awakened the echoes of their pavement. The far mountains (visible from the upper windows) had lost their tinge of sunset; the tranquil atmosphere grew leaden coloured as the golden stars appeared in the firmament; no wind ruffled the shrunk-up river which crawled lazily through the deepest channel of its wide and empty bed; the chimes of the Ave Maria had ceased, and the bell hung moveless in the open belfry: beauty invested a reposing world, and awe was inspired by beauty only. I walked through the rooms filled with sensations of the most poignant grief. He had been there; his living frame had been caged by those walls, his breath had mingled with that atmosphere, his step had been on those stones, I thought: – the earth is a tomb, the gaudy sky a vault, we but walking corpses. The wind rising in the east rushed through the open casements, making them shake; – methought, I heard, I felt – I know not what – but I trembled. To have seen him but for a moment, I would have knelt until the stones had been worn by the impress, so I told myself, and so I knew a moment after, but then I trembled, awe-struck and fearful. Wherefore? There is something beyond us of which we are ignorant. The sun drawing up the vaporous air makes a void, and the wind rushes in to fill it, – thus beyond our soul's ken there is an empty space; and our hopes and fears, in gentle gales or terrific whirlwinds, occupy the vacuum; and if it does no more, it bestows on the feeling heart a belief that influences do exist to watch and guard us, though they be impalpable to the coarser faculties.

I have heard that when Coleridge was asked if he believed in ghosts, – he replied that he had seen too many to put any trust in their reality; and the person of the most lively imagination that I ever knew echoed this reply. But these were not real ghosts (pardon, unbelievers, my mode of speech) that they saw; they were shadows, phantoms unreal; that while they appalled the senses, yet carried no other feeling to the mind of others than delusion, and were viewed as we might view an optical deception which we see to be true with our eyes, and know to be false with our understandings. I speak of other shapes. The returning bride, who claims the fidelity of her betrothed; the murdered man who shakes to remorse the murderer's heart; ghosts that lift the curtains at the foot of your bed as the clock chimes one; who rise all pale and ghastly from the church-yard and haunt their ancient abodes; who, spoken to, reply; and whose cold unearthly touch makes the hair stand stark upon the head; the true old-fashioned, foretelling, flitting, gliding ghost, – who has seen such a one?

I have known two persons who at broad daylight have owned that they believed in ghosts, for that they had seen one. One of these was an Englishman, and the other an Italian. The former had lost a friend he dearly loved, who for a while appeared to him nightly, gently stroking his cheek and spreading a serene calm over his mind. He did not fear the appearance, although he was somewhat awe-stricken as each night it glided into his chamber, and, 'Ponsi del letto in su la sponda manca'.[21]

This visitation continued for several weeks, when by some accident he altered his residence, and then he saw it no more. Such a tale may easily be explained away; – but several years had passed, and he, a man of strong and virile intellect, said that 'he had seen a ghost.'

The Italian was a noble, a soldier, and by no means addicted to superstition: he had served in Napoleon's armies from early youth, and had been to Russia, had fought and bled, and been rewarded, and he unhesitatingly, and with deep belief, recounted his story.

This Chevalier, a young, and (somewhat a miraculous incident) a gallant Italian, was engaged in a duel with a brother officer, and wounded him in the arm. The subject of the duel was frivolous; and distressed therefore at its consequences he attended on his youthful adversary during his consequent illness, so that when the latter recovered they became firm and dear friends. They were quartered together at Milan, where the youth fell desperately in love with the wife of a musician, who disdained his passion, so that it preyed on his spirits and his health; he absented himself from all amusements, avoided all his brother officers, and his only consolation was to pour his love-sick plaints into the ear of the Chevalier, who strove in vain to inspire him either with indifference towards the fair disdainer, or to inculcate lessons of fortitude and heroism. As a last resource he urged him to ask leave of absence; and to seek, either in change of scene, or the amusement of hunting, some diversion to his passion. One evening the youth came to the Chevalier, and said, 'Well, I have asked leave of absence, and am to have it early to-morrow morning, so lend me your fowling-piece and cartridges, for I shall go to hunt for a fortnight.' The Chevalier gave him what he asked; among the shot there were a few bullets. 'I will take these also,' said the youth, 'to secure myself against the attack of any wolf, for I mean to bury myself in the woods.'

Although he had obtained that for which he came, the youth still lingered. He talked of the cruelty of his lady, lamented that she would not even permit him a hopeless attendance, but that she inexorably banished him from her sight, 'So that,' said he, 'I have no hope but in oblivion.' At length he rose to depart. He took the Chevalier's hand and said, 'You will see her to-morrow, you will speak to her, and hear her speak; tell her, I entreat you, that our conversation to-night has been concerning her, and that her name was the last that I spoke.' 'Yes, yes,' cried the Chevalier, 'I will say any thing you please; but you must not talk of her any more, you must forget her.' The youth embraced his friend with warmth, but the latter saw nothing more in it than the effects of his affection, combined with his melancholy at absenting himself from his mistress, whose name, joined to a tender farewell, was the last sound that he uttered.

When the Chevalier was on guard that night, he heard the report of a gun. He was at first troubled and agitated by it, but afterwards thought no more of it, and when relieved from guard went to bed, although he passed a restless, sleepless night. Early in the morning some one knocked at his door. It was a soldier, who said that he had got the young offficer's leave of absence, and had taken it to his house; a servant had admitted him, and he had gone up stairs, but the room door of the officer was locked, and no one answered to his knocking, but something oozed through from under the door that looked like blood. The Chevalier, agitated and frightened at this account, hurried to his friend's house, burst open the door, and found him stretched on the ground – he had blown out his brains, and the body lay a headless trunk, cold, and stiff.

The shock and grief which the Chevalier experienced in consequence of this catastrophe produced a fever which lasted for some days. When he got well, he obtained leave of absence, and went into the country to try to divert his mind. One evening at moonlight, he was returning home from a walk, and passed through a lane with a hedge on both sides, so high that he could not see over them. The night was balmy; the bushes gleamed with fireflies, brighter than the stars which the moon had veiled with her silver light. Suddenly he heard a rustling near him, and the figure of his friend issued from the hedge and stood before him, mutilated as he had seen him after his death. This figure he saw several times, always in the same place. It was impalpable to the touch, motionless, except in its advance, and made no sign when it was addressed. Once the Chevalier took a friend with him to the spot. The same rustling was heard, the same shadow steps forth, his companion fled in horror, but the Chevalier staid, vainly endeavouring to discover what called his friend from his quiet tomb, and if any act of his might give repose to the restless shade.

Such are my two stories, and I record them the more willingly, since they occurred to men, and to individuals distinguished the one for courage and the other for sagacity. I will conclude my 'modern instances,' with a story told by M. G. Lewis, not probably so authentic as these, but perhaps more amusing. I relate it as nearly as possible in his own words.

'A gentleman journeying towards the house of a friend, who lived on the skirts of an extensive forest, in the east of Germany, lost his way. He wandered for some time among the trees, when he saw a light at a distance. On approaching it he was surprised to observe that it proceeded from the interior of a ruined monastery. Before he knocked at the gate he thought it proper to look through the window. He saw a number of cats assembled round a small grave, four of whom were at that moment letting down a coffin with a crown upon it. The gentleman startled at this unusual sight, and, imagining that he had arrived at the retreats of fiends or witches, mounted his horse and rode away with the utmost precipitation. He arrived at his friend's house at a late hour, who sate up waiting for him. On his arrival his friend questioned him as to the cause of the traces of agitation visible in his face. He began to recount his adventures after much hesitation, knowing that it was scarcely possible that his friend should give faith to his relation. No sooner had he mentioned the coffin with the crown upon it, than his friend's cat, who seemed to have been lying asleep before the fire, leaped up, crying out, "Then I am king of the cats"; and then scrambled up the chimney, and was never seen more.'

6.9 Sir Walter Scott (1771–1832), 'On the Supernatural in Fictitious Composition; and particularly on the Works of Ernest William Hoffmann' (1827)

The following extract represents the conclusion of a much longer essay. One aspect of the essay's interest for the historian of Gothic is Scott's flair for making fine generic distinctions. Here, Scott introduces and refines on the notion of the 'fantastic'. Although omitted for reasons of space, the first section of the essay is no less interesting, albeit for different reasons: like Mary Shelley and Charles Lamb, Scott is eager to establish the universality of the predisposition to fear of the supernatural. His sensitivity to the charge of appearing sympathetic to Catholicism makes the essay worth seeking out for those interested in shifting debates on religion.

Source: *Foreign Quarterly Review*, vol. 1 (1827), pp. 312–15, 325–6.

★

. . . We have thus slightly traced the various modes in which the wonderful and supernatural may be introduced into fictitious narrative; yet the attachment of the Germans to the mysterious has invented another species of composition, which, perhaps, could hardly have made its way in any other country or language. This may be called the FANTASTIC mode of writing, – in which the most wild and unbounded license is given to an irregular fancy, and all species of combination, however ludicrous, or however shocking, are attempted and executed without scruple. In the other modes of treating the supernatural, even that mystic region is subjected to some laws, however slight; and fancy, in wandering through it, is regulated by some probabilities in the wildest flight. Not so in the fantastic style of composition, which has no restraint save that which it may ultimately find in the exhausted imagination of the author. This style bears the same proportion to the more regular romance, whether ludicrous or serious, which Farce, or rather Pantomime, maintains to Tragedy and Comedy. Sudden transformations are introduced of the most extraordinary kind, and wrought by the most inadequate means; no attempt is made to soften their absurdity or to reconcile their inconsistencies; the reader must be contented to look upon the gambols of the author as he would behold the flying leaps and incongruous transmutations of Harlequin, without seeking to discover either meaning or end further than the surprise of the moment.

Our English severity of taste will not easily adopt this wild and fantastic tone into our own literature; nay, perhaps will scarce tolerate it in translations. The only composition which approaches to it is the powerful romance of *Frankenstein*, and there, although the formation of a thinking and sentient being by scientific skill is an incident of the fantastic character, still the interest of the work does not turn upon the marvellous creation of Frankenstein's monster, but upon the feelings and sentiments which that creature is supposed to express as most natural – if we may use the phrase – to his unnatural condition and origin. In other words, the miracle is not wrought for the mere wonder, but is designed to give rise to a train of acting and reasoning in itself just and probable, although the *postulatum* on which it is grounded is in the highest degree extravagant. So far *Frankenstein*, therefore, resembles the *Travels of Gulliver*, which suppose the existence of the most extravagant fictions, in order to extract from them philosophical reasoning and moral truth. In such cases the admission of the marvellous expressly resembles a sort of entry-money paid at the door of a Lecture-room, – it is a concession which must be made to the author, and for which the reader is to receive value in moral instruction. But the *fantastic* of which we are now treating encumbers itself with no such conditions, and claims no further object than to surprise the public by the wonder itself. The reader is led astray by a freakish goblin, who has neither end nor purpose in the gambols which he exhibits, and the oddity of which must constitute their own reward. The only instance we know of this species of writing in the English language, is the ludicrous sketch in Mr. Geoffrey Crayon's tale of *The Bold Dragoon*, in which the furniture dances to the music of a ghostly fiddler. . . .

6.10 Thomas Carlyle (1795–1881), 'The Age of Romance' (1837)

Thomas Carlyle was regarded as a sage by many contemporaries; he was an historian, philosopher, political commentator, and satirist. In this essay, he argues against the common feeling that the age of romance is over, and that modern life is prosaic. Carlyle finds romance in the phantasmagoria (22) of common experience; romance exists 'in Reality alone.' The logic of Carlyle's position is that one should no longer seek the supernatural in the manners of the Middle Ages, and therefore in Gothic romances; one finds it, rather, in the theatre of everyday life. This paradox is related to the collapse of the old religious scaffolding, and to the absence of any modern intellectual structure that would enable us to gain a true glimpse of the transcendental. In this state of metaphysical chaos, quackeries and impostures naturally abound. One such 'small Romance' is dealt with here. The Diamond Necklace Affair rocked pre-Revolutionary France. Jeanne de la Motte, masquerading as a confidante of Marie Antoinette, tricked the Cardinal de Rohan into negotiating secretly for a particularly lavish necklace which the Queen supposedly coveted. It was, however, an elaborate scam: the Queen had no part in it, and the necklace ended up in London, where it was fenced by de la Motte's accomplice. However, such was the sensitivity of the issue, and the strength of anti-Royalist feeling at the time, that the Queen found it difficult to clear her name. Indeed, many believed that as an episode of outrageous royal consumption it hastened the Revolution (Schama, 1989, pp. 203–10). The connection between the bizarre micro-history of the Diamond Necklace and the epochal events of the French Revolution fascinates Carlyle. Looking back fifty years, he draws lessons material to his own time. His manner of doing so is idiosyncratic, oblique, and frequently ironic; the result of a long-standing interest in German Transcendental philosophy. Ideas are mediated by the mannered style of an authorial persona, or sometimes, personae (cf. the debate around Burke's 'gothic' language, 5.2, 5.6, 5.7). Although Carlyle appears to affirm the existence of a transcendental realm, his clamorous and digressive prose hints at the difficulty of arriving at a perception of the noumenal.

Source: First published in *Fraser's Magazine*, vols 85–6 (1837). Quoted from Thomas Carlyle (1869), *Critical and Miscellaneous Essays*, 7 vols, London: Chapman & Hall, vol. V, pp. 131–6.

★

The Age of Romance has not ceased; it never ceases; it does not, if we will think of it, so much as very sensibly decline. 'The passions are repressed by social forms; great passions no longer show themselves?' Why, there are passions still great enough to replenish Bedlam, for it never wants tenants; to suspend men from bedposts, from improved-drops at the west end of Newgate. A passion that explosively shivers asunder the Life it took rise in, ought to be regarded as considerable: more no passion, in the highest heyday of Romance, yet did. The passions, by grace of the Supernal and also of the Infernal Powers (for both have a hand in it), can never fail us.

And then, as to 'social forms,' be it granted that they are of the most buckram quality, and bind men up into the pitifulest straitlaced commonplace existence, – you ask, Where is the Romance? In the Scotch way one answers, Where is it not? That very spectacle of an Immortal Nature, with faculties and destiny extending through Eternity, hampered and bandaged up, by nurses, pedagogues, posturemasters, and the tongues of innumerable old women (named 'force of public opinion'); by prejudice, custom, want of knowledge, want of money, want of strength, into, say, the meagre Pattern-Figure that, in these days, meets you in all thoroughfares: a 'god-created Man,' all but abnegating the character of Man; forced to exist, automatised, mummy-wise (scarcely in rare moments audible or visible from amid his wrappages and cerements), as Gentleman or Gigman;* and so selling his birthright of Eternity for the three daily meals, poor at best, which Time yields: – is not this spectacle itself highly romantic, tragical, if we had eyes to look at it? The high-born (highest-born, for he came out of Heaven) lies drowning in the despicablest puddles; the priceless gift of Life, which he can have but *once*, for he waited a whole Eternity to be born, and now has a whole Eternity waiting to see what he will do when born, – *this* priceless gift we see strangled slowly out of him by innumerable packthreads; and there remains of the glorious Possibility, which we fondly named Man, nothing but an inanimate mass of foul loss and disappointment, which we wrap in shrouds and bury underground, – surely with well-merited tears. To the Thinker here lies Tragedy enough; the epitome and marrow of all Tragedy whatsoever.

But so few are Thinkers? Ay, Reader, so few think; there is the rub! Not one in the thousand has the smallest turn for thinking; only for passive dreaming and hearsaying, and active babbling by rote. Of the eyes that men do glare withal so few can see. Thus is the world become such a fearful confused Treadmill; and each man's task has got entangled in his neighbour's, and pulls it awry; and the Spirit of Blindness, Falsehood and Distraction, justly named the Devil, continually maintains himself among us; and even hopes (were it not for the Opposition, which by God's grace will also maintain itself) to become supreme. Thus too, among other things, has the Romance of Life gone wholly out of sight: and all History, degenerating into empty invoice-lists of Pitched Battles and Changes of Ministry; or, still worse, into 'Constitutional History,' or

* I always considered him a respectable man. – What do you mean by respectable? He kept a Gig. – *Thurtell's Trial.*

'Philosophy of History,' or 'Philosophy teaching by Experience,' is become dead, as the Almanacs of other years, – to which species of composition, indeed, it bears, in several points of view, no inconsiderable affinity.

'Of all blinds that shut-up men's vision,' says one, 'the worst is Self.' How true! How doubly true, if Self, assuming her cunningest, yet miserablest disguise, come on us, in never-ceasing, all-obscuring reflexes from the innumerable Selves of others; not as Pride, not even as real Hunger, but only as Vanity, and the shadow of an imaginary Hunger for Applause; under the name of what we call 'Respectability'! Alas now for our Historian: to his other spiritual deadness (which however, so long as he physically breathes, cannot be considered coomplete) this sad new magic influence is added! Henceforth his Histories must all be screwed-up into the 'dignity of History.' Instead of looking fixedly at the *Thing*, and first of all, and beyond all, endeavouring to see it, and fashion a living Picture of it, not a wretched politico-metaphysical Abstraction of it, he has now quite other matters to look to. The Thing lies shrouded, invisible, in thousand-fold hallucinations, and foreign air-images: What did the Whigs say of it? What did the Tories? The Priests? The Freethinkers? Above all, What will my own listening circle say of *me* for what I say of it? And then his Respectability in general, as a literary gentleman; his not despicable talent for philosophy! Thus is our poor Historian's faculty directed mainly on two objects: the Writing and the Writer, both of which are quite extraneous; and the Thing written-of fares as we see. Can it be wonderful that Histories, wherein open lying is not permitted, are unromantic? Nay, our very Biographies, how stiff-starched, foisonless, hollow! They stand there respectable; and – what more? Dumb idols; with a skin of delusively-painted waxwork; inwardly empty, or full of rags and bran. In our England especially, which in these days is become the chosen land of Respectability, Lifewriting has dwindled to the sorrowfulest condition; it requires a man to be some disrespectable, ridiculous Boswell before he can write a tolerable Life. Thus too, strangely enough, the only Lives worth reading are those of Players, emptiest and poorest of the sons of Adam; who nevertheless were sons of his, and brothers of ours; and by the nature of the case had already bidden Respectability good-day. Such bounties, in this as in infinitely deeper matters, does Respectability shower down on us. Sad are thy doings, O *Gig*; sadder than those of Juggernaut's Car: that, with huge wheel, suddenly crushes asunder the bodies of men; thou, in thy light-bobbing Long-acre springs, gradually winnowest away their souls!

Depend upon it, for one thing, good Reader, no age ever seemed the Age of Romance to *itself*. Charlemagne, let the Poets talk as they will, had his own provocations in the world: what with selling of his poultry and pot-herbs, what with wanton daughters carrying secretaries through the snow; and, for instance that hanging of the Saxons over the Weser-bridge (four thousand of them, they say, at one bout), it seems to me that the Great Charles had his temper ruffled at times. Roland of Roncesvalles too, we see well in thinking of it, found rainy weather as well as sunny; knew what it was to have hose need darning; got tough beef to chew, or even went dinnerless; was saddle-sick, calumniated, constipated (as his madness too clearly indicates); and oftenest felt, I doubt not, that this was a very Devil's world, and he, Roland himself, one of the sorriest caitiffs there. Only in long subsequent days, when the tough beef; the constipation and the calumny had clean vanished, did it all begin to seem Romantic and your Turpins and Ariostos found music in it.[23] So, I say, is it ever! And the more, as your true hero, your true Roland, is ever *unconscious* that he is a hero: this is a condition of all greatness.

In our own poor Nineteenth Century the Writer of these lines has been fortunate enough to see not a few glimpses of Romance; he imagines this Nineteenth is hardly a whit less romantic than that Ninth, or any other, since centuries began. Apart from Napoleon, and the Dantons, and Mirabeaus, whose fire-words of public speaking, and fire-whirlwinds of cannon and musketry, which for a season darkened the air, are perhaps at bottom but superficial phenomena, he has witnessed, in remotest places, much that could be called romantic, even miraculous. He has witnessed overhead the infinite Deep, with greater and lesser lights, bright-rolling, silent-beaming, hurled forth by the Hand of God: around him and under his feet, the wonderfulest Earth, with her winter snow-storms and her summer spice-airs; and, unaccountablest of all, himself standing there. He stood in the lapse of Time; he saw Eternity behind him, and before him. The all-encircling mysterious tide of FORCE, thousand-fold (for from force of Thought to force of Gravitation what an interval!) billowed shoreless on; bore him too along with it, – he too was part of it. From its bosom rose and vanished, in perpetual change, the lordliest Real-Phantasmagory, which men name *Being*; and ever anew rose and vanished; and ever that lordliest many-coloured scene was full, another yet the same. Oak-trees fell, young acorns sprang: Men too, new-sent from the Unknown, he met, of tiniest size, who waxed into stature, into strength of sinew, passionate fire and light: in other men the light was growing dim, the sinews all feeble; they sank, motionless, into ashes, into invisibility; returned *back* to the Unknown, beckoning him their mute farewell. He wanders still by the parting-spot; cannot hear *them*; they are far, how far! –

It was a sight for angels, and archangels; for, indeed, God himself had made it wholly. One many-glancing asbestos-thread in the Web of Universal-History, spirit-woven, it rustled there, as with the howl of mighty winds, through that 'wild-roaring Loom of Time.' Generation after generation, hundreds of them or thousands of them, from the unknown Beginning, so loud, so stormful-busy, rushed torrent-wise thundering down, down; and fell all silent, – nothing but some feeble reëcho, which grew ever feebler, struggling up; and Oblivion swallowed them *all*. Thousands more, to the unknown Ending, will follow: and *thou* here, of this present one, hangest as a drop, still sungilt, on the giddy edge; one moment, while the Darkness has not yet ingulfed thee. O Brother! is *that* what thou callest prosaic; of small interest? Of small interest and for *thee*? Awake, poor troubled sleeper: shake off thy torpid nightmare-dream; look, see, behold it, the Flame-image; splendours high as Heaven, terrors deep as Hell: this is God's Creation; this is Man's Life! – Such things has the Writer of these lines witnessed, in this poor Nineteenth Century of ours; and what are all such to the things he yet hopes to witness? Hopes, with truest assurance. 'I have painted so much,' said the good Jean Paul,[24] in his old days, 'and I have never seen the Ocean: – the Ocean of Eternity I shall not fail to see!'

Such being the intrinsic quality of this Time, and of all Time whatsoever, might not the Poet who chanced to walk through it find objects enough to paint? What object soever he fixed on, were it the meanest of the mean, let him but paint it in its actual truth, as it swims there, in such environment; world-old, yet new and never-ending; an indestructible portion of the miraculous All, – his picture of it were a Poem. How much more if the object fixed on were not mean, but one already wonderful; the mystic 'actual truth' of which, if it lay not on the surface, yet shone through the surface, and invited even Prosaists to search for it!

The present Writer, who unhappily belongs to that class, has nevertheless a firmer and firmer persuasion of two things: first, as was seen, that Romance exists; secondly, that now, and formerly, and evermore it exists, strictly speaking, in Reality alone. The thing that *is*, what can be *so* wonderful; what, especially to us that *are*, can have such significance? Study Reality, he is ever and anon saying to himself; search out deeper and deeper *its* quite endless mystery: see it, know it; then, whether thou wouldst learn from it, and again teach; or weep over it, or laugh over it, or love it, or despise it, or in any way relate thyself to it, thou hast the firmest enduring basis: *that* hieroglyphic page is one thou canst read on forever, find new meaning in forever.

Finally, and in a word, do not the critics teach us: 'In whatsoever thing thou hast thyself felt interest, in that or in nothing hope to inspire others with interest'? – In partial obedience to all which, and to many other principles, shall the following small Romance of the *Diamond Necklace* begin to come together. A small Romance, let the reader again and again assure himself, which is no brainweb of mine, or of any other foolish man's; but a fraction of that mystic 'spirit-woven web,' from the 'Loom of Time,' spoken of above. It is an actual Transaction that happened in this Earth of ours. Wherewith our whole business, as already urged, is to paint it truly.

For the rest, an earnest inspection, faithful endeavour has not been wanting, on our part; nor, singular as it may seem, the strictest regard to chronology, geography (or rather in this case, topography), documentary evidence, and what else true historical research would yield. Were there but on the reader's part a kindred openness, a kindred spirit of endeavour! Beshone strongly, on both sides, by such united twofold Philosophy, this poor opaque Intrigue of the Diamond Necklace might become quite translucent between us; transfigured, lifted up into the serene of Universal-History; and might hang there like a smallest Diamond Constellation, visible without telescope, – so long as it could.

6.11 Anon., 'The Historical Romance' (1845)

A measure of the difference between the final document and material from earlier chapters is that here the 'Gothic', in the shape of Scott's version of historical romance, supports the cause of conservative idealism. This thesis is antithetical to that of the essay by Godwin, with which this chapter began, and demonstrates the way in which Gothic writing remains a site of contention.

Source: *Blackwood's Magazine*, vol. 58 (1845), pp. 341–2, 345–6.

★

We are constantly told that invention is worn out; that everything is exhausted; that all the intellectual treasures of modern Europe have been dug up; and that we must look to a new era of the world, and a different quarter of the globe, for new ideas or fresh views of thought. It must be confessed, that if we look to some parts of our literature, there seems too good reason for supposing that this desponding opinion is well founded. Every thing, in some departments, does seem worked out. Poetry appears for the time wellnigh extinguished. We have some charming ballads from Tennyson; some touching lines from Miss Barret; but where are the successors of Scott and Byron, of Campbell and Southey? Romance, in some branches, has evidently exhausted itself. For ten years we had novels of fashionable life, till the manners and sayings of lordling and right honourables had become familiar to all the haberdashers' apprentices and milliners' girls in London. That vein being worked out, literature has run into the opposite channel. Action and reaction is the law, not less of the intellectual than the physical world. Inventive genius has sought out, in the lower walks of life, those subjects of novel study and fresh description which could no longer be found in the higher. So far has this propensity gone, so violent has been the oscillation of the pendulum in that direction, that novelists have descended to the very lowest stages of society in the search of the new or the exciting. Not only have the manners, the selfishness, the vulgarity of the middle ranks been painted with admirable fidelity, and drawn with inimitable skill, but the habits and slang of the very lowest portrayed with prurient minuteness, and interest sought to be awakened in the votaries of fashion or the Sybarites of pleasure by the delineation of the language and ideas of the most infamous wretches who ever disgraced society by their vices, or endangered it by their crimes.

'Whatever,' says Dr Johnson, 'makes the PAST or the FUTURE predominate over the present, exalts us in the scale of thinking beings.' The words are familiar till they have become trite; but the words are often repeated when the sense is far off. It is in the general oblivion of the thought of the philosopher, while his words were in every mouth, that the cause of the want of originality in modern words of the imagination is to be found. If to the 'Past' and the 'Future,' enumerated by Johnson, we add the 'DISTANT,' we shall have an effectual antidote, and the only one which is effectual against the sameness of the present ideas, or the limited circle of present observation. The tendency to *localize* is the propensity which degrades literature, as it is the chief bane and destroyer of individual character. It is the opposite effect of engendering a tendency to expand, which constitutes the chief value of travelling in the formation of character. If the thought and conversation of individuals are limited to the little circle in which they live, or the objects by which they are immediately surrounded, we all know what they speedily become. It is in the extensions of the interest to a wider circle, in the admission of objects of general concern and lasting importance into the sphere of habitual thought, that the only preservative against this fatal tendency is to be found. It is the power of doing this which forms the chief charm of the highest society in every country, and renders it in truth every where the same. A man of the world will find himself equally at home, and conversation flow at once with equal ease, in the higher saloons of London or Paris, of Rome or Vienna, of Warsaw or St Petersburg. But he will find it scarcely possible to keep up conversation for a quarter of an hour in the *bourgeois* circle of any of these capitals. It is the same with literature, and especially that wide and important branch of literature which, aiming at the exciting of interest, or delineating manners, should in an especial manner be guarded against the degradation consequent on a restriction of its subjects to matters only of local concern.

The prodigious success and wide-spread popularity which have attended some of the most able novels of this new school of romance in late years, as well as the great ability which their composition evinces, must not blind our eyes to the degrading tendency of such compositions upon the national literature. Immediate circulation, great profit to the bookseller, a dazzling, reputation to the author, are by no means to be relied on as heralds of lasting fame. In cases innumerable, they have proved the reverse. Still less are they to be considered as proofs that the writer, be his abilities what they may, has worthily performed his mission, or elevated himself to the exalted level of which is art is susceptible. The most pernicious romances and poems that ever appeared have often been ushered into the world by the most unbounded immediate applause; witness the *Nouvelle Heloise* of Rousseau, and *Pucelle* of Voltaire. It was just their dangerous and seductive qualities which gave them their success . . .

Where now are all the novels portraying fashionable life with which the shops of publishers teemed, and the shelves of circulating libraries groaned, not ten years ago? Buried in the vault of all the Capulets. Where will the novels portraying manners in the lowest walks of life be ten years hence? He is a bold man who says they will be found in one well selected library. We are well aware of the fidelity with which they have painted the manners of the middle class, previously little touched on in novels; we fully admit the pathos and power of occasional passages, the wit and humour of many others, the graphic delineation of English character which they all contain. But, admitting all this, the question is – have these productions come up to the true standard of novel-writing? Are they fitted to elevate and purify the minds of their readers? Will the persons who peruse, and are amused, perhaps fascinated, by them, become more noble, more exalted, more spiritual beings, than they were before? . . .

These two extremes of novel-writing – the Almack and Jack Sheppard schools[25] – deviate equally from the standard of real excellence. The one is exclusively devoted to the description of the high, the other of low life. The one portrays a style of manners as artificial and peculiar as that of the paladins and troubadours of chivalry; the other exhibits to our view the lowest and most degraded stages of society, and by the force of humour or the tenderness of pathos interests us too often in the haunts of vice or the pursuits of infamy . . .

All these extravagances in the noble art of romance originate in one cause. They come of not making 'the past and the *distant* predominate over the present'. . . .

Sir Walter Scott, as all the world knows, was the inventor of the historical romance. As if to demonstrate how ill founded was the opinion, that all things were worked out, and that originality no longer was accessible for the rest of time, Providence, by means of that great mind, bestowed a new art, as it were, upon mankind at the very time when literature to all appearances was effete, and invention, for above a century, had run in the cramped and worn-out channels of imitation. Gibbon was lamenting that the subjects of history were exhausted, and that modern story would never present the moving incidents of ancient story, on the verge of the French Revolution and the European war – of the Reign of Terror and Moscow retreat. Such was the reply of Time to the complaint that political incident was worn out. Not less decisive was the answer which the genius of the Scottish bard afforded to the opinion, that the treasures of original thought were exhausted, and that nothing now remained for the sons of men. In the midst of that delusion he wrote *Waverley*; and the effect was like the sun bursting through the clouds . . .

Considered in its highest aspect, no art was ever attempted by man more elevated an ennobling than the historical romance. It may be doubted whether it is inferior even to the lofty flights of the epic, or the heart rending pathos of the dramatic muse. Certain it is that it is more popular, and embraces a much wider circle of readers, than the *Iliad* or the *Paradise Lost*. Homer and Tasso never, in an equal time, had nearly so many readers as Scott. The reason is, that an interesting story told in prose, can be more generously understood, and is appreciated by a much wider circle, than when couched in the lofty strains, and comparative obscurity of verse. It is impossible to over-estimate the influence, for good or for evil, which this fascinating art may exercise upon future ages. It literally has the moulding of the human mind in its hands; – 'Give me,' said Fletcher of Saltoun, 'the making of ballads, and I will give you the making of laws.' Historical romances are the ballads of a civilised and enlightened age. More even than their rude predecessors of the mountains and the forest, they form those feelings in youth by which the character of the future man is to be determined. It is not going too far to say, that the romances of Sir Walter Scott have gone far to neutralize the dangers of the Reform Bill. Certain it is that they have materially assisted in extinguishing, at least in the educated classes of society, that prejudice against the feudal manners, and those devout aspirations on the blessing of democratic institutions, which were universal among the learned over Europe in the close of the eighteenth century. Like all other great and original minds, so far from being swept away by the errors of his age, he rose up in direct opposition to them. Singly he set himself to breast the flood which was overflowing the world. Thence the reaction in favour of the institutions of the olden time in church and state, which became general in the next generation, and is now so strongly manifesting itself, as well in the religious contests as the lighter literature of the present day.

'Some authors,' says Madame de Staël, 'have lowered the romance in mingling with it the revolting pictures of vice; and while the first advantage of fiction is to assemble around man all that can serve as a lesson or a model, it has been thought that a temporary object might be gained in representing the obscure scenes of corrupted life, as if they could ever leave the heart which repels them as pure as that to which they were unknown. But a romance, such as one can conceive, such as we have some models of, is one of the noblest productions of the human mind, one of the most influential on the hearts of individuals, and which is best fitted in the end to form the morals of nations.' It is in this spirit that romances should be written – it is in this spirit that it has been written by some of the masters of the art who have already appeared, during the brief period which has elapsed since its creation. And if, in hands more impure, it has sometimes been applied to less elevated purposes; if the turpid waters of human corruption have mingled with the stream, and the annals of the past have been searched, not to display its magnanimity, but to portray its seductions; we must console ourselves by the reflection, that such is the inevitable lot of humanity, that genius cannot open a noble career which depravity will not enter, nor invent an engine for the exaltation of the human mind, which vice will not pervert to its degradation.

Notes

1. Gaius Sallustius Crispus (86–35 BC) was a Roman historian. His partisan and moralising histories of Caesear's campaigns precluded detailed or analytic treatments of his material.
2. Historical (as opposed to poetic) licence.
3. E. A. Clarendon, later Baron Hyde, was a Royalist historian of the Civil War.
4. David Hume was a Scottish philosopher (1711–76). His immensely influential *History of Great Britain* (1757–62) attacked many of the current Whig orthodoxies.
5. A rough translation of '*incredulous odi*'. See 4.1.
6. A reference to *Caleb Williams.*
7. For a history of the reception of the German 'Gothic' novel, see Hadley 1978; for examples of anti-German reviewing, see Reiman 1977.
8. For the origins of this assertion, see 3.10.
9. Count Cagliostro was the alias of Joseph Balsamo, a small-time Italian crook and pimp who caused a sensation throughout Europe as the purveyor of Egyptian mysteries. A self-confessed Freemason, he was linked to the shadowy world of Illuminist conspiracy, largely through rumour, innuendo, and politically motivated smears (see 5.10).
10. *The Fatal Revenge: or, The Family of Montorio, A Romance* (1807) was Maturin's first romance.
11. See John Allen Stevenson, '*Tom Jones,* Jacobitism, and the Rise of the Gothic', in Smith and Sage (1994, pp. 16–22).
12. A reference to Leigh Hunt's eldest son, Thornton Hunt.
13. Barry Cornwall was the pseudonym of Brian Waller Proctor (1787–1874); Lamb is alluding to Cornwall's *Dramatic Scenes* (1819).
14. Ino Leucothea was a Greek sea-goddess.
15. Mungo Park (1771–1806) was the first European to explore the upper reaches of the Niger; the captain of the *Hecla* was William Parry (1790–1855), who led two expeditions to find the north-west passage.
16. Thetis was a Nereid and the mother of Achilles.
17. From Shakespeare's *Troilus and Cressida,* III.ii.188–9.
18. A reworking of Obadiah, 16.
19. P. B. Shelley, *The Cenci,* II.i.179–80.
20. The references are to Matthew Lewis, *The Monk* (1796); Thomas Moore, 'The Ring, a Tale', *The Poetical Works of the Late Thomas Little, Esq.* (1801); and *Fantasmagoria, ou Recuel d'Histoires d'Apparitions de Spectres, Revenans, Fantômes, etc.* (1812).
21. 'Lay down on the left side of the bed'; a line from Petrarch's *Rime Sparse,* 359.3.

22 For a history of the word 'phantasmagoria', which came into popular use at around this time, see Castle, 1995, pp. 140–67.

23 Roland was the most famous of Charlemagne's Paladins (or peers). His disastrous adventures in the Pyrenees were transformed by legend into heroic exploits, as in, for instance, the *Chanson de Roland.* Archbishop Turpin was attributed (erroneously) with the authorship of a fabricated twelfth-century, Latin version of the chronicle. Ludovico Ariosto (1474–1535) also used the legend in *Orlando Furioso.*

24 Jean Paul Friedrich Richter (1763–1825) was a German novelist. 'Jean Paul' was his pen name.

25 Almack's Assembly Rooms (named after William Almack) were a fashionable gathering place from around 1750 to 1850. Jack Sheppard (1702–24), a notorious thief and highwayman, was hanged at Tyburn.

Bibliography

Albrecht. W. P. (1975) *The Sublime Pleasure of Tragedy: A Study of Critical Theory from Dennis to Keats*. Lawrence, Kansas: University of Kansas Press.

Ashfield, Andrew and de Bolla, Peter, eds (1996) *The Sublime: A Reader in British Eighteenth-century Aesthetic Theory*. Cambridge: Cambridge University Press.

Ashton, John (1966) *Chap-books of the Eighteenth Century* [1882]. Reprint, New York: Benjamin Blom.

Babcock, Robert Witbeck (1964) *The Genesis of Shakespeare Idolatry 1766–1799: A Study in English Criticism of the Late Eighteenth Century*. New York: Russell & Russell.

Baine, Rodney (1968) *Daniel Defoe and the Supernatural*, Athens, Georgia: University of Georgia Press.

Baker, E. A. (1934), *The History of the English Novel*, vol. 5, *The Novel of Sentiment and the Gothic* Romance. London: Witherby.

Boone, Troy (1994) 'Narrating the Apparition: Glanvill, Defoe and the Rise of Gothic Fiction', *The Eighteenth Century*, 35 (2), pp. 173–89.

Boulton, James (1963) *The Language of Politics in the Age of Wilkes and Burke*. London: Routledge & Kegan Paul.

Brunstrom, Conrad (1997) 'James Beattie and the Great Outdoors: Common Sense Philosophy and the Pious Imagination', *Romanticism*, 3 (1), pp. 20–34.

Butler, Marilyn, ed. (1984) *Burke, Paine, Godwin, and the Revolution Controversy*. Cambridge: Cambridge University Press.

Castle, Terry (1995) *The Female Thermometer: Eighteenth-century Culture and the Invention of the Uncanny*. New York and Oxford: Oxford University Press.

Clery, E. J. (1995) The *Rise of Supernatural Fiction, 1762–1800*. Cambridge: Cambridge University Press.

Colton, Judith (1976) 'Merlin's Cave and Queen Caroline: Garden Art as Political Propaganda', *ECS*, 10, pp. 1–20.

Cooke, Arthur L. (1951) 'Some Side Lights on the Theory of the Gothic Romance', *Modern Language Quarterly*, 12, pp. 429–36.

Danziger, Marlies K. (1959) 'Heroic Villains in Eighteenth-century Criticism', *Comparative Literature*, 11, pp. 35–46.

de Montluzin, Emily Lorraine (1988) *The Anti-Jacobins, 1798–1800: The Early Contributors to the 'Anti-Jacobin Review'*. Basingstoke: Macmillan.

Engell, James (1981) *The Creative Imagination: Enlightenment to Romanticism*. Cambridge, Massachusetts: Harvard University Press.

Fairchild, H. N. (1928) *The Noble Savage: A Study in Romantic Naturalism*. New York: Columbia University Press.

Ferguson, Frances (1992) *Solitude and the Sublime*. London: Routledge.

Frayling, Christopher (1991) *Vampyres: Lord Byron to Count Dracula*. London and Boston: Faber & Faber.

Galloway, W. F. (1940) 'The Conservative Attitude to Fiction 1770–1830', *PMLA*, 55, pp. 1041–59

Gerard, Alexander (1774) *An Essay on Genius*. London and Edinburgh: Cadell & Creech.

Graham, John (1966) 'Character Description and Meaning in the Romantic Novel', *Studies in Romanticism*, 5, pp. 208–18.

Grant, Douglas (1965) *The Cock Lane Ghost*. New York: St Martin's.

Hadley, M. (1978) *The Undiscovered Genre: A Search for the German Gothic Novel*. Berne, Frankfurt am Main and Las Vegas: Peter Lang, (1978).

Henn, T. R. (1934) *Longinus and English Criticism*. Cambridge: Cambridge University Press.

Christopher Hill (1954) 'The Norman Yoke', *Democracy and the Labour Movement*, ed. John Saville. London: Lawrence & Wishart, pp. 42–54.

Hipple, W. J. (1957) *The Beautiful, the Sublime and the Picturesque*. Carbondale: Southern Illinois University Press.

Hunt, Lynn, (1993) 'Pornography and the French Revolution' in *The Invention of Pornography: Obscenity and the Origins of Modernity, 1500–1800*. New York: Zone Books, pp. 301–39.

Jacob, Margaret C. (1981) *The Radical Enlightenment: Pantheists, Freemasons, and Republicans*. London: Allen & Unwin.

Johnson, Claudia L. (1995) *Equivocal Beings: Politics, Gender and Sentimentality in the 1790's: Wollstonecraft, Radcliffe, Burney, Austen*. Chicago: University of Chicago Press.

Jones, Chris (1993) *Radical Sensibility: Literature and Idea in the 1790s*. London and New York: Routledge.

Kilgour, Maggie (1995) *The Rise of the Gothic Novel*. London: Routledge.

Klancher, Jon (1995) 'Godwin and the Republican Romance: Genre, Politics, and Contingency in Cultural History', *Modern Language Quarterly*, 56 (2), pp. 145–65.

Kliger, Samuel (1945) 'The "Goths" in England: An Introduction to the Gothic Vogue in Eighteenth-century Aesthetic Discussion', *Modern Philology*, 43, pp. 105–17.

—— (1949) 'Whig Aesthetics: A Phase of Eighteenth-century Taste', *English Literary History*, 16, pp. 135–50.

—— (1952) *The Goths in England: A Study in Seventeenth- and Eighteenth-Century Thought*. Cambridge, Massachusetts: Harvard University Press.

Lévy, Maurice (1996) *The Roman 'Gothique' Anglais, 1765–1824* (1968), new ed. Paris.

Lipking, Laurence (1970) *The Ordering of the Arts in Eighteenth-century England*. Princeton, New Jersey: Princeton University Press.

Lonsdale, Roger, ed. (1969) The *Poems of Thomas Gray, William Collins, Oliver Goldsmith*. London and Harlow: Longman.

Loomis, Emerson Robert (1957) 'The Anti-Gothic Novel', Unpublished doctoral dissertation, Florida State University.

McCalman, Iain (1996) 'Mad Lord George and Madame La Motte: Riot and Sexuality in the Genesis of Burke's *Reflections on the Revolution in France*', *Journal of British Studies*, 35 (July), pp. 343–67.

—— (1993) *Radical Underworld: Prophets, Revolutionaries, and Pornographers in London, 1795–1840*. Oxford: Clarendon Press.

McCarthy, Michael (1987) *The Origins of the Gothic Revival*. New Haven and London: Yale University Press.

McKeon, Michael (1987) *The Origins of the English Novel*. London: Hutchison.

McKillop, Alan D. (1921) 'Jane Austen's Gothic Titles', *Notes & Queries*, New Series, 9, pp. 361–2.

—— (1932) 'Mrs Radcliffe on the Supernatural in Poetry', *Journal of English and German Philology*, 33, pp. 352–9.

McKinney, David D. (1990) 'The Castle of My Ancestors: Walpole and Strawberry Hill', *British Journal of Eighteenth-Century Studies* 13 (2), pp. 199–214.

McManners, John (1985) *Death and Enlightenment: Changing Attitudes to Death Among Christians and Unbelievers in Eighteenth-century France*. Oxford and New York: Oxford University Press.

Madoff, Mark (1979) 'The Useful Myth of Gothic Ancestry', *Studies in Eighteenth Century* Culture, 9, pp. 337–50.

Mayo, Robert (1943) 'How Long Was Gothic Fiction in Vogue?', *Modern Language Notes*, 58, pp. 58–64.

—— (1950) 'Gothic Romance in the Magazines', *Proceedings of the Modern Language Association*, 65, pp. 762–89.

Monk, Samuel H. (1960) *The Sublime: A Study of Critical Theories in XVIII-century England*. Ann Arbor: University of Michigan Press.

Moretti, Franco (1983) *Signs Taken For Wonders: Essays in the Sociology of Literary Forms*, trans. Susan Fischer *et al.* London: Verso.

Mulvihill, James (1995) 'Peacock's *Nightmare Abbey* and the "Shapes" of Imposture', *Studies in Romanticism*, 34, pp. 553–68.

Paine, Thomas (1987) *The Thomas Paine Reader*, eds Michael Foot and Issac Kramnick, Harmondsworth: Penguin.

Parraux, André (1960) *The Publication of 'The Monk': A Literary Event 1796–1798*. Paris: Librarie Marcel Didier.

Parsons, C. O. (1943) 'The Interest of Scott's Public in the Supernatural', *Notes and Queries*, 185, pp. 92–100.

—— (1956) 'Ghost-stories Before Defoe', *Notes and Queries*, 201, pp. 293–8.

Percy, Thomas (1966) *Reliques of Ancient English Poetry*, revised edition by Henry B. Wheatley, 3 vols. New York: Dover Publications.

Percy, Thomas (1893), *Reliques of Ancient English Poetry*, ed. R.A. Willmot. London: George Routledge & Sons.

Phillips, Patricia (1984) *The Adventurous Muse: Theories of Originality in English Poetics, 1650–1760*. Uppsala: University of Uppsala.

Pittock, Joan (1973) *The Ascendancy of Taste: The Achievement of Joseph and Thomas Warton*. London: Routledge & Kegan Paul.

Pocock, J.G.A. (1987) *The Ancient Constitution and the Feudal Law: A Study of English Historical Thought in the Seventeenth Century* (1957; reissue with retrospect). Cambridge: Cambridge University Press.

—— (1985) 'The Varieties of Whiggism from Exclusion to Reform: A History of Ideology and Discourse', in *Virtue, Commerce and History*. Cambridge: Cambridge University Press.

Prior, Moody E. (1932) 'Joseph Glanvill, Witchcraft and Seventeenth-century Science', *Modern Philology*, 30, pp. 167–93.

Rice-Oxley, L. (1924) *Poetry of the Anti-Jacobin.* Oxford: Basil Blackwell.

Richter, David H. (1988) 'The Reception of the Gothic Novel in the 1790s', in *The Idea of the Novel in the Eighteenth Century,* ed. Robert W. Uphaus. East Lancing, Michigan: Colleagues Press.

Roberts, Marie Mulvey (1990) *Gothic Immortals: The Fiction of the Brotherhood of the Rosy Cross.* London: Routledge.

Reiman, D. H. (1977) *The Romantics Reviewed,* vol. 1. New York and London: Garland Publishing.

Sadleir, Michael (1944) '"All Horrid?": Jane Austen and the Gothic Romance', in *Things Past.* London: Constable.

Sage, Victor and Allan Lloyd Smith, eds (1994) *Gothick Origins and Innovations.* Amsterdam and Atlanta, Georgia: Rodopi.

Samson, John (1986) 'Politics Gothicized: The Conway Incident and *The Castle of Otranto*', *Eighteenth Century Life,* 10 (3), pp. 145–58.

Schama, Simon (1989) *Citizens: A Chronicle of the French Revolution.* Harmondsworth: Penguin.

Schonhorn, Manuel (1965) Introduction, *Accounts of the Apparition of Mrs Veal.* Augustan Reprint Society no. 115, Los Angeles: University of California Press.

Schuchard, Marsha Keith (1992) 'Blake's "Mr. Femality": Freemasonry, Espionage, and the Double-Sexed', *Eighteenth Century Culture,* 22, pp. 51–71.

—— (1995) 'William Blake and the Promiscuous Baboons: A Cagliostroan Séance Gone Awry', *British Journal for Eighteenth-century Studies,* 18 (2), pp. 185–200.

Shaw, Harry E. (1996). *Critical Essays on Sir Walter Scott: The Waverley Novels.* New York: G. K. Hall.

Shepperson, Archibald Bolling (1936) *The Novel in Motley: A History of the Burlesque Novel in English.* Cambridge, Massachusetts: Harvard University Press.

Sickels, Eleanor M. (1969) *The Gloomy Egoist: Moods and Themes of Melancholy from Gray to Keats.* New York: Octagon Books.

Smith, Allan Lloyd and Victor Sage eds (1994) *Gothick Origins and Innovations.* Amsterdam and Atlanta, Georgia: Rodopi.

Smith, Olivia (1984) *The Politics of Language, 1791–1819.* Oxford: Clarendon Press.

Smith, R. J. (1987) *The Gothic Bequest: Medieval Institutions in British Thought, 1688–1863.* Cambridge: Cambridge University Press.

Spacks, Patricia Meyer (1962) The *Insistence of Horror: Aspects of the Supernatural in Eighteenth-century Poetry.* Cambridge, Massachusetts: Harvard University Press.

Swedenberg, H. T. (1938), 'Fable, Action, Unity and Supernatural Machinery in English Epic Theory, 1650–1800', *Englische Studien,* 73, pp. 39–48.

Taylor, John Tinnon (1943) *Early Opposition to the English Novel.* New York: King's Press.

Thomas, Keith (1971) *Religion and the Decline of Magic.* Harmondsworth: Penguin.

Thompson, E. P. (1970) *The Making of the English Working Class.* Harmondsworth Penguin.

Thorp, Willard (1928) 'The Stage Adventures of Some Gothic Novels', *PMLA,* 43, pp. 476–86.

Tucker, Susie L. (1972) *Enthusiasm: A Study in Semantic Change.* Cambridge: Cambridge University Press.

Weiss, Harry B. (1969) *A Book About Chapbooks: The People's Literature of Bygone Times* [1942], Hatboro: Folklore Association.

Westcott, Isabel M., ed. (1958) *Seventeenth-century Tales of the Supernatural*. Augustan Reprint Society, no. 74, Los Angeles: Clark Memorial Library, UCLA.

Whitney, L. (194) *Primitivism and the Idea of Progress in English Popular Literature of the Eighteenth Century*. Baltimore: Johns Hopkins University Press.

Wood, Theodore E. (1972) *The Word 'Sublime' and its Context 1650–1760*. The Hague: Mouton.

Index

Note: 'n' after a page reference indicates a note number on that page.